ENOUGH ROPE

P. L. Doss

WINNER, BRONZE IPPY

Independent Publisher Book Awards,

Suspense/Thriller Category, 2014

Praise for ENOUGH ROPE

… Doss' twisty, curvy plot dishes out the goods: scandalous secrets, including blackmail and extramarital affairs.… The lengthy list of suspects is impressive, and readers won't find it easy pinpointing the killer's identity.… A murder mystery that sneaks up, takes hold and refuses to let go.

- *Kirkus Indie*

… An exceptional debut that becomes more and more complex as the evidence builds and the tale unfolds. …The author has seamlessly woven themes of fallible human nature, deceit, greed, betrayal, and family secrets. …The characters are wonderfully drawn, especially Halloran and Hollis, but the minor members of the cast are also well characterized. … The author has masterfully woven together a well-crafted tale.

- Gali, OnlineBookClub.org (https://onlinebookclub.org/)

ENOUGH ROPE is a labyrinthine tale of murder, lust, revenge, and secret histories. … Will keep your interest until the explosive conclusion.

- Star, Goodreads

…With every page I turned the mystery of the murders became more complex and the plot thickened …. A thrilling and wonderfully written murder mystery read …

- Charlie, Girl of 1000 Wonders (https://girlof1000wonders.wordpress.com)

It is always exciting to find a new author, and P.L. Doss is quite a find. The characters are sympathetic and the story is exciting. Can't wait until the next in the series!

- Beverly M, NetGalley

A twisty puzzle with plenty of suspects and old secrets that have far-reaching effects.

- Jen, Goodreads

ENOUGH ROPE

P. L. Doss

**Mayfair
Press**

Enough Rope
P. L. Doss

Published in the United States.

Edition ISBNs
Trade Paperback: 978-0-9890934-0-8
eBook: 978-0-9890934-1-5

Cover design by John Martucci
Author photo by John Martucci
Book design by Christopher Fisher

This edition was prepared for printing by The Editorial Department
7650 E. Broadway, #308, Tucson, Arizona 85710
www.editorialdepartment.com

TO CLAYTON BRADLEY DOSS, JR
November 19, 1945—February 7, 2008

He was both Halloran and Joplin…and everything to me.

ACKNOWLEDGMENTS

This book could not have been written without the help of many people. They have all given me their time, expertise, support, advice, ideas, and, perhaps most importantly, their honest opinions. I am extremely grateful and indebted to the following:

First, the professionals: Dr. Gerald Gowitt, Chief Medical Examiner of Dekalb County, Georgia vetted my autopsy chapters and corrected any misspellings of medical terms. Deloris Roys, Phd., now Director Emeritus of the Highland Institute for Behavioral Change, who often advised me when I supervised sex offenders, answered many questions about the practice of autoerotic asphyxia and helped make sure that Dr. Woodley's article on the subject was sound. Dr. Nathan Segal and Dr. Eric Baret provided medical expertise whenever I needed it. Jane Sams, Justin Browder, and Drake Chandler, three of my favorite attorneys, shared their knowledge of the law—and of law practices—with me. Any mistakes or liberties I took with reality for the sake of my fictional world are strictly mine.

Next, to all my readers: Kathy Hawthorne and Les Pickering from my writing group, Brenda Smith, Arline Browder, Justin Browder, Katherine Lee, Ed Beeson, Carlin Kriegle, Nicole Rose, Sue Crawford, Beth Beasley, Jane Sams, Terry Leite, Angela Phillips, Sarah Doss and Tom Armentrout. They not only found typos and discrepancies, they enriched the book by providing insight into characters and asking questions that I should have asked myself. I sincerely hope I haven't forgotten anyone.

Lastly, to my family: My mother, Dorie Leite Aul, and my son and daughter-in-law, Clayton and Kristina Doss, have given me their support, encouragement, and love. My sister, Terry Leite, proved to be an excellent editor—and an indefatigable cheerleader. My daughter, Nicole

Rose, was one of my earliest supporters and never let me give up on this book. She is the main reason it made it into print.

I also want to thank John Martucci of Martucci Design, who created the incredible book cover, as well as everyone at The Editorial Department who helped to make this book a reality, especially Morgana Gallaway, Christopher Fisher, Betsy White, and Jane Ryder.

"Give him enough rope and he'll hang himself."

English Proverb

ENOUGH
ROPE

Prologue

THE THOUGHT OF HOW HE WOULD LOOK in death gave Elliot Carter the strength to kick his legs out. The stepladder had been knocked over, but his feet made contact with the tree, and he pushed himself away to gain momentum. If he could just get close enough to grab hold of the trunk when his body swung back, maybe he'd have a chance. But the bindings around his thighs and chest restricted his arm movement, and his sudden, jerking motions caused the rope around his neck to tighten even more. A roaring noise began reverberating inside his head. Convulsively, he gulped in air, unaware that any oxygen his lungs received would never reach his brain.

Panic seized him, scattering his thoughts and obliterating all concentration. The roaring in his head grew in excruciating intensity. It was then that Carter knew with certainty that he was going to die and that everything he had achieved in his life would be destroyed. How could he have let things get so out of control? None of it was worth dying for.

Certainly not this way.

This agonizing thought lasted only a few seconds and was replaced by an almost euphoric sense of well-being as his brain was depleted of oxygen. Elliot Carter stopped struggling. His body began to swing in a gentle arc, accompanied by the soft creaking of the tree branch. A few hundred feet away, the late-night traffic was moving briskly along Piedmont Road.

1

THE JOGGER HEADED DOWN Seventeenth Street to Peachtree Circle and then to The Prado, the main street in the Ansley Park neighborhood. Within ten minutes, he had reached Piedmont Road. Further on, he passed the Driving Club, which sat in sprawling splendor behind a white picket fence lined with jonquils. As he entered the heavy iron gates of Piedmont Park at 14th Street, the light was becoming stronger; he could now see white and pink dogwoods dotting the landscape, a specialty of an Atlanta spring. It was still cold in the mornings, but would warm up later in the day. He filled his lungs with the fresh, chilled air, then exhaled slowly, watching his breath plume out in front of him.

A gusty wind rifled the trees as the jogger approached the Noguchi Playscapes. When he was about fifty yards away, he saw a movement near the rectangular slides like the slow swing of an old clock's pendulum. At first, in the still-feeble light, he thought it was made by another piece of equipment, maybe a tire swing. But as he drew closer, he realized that he was looking at a body—a human being—hanging from the branch of a large elm tree.

The jogger picked up speed as adrenaline hit his bloodstream. At twenty yards away, he saw that the body was that of a rather large woman, facing away from him. She had short, dark hair and was dressed in only a bra, thong underwear, and high-heeled sandals. He raced headlong to reach her now, knowing that he needed to see if the woman were still alive. He tried to remember the steps of CPR; tried to think of what he could use to cut her down from the tree.

When he was only about five yards away, the jogger realized that it was not a woman hanging from the tree; coarse hair covered the arms and legs. He rushed up and grasped the legs, intending to lift the body up and ease the rope's compression on his neck. But as soon as he did, he knew that whatever aid he could give would be useless. The man's legs were too stiff, too cold, even for a chilly spring morning. Deciding to check for a heartbeat anyway, he turned the body around, but then he received another shock: the bulging eyes staring out at him belonged to a man he knew.

A man who was like a brother to him.

2

HOLLIS JOPLIN WALKED INTO the kitchen, trying to remember where he'd put the Extra Strength Tylenol. Two cups of coffee had done nothing to dull his headache, and he hadn't slept much the night before. In fact, he hadn't been sleeping well for the past few weeks. He'd been trying to ward off one of his legendary "blue funks," but the murder-suicide scene he'd handled the day before threatened to put him over the top.

The victims were Cecil and Mary Heard, an elderly couple whose bodies hadn't been discovered for a week. They had no living children, and their newly gentrified street off Monroe Drive was filled with two-career couples who had neither the time nor the interest to check on them. Cecil Heard, ill with terminal cancer, had shot Mary, who had Alzheimer's, and then himself. The UPS man, delivering Cecil's medications, alerted police when the stench of something rotting wafted through the open bedroom window on the floor above him.

What had happened was terrible and sad, but what really bothered him, Joplin decided as he rummaged through the cabinet over the stove, was that no one had cared about the old couple. No one. He finally found the Tylenol behind a bag of Dixie Crystals and palmed two tablets into his mouth, gulping water from the faucet to wash them down. Telling himself that he had to let the case go for now, he walked back to his bedroom.

Quincy looked up sleepily from the bed, where he had curled into a tight, feline ball, then gave a supremely indifferent yawn and settled back down on the comforter. Joplin envied the cat's total self-involvement. Determined to put some distance between himself and the Heard case, he took a deep breath, then slowly exhaled through his mouth, the way the instructor of a stress management training course had demonstrated. It seemed to work. Heading for the bathroom and a long, hot shower, he felt better.

The jarring ring of the phone stopped him. Startled, Quincy scrambled off the bed and faded from the room as Joplin reached for the receiver. "This is Joplin," he said, trying to keep the irritation out of his voice. He looked at his watch; it was only 7:10 a.m.

"It's Simmons, Hollis. Got a scene here with your name on it."

"It must have Crawford's or Rodriguez's name on it, Ike. My shift doesn't start until eight."

Joplin, Viv Rodriguez and Deke Crawford were part of three night/ day teams of investigators with the Milton County Medical Examiner's Office who were responsible for going out on crime scenes during a particular 24-hour period, with two people assigned to the 8 a.m. to 4 p.m. day shift, two to the 4 p.m. to midnight shift, and the other two taking the midnight to 8 a.m. shift on a rotating basis. Some wag had dubbed it the "Menstrual Cycle" years ago, since it changed weekly over a twenty-eight-day period. Deke and Viv, who had the midnight shift Tuesday night were technically still on duty. The Homicide Unit was supposed to keep posted copies of each week's schedule.

"I know," said Simmons. "Just thought I'd save you a trip to the ME's office, is all. We got a body in Piedmont Park, discovered by a jogger 'bout six-forty this morning in the playground. White male, approximately forty years old. Apparent cause of death is asphyxiation by hanging."

"Gimme a break, Ike. I haven't even had a shower yet. Let's just let Crawford catch this one, okay? I'll call him myself."

"Suit yourself, Hollis. You white boys all look alike to me anyway," Simmons said, slipping easily into the jabbing camaraderie they'd had as partners at the Homicide Unit. "I doubt if I'll notice the difference. One of you better get there soon, is all. From what the uniform who called it in said, I think we got a gasper on our hands," he added, referring to the word police often used to describe a victim who'd died of autoerotic asphyxiation. "I sent Knox on ahead, but I don't want to take any chances on having that scene messed with. Captain Barrow would have my ass for breakfast, and that's a fact."

"He'd never be able to finish it, Ike. You must have put on twenty pounds in the three years since I left Homicide, and you had a backside the size of Stone Mountain then."

"Now, that hurts, Hollis," said Simmons, chuckling. "But I'm a Christian man, and I forgive you."

"That's big of you, Ike," Joplin said, feeling less cranky. He asked the homicide detective for the exact location of the body in the park, then said he'd meet him there in twenty minutes. He'd changed his mind about calling Crawford; an autoerotic hanging might be just the thing to take his mind off the Heard case.

Joplin took a two-minute shower and was dressed in another five. The navy blue windbreaker that identified him as an investigator with the Milton County Medical Examiner's Office was in the hamper with the rest of the clothes he'd worn yesterday. They all smelled too much like Cecil and Mary Heard. Instead, he grabbed a sport jacket from the closet and attached his ID tag to the pocket.

Quincy was already in the kitchen, meowing for his breakfast. Joplin looked at his watch, then pulled out a packet of Tender Vittles from the pantry closet and dumped it into the cat's dish. Quincy stared up at Joplin, his hazel eyes full of disbelief, then sniffed cautiously at the food. His suspicions confirmed, he began pawing the floor around the dish, covering the food with imaginary dirt.

"Sorry, Quince," said Joplin. "You can have fried chicken tonight, okay?" When the cat looked back up at him in disgust, he walked out, shutting the door behind him.

Joplin lived on Mathieson Drive in Buckhead, in an old apartment building that was destined to be sold, razed, and replaced by loft apartments in the future. The only thing that had preserved it so far was the bleak economy. Atlanta was so bloated by luxury, high-rise condominiums built five years ago that were now either totally empty or owned by tenants desperate to unload them, that there was little chance he'd have to move anytime soon. That suited him just fine; he liked living within the city limits. For one thing, he could get to work in roughly ten minutes, since the ME's office was on Cheshire Bridge Road, about five miles from his apartment.

Milton County, which shared the metropolitan area of Atlanta with Dekalb County to the east and Fulton County to the south, was almost the exact shape of Italy, due to what Joplin was sure was an ingenious bit of socio-economic gerrymandering when it was created in 2004. After many legal battles and legislative changes that reversed the political majority of the Fulton County Commission from Democratic to Republican, the county had been divided into two separate, but very unequal parts. The top of the boot was formed by the towns of Roswell, Alpharetta, and Sandy Springs, with Midtown making up the foot. Buckhead, considered the most upscale part of the city, was smack dab in the middle. These last two areas had originally been slated to remain with the newly-truncated Fulton County, but their moneyed homeowners and influential businesses had revolted, threatening to leave the county in droves. The Board of Commissioners had ultimately caved, leaving the county with only downtown Atlanta as the jewel in its very tattered crown.

Joplin had moved to Buckhead ten years ago, when the city was offering pay incentives to police officers to live in the areas where they worked. He'd just made detective and joined the Homicide Unit, so it seemed like a good move. His wife had been thrilled, even though their apartment in Cobb County had been much nicer. Now, both the extra pay and the wife were long gone, but he hoped he could find a way to stay there.

It was only about six miles from where he lived to Piedmont Park, but Joplin used his siren and portable flashing light anyway. If he didn't, at this hour of the day, the trip would take at least twenty minutes. He was convinced that half the people in New York and most of the people in the Midwest had moved to Atlanta since the '96 Olympics, and rapid transit, in the form of MARTA, was a joke. He turned left onto Peachtree and made it to Piedmont Road in just under a minute. As he wove his way through the heavy traffic heading to Midtown, his eyes were repeatedly drawn to the IBM Tower that glimmered like a beacon in the early morning light. Rising from an area of relatively low buildings in Midtown, and visible on a clear day from almost any spot within the city limits, its Gothic crown and graceful lines outclassed all the other skyscrapers.

Joplin usually preferred old buildings. He'd had a lifelong interest in architecture and had collected numerous books on the subject. But the Tower had been something special from the day it had been built, over thirty years ago. Even when IBM sold it, and it was renamed One Atlantic Center, longtime Atlantans clung to its old name, as well as the feeling that it was some kind of talisman of the city itself.

Reluctantly, as he reached Monroe Drive, Joplin pulled his eyes from the Tower and turned his thoughts to the body in the park.

3

A SMALL CROWD OF JOGGERS and early morning stirrers had begun to gather on the sidewalk by the time Hollis Joplin reached the Piedmont Road border of the park. He showed his ID to a uniformed cop who was blocking entry at the park gate. The scene had already been roped off, and after parking his car near the path that led to the playground and grabbing his black bag, he walked quickly over to where Knox and another uniform stood.

"Glad you could make it, Hollis," said Ricky Knox, touching the brim of his pork pie hat. All the detectives in the Atlanta PD Homicide Unit wore hats, and Knox, a tall, raw-boned man whose jacket sleeves never seemed long enough, was no exception.

"What've we got?"

"The deceased is a forty-four-year-old white male, name of Elliot Carter. Guy who found him is that big-shot attorney who's always on TV. Tom Halloran—you know the one?"

"Yeah," said Joplin. "The one who helps beautiful young widows of very rich old men get their inheritances."

"That's the one. Anyway, he says the deceased was his friend and also a partner at Halloran's law firm." Knox looked down at his notebook. "Healey and Caldwell," he added.

Joplin's eyebrows went up.

"Yeah, a little coincidental, huh? But Halloran lives in Ansley Park and says he jogs this way almost every morning. The deceased lived in the Ansley Towers on 14th Street across from Colony Square, so it's not so strange. We also found Mr. Carter's wallet under the tree he's hanging from and his car—a Jaguar—just down the street near the bicycle shop. The make and model were on the insurance card in his wallet."

"Good." Joplin turned to the uniformed cop and gestured toward the crowd, which had now almost doubled in size. "Officer Landers," he said, peering at the man's nameplate. "Think you could make some of these good citizens go on about their business?"

"I'll sure try," said Landers.

Joplin watched as the cop made an attempt to disperse the crowd. Only about a third of the people left; the rest continued gawking at Elliot Carter's poor, grotesque body, the wigged head lolling to its left and the rigid limbs swaying in the early morning breeze.

"D.C. eyeballers," Joplin muttered as he slipped under the yellow tape and set his evidence case on the grass. It was an expression he'd learned as a rookie, one that had originally been coined to describe the people who always seemed to gather whenever some poor fool, drunk or stoned or just plain crazy, was being arrested for disorderly conduct. It also applied on a number of other occasions, all of them involving varying degrees of catastrophe that people seemed to find so compelling.

Joplin understood better than most people that aspect of human nature which finds death, especially when it's violent or bizarre, as fascinating as it is fearful. But once he was on a case, he was protective of the victim. Legally, as a representative of the medical examiner's office, he had jurisdiction over the body until a manner of death had been preliminarily established; morally, he believed it was his duty to preserve the dignity of the dead as much as possible.

This didn't mean that he wouldn't indulge in some morgue humor during an autopsy. But that was among his colleagues, who dealt with death, in all of its tragic and ridiculous forms, on a daily basis. Sometimes a joke was the only shield available against despair or revulsion. But in Joplin's mind, the idly curious had no such rights, even in a case like the one before him, where in all probability the dead man had stripped himself of dignity.

Joplin paused for a minute to admire the Noguchi Playscapes, in all their orange and blue and yellow and green glory. He'd only been able to get to the park once since they'd been restored a few years back and was glad to see they were holding up well. But the bright colors and whimsical shapes were a startling background for such a grotesque death scene, he thought, as he pulled his camera from the case. Joplin had already made a quick survey of the area, so he knew what initial shots to get: the body, from several different angles and distances; Piedmont Road and the sidewalk area closest to the body; and the playground area as seen from the road. He took what pictures he could before moving into the protected area, then grabbed his case and ducked under the police tape.

Gross observation of the scene yielded nothing out of the ordinary. Slowly, Joplin moved from the orange and black slide toward the large tree where Elliot Carter was hanging, taking care not to disturb anything that might later prove to be evidence, but putting off a closer examination for later. He was a "body-to-perimeter" man, preferring to go over a scene by using the corpse as the zero point and working his way to the tape.

The body began to tell him things from ten feet away. It was facing away from him, suspended only about a foot from the ground. An over-turned stepladder lay a few feet away. The torso and arms were pale. Blood had pooled considerably in the hands and legs, purpling them and, in spots, stippling them with several small, petechial hemorrhages. This condition, called livor mortis, was one of the three factors used to estimate time of death, and what he saw indicated that Carter had been dead at least six hours. The extent of rigor mortis, which involved stiffening of the muscles caused by undissipated lactic acid, and algo mortis, the cooling process after death, might tell him a little more.

After snapping a few pictures of the ground beneath the body, Joplin set the camera down and moved in closer, pulling a notebook out of his back pocket as he did. Like an artist doing a quick sketch, he jotted down a description of the victim's clothing without looking at what he was writing. His eyes went from feet to head, taking in the high-heeled sandals, the white thong underwear and brassiere, and the chin-length brown wig. He then began to look for any external injuries. Except for the pressure marks he knew he would find under the neck ligature, there appeared to be none.

Joplin squatted down for a better look at the ground under the tree, which wasn't covered by the mulch spread carefully over the play area. He saw several footprints with ridges in them that looked like they'd been made by some kind of running shoe. There was also a set of prints with two holes where the heels would be, which seemed to correspond to the shoes on the body. He walked back over to his case and retrieved some gel strips so he could make casts of the prints. This accomplished, he made a note of what he'd observed, then grabbed the camera and took documenting pictures.

The front side of the body told him more. The man's penis wasn't exposed as in most cases of autoerotic hangings Joplin had investigated; he needed to include that in his notebook when he finished with the camera. The bra appeared to be stuffed with white jockey briefs and fastened in the front. There were no signs of any external injuries on this side either. Carter's eyes were open and revealed several prominent hemorrhages. The lenses were opaque, due to dehydration, another indication that several hours had passed since the victim's death. His tongue protruded slightly and was dried and blackened, which often occurred in an asphyxial death.

After photographing all of this, Joplin opened his case again and pulled on some latex gloves. He reached up and touched Carter's jaw, then tugged gently on the left arm and leg, careful not to disturb the ropes. He noted that the body appeared to be in full rigor, which added a few more hours onto his estimate as to time of death, since the entire process took from six to twelve hours. Livor mortis was complete, too; when he pressed a thumb into Carter's left calf, the dusky color didn't change. He would try to get a core temperature reading before he left the scene, but the dead man was too exposed for that at the moment. Inserting a rectal thermometer or even making a small incision over the liver to get a reading there wasn't something Joplin wanted the gawkers to see. Or the media to record, if reporters or TV vans had shown up.

Joplin focused on the ropes next. There appeared to be two separate pieces, with one wrapped around Carter's neck and the other resting loosely against his lower back, then encircling his right shoulder. They were all tied with slipknots. He made detailed notes, which included the direction of the loops, as well as his opinion that the second rope had formed a sling out of which Elliot Carter had slipped. He then took several more pictures. Although the knots themselves would be carefully preserved, once the body was cut down it would be almost impossible to reconstruct the bindings without such pictures. Joplin also stood in front of Carter to photograph what would have been the dead man's last sight of the world: a low, curved wall on a slope that served as the western border of the playground.

Puzzled, he underlined this note for further reflection. Why would Carter not position himself so he could see anyone who might approach the playground from the playing fields or the sidewalk near Piedmont Road? Although it was rare for deaths of this type to occur in public places, it happened now and then. He himself had investigated one in a parking tier at Lenox Square a few years ago, and when he was still with Homicide, there'd been one at the Georgia Tech stadium. But in both cases, the victim had placed himself so that he could see anyone who might enter his little recreational area. The enormous risk of exposure might contribute to the "high," but the control had to be there. This was extremely important to the players of this macabre game of sex and death.

Just behind the tree, but not visible from where the body hung, Joplin found the rest of Elliot Carter's clothes: a pair of Nike running shoes and a black warm-up suit. There was also an IPhone. After photographing these items, he retrieved his evidence case and bagged and sealed everything, then listed their contents in his notebook.

A careful tour of the rest of the death scene was next, with Joplin on the lookout for anything that might have been left there within the last twelve hours. Both the mulch covering the playground area and the grass bordering it were littered here and there with cigarette butts, but they were all either yellowed with age or still swollen with yesterday morning's rain. Satisfied, he walked back to the body and began to bag the hands and feet. If anything suspicious turned up at the autopsy, any fibers on them or scrapings from the nails might be a source of evidence. That done, he packed up his equipment. His eyes made one last sweep over the scene, then he walked briskly over to where Knox and Landers were talking to Ike Simmons, who must have just arrived.

"You can go ahead and call for transport," Joplin said to Landers. The cop nodded and headed in the direction of his squad car.

"We outta this one, Hollis?" asked Simmons, his hands in his pockets.

Joplin knew Ike had several pending cases that were definite homicides and needed to focus on them, so he didn't mention the few minor irregularities he'd noted. "I think so, unless the autopsy comes up with something different. He probably died sometime between ten and twelve last night, from what I can tell. Rigor's complete."

Ike Simmons nodded. "We'll stick around till you wrap things up here, then notify the wife, have her officially ID the body." He gestured toward a very tall man in a navy warm-up suit standing several feet away. "Mr. Halloran there says he can take her to the morgue. It turns out she and the deceased have been separated for a while; she lives nearby on The Prado, in Ansley. Any idea when the body'll be ready for visitors?"

Joplin looked at his watch. It was 8:20. "Let's say at about nine-thirty. If I'm not called out on another scene, I'll talk to the wife then and see if she had any idea he was into this. Maybe get her permission to check out where he lived and see if there's any supporting evidence of it. Could be she even knew about his 'hobby.' Maybe that was the reason for the separation."

Simmons nodded his agreement, then frowned. "Hey, Hollis, you ever hear of a brother doing this kind of thing?" he asked, gesturing toward Elliot Carter's body.

"I've never had a case involving a black male, Ike. There might be some examples in the forensic literature, though. I could check on it."

"That's okay. I was just wondering, is all." Simmons grinned at Joplin. "Personally, I don't think a brother would do something that stupid."

"You gonna let that pass, Hollis?" asked Ricky Knox, with a look of mock outrage.

Joplin laughed and shook his head. "Now I *will* have to do some research, Ike. You and I both know stupidity crosses all racial and socio-economic boundaries."

Simmons chuckled and raised his hands in surrender. "I take it back, Hollis. You don't need to be doing any extra work at the ME's office. From what I can tell, you have no social life whatsoever. I don't think you've been out with a woman since you dated that kooky aerobics instructor last year."

"Don't start on me, Ike."

Simmons glanced at his watch. "Suit yourself, Hollis. But you still need a life."

"I promise I'll put it on my to-do list," said Joplin, turning away, but he knew Simmons was just concerned about him. Most of his family was gone; his father had died in Vietnam when he was two, and his mother had succumbed to cancer a year ago. Joplin had no brothers or sisters. It was Ike who had helped him through his mother's death, as well as his divorce four years ago. They'd remained close even after he'd left Homicide, and, lately, his former partner had been nagging him about settling down again.

Maybe Ike was right, Joplin thought. Maybe he should ask Carrie Salinger out. Smart and funny and bordering on beautiful, Carrie was the new pathology resident from Grady Hospital who had started her thirty-day rotation at the ME's office the week before. Then again, it was never a good idea to get involved with someone where you worked, and besides that, he was probably far down on the food chain from the men she usually dated.

Joplin headed toward Tom Halloran, who was standing about thirty feet away. He seemed even taller up close, about six-four, with a rigid, almost military bearing and icy blue eyes set above prominent cheekbones. He also looked younger in person, probably around thirty-five. But even in jogging sweats, he exuded the confidence bordering on arrogance that Joplin had seen in his TV interviews, and he was sure the attorney wasn't a man used to being kept waiting. The scowl on his face and his crossed arms were easy clues that he wasn't a happy camper just then. The overall effect seemed deliberately intimidating, but after thirteen years in law enforcement, Joplin had built up an immunity to lawyers' tactics. Early in his career, he'd been sandbagged by defense attorneys in court more times than he liked to remember, and even the ADAs he'd worked with had tried to pull the rug out from under him on occasion. Winning seemed to be their only goal, no matter what the consequences. But he tried to keep in mind that this particular attorney had just lost a friend and deserved whatever empathy he could muster up.

It was all part of the job.

4

Tom Halloran couldn't take his eyes off Elliot's body. He hoped the police were going to cut him down from the tree soon; it was killing him that so many strangers were seeing Elliot so exposed, and under such gruesome circumstances. He heard footsteps and made himself turn away, watching as the man with the black case who'd been talking to the police officers earlier came toward him. The man looked to be in his late thirties and was only of medium height, but his large blond head and wide shoulders gave him a more imposing stature.

"Mr. Halloran? I'm Hollis Joplin with the Milton County Medical Examiner's Office." He had a slight drawl, and he spoke in the slow and measured way Halloran had heard other Southerners speak when they were being somewhat formal.

"Are you a pathologist?"

"No, sir, I'm an investigator. We usually go to death scenes instead of the pathologists. I've been examining the body and gathering evidence to take back to the ME's office. I'd like to ask you a few questions, if I could."

"Sure. If I can ask you a couple first."

"All right." The investigator's round, green eyes looked at him expectantly.

"First, could you explain why Sgt. Knox implied that Elliot's death was an accident?"

"Pending further investigation," Joplin said, "I believe that's what happened. Of course, the manner of death will have to be officially established by a medical examiner."

"But that's crazy!" said Halloran. "That makes even less sense than the idea of Elliot deliberately killing himself. What in the world could he possibly have been doing dressed in women's underwear? He wasn't gay, for Christ's sake! And he wouldn't have put a noose around his neck and tied it to a tree branch just for fun."

"As a matter of fact, Mr. Halloran, that's probably just what he *did* do."

"I don't think that's funny."

"It wasn't meant to be, sir."

"All right," said Halloran, keeping his voice even. "Tell me what you *did* mean."

Joplin let out a long sigh. "This particular explanation is usually given only to immediate family members."

"I'm also the executor of Elliot's estate. I think this is information I need to know."

"Okay," said Joplin. "But I warn you, except for insurance purposes, you're not gonna like what I tell you. Have you ever heard of autoerotic asphyxiation?"

Halloran stared at the man. "No," he said slowly, "but I think I can guess what it means. Obviously, it has something to do with masturbation and hanging."

"Actually, it's masturbation *while* hanging. Or while you have a plastic bag over your head or a rope or stocking twisted around your neck. Hanging isn't the only way."

"I know what asphyxiation means, Investigator Joplin. What I don't know is why anyone would *do* something like that."

"For the high, the rush. It's a real turn-on for them, flirting with death."

"You mean it's like Russian roulette?"

"In a way, although there's a lot more control. Usually some escape system has been set up. But there's also a physical component, a euphoric feeling brought on by lack of oxygen to the brain, which intensifies the sexual climax. Unfortunately, the light-headedness also affects judgment and sometimes causes these people to put off using their escape devices until it's too late, which is why deaths of this type are ruled accidental. They don't mean to kill themselves."

"But what about the way he was dressed? The wig, the high heels?"

"Cross-dressing is often an element in cases like this. It contributes to the sexual fantasies involved."

Halloran looked across the playground to Elliot Carter's body. They'd been not only colleagues, but also good friends for the past ten years. When he'd been hired by Healey and Caldwell, fresh out of Notre Dame law school and still reeling from the devastation caused by his father's fall from grace and subsequent suicide, Elliot had been his assigned mentor. But he'd become much more than that. They had both loved classical music and racquet ball, and their wives liked each other, so they'd spent a lot of time together outside the office. But it wasn't just their common interests that had started the friendship. He had come to trust Elliot more than any other person he knew. Trusted his judgment, his perceptions, and his personal integrity. As head litigator for the firm's tax and trust division and the youngest associate ever to make full partner, Halloran might have achieved a certain celebrity, but Elliot Carter had always been his role model.

"No," he said at last. "You're dead wrong. Elliot Carter was not the kind of person who would hang himself in a public park to get some kind of kinky thrill."

"I told you you wouldn't like it, Counselor."

"He was a normal guy, for Christ's sake!" Halloran insisted.

"When you do the kind of work I do, Mr. Halloran, you have a different perspective on 'normal guys.' A lot of them—maybe all of them—do things the people who know and love them would never imagine."

Halloran shook his head slowly. "Not this sort of thing, believe me. Elliot would never risk hurting his son like this. Not for a few minutes' pleasure."

"It's a compulsion, Mr. Halloran. He might have started doing it when he was a kid himself."

Emphasizing each word, Halloran said, "Not Elliot Carter."

"Have it your way, Counselor. But the only other possibilities are suicide and murder. And the reason you gave for Carter not being the victim of an autoerotic death would seem to hold true for suicide."

"Then it was murder," Halloran said stubbornly. "Somebody murdered him."

"Do you have anybody in mind? Maybe another woman who was the reason for his separation from his wife? A woman with a jealous husband or boyfriend?"

"No, of course not. We were also close to Anne, Elliot's wife, and I can assure you we would have heard about it if that were the case. In fact, according to my wife, Anne hired a private investigator right after Elliot moved out, but he didn't find anything like that. Actually, even Maggie—that's my wife—even Maggie and I don't really know what was behind the separation."

"You were all close friends, but he never told you why he left his wife?" Joplin said, his tone radiating disbelief.

Halloran hesitated, remembering how confused, and even a little hurt, he'd been when Elliot wouldn't answer any of his questions about the separation. "He just said he had his reasons. Elliot was a very private man."

The investigator cut his eyes to the body hanging from the oak tree; the point wasn't lost on Halloran. "Which is even more reason to believe that Elliot wouldn't do something like this," he added quickly.

"What was the name of the private investigator Mrs. Carter used?" asked Joplin.

"Maggie said she used an agency called Ace Investigations, but I don't know the name of the actual investigator."

"What about a financial motive? Who would benefit most from his death? Mrs. Carter?"

"Actually, no," Halloran said, deciding it would do no harm to give the investigator details that would be available to anyone in the near future. "It'll be a matter of public record soon, so I can tell you this: Elliot changed his will a few days after he moved out, back in early September. It revoked a joint trust that he and Anne had drawn up several years ago and specified that she was to receive only two properties—the house in Atlanta and one up in Highlands, which were in both their names. He then set up a revocable living trust for his son, Trip, who's seventeen."

"Could he do that?"

"Yes, in fact, it's advisable for people going through divorces to change their wills. A divorce decree in Georgia nullifies an existing will, but you're vulnerable in the interim."

"I guess what I mean is, wouldn't his wife, even if they were going through a divorce, have been entitled to half his estate?"

"Only if he had died intestate. Unlike many other states, Georgia doesn't have what's called an Elective Share statute, which guarantees a spouse one-third of an estate, even if a new will disinherits the person. Anne can petition the Probate court for temporary money under the Year's Support statue, and she'll also be able to claim whatever money will come to her from a prenuptial agreement, since there was a death clause, but that's it."

"It sounds to me like she'd still be taken care of pretty well."

"Not after taxes, and not in this economy, I'm afraid," Halloran said, trying not to sound condescending. He was sure that if the investigator knew that Anne would also collect $500,000 under the terms of the pre-nup, he'd be convinced that she had a motive to murder Elliot; it would seem like an incredible amount of money to a county employee. "And it was a drop in the bucket," he added, "compared to the money Elliot inherited from his father and would eventually inherit from his mother. He also made a substantial amount of money himself over the years."

"So how much are we talking about here? For the boy, I mean."

"That I *can't* tell you. Trusts don't have to go through probate, so the terms won't be made public. What I *can* say is that Anne stood a much better chance negotiating a settlement with Elliot than killing him, which is what she's been doing for the last seven months. She wasn't giving up without a fight."

"I take it she knew about the new will?"

Halloran nodded. "Elliot was required to notify her under the terms of the existing joint trust they had."

"Anybody else you can think of who might have had a motive to kill Mr. Carter?"

"Not offhand, but that doesn't prove he wasn't murdered."

"I promise you we'll look at every possibility," said Joplin. His attention was suddenly caught by the approach of a young black man wearing a navy windbreaker and pushing a folded table on wheels. "Excuse me for just a few minutes, okay?" he said, then motioned for the man to follow him.

Halloran watched as they ducked under the police tape and made their way over to Elliot's body. It would be a relief not to have to see him hanging from the tree branch, but he doubted that he'd be able to get the image out of his mind for a long time.

***

"Darrell, can you hold the body bag in front of me for a sec so I can get a temp without freaking the civilians?" Joplin asked as he squatted down beside his evidence case. Once hidden from view, he opened the case and pulled on another pair of latex gloves. Next he grabbed a scalpel and made a short incision just below the right rib cage. After bagging the scalpel, he pulled out an electronic thermometer. The ambient temperature reading was 48 degrees Fahrenheit. Shoving the same thermometer deep into the cut he'd made, he waited several seconds before retrieving it. The body's core temperature was now 80 degrees Fahrenheit. Joplin packed away the thermoprobe, then jotted down the readings in his notebook. He would do the math to get yet another estimate on time of death back at the office, where he could factor in the low temperature for that morning. It had probably sped up the cooling process.

It took only a few minutes to cut Carter down and slip him into the body bag, far less time than it had taken the man to rig up the elaborate harness and noose that had caused his death. But why do it in such a public place? Joplin wondered again as he walked along beside the body. And why the Playscapes in Piedmont Park, of all places? His years as a homicide cop made him suspicious of anything that didn't fit the usual pattern. And although there'd been that other autoerotic death at Lenox Square mall, he'd been very careful and thorough in that investigation, too. Finding further evidence that Elliot Carter was into autoerotic asphyxia would be important.

Halloran was still where he'd left him a few minutes earlier. "Listen, ordinarily I would ask the next of kin about this," Joplin said to him, "but given the situation, maybe you could handle it. I'd like to get into Mr. Carter's apartment, if possible."

"But why? It's not part of the death scene."

"No, but I might find other evidence that he was into this kind of activity," Joplin replied. "Or not," he added pointedly. "The ME will take everything into consideration in determining manner of death, and not finding corroborating evidence could have an impact on his ruling. As Mr. Carter's executor, you'd have the authority to allow me to search his apartment, right?"

"Yes, although I don't have any letters testamentary for that purpose yet. But I have a set of keys at the office that Elliot gave me when he signed the new will." Halloran looked at his watch. "I told Detective Knox that I would bring Mrs. Carter to the ME's office to make an official identification of the body, but I could meet you at Ansley Towers after that, say around eleven o'clock."

"I appreciate it, sir," Joplin said. "See you later on this morning then."

A WSB-TV news van was pulling up to the curb along Piedmont as Joplin walked back to his car, probably alerted by one of the gawker's cell phones. The crowd had begun to thin out now that the body had been removed. But there were still several people on the sidewalk talking to one another and occasionally pointing to the tree where Elliot Carter had been hanging. Joplin imagined they would still be there, even after he and the detectives had left.

Even when there was nothing left to see.

5

HALLORAN SAW THE TV VAN out of the corner of his eye as he headed toward the sidewalk and turned away, hoping he hadn't been recognized by anyone, especially the news crew. He'd refused an offer from Sgt. Knox to drive him home; he wanted to collect his thoughts before he saw Maggie. His cell phone rang as he was crossing Piedmont, and only then did he remember that he'd promised to call her back as soon as he knew more about what had happened to Elliot. He'd phoned her while waiting for the police to arrive, and now he felt guilty as he listened to her frantic questions. Halloran tried to calm her down, but his efforts only seemed to make things worse for both of them. He'd been able to stay focused when talking to the detectives and the ME's investigator, but now that he was alone, the full impact of Elliot's death was overwhelming.

"I'm sorry, Maggie," he said, rubbing his forehead in an attempt to clear his head. "I just didn't know what to say to you. I'm still having trouble believing this has happened."

He heard her take a deep breath. "Just tell me."

So he told her, at first trying to leave out the more gruesome aspects, then giving up on that as the story of what he'd seen and heard that morning came pouring out. He heard her crying off and on and wished he could do the same, but he just felt numb. Maggie didn't say anything for a while, but when she did, it was exactly what he himself had said.

"Elliot couldn't have done that to himself, Tom. He couldn't have."

"I know. I told them that. I also told them that it must have been murder. That somebody deliberately killed him."

This time he heard shock in the sharp intake of her breath. "I can only imagine what you felt, seeing Elliot like that. But murder? Do you really think that?"

"I don't know," Halloran said, sighing, "but it's sure better than thinking he killed himself or that he was into autoerotic asphyxia. Jesus! I didn't even know what that was until now! Did you?"

"There was an episode on *Law and Order* several years ago that dealt with it. And that was what David Carradine died from, you know. But to think one of your friends…"

"I *don't* think it," Halloran said firmly, trying to remember who David Carradine was. "Maybe I'm totally wrong, but right now I just can't believe it. And I don't think Anne will either. I mean, isn't that something a wife would know about?"

"I have no idea. But if Anne had known about something like this, I'm sure she would have used it to make Elliot give her more money."

"I guess I'll just have to ask her. In fact, as soon as I get home and change clothes, I'm heading over there. I told the police I'd take her to the ME's office to identify the body."

"I want to go with you."

"No," he said quickly. "Neither of us has seen Anne in months, Maggie, and I don't know how she's going to take this. Or whether she'll even talk to me, for that matter."

Halloran was forced to go over the same ground with Maggie when he reached home, but after he'd showered and dressed and was on his way to see Anne, he began to wonder if he'd made a mistake in not letting her come along. Maybe she'd be more of a comfort to Anne than he would. Then again, maybe comfort wouldn't be appropriate. The Carters had been married for eighteen years and, technically at least, were still married when Elliot died. Anne had been devastated when he'd left her the previous September, trying everything she could to get him back at first. But the months since then had been filled with acrimonious negotiations. Not to mention a new will that had disinherited her.

Halloran had hoped that he and Maggie could stay friends with both of the Carters, but the will had ruined any chance of that. Despite his assurances that he'd had nothing to do with devising it, she was convinced that he could have done something to stop Elliot if he'd wanted to. And when she found out that Elliot had named him executor and successor trustee for Trip, she'd stopped speaking to him and Maggie completely.

Maybe he'd simply been unrealistic, he decided as he turned right onto The Prado to drive the two blocks to the Carter house. Divorce seemed to wreak havoc on relationships, no matter what the circumstances. Even his relationship with Elliot had begun to deteriorate since the Carters' separation. They had still had lunch together in the firm's dining room several times a month and played racket ball every week, but the easy camaraderie that had been fostered by the constant interaction between their two families had slowly disappeared. Elliot's private nature seemed to contract even more. It was sadly true what Halloran had told the ME's investigator; he had no idea why his best friend had left his wife.

He also hadn't pushed for an explanation or tried to remedy the situation.

The only excuse Halloran could come up with for himself was that the economic crisis had eclipsed everything in the past four years, and he, along with Elliot and all the other partners, had been struggling to keep the firm afloat. Their clients' businesses and portfolios had all plummeted, resulting in legal retainers and budgets being slashed. Like King and Spalding, considered to be the premier Atlanta law firm, the smaller, but equally prestigious, Healey and Caldwell had begun laying off associates and support staff in the past two years. And even now, in 2012, the partners were still under as much pressure to bring in new business as the junior partners and the remaining associates. And, of course, all of their own portfolios had suffered, too. The resulting stress and tension had put them all on a financial and emotional roller-coaster that tended to put personal relationships on the back burner.

But that was no excuse for neglecting a close friendship, Halloran admitted to himself, and now it was too late to do anything. Regret surged through him, making him feel almost nauseated. He took a deep breath and forced himself to focus on the present, on what he *could* do. As trustee for Trip Carter, he would be able to advise and guide the boy in any number of areas that would affect his life. He also hoped to be a source of emotional support for Trip, something Halloran knew from personal experience that the boy would need more than anything else. But that would depend on his relationship with Anne, which was pretty rocky right now. If she decided to contest the will, it would get even worse.

Halloran rounded a curve, and the Carter house came into view. A small-scale Italianate villa in rose stucco, it was a showplace, even by Ansley Park's standards. Halloran noticed a grey Crown Victoria sedan parked in front of the house and decided it probably belonged to Detective Knox.

Wondering what, exactly, he should say to Anne, especially concerning his suspicions that Elliot had been murdered, Halloran sat in his car a few minutes, preparing himself. He had no idea if she were being told the circumstances of Elliot's death and if not, whether he should be the one to do so. He felt as if he were going to court totally unprepared, which was something he never did. Reluctantly, he made himself get out of the car and walk to the front door.

Pauletta, the housekeeper who'd been with the Carters since Trip was a baby, answered the doorbell. She was a tall, slender black woman in her fifties with a reserved manner and a natural grace that had always impressed Halloran. As usual, she was dressed in the crisp black and white uniform that Anne insisted upon, but her normally serene expression was now one of grief. Her eyes filling with tears, she quickly ushered him into the house.

"I'm so glad you're here," she said softly.

"It's been a while, hasn't it?" Halloran said, giving her a quick hug.

"Too long, if anyone was to ask me. Mrs. Carter's in the living room."

Halloran followed her there. Detective Knox was standing near the baby grand piano, talking into a cell phone and looking out of place among the Persian rugs and antique porcelain vases. He nodded, but didn't hang up. Anne was sitting on one of the two overstuffed white sofas that flanked the fireplace, her hands resting stiffly in her lap. She was wearing a peach-colored robe, her face tear-streaked and devoid of make-up. Halloran realized that he had never seen Anne when she wasn't elegantly dressed and expertly made up. But she was still lovely, with her wide-set blue eyes and her blond hair tied back in its usual sleek ponytail at the nape of her neck.

He wondered again how Elliot could have left her. To Halloran's knowledge, Anne had never worked outside the home. Instead, she had thrown herself into advancing her husband's career and standing in the community with an enthusiasm that had always impressed him. She entertained clients with an ease and elegance that set the standard at Healey and Caldwell. She was also heavily involved in Atlanta's cultural network, which was a prerequisite for social and corporate advancement. There wasn't an issue of *Jezebel* or *The Season* or *Atlanta Magazine* that didn't have pictures of Anne Carter in dazzling ball gowns or cocktail finery, looking like the quintessential Southern belle.

The woman Halloran saw now was nothing like the one he remembered from those pictures. He was no longer in doubt about Anne's reaction to Elliot's death; she was obviously grief-stricken, her face layered with bewilderment and shock. He went over to her and sat down, then wrapped an arm around her. She began to cry.

"I'm so sorry, Anne," he told her.

She wiped her eyes and looked at him. "This detective has been telling me about Elliot." She shook her head and closed her eyes.

"Mrs. Carter was so upset at the thought that her husband had killed himself," said Detective Knox, walking over to them as he pocketed his cell phone, "that I decided it might be better if I told her the circumstances."

Halloran was relieved that he wouldn't have to tell Anne the details himself, but now it seemed as though the police had already made up their minds about how Elliot had died, despite what the ME's investigator had told him. "I'm sure you were trying to be helpful, Sergeant," he said, "but no official decision will be made about the manner of Mr. Carter's death until after the autopsy has been completed, right?"

"Right," Knox quickly agreed. He turned to Anne. "Ma'am, I'm going to go on now, unless you have any more questions."

Anne shook her head slowly without looking up at him.

"Mr. Halloran said he'd take you down to the ME's office a little later to officially identify the body. Is that okay with you?"

"Yes," Anne answered, tilting her head and seeming to make an effort to focus on what the man was saying to her. "Thank you."

When Knox was out of the room, Halloran said, "Anne, I know you're upset, but I need to ask you something before we go to the medical examiner's office. Were you surprised when you heard about the way Elliot died? That it looked like autoerotic asphyxia, I mean?"

Now she turned toward him, her face looking even more dazed than when he'd first entered the room. "My God, Tom, how can you even ask me something like that? I was horrified! And I still don't believe it. This whole thing seems like some sort of terrible dream."

"That's exactly what I was hoping you would say."

"What do you mean?"

"It's just that—" Halloran hesitated, then said, "Anne, I don't know if I should even bring this up right now, but I think Elliot was murdered."

"What in the world are you talking about?" All the color had drained from Anne Carter's face. "Nobody has said anything about Elliot being murdered."

"Because the police don't think he *was* murdered. But I just can't believe that he would do this to himself. Can you?"

It was several seconds before Anne answered. She stared at him, but her gaze had turned inward. "I don't know what to think," she said finally. "I just don't know."

Halloran sighed. "You're in a state of shock. And I should take my own advice and just wait until the autopsy is completed before I jump to any conclusions about Elliot's death." He looked at his watch. "It's already almost nine. Do you think you could be ready to head to the ME's office in twenty or thirty minutes?"

Anne stood up. "There's no need for you to take me. I'll ask Paul—Dr. Woodley—to go with me. He's my therapist, and, frankly, I think I need him right now."

Halloran stood up, too. "Anne, I know we haven't been on good terms this past year, but I—"

"That's not important anymore, Tom. Really. I have an appointment scheduled with Dr. Woodley for ten this morning, and I don't think he'll mind meeting me at the medical examiner's office instead. Maybe he can help me make sense out of this whole thing and tell me what to say to Trip." Her face went white again. "My God… Trip! I haven't even been thinking of him. He left for school before the police got here. What is this going to do to him?"

"Let me go get him," urged Halloran. "This is too much for you to deal with right now. I'll tell Trip."

She shook her head. "I've got to talk to him myself."

"All right, but at least let me call Olivia," Halloran insisted. He didn't want to take any chances that Elliot's mother, who lived in Charleston, might hear about his death from someone who wasn't a family member or close friend.

"I'd appreciate that. We're not on the best of terms these days. And now I need to get dressed, Tom."

Realizing he'd been dismissed, Halloran awkwardly patted Anne Carter's arm, not knowing what else to do. "I'll be in touch," he said.

6

THE PHONE ON HOLLIS JOPLIN'S DESK rang as he was typing up his preliminary report on Elliot Carter.

"A Mrs. Carter is here to identify her husband's body," said Keisha, the front receptionist. "Should I send her back to the viewing room?"

"Yeah, I'll be right there."

The viewing room was the size of a large elevator, with a rectangular window that showed part of the autopsy suite when its blinds were opened. A body would be wheeled in on a stretcher, then the sheet covering it would be carefully peeled back by an attendant to reveal only the head. A blond woman, her hair in a low ponytail that brushed the collar of her black pantsuit, and a dark-haired man only slightly taller than she was stood facing the shuttered window as Joplin opened the door. The man was obviously not Tom Halloran, whom Joplin had been expecting to see again with Mrs. Carter. He turned and stared at Joplin with bespectacled eyes. He was wearing a grey tweed jacket and a navy bow tie.

Joplin extended his hand. "I'm Hollis Joplin. I'm an investigator with this office, and I was at the scene where Mr. Carter was found."

"Paul Woodley. I'm Mrs. Carter's doctor," he added, offering his own limp hand.

The woman now turned to face Joplin. She was one of the most beautiful women Joplin had ever seen, with a high forehead, luminous light-blue eyes, and a wide, sensuous mouth. He suddenly felt sixteen again, and fought the urge to search his pockets for the breath mints he'd always carried at that age. Anne Carter was every teenage boy's favorite cheerleader who'd also been on the honor roll, all grown up. He was grateful when she didn't offer a hand, certain his own would be clammy with sweat.

"Mrs. Carter? I appreciate your coming down. I know this must be difficult for you."

"Yes, very," she said, lowering her eyes. "I'd like to get this over with." The long lashes swept up again. "I need to go get my son at his school."

"Of course." Joplin moved closer to the window and rapped on it. The blinds opened slowly, and he heard Mrs. Carter gasp. Elliot Carter's blackened tongue had been pushed back into his mouth, but he still looked very dead.

Anne Carter's hand flew up to her face. She closed her eyes tightly and turned her head. Dr. Woodley quickly moved her away from the window, and Joplin asked if she needed to sit down, but she shook her head, eyes still closed. When she opened them, they looked unfocused, as if she were lost in thought, and then her hands began to shake. She seemed suddenly conscious of this and clasped them together.

"Yes, that's my husband," she said, her head moving rapidly up and down.

In the hall outside the viewing room, Anne Carter recovered quickly, her game face reapplied like fresh make-up. But Joplin was sure her reaction upon seeing her husband's body had been one of fear, more than shock, and he wondered why. Was she afraid that an investigation into Carter's death would involve intruding into his personal life, probably his sex life? Or was she concerned for herself or someone close to her?

"I need to ask you a few questions, Mrs. Carter," he said softly.

"Certainly."

"Do you know how your husband was found? I mean, how he died?"

"Yes. That sergeant who came to my house told me. But I didn't believe him."

"You had no idea that he might have been into…that sort of sexual practice?"

"Of course not. Because he wasn't," she added, her tone insistent.

"But you hadn't been living together for a while, right?"

"We had an extremely happy marriage—in *every* way," she insisted. "And then Elliot went through some kind of mid-life crisis. But I never saw any evidence of …what that police officer told me. Never."

"Well, did he ever have any strange or unexplained marks on his body or keep any closets or desk drawers in your house locked?"

She seemed to hesitate for a few seconds, as if she were suddenly remembering something, then said, "No, absolutely not."

"I think Mrs. Carter has answered enough questions for one day," Paul Woodley said tersely. "She's in a state of shock and needs to rest."

"I'm very sorry for your loss, Mrs. Carter," Joplin responded; the interview was obviously at an end. He received a slight nod from her in return. But as he watched them walk down the hall, he was certain that Elliot Carter's estranged wife *hadn't* answered enough questions. At least, not the right ones.

Whatever those were.

The door to Jack Tyndall's office was open. Joplin walked in and sat down on the ugly brown corduroy couch that was stretched against the wall opposite his desk.

"I'll be with you in just a minute, Hollis." Tyndall didn't look up from his computer. With his rumpled hair and a day's growth of beard, he looked more like a hacker who'd been up all night breaking into the World Bank than a pathologist. But Joplin knew that four out of five women would still pick Jack over him any day of the week. And it wasn't just because of his Black Irish good looks; he also had a sort of bad-boy charm that got them every time. Ordinarily, this didn't bother Joplin; they'd been friends even before he joined the ME's office three years ago, and they'd become even closer since then. But now that he was thinking of asking Carrie Salinger out, it occurred to him that it might be a problem.

"Take your time," said Joplin, picking up a forensic journal that lay on the couch. "I haven't read this one yet. Anything of yours in it?"

"A review of police car chase fatalities in Atlanta that I did with Diane Morgan."

"Another one with Diane? Jeez, Jack, that makes three articles in one year you got that poor girl to write for you. When did she have time to finish her residency?"

Tyndall shrugged. "She's a good writer. I didn't want to pass up the opportunity."

Joplin shook his head. "You know, you can talk anybody into doing just about anything, Jack. Is that how you got so many women to marry you?"

The pathologist swiveled around to face Joplin. His blue eyes were red with fatigue, but he was grinning. "Talking is just one of my many charms, Hollis."

"Too bad they don't stay very long."

"Hey, I was married to Lisa for almost four years," said Tyndall with mock outrage.

"Yeah, I think that was your personal best, Jack. But you still had to pay through the nose when she divorced you."

"Don't remind me. I write out child support and alimony checks in my sleep." He sat back in his chair and stretched. "I'm sure you didn't come in here to discuss my marital problems, Hollis. What can I do for you?"

"As a matter of fact, I wanted to know when you might get to the Carter autopsy."

"The autoerotic fatality you brought in? I promise, it's next on my list. I haven't even had time for a second cup of coffee this morning."

"You look like it," said Joplin. Due to the current budget crisis, an open pathologist's position hadn't been filled. On top of that, Lewis Minton, the chief ME, was still recuperating from a heart bypass, and another pathologist, Art Akbar, had been in court for the past two days. All of the others had been working overtime lately. "You been sleeping on the sofa here again?"

"It beats fighting the traffic on 400." Tyndall rubbed his eyes with both hands, then patted his unshaven cheeks. "Guess I could shave, at least. The morning kind of got away from me. Not that my patients will give a shit."

"But those of us still alive would appreciate it, Jack." Joplin frowned, then said, "Hey, listen, the Carter case might turn out to be a real headache."

"What do you mean?"

"Carter was a partner at Healey and Caldwell, one of the top law firms in the city."

"I know the one. I had to give testimony on some of David Healey's cases when he was head of the firm's medical malpractice department."

"Well, the man who discovered the body is none other than Tom Halloran."

Tyndall gave a low whistle and shook his head. "I managed to follow one of his cases on truTV a few months ago during my lunch breaks, and he's something else! He represented the family of that guy who owned about a dozen Waffle Houses, whose mistress wheeled him into her attorney's office about two weeks before he died from chronic alcoholism and got him to leave her everything. You shoulda seen the look on her face when she ended up with nothing but the Florida condo he'd bought her! It was priceless! Only time in my life I ever felt like giving a lawyer a thumbs-up."

"Problem is, Halloran's also a partner at Healey and Caldwell *and* he's executor of Carter's will. He claims there's no way the deceased was into autoerotic asphyxia."

Tyndall shrugged. "So? That's the usual reaction from family and friends."

"Yeah, and I said as much to Mr. Halloran. But he's absolutely convinced foul play was involved, and I think we need to be especially careful with this one."

Tyndall sat up, more alert now. "You wouldn't say that unless something about this case bothered you besides some celebrity lawyer, Hollis. What is it?"

"Just a few things that seemed a little unusual." Joplin pulled out his notebook. "For one thing, the body was found in a very public, open area of the park—the playground—and yet it was facing a low wall on the west side of the playground. There seemed to be no attempt made on Carter's part to conceal himself or even to monitor any comings and goings in the area."

"That *is* unusual," said Jack Tyndall, frowning. "Could he be seen from the street?"

"Only in the daylight, and only if you were looking at that particular spot. In the dark, he would've been virtually invisible, unless someone walked very near him. But he might not have noticed anyone even then because he was turned away and probably very wrapped up in what he was doing. Then again, maybe he didn't start out facing the wall. That was just the way he was found. He used two sections of rope," Joplin went on, reading from his notes, "one forming a noose, the other encircling his thighs and lower trunk. I think the rope around his legs was some type of support structure."

"Well, he could've slipped out of it, or one of the knots failed to hold, and—"

"And his position shifted then or when he was struggling to free himself," Joplin finished. "Those are certainly two possibilities, but I'd also like to find more evidence that Carter was really into this. I'm going to get the LUDS on his cell phone," he added, referring to the Local Usage Details provided by the phone company when subpoenaed, "and I'm also going to meet Mr. Halloran at Carter's apartment in Ansley Towers around eleven. As Elliot Carter's executor, he's the only one who can agree to let me search the place. The Carters were separated, and the wife lives in Ansley Park with the teenage son. I talked to her when she came here to make an official ID of the body."

"Did she know anything?"

"She claims her marriage was perfect right up until her husband left her. Says she never saw any evidence of any deviant sexual practices, and when I tried to ask her some more questions, she clammed up. Or rather, the doctor she was with, a Dr. Woodley—I think he's a shrink—did the clamming for her. Gave me his professional opinion that Mrs. Carter was in a state of shock and needed to rest."

Tyndall's eyebrows went up. "And what is *your* professional opinion as to Mrs. Carter's physical and mental state, Hollis?"

Joplin grinned. "Physically, the lady is in superb condition. I don't know why the deceased left her, but it wasn't because she'd let herself go."

"Well," said Jack Tyndall. "I might have to check this out myself."

"Jack, you're my personal hero when it comes to women, but you're not her type. And I think she might be involved with this Dr. Woodley."

"Hey, I'm a doctor, too. And I clean up pretty well when I have to go to court."

"Yeah, but you still smell like formaldehyde, and pretty soon you're going to be paying alimony to *two* ex-wives. Not only that, but if you were ever able to start a 401K on your measly government salary, it's gone to hell like everyone else's. This lady likes her men to smell—and look—like money. She's out of your class, Jack. Mine, too, if it's any consolation."

"I'll take that under advisement. Meantime, tell me about Mrs. Carter's mental state."

"That's not as easy to assess." Joplin closed his eyes, summoning up an image of Anne Carter. He had what he'd later found out was an "eidetic" memory, an ability to retain accurate, extremely detailed visual memories of things and see them in an almost three-dimensional way when he recalled them. It was an ability that had helped him as a homicide detective, and even more so now. One of the most important aspects of his job was to serve as each pathologist's "eyes and ears" during a particular case. In Milton County, as with most counties in large cities, it was rare for medical examiners to go to death scenes. The resident pathologists—not the ones from Emory Hospital or Grady Memorial who were doing thirty-day rotations, but those who had one-year fellowships and intended to go into forensics—were required to go to scenes whenever possible. But for the most part, the deputy examiners delegated this job to the investigators. They also learned to depend heavily on the investigators' instincts and observations.

Joplin knew that Jack Tyndall was counting on him to report anything that might have a bearing on his ruling as to Elliot Carter's manner of death. The only trouble was, he couldn't get a good reading on Carter's wife. He'd met plenty of women of her type before, of course. They were all good-looking and sweet-smelling and carefully dressed, and usually they smiled a lot and said all the right, polite things, even when they were overcome with grief or horror. Or when they were trying to *look* like they were overcome with grief or horror.

Most of the time he could tell the difference, but with Anne Carter, he had to admit that he'd tried and failed. She'd seemed genuinely upset over her husband's death, but whether it was because she loved him or because he'd left her with a big mess on her hands, Joplin couldn't tell. He saw her again, the high forehead arched in fleeting surprise when he'd asked about marks on Carter's body or locked drawers, the pale blue eyes slowly widening. He looked down at her clenched hands and then back up to her face, seeing once more a pulse in the hollow of her throat begin to beat wildly.

"Let's just say," Joplin said finally, opening his eyes, "that if the autopsy shows that Elliot Carter *was* murdered, I'd advise Homicide to concentrate on Mrs. Carter. She's not strong enough to have hung her husband from a tree branch in Piedmont Park, and she probably wasn't even involved, but I think she knows something."

Tyndall yawned and gave another long stretch, his arms held high in the air. "Well, I've got to finish typing up these notes on a Jane Doe case from yesterday, but I'll try to do Carter before lunch. I'd like to turn it back over to Homicide as soon as possible if foul play's involved."

He brought his arms back down on his desk with a thud, saying, "But, frankly, Hollis, the chances of someone faking a death of this type—"

"Are a million to one," finished Joplin. "I know."

"And this'll put me another whole day behind on my already back-logged cases."

"There are just too many people dying to see you, Jack." Joplin heaved himself up from the sofa. "I'm going to go find some coffee. Get hold of me as soon as you've finished that autopsy, okay? I'm sure Mr. Halloran will be breathing down my neck."

7

"IT MUST BE FASCINATING," Joplin said to Carrie Salinger. She was sitting at a table in the large room that served as a library and conference room, a pile of forensic journals in front of her.

Carrie looked up from the journal she was reading. She was wearing a white lab coat, but hardly any make-up, which he liked. Her hair was dark brown, parted on the side, and fell to her shoulders. She had eyes that seemed black, a slightly olive complexion, and a lower lip that was so full it gave her face a pouty, sensuous expression that probably gave a lot of men the wrong impression. Wrong, because Joplin had discovered in just a week's time that Carrie Salinger was a very serious, somewhat intense young woman who was pretty much focused on medicine and nothing else. But she also had a dry sense of humor that tempered her reserve and could crack him up when he least expected it.

"I'm sorry, what did you say?" she asked.

"The article you're reading. It sure must be fascinating. I came in and poured myself a cup of coffee, did a soft shoe, and sang the 'The Star Spangled Banner,' but you never even looked up. You know, usually people try to ignore me *after* they get to know me."

Carrie Salinger smiled. "I think I would have heard 'The Star Spangled Banner', Hollis. And I wasn't trying to ignore you, I promise. I just have a tendency to get all wrapped up in whatever I'm reading."

"You're forgiven." Joplin brought his coffee over to the table and sat down across from her. "What are you reading anyway?"

"An article on autoerotic deaths." She held up a copy of the *Journal of Forensic Science*. "'Methods of Asphyxia in Autoerotic Fatalities: A Review of Twenty-five Cases.'"

"That's a good one."

"Yes, have you read it?" She seemed surprised.

"All the way through. I got Jack to help me with the big words."

Carrie's cheeks turned red. It was the first time he'd seen a girl blush since he was in high school. "I'm sorry," she said. "I guess that did sound pretty condescending."

"Forget it," said Joplin. "I take it you've seen the body I brought in this morning."

"It was quite an experience." She made a face. "God, I can't believe some of the things people do to themselves. I mean, after all this time at Grady, I thought I'd seen everything, but I guess not."

"It's never dull around here, that's for sure."

"I know a little bit about this kind of deviancy, but not much. I thought I'd better read up on it before the autopsy."

"Good idea. This one might be a little more interesting than usual."

"What do you mean?"

"You ever hear of a law firm called Healey and Caldwell?" asked Joplin.

"Sure. I grew up in Atlanta. That's one of the best in the city."

"You got a lot of lawyers in your family?"

"A few."

"I figured as much." He took a sip of coffee, then looked up at her. "Hey, you said you grew up in Atlanta. Is your family *that* Salinger family? As in Salinger Furniture?" he added, referring to a very upscale store that had been an Atlanta icon for decades.

Carrie's cheeks reddened again, and this time he was sorry that he'd embarrassed her. "It's my parents' business," she said curtly. "I'm just a poorly paid medical resident," she added, more pleasantly.

"Message received," replied Joplin. He went on to tell her about Tom Halloran and his relationship to Elliot Carter, as well as the fact that the attorney thought Carter was murdered.

"Well, I've certainly heard of Tom Halloran, and I know you have to take him seriously, but…murder?" Carrie said, frowning. "Is that possible?"

"Anything is possible, but it would take someone who had a pretty expert knowledge of forensics and death scenes and this particular type of perversion to fool a pathologist. Or me," Joplin added, grinning.

"Yessiree, he's our star investigator, Dr. Salinger," said a voice behind Joplin. "Aren't you, Hollis?"

"No, sir, Chief, I'm not," said Joplin without turning around. "I just try to do my job."

Chief MacKenzie laughed, a low, throaty, good-ole-boy laugh that went with his paunch and Brylcreemed hair. He ambled to the coffee maker, filled his cup, then turned around, smiling broadly. "Don't eat all the grits this boy dishes out, Dr. Salinger. He's going places, for sure. You tell her you go to graduate school, Hollis?"

"Not yet, sir. I wanted her to like me for my looks and personality first."

MacKenzie shook his head and winked at Carrie Salinger. "You know, Doctor, I've taken to watchin' my back these days now that Hollis is gettin' so educated. Cause I know he'll be after my job here as chief investigator soon, for sure. Won't you, Hollis?"

"No, sir, I've got my heart set on being police commissioner."

"Then you better start workin' on your tan, son, if you want to go that high up in *this* town." MacKenzie winked again at Carrie, then headed toward the investigators' room.

"Is he always that—"

"Racist?" finished Joplin.

"Well, that, too. I'm new around here, but I get the distinct impression that you're not Chief MacKenzie's favorite investigator."

"Let's just say that if Chief MacKenzie had to choose between firing me or becoming police commissioner himself, he'd have a real hard time."

"That bad, huh?" said Carrie, smiling.

"My cross to bear in life. Listen, are you free for dinner tomorrow night?"

"Well, yes, but—"

"Why not, then? Am I too old for you? I'm thirty-eight, by the way. And you're what—about twenty-eight? So that's too big an age difference, right?"

She smiled again and shook her head. "I'm twenty-nine, but given your level of maturity, I'd say we're pretty evenly matched."

Joplin clutched his heart and sighed. "You got me there. So what is it? Do you only date doctors and lawyers and accountants?"

"Actually, I don't date *anyone* these days. Med school and my internship were nothing compared to these last three years of anatomic pathology."

"Are you going to apply for a fellowship here when you're through?"

"No, although I have to admit I'm really enjoying myself. But I'm going into pediatric pathology, so I've got two more years of clinical path."

"How about a study date? I've got a paper due for my Constitutional Law class."

"When in the world do you find time to go to graduate school, by the way?"

Joplin wondered if she were trying to switch the subject. "Every Tuesday, from eight a.m. to five p.m. Georgia State has a master's program in Criminal Justice for people already working in the field. I've taken two classes a quarter for the last eighteen months, and if all goes well, I'll be through with the course work in August."

"I'm impressed. No, really," she added, laughing. "And I need to do some research myself. We could go to the Emory library."

Joplin knew that Carrie had graduated from Emory Medical School and completed her internship at its teaching hospital on campus. She'd probably be more comfortable there than at the Georgia State library. "Fine with me. We'll go have dinner at a place I know in Virginia-Highlands first. But I haven't been back to Emory since I took my forensic pathology course. Do you think they'll let me in?"

"Only if you have a shirt and shoes on. No tank tops. And try not to drool."

"Okay, we're even. I promise to lay off the 'aw, shucks, ma'am' routine."

"And I'll leave my silver spoon packed away in the sideboard at home...the one from Salinger's," Carrie said. "Deal?"

"Deal. I'm off tomorrow, but I'll swing by here and pick you up about six."

"I'm looking forward to it," said Carrie Salinger, giving him a smile that drove all thoughts of an impending blue funk out of his mind.

8

THE VIEW OF THE CITY from the living room of Elliot Carter's apartment stopped Joplin in his tracks. The wall was entirely glass and diagonally overlooked the intersection of Peachtree and 14th Street. To the right was the Colony Square complex; on the left were Symphony Tower and the Proscenium building. In the very center was the tower at One Atlantic Center, rising like an ageless obelisk.

Marveling at the spectacular architectural splendor, he stood blinking in the late morning light for several seconds and then forced himself to turn his attention to the room itself. It was filled with antique furniture—or what looked like it anyway. But antique or not, Carter's furniture looked expensive and had been chosen and arranged by someone—probably a decorator—who knew a lot about furniture. Also color, Joplin realized, noticing the subtle shades of peach and gray set off by contrasting tones of black and rust.

"Not your average post-divorce apartment," he said, thinking of his own, which was filled with mismatched furniture that would never have made it through the delivery door of Salinger's.

Tom Halloran shrugged. "I told you Elliot was a wealthy man."

Joplin strode through the dining room and on into the spacious kitchen. Everything was spotless. The shiny copper cookware, hanging on pegs on one wall, and the large, built-in spice rack with its alphabet-ized spices bespoke a love of both cooking and orderliness. He opened the door of the stainless steel Sub-Zero refrigerator. As he'd expected, it was filled with fresh fruit and vegetables, all neatly arranged. Abruptly, Joplin shut the refrigerator door and walked out of the kitchen, shaking his head.

"What's the matter?" asked Halloran, following him.

"I've just never seen such an immaculate place in my life, especially when it belonged to a single man, living alone. You ought to see my apartment." He'd have to spruce up, he decided, if there were a chance he might bring Carrie there.

"Well, I know Elliot used a maid service offered by the management, but I'm not sure how often they came. He *was* an especially organized man, though, I have to admit."

Joplin walked back through the dining room and living room and back into the foyer. The door on his left opened into a bedroom that held twin beds, a tall bureau, a small armoire with a TV set and stereo in it, and a table and lamp between the beds.

"This was Trip's room when he stayed with Elliot," said Halloran.

A quick look into the closet showed it contained several pairs of jeans, khaki pants, casual shirts, and ski equipment, as well as some high tops and a pair of Nike running shoes. The bathroom was just like the bed-room: too clean and orderly for a teenager. Either the kid was just like his father, thought Joplin, or the maid service was exceptional.

He went into the master bedroom next, certain that if he were going to find any evidence of previous autoerotic activity, it would be there. Like every other room in the apartment, it was immaculate. The queen-sized, four-poster bed was tautly made; a pile of books on the bedside table (an old edition of Walker Percy's *The Moviegoer*, a biography of Thomas Jefferson, and a copy of a Lars Kepler mystery) was neatly stacked. The thick Oriental rug even had vacuum cleaner ridges in it. Joplin made a mental note to ask when the cleaning lady had last been there.

The enormous bathroom held both a shower and a square, travertine-tiled Jacuzzi, as well as an elaborate series of mahogany drawers and cabinets along one wall. Before looking around any further, he got a small step-stool from the foot of Carter's bed and carefully examined the top of the door that led from the bedroom.

"What are you looking for up there?" asked Halloran.

"Grooves or abraded areas. Anything that might show that a rope or a harness or any other piece of equipment has been used on the door as a hanging device."

"Find anything?"

"Not on this door," said Joplin, stepping off the stool. Another door on the opposite side of the bathroom led into the closet. He opened it, and a bright light came on, making it easy to see that this door had also not been used for the purposes of autoerotic asphyxia. Joplin sighed, feeling more and more uncomfortable about Elliot Carter's death. If Carter had really been into hanging, it seemed logical that he would have chosen one of these doors. He could have watched himself, all dolled up in his bizarre finery, in the three-way mirror from either one of them.

But it was only a few minutes later that he found, at the very back of Elliot Carter's neat, orderly closet, several places where there were scratches in the metal rod in familiar, snakelike patterns.

"Bingo," he said.

Halloran peered at the rod where Joplin was pointing and shook his head. "That could be anything."

"Maybe. But I bet there's more in here."

A further search produced two coils of soft rope in a shoebox, a stash of bondage magazines in a small cedar chest that held sweaters, and a Neiman Marcus box filled with a collection of women's bikini underwear on one of the overhead shelves. Silently, Joplin showed each find to Halloran, then gathered up the items and placed them in plastic bags that he'd stuck in his jacket pocket for just such a purpose. He also took some digital pictures of the closet rod.

"Does this mean you won't investigate Elliot's death any further?" the attorney asked.

"If Dr. Tyndall finds anything unusual or suspicious during the autopsy, the police will follow up on it," Joplin assured him.

"Listen," said Tom Halloran. "Please don't give up on Elliot. I know you think I'm crazy for still believing he was murdered, after you found all that stuff, but just consider the possibility that it might have been planted, okay? Will you at least consider that?"

"Sure. In fact, I'm going to go talk to security, find out who went in and out of the building last night. Want to come?"

Halloran looked at his watch. "I need to get back to my office for an emergency partners' meeting, but thanks for asking." He held out his hand. "I'll be in touch."

Joplin gripped the attorney's hand and smiled. "I'm sure you will, Counselor."

The interview with Brent Daniels, the security man on duty, didn't yield much. Joplin learned that visitors' names and the times at which they asked to see a resident were only recorded if the resident wasn't home. Otherwise, tenants were contacted by phone and told who was there to see them. No one had come to see Elliot Carter during Daniels' shift the day before, which began at 7 a.m. and ended at 3 p.m. He had seen Carter himself around seven-fifteen, which was the attorney's usual time to leave for his office in the morning, but not after that. The log book showed no visitors for him during the second shift. Joplin would have to talk to Will Pinkston, who had that shift, to find out when Elliot Carter returned. The only other piece of information he gained was that there was just an electronic security system after eleven p.m.. Tenants used card keys to enter or leave then.

After writing down the other security man's name and number, Joplin thanked Daniels and left the building, but images of Elliot Carter's apartment kept flashing through his mind. What he'd found in the master closet certainly seemed to confirm an autoerotic death, but it also seemed obscenely out of place. Not the sexual paraphernalia itself; that was all as neatly stored as the food in Carter's refrigerator, and Joplin had seen too many examples of perversion in well-kept, elegant surroundings to be surprised by that. No, it was the idea that a man like Elliot Carter, who, to all appearances, was a good father and a respected, organized, responsible, *careful* man, would engage in the type of extremely risky and self-destructive behavior that had resulted in that grotesque death scene in Piedmont Park. It just didn't seem to fit.

Like a snake in a bottle of milk.

9

As she scrubbed up before the next autopsy, Carrie Salinger felt a growing excitement. In the ten days she'd been with the ME's office, she had assisted at fifteen other autopsies: five gunshot victims (two self-inflicted), three drug-related deaths, five vehicular deaths, one accidental drowning, and one SIDS baby. They'd all been interesting, but still pretty routine for a morgue in a large city. The only ones out of the ordinary had been the elderly couple whose bodies hadn't been discovered for a week. She hadn't seen such an advanced state of decomposition during med school or her internship. But now she was going to have the opportunity to observe a death caused by highly deviant behavior. Smiling, Carrie finished checking the instruments she and Jack would be using. Then she looked over at the body on Table One, and her smile faded.

The wig and women's underwear had already been removed from Elliot Carter, but not the ropes from his neck and thighs. She'd learned that it was very important to check the bindings in cases like this, to make sure that the victim could have tied them himself. For the first time, Carrie realized how handsome the man must have been. Even in death, with his features distorted by pressure, she could see a certain elegance in the face.

Carrie knew that she would take from this man whatever she could to add to her knowledge about human beings and their capacity for self-destruction. Not that she was judgmental; her approach was strictly clinical. In spite of her religious upbringing, she had long ago shed the traditional concept of good and evil and sin. She was still very much a part of the relatively small, tightly-knit Jewish community in Atlanta, if not the Conservative synagogue to which her parents belonged. But her pursuit of medicine had left no room for what she now thought of as the superstitious baggage of religion.

Carrie's only brother had died of Tay-Sachs disease when she was eight, igniting an overwhelming need to discover the causes of suffering—of death, disease, mental and physical deterioration. It was what had led her into medicine and, ultimately, to pathology. She was convinced that genetics, biochemistry, disease, and physical and mental trauma were the roots of all behavior considered "evil" by people. Obviously, the autopsy on Elliot Carter wouldn't reveal the roots of his sexual deviancy, but a lot could still be learned. Her eyes strayed to a small sign above the door from the hall. It read: Mortui Vivos Docent: This Is The Place Where Death Delights To Serve The Living. What, she wondered, would this corpse teach her?

"You ready for me now?" asked Eddie Brewer, the technician on duty that day, as he came in from the receiving area. He was a burly black man in his forties with sad eyes and a surprisingly gentle manner. Surprising because of his great strength. Eddie seemed able to lift even the heaviest of the bodies he was prepping as if they were stuffed with cotton. And yet she remembered how delicately he had handled the tiny, four-month-old baby who'd died from SIDS.

"Not yet, Eddie. We haven't done any external exams yet." Carrie looked at her watch. "But you can probably prep Table One in about fifteen or twenty minutes, okay? And by the time you finish that, we'll be finished with Table Two."

"Sure thing," said Eddie. "Just let me know."

Carrie had learned that it was a common practice for the pathologists to work on at least two bodies at a time in assembly-line fashion. In addition to Elliot Carter, they would also autopsy one John Gorman, a MARTA bus driver who'd dropped dead the night before at a red light. Gorman was fifty-two and overweight; a heart attack was the likely cause of death. He'd been in the "cold room" since he'd been processed. All bodies were weighed and photographed in the receiving room when they first arrived at the morgue, with a calendar and a clock placed in each picture to show the date and record the time. Next they were stripped of clothing and effects, which were recorded and placed in sealed envelopes. They were then put into a storage room kept at 3640 degrees Fahrenheit. Identification by friends or relatives could take place after that.

"This one weird enough for you, Carrie?" asked Jack Tyndall as he entered the autopsy room, followed by Tim Meara, the photographer. He nodded toward Table One.

"I guess he'll have to do until something better comes along," she answered, smiling.

Tim rolled his eyes. "Jeez, what do you want?" He was a short, red-haired man in his late twenties with a mordant sense of humor. "Cannibal victims from Our Lady of Perpetual Hope Cancer Home?"

"There's no pleasing some women, Tim," said Jack, peering over his shoulder at them as he scrubbed up. His thick, almost black hair looked as if he'd just smoothed it down with his hands, but at least he'd shaved that morning. It made him look less tired than usual and even a little younger, Carrie decided, noticing the cleft in his chin for the first time. Not that he could be much older than forty. She knew from the ME office's website that he'd graduated from the Medical College of Georgia in 1998. But he was already working on a second divorce and had quite a reputation as a ladies' man, which made him considerably less attractive to her.

Tyndall pulled on latex gloves and adjusted his Plexiglas visor. "Okay, Tim, I want some close-ups of the bindings. Be sure you get some good ones of these ropes around his thighs, okay? I think he rigged them up to form some kind of seat, but we'll have to try to reconstruct it." He turned to Carrie while Tim was taking the pictures. "Can you give me a hand turning him over? I need to see how they look in the back."

"Sure." Carrie grasped Carter's left hip and shoulder and pulled them toward her as Jack pushed. The muscles in his extremities had relaxed somewhat, but his torso was still quite rigid. Tyndall looked carefully at every inch of the back side of Carter's body.

"Okay, Tim, get this rope burn on his back," he said at last. "Right there, see? Looks like he slipped out of the part he was sitting in, and it went up around his chest and back."

"Was there any protective padding found on the body anywhere?"

asked Carrie. "I mean, to prevent rope burns, like under the neck liga-ture? I've read that that's usually a component of these deaths, and it also shows evidence of previous autoerotic sessions."

"Good question," said Jack. "No, our friend here used a good qual-ity cotton rope, which wouldn't ordinarily have caused rope burns. But he apparently slipped out of the support structure and dropped several inches, with the rope cutting into his back—and of course his neck, once there was nothing to support the weight of his body. Okay, let's turn him back over. Tim, as soon as I cut these ropes off, I want you to get shots of all the marks." Jack looked down at the body. "According to Hollis, this guy had it all: partner in a top law firm, rich out the wazoo, standing in the community. What a waste."

"I'll go get Eddie," Carrie said, feeling her face begin to flush. She had been thinking only of what this man's death could teach her, giving no thought to his life and the person he might have been. Maybe that was simply a protective device, she thought, but if so, it wasn't one she wanted to rely on.

It made her feel a little dead herself.

10

JACK WAS MAKING NOTATIONS on Carter's "body sheet," a front and rear illustration of the human body, when Carrie and Eddie returned to the autopsy room. "Hey, buddy," he said to the technician. "You can get going on Table One now."

"You got it, Jack."

Carrie had noticed that all the secretaries and technicians called Tyndall by his first name. The other pathologists were addressed more formally. She wondered if it were because, as the chief deputy ME, Jack had been there longer than the other pathologists. Except for Dr. Minton, of course.

The next several minutes were taken up by Gorman's external exam. During this time, Eddie made a y-shaped incision in Elliot Carter's body which ran from the top of his chest to his genitals. He then propped the head on a block to make dissection of the throat area easier. This done, he began the delicate task of uncovering the laryngeal structures, slicing through the skin and overlying muscles and gently folding them back. Next, he removed the chest plate to expose the heart and lungs. He used a small circular saw for this, its electric whine becoming a weird sort of background music as Carrie and Jack discussed Gorman's case. The cracking sound of ribs being pried open came next, and Carrie found it hard to focus on what Jack was saying.

"I'm through here, Jack," said Eddie several minutes later. He stripped off his gloves, dumped them in a special container, and got another pair at one of the sinks.

"Same here, buddy," Jack said. "I'll trade you." He and Carrie also replaced their used gloves with fresh ones. Jack then began examining Carter's neck and throat area. "The hyoid bone is still intact," he said, "so it's not likely that he was manually strangled first and then strung up to make it look like an autoerotic death." Gently, he probed the area where the spinal cord joined the brain stem. "I can't see any external signs of tearing here, but we'll have to check that out when we get into the cranium."

"Did you expect to see tearing there?" Carrie asked.

"I would've been surprised if I had, actually. It's usually only in judicial hangings—executions—that you see that type of damage and cause of death. There's a drop of at least six to ten feet when the trap door is opened in the platform, and that's what does it. Of course, you'd get the same result if you tied a rope around your neck, secured it to something and then jumped off, say, the roof of a house."

"How about if someone stood on a chair and then knocked it over?" asked Tim.

Tyndall shook his head. "Not enough of a drop." He turned back to Carter's exposed throat and began probing again, this time lower down.

"Could it crush the windpipe?" asked Tim.

"Nope. It takes at least thirty pounds of pressure exerted on the trachea to close it off or crush it, and that usually means manual strangulation. If someone stood on a chair with a noose around his neck and the chair was kicked out of the way, death would be caused by compression of the blood vessels leading to and from the brain— either the carotid artery or the jugular vein. Same as in an autoerotic death." He frowned and leaned closer to the body, then said, "But maybe not in this particular case."

"What do you mean?" Carrie moved to get a better view of the thoracic area.

"Hand me that basin." Tyndall made two quick cuts, then dropped a quarter-sized piece of tissue into the basin. He took this over to a microscope on the counter, carefully slid the tissue onto a slide and peered into the scope. "I'll have the histologist look at this under a more powerful microscope, but I think this is what killed Mr. Carter."

"What the hell is it?" asked Tim.

"A carotid baroreceptor," answered Carrie.

"A *crushed* carotid baroreceptor," said Jack. "Its function is to help regulate the heart, along with the vagus nerve. In very simple terms, if this thing is compressed, the heart is slowed and ultimately stops beating altogether. If so, Peggy should see copious quantities of recent hemorrhages when she examines it. I can see some of that even with this microscope." He returned the tissue to the basin and handed it to Carrie, who poured formaldehyde over the tissue to keep it from drying out.

When she turned back, Jack had cut through the pericardium and was drawing blood from the heart for analysis by the State Crime Lab. Removal of the heart itself would come next. At Emory, she had been taught to use the "en bloc" method, in which all the organs are taken out at once in a straight line, then examined and sectioned. This worked better when groups of students were handling one cadaver. But here, the pathologists used the Rokatansky-Virchow method. Each organ was examined in place, fluid was drawn from selected ones such as the heart and urinary bladder, and then each was removed individually. As Jack inspected each one and then cut it free from the body cavity, he handed it to Carrie, who placed it in a basin.

"Gross observation of all organs, as well as sectioning, shows excellent health," said Tyndall a little later. They had carefully preserved and labeled samples from each organ, as well as fluid samples and cavity smears, for analysis by the crime lab. "No fatty liver, no chronic irritation of the esophagus or stomach lining. His heart isn't enlarged, his arteries aren't clogged, and his lungs look pink and fluffy."

"But both the stomach and the small intestine are empty," Carrie said. "That means he hadn't had anything to eat in at least eight hours—probably more if he died around eleven o'clock last night. Why didn't he eat dinner, if this was just a normal day, topped off with a little kinky sex? And on an empty stomach, even a few drinks would cause some irritation we could see, right?"

"Not really. If he'd gone on a big binge, maybe we'd see some gastric irritation, but then he couldn't have tied those elaborate knots, could he? We'll have to test for ethanol in his system to be sure. But what's your point?"

Carrie pursed her lips and shook her head. "I don't know, maybe I'm making too much of it, but almost every case of autoerotic death I read about today showed alcohol or drug use prior to death. And usually a history of abuse. This guy's liver is in perfect shape, and when I examined them during the postmortem, his nasal passages didn't show signs of cocaine abuse."

"Well, the tox report might show some other kind of recreational drug use," said Jack. "And, as I said, he might have had a few drinks first." He peeled off his gloves, snapped on another pair and moved over to Table Two, where Eddie had finished prepping the remains of John Gorman. "I'll trade you again, buddy."

As Eddie moved out of the way, Jack looked over at Carrie. "To get back to what you just said, it's possible that Mr. Carter was a teetotalling, antidrug type of kinky person who was kind to small animals and always ate from the four basic food groups, but that would be atypical. And that's what we're always on the lookout for in this place: whatever doesn't fit the usual pattern." Jack peeled off his gloves again and threw them in the waste receptacle. "But even if the tox screen is negative for drugs or alcohol, that wouldn't be enough to support a ruling of homicide."

"What would be enough?" Carrie asked.

Jack drew on another pair of gloves. "It would be extremely difficult to fake this type of death. There are too many things to screw up. Problems with the death scene, for one. Maybe something that Hollis noted won't check out later. Or when he starts looking into the victim's background, we might find something wrong. Maybe there won't be any evidence of previous autoerotic activity. That would be a red flag. Or maybe when we check out the bindings found on the body, we'll discover that he couldn't possibly have tied them himself. Say he's right-handed, but they could only have been tied by a left-handed person or a right-handed person facing him as he tied Carter up. Any one of these things could affect my ruling as to the manner of death."

"So even though you haven't found much to support a ruling of homicide, you're not ruling it out yet."

"Exactly. We have to be very cautious here. We're dealing with a lot of complex legal issues, not just the scientific ones. That's what makes this job so interesting." Jack turned to look at her. "By the way, you'd make a terrific forensic pathologist. I know you're planning on going into pediatric pathology, but have you even considered it?"

Carrie turned to get another pair of gloves. Jack's praise made her feel ridiculously happy. Why did the man have this effect on her? she wondered. But her voice was steady when she answered. "Not really."

"Well, the pay sure sucks in the public sector. Trying to support an ex-wife, an almost ex-wife, and four children on my salary is no easy task, I assure you."

"Then why do you stay? Even teaching is more lucrative."

"I might teach someday," said Jack as he probed Gorman's thoracic area. "After I've found out all I can from human beings. From death itself. And," he added, grinning, "after I've written hundreds of forensic articles and made a national reputation." He looked sideways at Carrie, his head tilted. "By the way, would you be interested in collaborating on an article with me? If you do all the research and the lit review and the actual writing, I'll let you be first author. What do you say?"

"And what will you do?" she asked, laughing.

"The most important part: I'll come up with the topic."

"Sure," she answered, surprising herself. "It might be interesting."

"Big mistake," said Tim, shaking his head. "Jack's got the bodies of several dozen young and formerly juicy residents neatly wrapped and dangling from a huge web in his office. By the time he finished with them, they were too drained to finish their training."

"Thanks for the warning," Carrie said, smiling at Tim. But her words were almost drowned out by the sound of the tiny buzz saw that Eddie was using to split Elliot Carter's skull in two. She turned to look and saw that the technician had made an ear-to-ear incision in Carter's scalp and peeled his face down like the skin of a banana. Now even the vestiges of his elegant and handsome features were gone, and the discomfort Carrie had felt earlier over failing to see this man as a human being was replaced by a sadness that surprised her with its intensity.

11

Tom Halloran sat in Alston Caldwell's office and tried to think of any details he might have left out. Although he wasn't happy that David Healey, Jr., the firm's managing partner—and a first-class jerk in his opinion—was there, he knew Caldwell needed to know as much as possible about Elliot's death before they met with the other partners. But there was one thing he hadn't discussed with them yet, and he needed to get it over with before they moved into the large conference room.

"I'm not convinced yet that this was some kind of…accident," he said. "I think Elliot might have been murdered."

There was only a fleeting look of surprise on Caldwell's face. "Well, now, Mister Tom," he said in his slow, courtly drawl. A handsome and still vigorous man in his seventies, he often addressed the associates and younger partners this way. Halloran considered it peculiarly Southern and oddly charming. "Please elaborate. I've known Elliot's family all my life, and as distressing as it would be to know he was murdered, it would be better than thinking he did this to himself."

Halloran shook his head. "I just can't accept that he was into auto-erotic asphyxia."

"Are you sure you're not letting the facts be obscured by your personal feelings? After all, you just told us that the investigator from the ME's office found corroborating evidence in Elliot's apartment. I know it's a terrible thing to learn about a friend—good lord, I don't believe most of us here have even *heard* of this sort of…of—"

"Perversion?" David Healey offered. He was a tall, gray-templed man, who might easily have been cast to play an attorney on TV.

A ruthless, sanctimonious attorney, thought Halloran.

"You're probably right, sir," he said, ignoring Healey. "But the investigation is still ongoing. Evidence may turn up that could put a different light on things."

"I just want to know how much of this is going to get into the media," Healey said. "All this stuff about Elliot wearing a wig and women's underwear and diddling himself in Piedmont Park! How the hell do you think that's going to make the firm look?"

"I don't think that should be our major concern right now," Halloran responded.

"Is that so?" Healey said, cocking his head. "I know you think of yourself as the star of this firm, Tom, but if Healey and Caldwell's reputation is destroyed, you won't shine so brightly either. The media will have a field day with this unless we contain the damage."

David had been the only partner to keep the vote from being unanimous when Halloran had been made a full partner at the unheard of age of thirty. After five years, the decision still seemed to pain him.

"I'm more concerned with Elliot's reputation than mine, David. And I think the firm is capable of weathering this."

"Really," Healey said patronizingly. "Well, let me ask you this before you engage is some kind of pyrrhic victory that might pull us all down: How do you presume to know what Elliot was or wasn't into, sexually? Do you think he'd tell you about something like that if he were?"

These were the same questions Halloran had been asking himself all morning, but coming from David Healey they sounded obscene. He knew Healey and Elliot Carter had never been friends, even though they'd known each other since their law school days at the University of Georgia, but Halloran hadn't realized until now that they had probably been enemies. Why, he didn't know. Elliot had never discussed the subject with him, merely cautioning him to watch his back whenever he had complained about David's directives on billing or his practice of accessing computer files on other attorneys' clients whenever it suited him. For his part, David Healey had been almost deferential to Elliot at meetings. Halloran had attributed this to Alston Caldwell's obvious esteem for Elliot, but now that Elliot was dead, David didn't even try to conceal his hostility.

"No, David, I don't think he would've told me about it," he answered coldly. "Elliot Carter was one of the most private people I've ever known. He was also sensitive, discreet, and highly considerate of other people's feelings. All of which are reasons why I can't believe he caused his own death in this particular manner, and in a public park."

"And that's all the more reason for us to protect Elliot's privacy and reputation right now," Alston Caldwell interjected smoothly. "If an investigation shows that he was murdered, a big part of the murderer's intent must have been to destroy Elliot's good name, too. But, the public will be left with that horrible image of Elliot, the one the media are going to give them, unless we try to do something about it."

It was a good argument, and Halloran knew it. "All right, what do you have in mind?"

"Well, for starters, I think we should put a little pressure on the local TV stations and the managing editor of the *Atlanta Journal-Constitution* to leave out certain details of Elliot's death in their coverage," said Healey. "We've got a PR company on retainer for things like that. And a few phone calls from Alston to the right people wouldn't hurt."

"One will be to Lewis Minton, the chief ME," said Caldwell. "We go back a long way together, and I think if I ask him to look into the case personally, he will."

"But I don't want Investigator Joplin to think we're going over his head," Halloran protested. "I'd like to keep the lines of communication open with him."

"I'm sure Lewis will be discreet, Tom," said Caldwell.

Halloran nodded and turned to David Healey. "Was Elliot working on anything controversial lately, anything that—"

"Might cause one of his clients to string him up in Piedmont Park?" Healey finished sarcastically. "Do you really think that could've happened, Tom? It's simply not within the realm of probability that a client—or one of us, for that matter, since I'm sure you'll get to that next—would murder Elliot over a legal or business matter."

"I don't know about that, son," said Caldwell. "You'll find when you've practiced law as long as I have that people do the most amazing things for what seem like trivial reasons. And losing money is anything *but* trivial, I think you'll grant me, especially during these hard financial times. And especially in this town." He pursed his lips thoughtfully. "I do happen to agree with you on one point, David: If Elliot was, in fact, murdered, I don't think it was over a business dealing."

"What makes you say that, Alston?" Halloran asked.

The old gentleman's eyes narrowed. "If somebody *did* kill Elliot, then as I said, a big part of the reason was to destroy his reputation. But it had to be more *personal* than that to make him do it in this manner. This was spite, if you ask me. Pure and simple spite."

Several long seconds of silence passed after this pronouncement, as if the possibility that Elliot Carter had been murdered was being considered by the two men for the first time. It was finally broken when Caldwell looked at his watch.

"Let's take a little break before the partners' meeting, gentlemen," he said, standing up. "You've given us a lot to think about, Tom."

"I'll put in a call to our PR people," Healey said.

Halloran returned to his own office, stopping to ask Joan, his secretary, to have a sandwich sent up. He realized he hadn't had any breakfast and didn't want to go to the meeting completely unfortified, even though he wasn't really hungry. His mind kept replaying everything that had happened that morning, the images flashing at him like a DVD in fast forward. He was overwhelmed again by guilt that he hadn't been much of a friend to Elliot in the past year; that he didn't even know what was going on in his life during the past few months. The Carters' messy divorce was no excuse; if anything, he should have tried harder to stay connected to Elliot because of it. And Elliot's own reluctance to discuss personal matters was something Halloran now realized he should have tried to overcome. Instead, he had taken the path of least resistance, too caught up in the firm's financial problems to see that his friend might be in trouble.

But what kind of trouble? Halloran wondered. Had Elliot become compulsively drawn into the practice of autoerotic asphyxia, as the investigator believed, escalating both the risk of discovery and the danger to himself? Or was it something entirely different; something that led to the necessity of his being killed, and in a way that would ruin his reputation? Alston had used the word "spite" as a possible factor, and Halloran tried to think of anyone who could have harbored that emotion for Elliot.

Anne came to mind, of course. The bitterness she felt toward Elliot had been apparent to everyone who knew them. But the grief he'd seen on her face today had been real, too; he was convinced of that. And Anne certainly wasn't capable of dressing Elliot in that ghastly costume and hoisting him onto a tree limb in Piedmont Park.

The shrill ringing of the phone startled Halloran, causing him to jump.

"Mr. Halloran, Trip Carter's here to see you," said Joan, sounding shaken.

"I didn't know where else to go," Trip said before Halloran could get over to the door and wrap an arm around him. The boy sagged against him and sobbed, so he held him for a while, then walked him over to the sofa on the opposite wall and gently sat him down.

"You came to the right place," Halloran said, sitting down beside him, his arm still around the boy. "I'm so sorry about your dad, Trip. He was my best friend. I still can't believe he's gone, and if *I* can't believe it, I can only imagine how you must be feeling." He continued to hold Elliot's son, letting him cry for as long as he needed. Finally, he pulled a clean handkerchief out of his pants pocket and gave it to him.

Trip wiped his eyes and blew his nose, then looked up at Halloran. He was a handsome, dark-haired teenager with his father's rangy build and his mother's blue-green eyes, now rimmed with red. "Mom said you found him. In the park."

"I did," said Halloran cautiously, unsure about what he should say to Trip. He had no idea what Anne had told him about the circumstances of Elliot's death. "And I'll try to answer any questions you might have about that."

Tears welled up in Trip's eyes again and spilled over. "He didn't kill himself. Not…that way. The way the police think he did. But I don't want to talk about that right now, okay?" He looked down at the table. "I just can't. But I know he didn't do that to himself." He ran his hand through his hair in a circular motion. It was something Halloran had seen him do ever since he was a little boy, whenever he was nervous or upset about something. "We were supposed to get together last night at the Vortex for dinner. I got there at seven-thirty, but he wasn't there. So I waited about twenty minutes and then tried calling him at home and on his cell phone, but never got him."

"Had your dad left a message for you on your cell or at the restaurant?"

"No, and that wasn't like him at all. I called home, but got voicemail, so I figured my mom was out, too. I finally just left."

"What did you do then?"

"I decided to just go home. I thought Dad would get in touch with me later."

"And did he?"

Trip exhaled deeply. "No. Mom came in about nine, but she didn't know anything." He frowned. "She just said something probably came up."

"Your parents' separation has been pretty hard on you, hasn't it, Trip?"

"Yeah, I guess. Pretty much."

"Maggie and I were really surprised when your dad told us he was leaving. We always thought your parents had a good marriage."

"They *did*," Trip insisted. "I mean, I never even saw them argue." His face relaxed as he recalled a happier time. But then, almost immediately, the tightness returned. "At least, not until the night before Dad left. They had a real bad fight that night. I could hear Mom screaming at him and crying and carrying on. The next day, he just left."

"Did he ever talk to you about it, tell you why he was leaving?"

Trip looked down at his knees, then stared off into space. "Not really."

"I don't mean to be prying, Trip, it's just that—"

"Sure, I know. You're just trying to figure out what happened. But I honestly don't know why Dad left. Sometimes I felt like he *wanted* to tell me, but he couldn't. All I really know is what my mother told me."

"Can you tell me what that was?"

"That Dad must have found somebody else. That he had left her for another woman." Trip suddenly looked up at him. "Do you think she was right?"

"I don't know, Trip. It's possible, I guess. Things like that happen a lot more than married people like to admit. Did your dad ever introduce you to any women friends after he moved out? Anyone you thought he might be interested in?"

Trip shook his head. "No. Never. Mom always used to ask me that, too." His eyes filled up again. "I think it was about me, Mr. Halloran. I think he left because of me."

"Trip, a lot of kids think that when their parents divorce, but they're wrong."

"But, see, I know," said the boy. "I couldn't really make out what they were talking about, but I kept hearing Mom say my name when she was screaming at him that night. They were fighting about me! It had to be something *I* did. They both told me it had nothing to do with me, but I didn't believe them. I've tried and tried to think what it could have been, but I just can't," he added, and then broke down again.

"Maggie and I will come back and get your car," Halloran said over Trip's protests as they rode the elevator to the parking garage. "I don't want you to drive right now."

"But I'm okay now, I swear."

"Then just humor me."

A few minutes later, they were in Halloran's BMW. He didn't say anything until they were out on Peachtree Street. When they stopped for a red light, he glanced at the boy, who was staring ahead, dry-eyed now, but still looking lost and overwhelmed. "I want you to listen to me for a few minutes, Trip. Just listen." He took a deep breath. "When I was in law school, my father died…like your father's dad did. We had that in common, both losing fathers when we were young. But unlike your grandfather, my dad died in disgrace. He got caught up in a business scandal, and then he…he killed himself."

Trip turned to look at him. "I never knew anything about that. I'm sorry."

"It was a long time ago." The light changed, and Halloran moved into the intersection. "Our family lost just about everything, including all the friends we thought we had in Chicago. The whole thing made me very bitter and full of anger, and I came to Atlanta determined to make as much money and as big a name for myself as I could. No matter what I had to do, or whom I had to hurt in the process. But when I won my first big trial after nearly destroying the other side, your father helped me see that I was destroying *myself* in the process, and that winning wasn't everything. Not even at a firm like Healey and Caldwell. At least, not the way that I was going about it. He was one of the finest, most honorable men I've ever known, and he loved you more than anything else in the world. When he left home, it had to be in *spite* of that, not because of anything you did. Now, that's fact number one. Fact number two is that your father didn't kill himself, either accidentally or on purpose."

"What do you mean?"

He knew that he shouldn't be raising the boy's hopes when he had no proof whatsoever of what he'd said, what he'd been saying all morning. It was irresponsible and possibly even cruel. But it seemed to be all he could do for Elliot's son at the moment, and somehow, he had to find the proof.

"I mean that I think he was murdered, Trip. And that I'm going to do everything in my power to convince the police of that. But whether or not I succeed, I'm going to find out why he was killed and by whom. I promise you that."

12

ACE INVESTIGATIONS, INC. WAS in a ten-story office building on Peachtree in the Pershing Point area. Hollis Joplin rode the elevator to the fifth floor and found the detective agency at the end of a long hall that, along with its tan carpeting, had seen better days. The front office was in much better shape, however, with a number of plants, a burgundy rug, and gray upholstered furniture. In fact, it looked a lot better than most of the private agencies Joplin had seen in his time. From behind her computer, a fortyish, attractive black woman with a high, rounded forehead and softly sculpted hair looked up at him.

"May I help you?"

When Joplin explained who he was and that he was investigating the death of Elliot Carter, the woman put her hand to her mouth and stood up. Without a word, she turned and walked over to a door to her right, knocked softly, and then let herself in. Almost immediately, a middle-aged man, wearing a blue shirt, the sleeves rolled up and his tie pulled loosely down around the collar, came out of the room.

"I'm Jim Ferguson," he said, running a hand through his thinning gray hair as he walked over to Joplin. "What's this about Elliot Carter being dead?"

"He was found this morning in Piedmont Park. I was told his wife is one of your clients."

Ferguson stared hard at Joplin, then said, "I think we'd better go into my office. Janna, please hold all calls."

Ferguson's office had more of the gray and burgundy, but splashes of green had been added, and his desk was larger than the secretary's. Joplin was impressed. "You get a lot of work from law firms?" he asked.

"A fair amount."

"Is Healey and Caldwell one of them?"

"No, as a matter of fact."

"But Elliot Carter's wife, Anne Carter, *was* a client."

Ferguson sat at his desk and indicated a chair in front of it for Joplin. "I'm really not at liberty to answer that. Why don't you tell me what happened to Carter?"

"Well, it looks accidental, but I'm checking a few things out. You ever on the job?" Joplin asked, knowing most private detectives had police backgrounds.

"Ten years at Dekalb PD, which is why I know it's a little unusual for an ME's investigator to be 'checking a few things out.' That's Homicide's job."

"Yeah, well, this *case* is a little unusual." Joplin knew he could push the envelope and demand information from Ferguson, but he might get more out of the former cop if he treated him like a colleague. He decided to let him in on some of the details of Elliot Carter's death, what he'd found at Carter's apartment, and the fact that Carter's law partner was insisting that he'd been murdered.

"Sounds accidental to me," said Ferguson, shrugging. "No matter what Tom Halloran says. Those hot-shot lawyers are all alike. He's probably just thinking of how this will make his firm look."

"Then why do you still look so worried?" Joplin asked.

Ferguson stared at him, then took a deep breath and exhaled slowly. "Because Elliot Carter was here in this office yesterday."

"*Elliot* Carter?"

The private detective nodded, then pressed an intercom button. "Janna, could you bring me Ben's file on Anne Carter, please? Look," he said to Joplin, "I know I could probably hold off on giving up client information until you have more than just that attorney's suspicions, but I'm worried about Ben."

"Who's Ben?" Joplin asked.

"He's my partner. Ben Mashburn, also an ex-cop. He was handling the Carter case. And no one's seen or heard from him since yesterday afternoon."

Joplin frowned as he processed this latest wrinkle. "Has anyone checked the hospitals?"

Ferguson nodded. "Jane, Ben's wife, called me this morning after doing that. My wife and I were in Augusta visiting our daughter and her family this week, and after talking to Jane, I decided I'd better come on back to Atlanta. I just got here an hour ago. Janna said Ben got a phone call at four-forty yesterday afternoon that she put through to him. A few minutes later, he came out to the front desk and said he was staying a little late and to go on home, that he'd lock up. Nobody has seen him since."

"Have you called Missing Persons?"

Ferguson hesitated, then said. "Ben's a recovering alcoholic. This sort of thing has happened before, so we thought we'd give it a little more time."

Before Joplin could respond to this, the door opened, and the secretary rushed in. "I can't find the Carter file," she said.

"Can't find it?" Ferguson repeated, looking dumbstruck.

"I checked Ben's file cabinet and searched his desk, too."

Jim Ferguson swiveled to the computer on the left side of his desk and began typing. His face grew even more pinched with concern as he stared at the screen. He clicked the mouse twice, then moved it along the pad on his desk. Turning back to Joplin, he said, "There's nothing about the Carter case in either his or Janna's computer files. Not from last September, or this past Monday, when Mrs. Carter hired him again."

"Anne Carter hired Mashburn *twice*?" said Joplin.

"He phoned me in Augusta on Monday to say Mrs. Carter had called and asked to see him that afternoon. Ben hadn't been able to come up with anything she could use in her divorce case last fall, but he seemed to think the case was pretty hot this time around and that it could be a big thing for the agency."

"Did he say what he meant by that?"

"No, he said he'd know more in a few days."

"I'm almost sure it was Mrs. Carter who called Ben yesterday afternoon," offered Janna. "Just before he told me to go on home."

"Tell me about Elliot Carter's visit here yesterday," said Joplin.

The secretary looked at Ferguson, who gave her a curt nod. "Like I told Mr. Ferguson, it was about three-thirty. He came in looking real upset and asked to see Ben. Gave me his name, but wouldn't sit down until Ben came out. Then they went back into Ben's office."

"How long were they in there?"

"About forty-five minutes. He looked a whole lot calmer when he came out."

"Did Mashburn come out with him?"

Janna shook her head. "I didn't see him until he told me I could leave," she said. "And I haven't seen him since then," she added, her voice choking up.

A navy Jaguar was in the driveway of the Carter house when Halloran and Trip arrived. He pulled in behind it, wondering if it belonged to the helpful Dr. Woodley. If so, it didn't make much of an impression on Trip, who didn't even glance at it as he walked between the two cars. As they made their way up the brick path, the front door opened, and Anne burst out.

"Trip!" she said, coming quickly down the front steps to meet them. She was now carefully made up and dressed in a black pantsuit. Trip seemed to stiffen as she hugged him. "I've been so worried about you! Where have you been all this time?"

"I needed to be by myself, okay? I just want to go to my room now."

"Okay, honey, but wouldn't you like some company? Dr. Woodley is here, and—"

"I don't want to talk to anybody right now, Mom," the boy said as he pulled away and hurried into the house.

"I think he's feeling overwhelmed by everything right now, Anne," said Halloran, seeing the stricken look on her face.

"I went over to Westminister to get him," Anne said as they walked up the front steps. She ushered him into the living room and over to one of the white sofas. "I didn't want him to hear about Elliot from anybody else, and I decided I'd better tell him everything, in case it was on the news. But when I did, he just went crazy! He ran out of the headmaster's office before anyone could stop him."

"He came to my office about an hour ago. We talked for a while, but I don't know how much good it did." Halloran felt the sadness of the whole situation sweep through him again. "This is a hell of a thing for someone his age to handle, Anne."

"I know that, Tom. And I appreciate what you did. Really."

A tall man with sandy-gray hair came into the room then, carrying a glass of ice water. He wore tortoise-shell glasses and had an exceptionally high brow, giving him a studious appearance. The gray tweed jacket and white Oxford shirt accentuated this.

"I brought you some Tylenol, Anne." Ignoring Halloran, the man walked over to Anne and offered her two tablets. Obediently, she took the pills and the water.

"This is Paul—Dr. Woodley," she said as Halloran stood up.

Woodley offered his hand, but there was no warmth in either his manner or his grip.

"Tom Halloran. Nice to meet you."

"Tom brought Trip home," Anne said, when Woodley didn't respond to this.

"I see," said the doctor mildly. He pushed his glasses up on the bridge of his nose.

Halloran decided he disliked the man intensely.

"Paul, Trip went up to his room," Anne said. "Is it all right for him to be alone at a time like this?"

"I think he'll be fine. You can coax him out when his grandmother gets here."

"Olivia called and said she'd be here by mid-afternoon," Anne explained.

"Good," said Halloran. "I got hold of her about nine-thirty this morning, and she told me she was going to get here as soon as she could. By the way, I made Trip leave his car in the One Ninety One building parking garage. I can bring it back when I leave the office tonight and Maggie can meet me here. I know she'd like to see you, Anne."

"I'm sure we can get a couple of Trip's friends to go pick it up," said Paul Woodley before Anne could answer him.

Anne looked up at him, clearly surprised, then stood up and turned to Halloran. "Thank you for all your help, Tom," she said quietly.

The psychiatrist saw him out. The front door slammed shut a little too loudly, confirming Halloran's feeling that Paul Woodley had settled in at the house as if he owned it.

Or thought he might someday.

***

After calling Maggie on his cell and filling her in on taking Trip home and his unsettling meeting with Anne's therapist, Halloran decided to make one more stop before returning to the office. He'd already missed the partners' meeting anyway.

The Milton County Medical Examiner's Office was on Cheshire Bridge, a busy street that forked off Piedmont Road, just north of Monroe Drive. The building was a wide, one-story stucco affair that was as deep as it was wide and looked out of place among the strip clubs, liquor stores, and tacquerias surrounding it. Halloran parked and went inside to a narrow green waiting room. A frosted glass window opposite the door opened and a receptionist greeted him. He gave his name, explaining that he was Elliot Carter's executor, and asked whether the autopsy had been performed.

The receptionist was pleasant and sympathetic, but he got very little information from her. She spoke briefly to someone named Angie on her phone, then looked up at him and smiled. "The autopsy was completed earlier this afternoon, Mr. Halloran, but the report hasn't been released yet," she said.

"Well, could I at least speak with the pathologist who performed it?"

"Dr. Tyndall is doing another autopsy right now, but I can ask him to call you."

"I'd appreciate that," said Halloran. He pulled out his wallet and handed her a business card. "Is Investigator Joplin here by any chance?"

"I'm afraid he's out of the office."

Halloran thanked her again and walked outside. A TV van was pulling up to the curb in front of the building. He walked quickly to his car without glancing back, hoping no one in the van had seen his face. Unless some gory triple murder had just occurred, he was sure the video crew getting out of the van was there to cover Elliot's death. This was one situation where publicity would do neither him nor Healey and Caldwell any good.

And certainly not Elliot Carter.

13

"ELLIOT CARTER WENT TO SEE the private detective Anne hired?" Tom Halloran's voice was so loud Joplin had to hold the cell phone several inches from his ear.

Joplin had called the attorney, albeit reluctantly, after filling Ike Simmons in on the latest developments. He'd been afraid that once Halloran heard what he'd discovered at Ace Investigations, he would see it as irrefutable evidence that his friend had been murdered. But there was a strong possibility that Ben Mashburn might turn up dead, and Joplin also wanted to find out more about the Carters' legal situation to pass on to Simmons. Ike had talked to Jack, who'd told him that Elliot Carter's autopsy hadn't revealed anything to contradict the assumption that it was an autoerotic fatality. That meant that Homicide wouldn't officially take over the case. Because of all the budget cuts and unfilled positions at Atlanta PD in the past two years, they simply didn't have the man power. As a result, Joplin often extended his own investigation on cases where a ruling as to manner of death was uncertain or delayed for some reason, partly out of a sense of duty and partly because it was hard to break old work habits. Besides, it helped fill in the blanks for the pathologist and kept the case warm for Homicide if murder were ultimately proven. Otherwise, too much time would be lost.

"According to the secretary, it was about three-thirty yesterday afternoon," he said now to Tom Halloran.

"Well, that's possible, anyway. I went over Elliot's schedule for yesterday with his secretary a little while ago. He had appointments until noon, when he left for lunch. He told the secretary he wouldn't be back until four, because he had a meeting with a client at One Atlantic Center. But then around three o'clock, he called in and told her to cancel his last two appointments. Told her something had come up and he wouldn't be back."

Joplin puzzled over this. "It sounds like Mashburn must have called him while he was out, which means he somehow had Carter's cell phone number."

"Anne must have given it to him," said Halloran. "But why? And what could Mashburn have said to Elliot to make him go to his office?"

"Maybe that he had something damaging on Carter and wanted to discuss it."

"You said the file Mashburn had detailing his investigation was missing. Do you think he could have given it to Elliot and then deleted everything from his computer?"

"From what I could tell, the agency seemed pretty reputable," Joplin replied. "It wouldn't stay in business very long if its detectives sold out their clients. Ferguson only talked to me because I'm conducting a death investigation."

Halloran didn't respond for several seconds. When he did, his voice sounded tight, as if he were trying to keep himself under control. "Another possibility is that someone killed Elliot and probably Ben Mashburn, too, and then destroyed all the files."

"I thought of that myself, Counselor," Joplin assured him. "I advised Mr. Ferguson to file a missing persons report immediately, and then I called Ike Simmons at the Homicide Unit and told him everything I just told you. He's going to make sure Missing Persons makes this a priority."

"Good," said Halloran, sounding relieved. "Is he also going to talk to Anne and find out what she knows?"

"I'm sure he will," Joplin replied, deliberately being vague. "Can I ask you a few questions about the Carters' legal situation? It might help when he interviews her."

"Well, that depends on what you want to know."

"First off, did Elliot Carter have an attorney handling his divorce?"

"Yes, Bart Lawson, who's tops in our domestic law department. Elliot wanted him to handle the litigation if a settlement couldn't be reached."

Joplin wrote Lawson's name down in his notebook. "Was that likely to happen?"

"Yes." The attorney didn't say anything more for a few seconds, and Joplin could tell he was reluctant to say anymore. Then Halloran said, "Elliot told me he had agreed to compensate Anne for her contributions to his career, as well as sign over both houses to her so that Trip wouldn't be uprooted, but Anne was also trying to get the prenuptial agreement thrown out."

"On what basis?"

"Probably that she was pressured into signing it by the family, but you'd need to ask Bart about that."

"Okay. Let's move on to Carter's will. Who's the trustee for the son?"

Again there were several seconds of silence. "I am," Halloran finally said, "now that Elliot is dead. He named me as successor trustee."

"I see," said Joplin slowly. "So in addition to collecting fees as executor, you'll also be in charge of a sizeable estate for several years *and* be paid to be the boy's trustee. Some people might call that a pretty good motive for murder, Mr. Halloran."

"Maybe so, but if that were the case, I doubt I'd be running around trying to make everyone believe he was murdered, would I?"

Joplin grinned and said, "You've got me there, Counselor. Listen, thanks for talking to me. This'll help a lot."

"I hope so, but getting Anne to talk won't be easy."

Joplin listened intently as Tom Halloran related meeting Anne's therapist when he took Trip Carter home. It jibed with his own impression that Paul Woodley seemed to be overly protective of his patient. Maybe even proprietary. "Do you think there's more than a doctor/patient relationship going on?" he asked.

"Yes, but I'm not exactly sure what it is."

"Well, maybe I can find out," said Joplin. He had told Jack Tyndall earlier in the day that if it turned out that Elliot Carter had been murdered, Homicide should concentrate on Mrs. Carter. Since it was still technically his case, he could start concentrating on the deceased's beautiful widow himself.

And Dr. Paul Woodley as well.

***

The Pershing Point area, where Ace Investigations was located, was just a five-minute drive from the Carter house in Ansley Park. Although it was already after five, Joplin decided to try to see Anne Carter before he headed for home.

He walked up the driveway as slowly as possible, so that he could admire the large, rose-colored stucco house. Joplin was sure it had been designed by Phillip Schutze, one of Atlanta's most famous architects in the early part of the twentieth century. It was in the style of a Palladian villa, like a smaller version of the Swan Coach House in Buckhead, which Schutze had also designed. He wished he could spend more time checking it out, even get a few pictures, but decided that wouldn't go over too well with the lady of the house.

The housekeeper ushered him into a two-story entry hall with black and white marble tiles. "I'll see if Mrs. Carter is available," she said politely, then disappeared down a hallway to the left of the wide staircase.

Joplin barely had a chance to peer into the handsome, book-lined study on the left side of the entry hall before Anne Carter appeared. There was a puzzled expression on her face, and her head was tilted to one side. She was definitely not expecting to see him.

"Mr. Joplin?" she inquired. "Did I get your name right? I'm afraid I wasn't in very good shape when I met you this morning."

"You got it right, ma'am. I've been admiring your house. Is it a Phillip Schutze?"

She smiled at him. "Yes, it is. He designed it in 1932."

"I thought so. I'm sort of an architecture buff, and this is a real treat for me. I don't have many opportunities to go into houses designed by Phillip Schutze. It's beautiful."

"How nice of you to say so," she said, inclining her head in a faintly regal manner. "But I'm sure you came here on official business. Is it about the autopsy?"

"Actually, I need to talk to you about Ben Mashburn, the private investigator you went to see on Monday," Joplin said, deciding to switch gears abruptly. "He's missing."

The gear-switching had the desired effect. Anne Carter's mouth opened as she stared at him. "I don't know what you're talking about," she said abruptly.

"Mrs. Carter, I just spent an hour at Ace Investigations, talking to Jim Ferguson. I think you met him last September when you hired Ben

Mashburn to investigate your husband. He told me you hired Mashburn again this past Monday. His secretary also remembers meeting you—both times," Joplin added, to forestall a second denial.

She ignored this and said, "What happened to Ben?"

"We don't know. Nobody's seen him since late yesterday afternoon. He got a phone call from a woman about twenty to five. The secretary is pretty sure it was from you. Mashburn's wife says he never made it home last night."

"Well, I'm certainly sorry to hear that, but I don't see what it has to do with me."

"Was it you who called him yesterday?" asked Joplin.

Anne Carter fingered the pearls at her neck. "Yes, but he said he'd have to call me back. Only he never did. I forgot all about that, what with everything that's happened."

"I can understand that. What was it you went to see him about on Monday?"

With raised eyebrows, she said, "You mean Jim Ferguson didn't tell you that, too? I had the impression he didn't understand the meaning of the word 'confidential.'"

"Private investigators aren't like doctors or lawyers, Mrs. Carter. They can't keep things confidential during an official investigation."

"Then why are you asking me? I'm sure you know all about it."

"I'd like to hear about it from you," Joplin bluffed.

Her facial expression relaxed, and Joplin knew she hadn't bought it. "I'd really rather not go into it," she said. "It's all very personal."

"The written file, as well as all the information in the office computers, has mysteriously disappeared," Joplin said, deciding he did better with her when he used ambush techniques. "All Ferguson could tell me about were the results of the first investigation. That Mashburn hadn't come up with anything incriminating."

"Then I think I'll let things stay as they are. My husband is dead. Whatever I talked to Ben Mashburn about is irrelevant now. There's no sense in dragging Elliot's name through the mud; I have my son to think about. Besides, my mother-in-law just got here from Charleston, and I need to get back to her."

"Mrs. Carter, I'm trying to conduct an investigation into your husband's death. Refusing to answer my questions could result in your being charged with obstruction."

Anne Carter lifted her chin, and her eyes glittered with a hardness Joplin hadn't seen before. "As far as I know, no crime has been committed, so I'm not obstructing anything. An Atlanta police detective stood right here this morning," she added, pointing to the floor, "and told me that my husband had died accidentally. And *he* was with the Homicide Unit. In fact, I think you're going *way* outside the scope of your job in questioning me like this."

"Actually, Mrs. Carter, this *is* within the scope of my job, which is to assist the ME'S office—specifically, Dr. Tyndall, in this case—in determining the manner of your husband's death. The police—"

"Dr. Tyndall?" she said, interrupting him.

Joplin was sure she was trying to switch the subject and throw him off, but he answered her patiently. "Dr. Tyndall is the pathologist who performed the autopsy earlier this afternoon. Now, as I was saying, the police don't have the authority to declare a death accidental. And what I'm trying to do is rule out anything that would point to homicide."

She looked past him, at a spot just behind his left shoulder, and didn't reply right away. Joplin began to hope that he might be getting through to her. Then her face tightened and her eyes turned hard again.

"Isn't that what an autopsy is for?" she asked, sarcasm in her tone.

"Yes, but there are other factors to consider, such as the fact that one of the last people to see your husband alive is now missing himself."

"Ben Mashburn could be out on a bender, for all you know. So unless Elliot's death is ruled a homicide or Ben is found murdered, I'm not going to say any more."

Joplin decided not to force the issue, but he wasn't ready to give up entirely. "How did you know that Ben Mashburn had a drinking problem?"

"Because he told me so," she said, folding her arms. "He called me one night last October to give me a report on his progress, and I was… I'd had a few glasses of wine. So he told me that he was a recovering alcoholic and talked to me for a while. He didn't want to see me 'escape into a bottle,' as he put it." The hardness slowly melted from her face. "He was a nice man, Mr. Joplin, and if I could help you find him, I would. Now please go away and leave me alone."

Anne Carter walked hurriedly to the front door, her high heels clattering on the marble floor. She swung it open, staring pointedly at him.

"Thank you for your time," Joplin said.

"That's all you're going to get of it, I assure you."

Joplin nodded and walked through the door, certain he wouldn't be invited back into this particular Phillip Schutze house again.

14

By the time Tom Halloran pulled into the driveway of his house, it was almost seven-thirty. He was bone-tired. He'd spent the afternoon gathering paperwork and dictating a petition regarding Elliot's will to file in probate court the next day, hoping to get everything completed by the time of his meeting with Olivia Carter at six that evening. Joplin's call had made this nearly impossible; he found himself unable to concentrate after hanging up. But when Olivia phoned and rescheduled for the following day at noon, saying she wanted to spend more time with Trip, Halloran had pushed himself to finish. An hour later, he phoned Maggie to say he was on his way home, satisfied he'd done all he could on that long, terrible day. He also gave her a short version of what Joplin had told him about the disappearance of Ben Mashburn.

The entry hall was dark when Halloran let himself into the house. A light shone from the kitchen, however, and he could hear the rumble of the television coming from the back of the house, so he headed that way.

Maggie was sitting at the kitchen table, a glass of white wine in her hand and her long legs stretched out on a second chair. Her skin was usually the pale cream that goes with being a redhead, but tonight it seemed ashen, and her green eyes were bloodshot. She looked up at him. "You look exhausted. You want wine or something stronger?"

"Stronger sounds good. I'll get it." Halloran walked over to the Beaux Arts secretary that served as their bar and pulled a bottle of Glenlivet out of the top cabinet.

"I cancelled my meeting with Tory Baxter," said Maggie tiredly. "It just didn't seem right to be going through pictures of Lindsey and Cameron on their pony today."

Maggie was a well-known children's photographer who'd developed a uniquely personal style of shooting families in their homes and various other pertinent sites in the Atlanta area. Until the recession, she'd been in great demand, both by prominent families as well as on the charity circuit. Now, only her wealthiest clients were still able to afford her fees, and even that group was dwindling.

"I think I'll be able to come up with the mortgage money this month," Halloran said, turning to smile at her. "I couldn't concentrate on anything except starting probate on Elliot's will myself. And even that was pretty overwhelming."

"Anything new on the private investigator? Has he turned up?"

"Not that I know of," Halloran said, going to the refrigerator for ice. "The investigator did say he'd call if there's anything to report." He sat down next to her at the table. "Frankly, I think they're going to find him dead."

Maggie tugged on a few strands of her cropped hair and frowned. "I certainly don't want the man to be dead, but won't that prove that Elliot was murdered?"

"I just don't know. I don't know if the police will even find a connection. And his body might not be found any time soon. The ME will have to rule Elliot's death accidental, if no new evidence turns up. And I'm afraid the media is going to have a field day with it once the details get out." He let out a long breath. "God, I wish I could at least spare Trip that."

Maggie reached out and touched his face. "I'm sure it brings back a lot of bad memories for you, Tom."

Halloran took her hand and kissed it, then nodded slowly. "It does."

"How do you think Trip's doing? Did Olivia say?"

"Not well. That's why she wanted to stay with him longer." Halloran took a big sip of his drink, then set the glass down. "Maggie, what if Ben Mashburn turns up dead and the police *do* connect it to Elliot's death? Anne might become the prime suspect. I don't think Trip would ever recover from that."

"You've got to be kidding, Tom! How in the world could Anne Carter, who weighs all of a hundred and ten pounds, dress a man Elliot's size in women's underwear and then hang him from a tree in Piedmont Park?"

Halloran shrugged. "She'd have to have help, of course."

Maggie stared at him, open-mouthed. "Tom, you don't seriously think Anne would've done something like that, with or without help, do you?"

"No, of course not. Especially since Elliot had changed his will. She won't be able to maintain both houses. And even if she sells them, she won't get anything like their value four years ago. The best chance she stood of getting more money out of him was through a divorce settlement. And with Elliot dead, that avenue is closed."

"Well, I don't believe Anne killed him, but couldn't she contest the will?"

"Yes, but that might take years. In fact, since I'd be handling the case, I'd make sure of it. And I can't see her tying herself up in endless litigation when negotiation would've done the trick."

"But why did Elliot cut her out of the will so quickly? It's as if he never even considered the possibility of a reconciliation. We assumed he was going through some mid-life crisis when he moved out, but what if *Anne* were seeing someone? It would explain why she didn't have much negotiating power."

Halloran had to admit it made sense. It would also explain why Eliot had refused to say anything about his reasons for moving out. "It's certainly a possibility," he said. "Her psychiatrist is a good candidate. He and Anne seem to have more than a doctor/patient relationship. In fact, maybe he's never really been her therapist at all."

"You mean that was just a cover?" asked Maggie.

"Exactly." Another possibility occurred to Halloran. "Could it have been David?"

Maggie's surprise was obvious. "David Healey? What made you think of him?"

Halloran shrugged. "He and Elliot were always a little cool towards each other, but today at the meeting with Alston, David was downright hostile about Elliot."

"Carol Freeman did tell me that she saw David and Anne having lunch at Chops last July. I dismissed it at the time because Carol's such a gossip, and I figured they were just planning a firm function, but it's a possibility."

"Well, if Elliot *did* catch Anne in an affair, that explains why she hired Ben Mashburn right after he left her. She was probably hoping to find something on Elliot and level the playing field. What I can't understand is why she hired him a second time."

Maggie stared down into her wineglass, twisting it around by the stem. "I guess we won't know for sure unless Mashburn turns up—alive, I mean."

"Or unless Joplin got her to tell him what was going on. He said he was going to interview her again."

The door from the TV room suddenly burst open, and Megan and Tommy spilled into the kitchen. "Hi, Daddy," said Tommy. "What're you doing here?"

"Very funny, sport." Halloran gave his son a fake roundhouse punch, regretting all the late nights he'd spent at the office in the past several months. When Megan asked if he would watch *America's Funniest Videos* with them, he quickly agreed and followed the kids back into the den.

He took the glass of scotch with him.

Maggie fixed an omelet after they put the kids to bed, then they turned in themselves. It had been one of the longest days of Halloran's life, and certainly one of the worst. He lay awake a long time, however, exhausted but unable to sleep. Maggie suddenly rolled over and clutched him tightly. He hugged her back and kissed her face, tasting salty tears. Tentatively at first, they began to touch and caress each other. Soon they lost themselves in the usual rhythms and urgencies of sex, grateful for its release.

15

HOLLIS JOPLIN WAS LYING UNDER a tree next to the Chattahoochee River, his fishing pole tethered to a stake in the ground. His eyes were closed, and the sun felt warm on his face. A large fly landed on his cheek. He brushed it away, but soon it was back, lighting on his other cheek this time. He turned on his side, covering his face with his right arm, but the fly wouldn't give up. It began to walk up and down on his body, then finally perched itself on his shoulder and meowed softly into his ear.

"Leave me alone, cat," muttered Joplin. He twitched his shoulders, forcing Quincy to leap from the bed. Soon, however, he heard the sounds of a favorite wake-up game: bag rustling. Groaning, he pulled the covers up over his head. How had the damned cat managed to find the new hiding place for his emergency clothes *this* time?

Joplin wasn't fanatical about doing the laundry, which in the past had often led to a critical shortage of clean clothes. Periodically, he would go to Target and buy three or four white shirts, four or five pairs of socks, and half a dozen pairs of Jockey briefs. Then, whenever he was in a rush to go out on a scene and had nothing clean to wear, he knew he was safe. It was a perfect system, except for one hitch: Quincy. The cat loved to bat around the plastic bags filled with clothes and then climb into them. He had also discovered that this got Joplin up and out of bed.

The phone rang, and he lifted the covers to see the clock on the bed-side table; it was seven-twelve a.m. Reluctantly, he answered it.

"It's Ike, Hollis. Thought you might want to know we found your missing detective."

"Mashburn?" Joplin asked, surprised. "You found Ben Mashburn?"

"Yep. Found him before Missing Persons did, in fact. We're here in the parking lot of the Urbana Motel, and he's sittin' in his car. Only trouble is, he's dead."

"Shit."

"My sentiments exactly. 'Specially since it looks like he did himself in. Now ordinarily, that means we won't have this case long, but I don't think that's gonna happen here. Not since you've connected it all up with the Carter case, which is beginning to look more and more like a homicide. And unless I miss my guess, this one does, too. I know you're off today, but seein' as how you know so much about this case—"

"I'm on my way."

Joplin had been called to scenes at the Urbana Motel on Fourteenth Street, near the expressway, a few times since he'd been with the ME's office, and several prior to that when he'd been with the Homicide Unit. The motel had done a pretty brisk business in the fifties and early six-ties, before all the high-rise hotels had changed the skyline of Atlanta. Now its clientele consisted of people getting together without their proper spouses and businessmen holed up with bottles of Jack Daniels, on three-day binges. Sometimes people from the first group had heart attacks; the ones in the second group sometimes decided to end it all after a few days of nonstop drinking. But they were all just as dead when Joplin saw them.

As he pulled into the courtyard, he noticed that the fountain in the center was a mere trickle of its former self, its turquoise paint peeling in several places. A portable sign nearby announced that the rooms had cable TVs and advised prospective clients to ask about the Urbana's low weekly rates. Joplin drove to the rear of the motel and turned into a nar-row strip of road that ran the length of the building and was lined on both sides by parking spaces. Most of them were empty, which was usual for that time of day. Three APD cars surrounded a tan Acura at the far end of the spaces to the right of the road. The two front doors of the car were open, and as Joplin approached it, Ike Simmons was backing out on the passenger side, a handkerchief pressed against his nose. Joplin eased into a parking spot on the other side of the road, adjacent to the motel, then got out of the car, taking his black bag with him.

"Appreciate you comin', Hollis," said Simmons, straightening up and stuffing the handkerchief into his pocket as Joplin reached the car. He had been leaning over the body, which had fallen sideways onto the passenger seat, the legs and hips still behind the wheel. "I want to be extra careful with this one."

Joplin looked down at the remains of Ben Mashburn, his brain automatically sorting out the commingling odors of decomposing body, blood, alcohol, and gunpowder. "You sure it's Mashburn?"

Simmons nodded. "His driver's license was in his wallet in his left rear pants pocket."

"When was he found?"

"About six-thirty-five this morning. One of the maids went to empty garbage into the dumpster over there and remembered seeing the car yesterday. She decided to take a look inside because none of the rooms on this side was still occupied by then."

"Yeah, isn't checkout something ungodly like eight-thirty a.m. at this dump?"

"Eight, to be exact. This side of the motel is for daily, not weekly guests, so they like to try to hustle people out of here and clean the rooms before the noon rush starts."

Joplin snorted. "You mean 'nooner' rush, don't you, Simmons?"

The detective raised his eyebrows in mock surprise. "Why, Hollis, this is a perfectly respectable motel. The manager told me so himself."

"He should know," said Joplin, setting his case down on the pavement.

"Anyway, when the maid saw Mashburn's body, she hightailed it to the manager's office, and he called it in. We're lucky she got curious, because he might not have been found until he *really* started smelling. The body isn't visible unless you're standing right next to the car, and most people who come here aren't interested in their neighbors."

Joplin was reminded of Cecil and Mary Heard. Their neighbors hadn't been interested in them either. "Did anybody hear any gunshots?"

Simmons gestured toward the other cars in the parking lot. "These belong to employees, and they don't remember hearing anything that sounded like a gunshot in the past two days. The uniforms are still checking with the weekly residents. The manager said he'd give us a copy of the registration during that time period, but it'll probably be filled with a lot of fake names, unless some of them used credit cards."

"Was Mashburn registered?"

"If he was, it was under another name. We showed the manager the DL picture, but he didn't recognize him. We may have better luck with the night manager." Ike paused and cocked his head to the left. "I'm thinking maybe Mashburn used to hole up here when he'd go on one of those benders you told me about."

"You think that's what he was doing here?" asked Joplin.

"Well, if not, somebody sure tried to make it look like that."

Joplin put on latex gloves, then leaned into the driver's side of the car. For a few minutes, he studied the blood and bone and brain matter that coated the headrest on the driver's side and had splattered the seat behind it. Mashburn was dressed in a gray plaid jacket, gray slacks, a white shirt, and a red paisley tie. He had been a tall, big-boned man with an athletic build turned flabby. Probably from years of hard drinking and endless hours spent in parked cars, watching motels just like this one, thought Joplin. He looked like the ex-cop he was, and an ex-cop would know that eating the gun was the best way to make sure that he would die, not just end up a vegetable in a nursing home. Most of the back of his balding head had been blown off.

Ben Mashburn's right arm was under him, the hand sticking out past the edge of the seat. A .38 Smith and Wesson dangled from his thumb. Joplin squatted down so that he was eye-level with the body; the smell of alcohol was even stronger from that position. A bottle of Cutty Sark stood upright on the floor, three-fourths of it gone. Joplin reached into his black bag and pulled out his camera. He took a few pictures, then stood up and photographed the body from different angles. He set the camera down and felt the side of Mashburn's neck, then gently pulled up on the corpse's left arm. It took a few minutes to get the man's belt undone so that he could pull up the shirt and under-shirt and examine the abdomen. It was a dull green, as he expected, and no longer hard.

"Rigor's almost completely gone," he said to Simmons. "And according to his partner, nobody's seen him since about five o'clock on Tuesday."

"You think he's been dead since then?"

"My guess is he died the same night Elliot Carter did, but maybe around eight or nine o'clock. The inside of this car got pretty hot yesterday, so that jump-started the decomposition process."

Simmons frowned. "Could he have drunk that much Scotch by eight or nine o'clock?"

"He was an alcoholic. Who knows what his tolerance was? The real question is, could he have been capable of deciding to kill himself and then actually carrying out that decision after drinking that much, or would he have just passed out at that point?"

"And what do you think, Hollis?"

Joplin smiled at his former partner. "I think I'll wait for the autopsy."

"Holdin' your cards kinda close to your chest, aren't you?"

"Like you said, we want to be extra careful with this one, Ike."

Simmons smiled and nodded. "I did say that, didn't I? CSU should be here in a few. I'll have them go over the car with a fine-toothed comb. Maybe we'll get lucky and turn up something on the gun and the scotch bottle."

"Good," said Joplin. "I'll bag the hands before I leave and then look around the outside of the car, see if anything turns up. But if you want my advice, I'd treat it like it's yours for the time being, if you can. This case is beginning to smell to high heavens."

"Just like my grandmama's back porch when she made chitlins," said Simmons, his expression grim now. "Which is why I never ate them."

Joplin called Healey and Caldwell and learned that Halloran wasn't expected to be in the office until nine. He punched in the home number the attorney had given him, and Halloran answered after the first ring.

"Did you find Ben Mashburn?" he asked quickly, after Joplin had identified himself.

"Unfortunately, yes. His body was found in his car this morning at the Urbana Motel. It looks like suicide, but we're not treating it that way."

"I'm glad of that, anyway. But I'm not glad Mr. Mashburn's dead. How did he die?"

"A gun was put into his mouth and fired. I'm not so sure Mashburn did the firing. He was a recovering alcoholic, but it looked like he'd drunk most of a fifth of scotch, and I don't think he would've been able to pull the trigger."

"When will the autopsy be done?"

"Probably this afternoon. I don't know the exact time."

There was a silence and then Halloran said, "This changes things, doesn't it?"

"It could," said Joplin guardedly.

"Were you able to talk to Anne Carter yesterday?"

"Yes, but I didn't get anything out of her. She's refusing to talk about why she went to see Mashburn on Monday unless this officially becomes a homicide investigation, and I can't really force her at this point."

"Do you want me to talk to her?"

"No, sir, I don't," said Joplin firmly, beginning to regret calling the attorney.

"But she might open up to *me* now that Mashburn's been found," Halloran protested.

"You need to just let us do our jobs, Counselor, okay? I appreciate your putting me onto Ben Mashburn, but now you need to step back. I promise I'll tell you what I can."

"Okay," Halloran said, but Joplin could hear the reluctance and disappointment in his voice. "I understand. Thanks for calling me."

Joplin ended the call, totally unconvinced that Tom Halloran would be able to stay out of the investigation. Despite the help he'd given, the attorney was fast becoming a colossal pain in the butt. Joplin hadn't had a partner in over three years, and he wasn't looking for one now.

It was time to stop this budding bromance.

16

HALLORAN SAT AT THE KITCHEN TABLE and stared at his half-eaten bowl of cereal. Instead of finishing it, he tried to take his mind off the death of Ben Mashburn and what it might mean by checking the newspaper to see how they'd handled Elliot's death. He was relieved to see that the *Atlanta Journal/Constitution* had only given it three paragraphs in the Metro section. The PR firm had certainly earned its retainer, at least for the moment. The article not only left out the more lurid circumstances, but there was a hint that Elliot might have been murdered. The last sentence read, "Foul play has not been ruled out." There was no guarantee, however, that the media restraint would last long.

Anxious to do anything that might help, Halloran reached for the phone and dialed Anne Carter's number, deciding that letting her know about Mashburn's death wasn't really interfering in the official investigation. The phone rang several times before Anne answered.

"Anne? It's Tom Halloran. Did I wake you?"

He heard what sounded to him like a sigh. "No, I just didn't get much sleep last night."

"Maybe Dr. Woodley can prescribe something for you."

"I really don't like to take pills. Tom, if you're calling about Trip's car—"

"No, Anne, I need to talk to you. As soon as possible. Can I stop by in a little while?"

"Actually, I was just about to leave the house," Anne said quickly.

"I can be there in five minutes, and I won't stay long," Halloran insisted.

There were several seconds of silence. "All right," she said finally. "I'll be here."

Halloran was about to thank her, when he realized she'd already hung up. He made a quick call to his secretary to tell her he'd be in even later, then grabbed his briefcase and headed for the door. He was glad Maggie had already left for her rescheduled appointment with Tory Baxter; he wouldn't have to explain his visit to Anne. He was acutely aware that he had just done exactly what he'd told Hollis Joplin he *wouldn't* do, not ten minutes earlier. All he had to do was tell Anne that Ben Mashburn was dead; that wouldn't have violated his agreement with the investigator. But he couldn't seem to help himself. It was as if he felt compelled, now that Elliot was dead, to involve himself in the most intimate details of his friend's life: the reasons why he had left his wife, changed his will so quickly, and distanced himself from the people who cared about him. These were things that Elliot had not chosen to share with him when he was alive, and he had tried to respect that. But now he wondered if they had somehow led to his death.

Sadly, there was no longer any reason to respect Elliot's feelings. And maybe every reason Halloran should ask the questions he hadn't asked months ago.

He could believe Anne hadn't gotten much sleep when she opened the front door. Although she'd put on make-up and fixed her hair, the results were far below her usual standard of perfection. She suddenly looked every bit her age.

"Come into the study, Tom. Pauletta's vacuuming, and I can't hear myself think."

Halloran did hear the drone of a vacuum cleaner as he stepped into the entry hall, but it sounded far away. He followed Anne into the room he had always thought of as exclusively Elliot's. It was a very masculine room, with rich oak paneling and a handsome leather sofa. But the look was softened by a lovely old Chippendale desk and several paintings done in the Impressionist style. For all Halloran knew, they were real

Renoirs or Monets that had been in Elliot's family for years. If so, he hadn't bothered to take them with him when he'd moved out. He had also left behind the huge black and white photograph of Anne over the fireplace that Maggie had given him as a Christmas present two years ago. She'd managed to capture a sort of sweet melancholy in Anne's face, and Elliot often said it was one of his most prized possessions.

Anne motioned him to the leather sofa, then turned to close the double doors behind her. She was dressed in cream-colored pants and a long, pink, cotton sweater, but wore no jewelry. Her ears looked oddly naked. In addition to her blond ponytail, large earrings were a trademark of Anne's, and Tom realized that he'd never seen her without them.

"Anne, you look worn out. Are you doing okay?"

Before she could answer, the phone on the Chippendale desk rang. Anne turned her back to him as she picked it up, but Halloran could tell that she was talking to her mother.

Lucille and Ray Landrum lived in McRae, a tiny town in South Georgia. They were frequent visitors, and their pride in their daughter's social position in Atlanta was obvious. Halloran had never really felt comfortable around them; there was something a little too deferential about them.

"No, Mama, I'd really rather you wait until I know what the funeral plans are," Anne was saying now. "I'm doing fine, really…Yes, I'll call you as soon as I know. Tell Daddy I'm okay." She hung up, then came and sat down beside him on the sofa, crossing her legs and clasping her hands tightly around the top knee.

"Is Trip here?" Halloran asked, wondering if Anne's putting off her parents had anything to do with Dr. Woodley.

"He went to have breakfast with Olivia."

"How's he doing?"

Anne shook her head. "I don't know. He's not really talking to me—at least, not about how he feels." She stared past him for a few seconds, then said, "By the way, Tom, I called the medical examiner's office and they're releasing Elliot's body today."

"Really? Has there been a ruling as to the manner of death yet?"

"No, but Dr. Tyndall said I could go ahead and make funeral arrangements now."

"I'm afraid that'll be up to Olivia," Halloran said evenly. "I'm sorry, but Elliot specifically named her to handle the funeral."

Anne gave an odd little smile that looked more like a grimace. "I guess I knew that was coming," she said. "I hope I'll at least be allowed to attend it. In spite of everything that's happened in the past year, I'm still Elliot's wife, you know."

"I'm sure Olivia would be happy to have you there," Halloran replied diplomatically, hoping it was true. He was also hoping that what Anne had said wasn't a sign of her intention to contest Elliot's will. It certainly sounded like it.

"She will be—if you tell her to, Tom," said Anne pointedly. Then she rearranged her face into a more relaxed expression and added, "I'm sure you didn't come here to talk about the funeral, though."

"No, actually, I didn't," he said, unsure how to begin. Once again, he was conscious of going back on his word to Joplin. It was a little late, however, to change course, and maybe he would learn something helpful. "I'm here about Ben Mashburn, the private detective you hired," he said finally, discarding any pretense of what he was doing.

"Well, I can guess who's been talking to you. I may have to lodge an official complaint about that investigator before this is over. He's way out of line."

"Joplin's just doing his job, Anne," Halloran responded, deciding it was better not to tell her he'd been the one to put the investigator on to Ace Investigations. "He did tell me he'd learned from Mashburn's partner that you had hired him again this past Monday and that he was missing. He also found out that Elliot was in Mashburn's office on Tuesday afternoon. This morning, Joplin called me and told me Ben Mashburn was found dead in his car. I thought you should know."

All the blood in Anne's face drained away, making the blush she'd applied stand out in pink, ragged circles. Her lips started to form a word and then abruptly closed. She shook her head. "Oh, my God, you can't mean it."

"Believe me, I wish it weren't true."

Anne touched her forehead as if she were feeling faint. "Ben is dead," she said in an almost inaudible voice. "I can't believe this. And what was *Elliot* doing in Ben Mashburn's office?"

Halloran realized that Joplin had never given her that bit of information and wished he'd simply told her about Mashburn's death. "I was hoping you could tell *me* that," he said.

"I have no idea, Tom. You have to believe me."

Despite all of her evasions, Anne sounded—and looked—sincere. Halloran found it difficult *not* to believe her, but he still had reservations. "Why did you go to see Mashburn again on Monday? At least tell me that."

She sighed deeply. "First tell me how Ben died."

"A gunshot wound. It evidently looked like suicide at first, but the police are treating it like a homicide. I'm not sure why. I don't know many details."

"But it could still turn out to be suicide?" Her eyes were hopeful.

"Yes, but I don't think it will. I believe Mashburn was murdered. Just as I believe Elliot was. The connection between them is whatever it is that Mashburn discovered."

Several different emotions surfaced on Anne Carter's face as she stared at a picture of herself and Elliot and Trip on the desk. He saw fear and pain and terrible indecision grip her in turn, and then all at once she stood up.

"I'll be right back."

Halloran felt his heart speed up, half worried that he'd blundered again and half hopeful that what he'd said to Anne might produce some real information. Minutes later, Anne returned, carrying a large manila envelope. She walked stiffly to the sofa and sat down, tossing the envelope onto the cushion next to her as if she couldn't bear to be in contact with it any longer.

"I went up to the house in Highlands last week and found that taped to the bottom of a drawer in Elliot's closet," she said. "I was checking to see if he'd cleared everything out and the drawer got stuck when I opened it."

Halloran slowly picked up the envelope. He was conscious of Anne's eyes on his face as he lifted the flap and reached into it.

There were eight photographs. Each showed young or prepubescent children of both sexes engaged in various sexual acts with an adult male. He felt bile rising in his esophagus and closed his eyes, trying to keep from vomiting.

"At first, all I wanted to do was destroy those pictures," Anne said. "But then I realized what they meant—that Elliot might be a pedophile, for God's sake! I didn't want to go to the police, so I called Ben Mashburn

Monday and asked him to meet with me. When I showed him the pictures, he agreed to look into it. He said I didn't really have enough evidence to go to the police anyway. That I couldn't prove where I'd gotten the pictures, and it would just look like I was trying to get back at Elliot."

Halloran nodded slowly in agreement, still trying to get his stomach under control. "That's true. So did Mashburn find anything? Something you could take to the police?"

"That's just it—I don't know. Ben called me Tuesday morning and said he was on to something, but he needed a little longer to check it out. Later that afternoon, when I hadn't heard from him, I called his office. He told me he wanted to talk to me, and that he'd come by the house that night around six-thirty. But he never got here. And when I tried the office again about seven, there was no answer."

"Anne, why didn't you tell me all this yesterday morning?"

She shook her head slowly. "I don't know, Tom. All I could think of was that Elliot was dead. Why drag his name through the mud? I still didn't have any proof of anything, but what if I had? The man was dead!"

"But why do you still have the pictures? I mean, why didn't Mashburn keep them to use in his investigation?"

She seemed startled by the question. "But he did take the pictures—at least some of them. There were about eleven or so, and he took…let me think… I guess about three of them. He said to keep the others in a safe place."

"One more question: Did Mashburn tell you how he was going to pursue this?"

"No." She leaned forward and looked him in the eye. "Tom, what are you going to do about this? Are you going to tell the police?"

Halloran stood up, his only thought to get out of that house as soon as he could. "I don't know. I'm still in a state of shock over the whole thing. First the way Elliot died, and now this. I think I need to take those pictures with me, though."

Anne Carter stood up, too. "That's fine with me," she said, quickly handing him the envelope. "I never want to set eyes on them again."

17

STILL REELING FROM EVERYTHING Anne had told him, Halloran emerged from Ansley Park at Sixteenth Street and turned south on Peachtree. He didn't feel like going into the office, much less visiting Olivia Carter, but he knew he needed to do both. At Tenth Street, the light turned red, and he punched in his secretary's number on the car phone.

"Mr. Halloran's office."

"Joan, I'm on my way to see Elliot's mother at the Ritz-Carlton. Anything going on?"

"Nothing that can't wait," she said crisply. "David Healey's been throwing his weight around, complaining about your absence. I essentially told him to put a sock in it."

"I'm going to give you a raise for that one, Joanie."

"It was my pleasure, I assure you. Are you okay, Mr. Halloran?"

"Roughly speaking. I might stay and have lunch with Mrs. Carter. I'll call you."

The light changed. Halloran pressed the gas pedal, his actions on autopilot while he tried to make sense of the latest revelations. Was it possible that Elliot could have been a pedophile *and* into autoerotic asphyxia? He knew a bit about pedophilia, but until yesterday he'd never even heard of the other practice. He realized he was abysmally ignorant about such things.

And then something occurred to him that made even this quandary pale in comparison: What if Elliot were something far worse? What if he were a murderer? Maybe Ben Mashburn had decided to sell Anne Carter out, despite what Joplin thought. He had invited Elliot to his office and shown him the pictures, then agreed to delete everything damning from his files and meet him somewhere to be paid off.

But instead of paying him off, Elliot had killed him.

As far as Halloran knew, Elliot was the only person who could have benefited from Mashburn's death and the disappearance of those files. Even though he might have discovered that Anne still had some of the photographs, he would have known, like Mashburn, that she couldn't prove where she'd found them. Or maybe Mashburn had agreed to retrieve the other photographs, and that was why he'd arranged to go to her house that night. Elliot could have given the detective a sum of money for erasing the computer files and giving him the hard copy, then promised him more when he got the other pictures. They might have arranged to meet sometime later that night.

But why, then, hadn't Mashburn kept his appointment with Anne at six-thirty that night? Had it been something as simple as the need for a drink? Guilt over selling out to Elliot Carter or a desire to celebrate his windfall might have made him a very thirsty man. Maybe he stopped at a liquor store and bought a bottle. He probably started drinking and couldn't stop. Maybe he was passed out in his car by the time Elliot arrived. The idea of murdering Mashburn might not have occurred to Elliot until then, but he would have realized how vulnerable he'd be to either exposure or blackmail in the future.

A car behind him honked loudly, and Halloran realized that he'd stopped for another light that was no longer red and he was now holding up traffic. He drove on, his heart pounding, feeling both stressed and guilty. How could he possibly consider Elliot capable of murder?

Out of the corner of his eye, he saw the manila envelope that Anne had entrusted to him. He wished that he could pitch it out of the car and forget that he had ever laid eyes on the revolting images it contained. Seeing those photographs, more than anything else, had brought him to the point of believing his best friend capable of murder.

Without taking his eyes off the road, Halloran reached across the seat and opened his briefcase, then slid the envelope into it. Until Mashburn's death was ruled a homicide or he could discover any corroborating evidence that Elliot was a pedophile, he would refuse to consider the possibility that Elliot might have killed Ben Mashburn. This meant he couldn't tell Hollis Joplin about the photographs, at least, not right away. He'd be going way beyond breaking his agreement with Joplin not to involve himself in the investigation and well into actually withholding evidence and obstructing justice. But he felt he owed it to Elliot to keep something so damning—true or not—from being exposed.

Maybe, he thought, Anne Carter had manufactured the whole scenario about finding the photographs at the house in Highlands. She might have figured she could wave those photographs at Elliot and get him to give her more money to keep her from claiming they were his; the charge alone would be intimidating. But why, then, would she involve Ben Mashburn in her scheme? That was something he could think about later, he decided; meanwhile, he wasn't going to tell Joplin or the police about the pictures. It would be taking a big risk; possession of child pornography by itself was a felony offense—and one that could get him disbarred. But it was a risk Halloran felt he must take for Elliot.

This decision made, he felt much calmer and able to face Olivia Carter.

Halloran had to ring the buzzer of Suite 1036 in the downtown Ritz-Carlton twice before Olivia Carter answered it. A tiny woman, she now she seemed almost shrunken, her skin paper thin, but still elegant as always. Her black and white suit complemented her silver hair, cut in a stylish bob. After hugging him tightly, she led him into the sitting room of the suite. A huge flower arrangement dominated the coffee table, and Halloran almost expected Elliot to be lying in state in the next room.

"I thought maybe Trip might still be here," he said, looking around the room.

"He left about half an hour ago," said Olivia, motioning for him to sit down next to her. "I'm terribly worried about him, Tom. About the only thing keeping him going right now is that you told him his father didn't kill himself—that he was murdered. And that you would find the person who did it."

He smiled and took her hand. "You always were a very direct person, Olivia, so I'll be just as direct with you. Do you know how Elliot died?"

"I do," she said, looking right into his eyes. "Anne told me everything."

"According to an investigator at the scene, this type of behavior often begins during adolescence. Do you have any knowledge—or even any suspicions—that Elliot might have done this sort of thing when he was growing up?"

Olivia didn't answer right away. Finally, she said, "Tom, I want you to understand something. I would tell you if I did because I'm an old woman, and I've been around money and power all my life. I know what it can do, and what it can't. It can't save you from heartbreak or death, but it can buy a lot of silence. If I had any fears whatsoever that an investigation into Elliot's death would ruin his reputation, I'd tell you to bury him quickly and try to pay off every reporter in this town. Does that answer your question?"

"It does. Thank you. What if I were to tell you that Anne showed me pictures—sexually explicit pictures—of young children and said that she had found them in Elliot's bureau in the Highlands house last week?"

Olivia Carter didn't even flinch. "I would tell you that Anne is lying. Why she's lying, I don't know, but she's lying." Olivia sighed and sank into the cushions. "Tom, Elliot was a normal, healthy teenager and young man in every way. I might seem biased, but I can't believe that he was ever involved in that sort of thing."

"Neither could Anne."

"Well, that's something, I guess," said Olivia dryly.

"I take it Anne isn't your favorite person."

"Things have been very…trying this past year."

"Olivia, do you know why Anne and Elliot separated? Elliot wouldn't discuss it, and Anne stopped talking to Maggie and me. But before she did, she told Maggie that Elliot was just going through some kind of midlife crisis. She even hired a private investigator."

Olivia Carter's lips twisted in a grimace of distaste. "She never bothered to tell me that little detail in any of her many phone calls last fall."

"Why was Anne calling you?"

"She wanted me to help her get Elliot back. She was sure if I told him to, he'd do it. Just like the last time."

"What do you mean?"

"About seven years ago, Elliot found out that Anne was…involved with someone. She begged him not to leave her and said it only happened because she felt so devastated that she couldn't have another baby.

That she felt like a failure as a woman and needed what she called 'reassurance' at the time."

"I remember that time," said Halloran slowly. "It was a rough period for both of them, but Maggie and I had no idea that anything else was going on. I'm glad he at least talked to you, Olivia."

"It was the only time he ever came to me with any kind of personal problem between them, but he was so distraught, he couldn't think straight. Trip was only ten at the time, and Elliot couldn't imagine leaving him. So I told him that if he could find it in his heart to forgive her, he might be able to put his marriage back together."

"Apparently, he did," said Halloran. "Or at least until last September. Did Elliot ever tell you why he left then?"

She shook her head. "He just told me it was over. I did ask him if he had seriously considered everything before taking this step, and he told me he had. So I never said another word about it to him. Just kept in touch with him and Trip and tried to be pleasant when Anne called me. The phone calls tapered off when she realized I wasn't going to get involved again, and stopped altogether by Christmas."

"Did anything happen last summer that seemed to be connected with Elliot's leaving?"

She frowned in concentration, then shook her head slowly. "The only thing that concerned me at the time was that Elliot mentioned he was going to see a specialist—a urologist. He assured me it was for a minor problem, but I was very concerned because I had taken DES when I was pregnant with Elliot to prevent a miscarriage."

"DES?"

"Yes, I think it stands for diethyl something. Diethyl stylbestrol—that's it. I had a miscarriage not too long before I got pregnant with Elliot, and my husband and I didn't want to take any chances, so I took this DES. The doctors said it was perfectly safe, of course." She made a face. "Don't they always? But later on, they came out with all kinds of research that it was causing sterility, as well as vaginal and testicular cancer in the adult children whose mothers took it while pregnant. So when Elliot told me about the urologist, I reminded him about that and made him promise to call me as soon as he saw the doctor."

"And did he?"

"No. A few days went by, and I finally called him, frantic. But Elliot told me it was nothing to worry about. Then he told me he had left Anne."

She shrugged. "I don't see how the two events are connected, Tom, but you asked me about last September."

"Yes, I did," he said, taking both of her hands, while his mind made a few connections that Olivia hadn't. He could feel the tiny, birdlike bones directly beneath the skin, and realized again how frail she was despite her strong demeanor. "And you've answered everything as honestly and directly as you always do. Just one more question: Did Elliot ever undergo any fertility testing when Anne did? Don't they usually test both partners?"

"Yes, but it wasn't necessary because the problem was with Anne, you see. Something to do with scarring in her Fallopian tubes, she said. Elliot was scheduled to have tests done after her, but Anne insisted he cancel the appointment."

"Well, that sounds logical," said Halloran noncommittally. "And now I hope you'll let me take you to lunch. We'll talk about Elliot some more, but only about the good times, okay?"

"I'd like that very much," she said, at last tearing up, her armor momentarily falling away.

18

HALLORAN MADE IT TO HEALEY AND CALDWELL a little after two o'clock that afternoon..

"David Healey's in Mr. Carter's office," said Joan as he approached her desk. Her voice was tight with anger. David had never been a favorite with the secretaries, not even his own. "Delia called me—she wasn't about to tangle with him. I wasn't any better, though. He declined my offer to help him find anything he needed."

"How long has he been in there?"

"About twenty minutes."

"Did he say what he wanted?"

"Nope. Just let himself in and told Delia he wasn't to be disturbed."

Halloran handed Joan his briefcase. "I think I'll go disturb him."

The door to Elliot's office was locked. He used the key he'd gotten from Delia, Elliot's secretary, the day before, and wondered how David had gotten in. Maybe he and Alston Caldwell had keys to all the offices.

Healey was at Elliot's computer. His head jerked up in irritation as Halloran entered the room. "I told Delia not to let anyone in here."

"So did I. And I happen to be Elliot's executor."

"I assure you I'm doing nothing that would interfere with your fiduciary duties, Tom. And I don't need your permission to go into the files of an attorney in my own law firm. This is firm business."

"Is it?" Halloran asked, walking over to him. "You don't know the first thing about tax law, David. What are you looking for?"

Angrily, David Healey jabbed at a computer key. "None of your goddamn business."

"Was it firm business when you and Anne had lunch together last summer?"

"I don't know what the hell you're talking about."

"Someone saw the two of you at Chops last July."

Healey's face turned a dull red. "Anne is an old friend, Tom. She and Elliot and I all knew each other in college. Not that that's any of your business either." He stood up dismissively. "Now get out, or I'll call security."

"If you delete anything from Elliot's files, you could be charged with obstruction, David," said Halloran. "The police are very close to turning Elliot's death into a murder investigation."

"I have no intention of obstructing justice, Tom. Now, do you want me to call security?"

What Halloran really wanted to do was punch David Healey in the mouth. But a physical struggle between two partners in the office of a dead partner would set tongues wagging and do no one, Elliot included, any good. Abruptly, he turned and headed for the door.

"A Dr. Tyndall from the Medical Examiner's office called," said Joan, as Halloran reached her desk. "Shall I get him on the line for you?"

"Please."

The phone rang as he sat down at his own desk. "Dr. Tyndall? I really appreciate your calling me."

"Actually, Mr. Halloran, I'm not real comfortable discussing a case while the results are still pending," the pathologist said curtly. "But I received a call yesterday from Dr. Minton, our chief ME, who had gotten a call from your Mr. Caldwell, and I've been told to answer any questions you might have."

"I can tell that doesn't sit very well with you, and I'm sorry about that. I hope you can understand that this has really hit us all pretty hard."

"Yes, I can. But I can't wave a magic wand and change the facts of what happened. I didn't find anything during the autopsy that would rule out autoerotic asphyxia."

"Well, that's disappointing, but I'm sure you know about the death of the private detective that Anne Carter hired. And that Elliot was in his office the day he died. Doesn't that throw a new light on things?"

"I admit it seems a little too coincidental, but that detective's death might have been just what it looks like—a suicide."

Suddenly tired, Halloran rubbed his hand over his face. "And you found absolutely nothing suspicious during Elliot's autopsy?"

"Not really suspicious, just…unusual," Tyndall answered. "Usually the victims in cases like these use alcohol to prime themselves, to lower their inhibitions and get into the fantasy of it all. But it didn't look like Mr. Carter had had anything at all to drink. He also hadn't eaten since around noon."

"He was supposed to meet his son, Trip, for dinner that night, but he never made it. Could you place the time of death?"

"About eleven p.m., give or take an hour either way."

"I don't understand. He left Mashburn's office at four p.m. Where was he all that time?"

"Well," said Tyndall, "there is *one* possibility: Sometime between the hours of five p.m. and midnight, your friend might have been busy killing Ben Mashburn."

The pathologist had only voiced what Halloran himself had thought earlier, but it seemed more of a possibility coming from someone else. He stayed lost in thought for several minutes after he hung up, wondering again if it could be true, then reached for the phone again. Delia answered on the first ring.

"Delia, did you make Elliot's doctors' appointments for him?"

"Yes, Mr. Halloran."

"Do you know who his urologist was?"

"Urologist?" Her voice sounded puzzled. "Oh, wait! He did go to one last year sometime. Just a sec; I'm looking it up," she added. "Here it is: Dr. Robert Greer. He's in the 2045 building across from Piedmont Hospital."

After getting Dr. Greer's phone number, Halloran decided he'd better let Maggie know about Ben Mashburn's death, as well as the bombshell Olivia had dropped about Anne's affair, before calling the urologist. He got hold of her on her cell phone.

"Well, we did discuss that as a possibility," she responded after several seconds. "It's still upsetting to find out it's actually true, though. But tell me about Ben Mashburn. Do the police think he was murdered?"

"I think that investigator from the ME's office—Hollis Joplin—is beginning to think so. Which is what I told Anne when I went to see her this morning."

"You went to see Anne?"

"Yes, I thought she should know about Mashburn's death."

"And *you* had to be the one to tell her? Listen, Tom, I think you're getting far too involved in this. And Anne is evidently an expert at concealing things she doesn't want people to know. Let this man Joplin handle it. It's his job, not yours."

"I realize that now," Halloran admitted. "I think I bit off a little more than I can chew, as the saying goes," he added, then told her about the photographs.

"I don't believe it," said Maggie adamantly when he'd finished. "Anne must be lying about where or how she got them. Let me take a look at them tonight, Tom. I might be able to find out something about them. Something that would help *prove* she's lying."

Halloran had to smile at this. "Now who's getting too involved in the investigation?"

"I know, but—"

"It's okay. I appreciate the offer. We'll talk about it tonight," he added, and hung up when she agreed.

Dr. Greer's nurse did not seem pleased about scheduling an appointment for someone who wasn't a patient. After tersely informing Halloran that the doctor had been out of town for the past three days at a conference and would be extremely busy when he returned, she finally agreed to let him see Greer at eight a.m. the following Thursday, before his first appointment.

His next phone call was to Hollis Joplin; Halloran knew he at least had to tell the investigator about going to see Anne. When he'd finished telling Joplin what he could, there was complete silence on the line for several seconds.

"What is it about 'back off and let us do our jobs' you don't understand, Mr. Halloran?" asked Joplin, clearly irritated. "I realize you're a local celebrity—maybe even a *national* celebrity now that you've been on truTV—but I'm not impressed. You're way out of line."

"You have every right to be upset, but—"

"That's not the point. My concern is that you're going to screw things up. Big time. It's looking like this could turn into a homicide investigation and if so, I don't want to hand over a big mess to Detective Simmons. For instance, he may have wanted to drop the bombshell about Elliot Carter being at Mashburn's office on Mrs. Carter himself, so he could observe her reaction. But you've made that impossible."

"Well, if it means anything, I'm pretty sure she didn't know anything about Elliot's being there from the look on her face when I told her," Halloran offered.

"It *doesn't* mean anything. Not unless you've graduated from the police academy since yesterday."

"I've been a litigator for ten years, Investigator Joplin," replied Halloran, beginning to feel angry himself. "I know how to ask pertinent questions and gauge whether someone's telling the truth. And I *am* an officer of the court."

"Yeah, but you handle civil suits, Counselor. Criminal cases are a whole other ballgame."

Halloran was about to fire back that he also handled tax fraud cases when he remembered that the evidence he was holding might very well put him on the receiving end of his very own criminal case, Halloran decided to back down. It wasn't something he was used to doing, but under the circumstances, perhaps discretion was the better part of valor.

"Point taken," he said. "I promise to stay out of your way in the future."

"I'm going to make sure you keep that promise, Mr. Halloran," Joplin said tersely and then clicked off before Halloran could reply.

19

IT WAS SIX O'CLOCK WHEN JOPLIN turned into the employees' parking lot at the ME's office to pick up Carrie Salinger. He had seen her only briefly that morning while writing up his report on the Mashburn case, just long enough to make sure their date was still on. Then he had gone home and worked on the paper for his Constitutional Law class, at least until he'd received Tom Halloran's phone call about his visit to Anne Carter; his concentration wasn't as good after that.

Joplin was surprised to see Lewis Minton's old blue Cadillac, since the chief ME wasn't due back at work until the next week, and then only for half-days. He suspected that Minton's presence had something to do with the Carter case.

The secretaries had left for the day, but as Joplin walked down the main hall, he could hear the slow, deliberate cadence of Minton's dictating voice.

"...to the conclusion that the wounds, the condition and appearance of the body, the residue of gunpowder found on the right hand, as well as the subject's history of alcoholism and depression, are all consistent with suicide as the manner of death. The events preceding the subject's death raise questions which need to be answered before any official ruling can be made. The autopsy, however, pending the histology and toxicology reports, has produced no evidence of foul play."

"I know Mrs. Minton doesn't know you're here, or she'd skin you alive," said Joplin, standing in the door frame.

"Hollis!" said Lewis Minton warmly, looking up from the papers on his desk. "I was hoping I'd see you while I was here. Dr. Salinger said you were stopping by for her this evening. Fast work, son," he added, grinning.

"Yeah, well, I figured I'd better ask her out before she got to know me too well."

Minton laughed and shook his head. He was a large, bearlike man with a rugged face and warm brown eyes. Joplin had liked him immediately the first time he met him, over ten years ago. He'd grown to respect and admire him shortly after that.

In the world of bureaucracy, where the average appointed official saw his chief job as one of maintaining his turf, Lewis Minton was an exception. He had devoted his life to forensic medicine, and when he'd been appointed as the first Chief Medical Examiner in Milton County in 2004, he insisted on the highest standards and technology possible. He was also a man who inspired great loyalty in the people who worked for him.

"I'll give you five-to-one odds the tox report shows that Mashburn had too much ethanol in his system to keep his eyes open, much less fire a gun, Doc," said Joplin.

"I read your report, Hollis," Minton said, leaning back in his chair and lacing his fingers together. "The Carter report, too. I have the same reservations you do. Maybe the lab work will resolve things for us."

"Doc, I know you didn't just saunter in here and take over an autopsy without a good reason. Especially with a wife who's worried half to death about you."

Minton sighed. "I told Helen I was going to the Y for a swim. Figured she couldn't check up on me there. Truth is, I got a phone call from Alston Caldwell last night."

"As in Healey and Caldwell?"

"You got it. Alston and I have known each other for a long time, and he asked me to look into Carter's death as a personal favor."

"Sounds like Tom Halloran's been working overtime," said Joplin, trying to keep the irritation out of his voice. "He's the one who found the body, and he's also with Healey and Caldwell."

"Yes, I remember that from your report. And Alston told me about his insistence that Elliot Carter was murdered."

"Halloran also provided the connection between Mashburn and Elliot Carter. And he's been pushing to have this thing turned into a murder investigation from the very beginning. I don't think he'll give up easily."

Lewis Minton took off his glasses. He got a handkerchief out of his coat pocket and began to clean them. "The State Crime Lab may not send us the toxicology reports for six weeks, Hollis. You know how backed up they are. We need some answers badly. And soon. Not just because Alston Caldwell is a friend of mine, but because if these two deaths were murders, I want the Homicide Unit involved ASAP. If there's a killer out there intelligent enough to plan something like this, I don't want the trail to get cold."

"I'm way ahead of you, Doc," Joplin said, and went on to detail his own investigation into the two deaths. "I'm filling Simmons in as I go along. He's already proceeding as if Mashburn's death is a homicide."

"But it won't be given top priority until the ruling is official. The city hasn't been able to fill all the empty officer positions because of budget cuts. I want you to drop everything else and concentrate on finding out how both of these men died."

"Chief McKenzie isn't going to be very happy about that."

"You leave McKenzie to me. Now go take that nice young woman out to dinner."

"You look wonderful."

Carrie Salinger was standing on tiptoe, trying to wedge a bound forensic journal back into its place on the shelf. At the sound of Joplin's voice, she turned and smiled at him. She was wearing a pink sweater set over a slim floral skirt. It was the first time he'd seen her without a white lab coat. She had also put on makeup since he'd seen her that morning and tied her hair back in a low ponytail.

"And how do you like the front of me?" she asked.

Embarrassed, Joplin said, "It matches the back…I mean, you look great all over."

"Thanks," she said, laughing. "So do you. Let me just get my purse. Where are we going, by the way?"

"D'Angelo's, over in Virginia-Highland. You know it?"

Carrie shook her head. "No, but I've heard of it, and I love Italian food."

"Great. Come on, let's get out of here."

The restaurant was a long, narrow, high-ceilinged room with brick walls. It was owned by a transplanted New Yorker named Mike D'Angelo, who loved Atlanta with the fervor of a new convert. The food, however, was straight out of Little Italy. Joplin had made it a point to eat there at least once a month since it opened the year before. They were ushered to a booth near the back by Mike himself, who recommended the Tuscan white bean soup to start, followed by the salmon piccata. He looked approvingly at Carrie and slapped Joplin on the back, then went off in search of their waiter. Joplin ordered a bottle of Chianti Classico, and they sat silently and almost shyly as the waiter poured it.

"I haven't gone out much this past year," Joplin said after the first few sips. "I think Mike always thought I was gay."

Carrie laughed and set her glass down. "He did seem a little thunderstruck. Do you mean to tell me you've never brought a woman here besides me?"

Joplin shrugged. "I went out a lot right after my divorce, when I was still with Homicide. After I got through that stage, I tried to have a few 'meaningful relationships,' as they say. They usually broke up because of my job. It's hard to have a relationship with somebody who's either on call or half asleep."

Carrie nodded slowly in agreement. "Whenever I tried to date another doctor, our schedules conflicted. And when I dated someone who wasn't a doctor, he didn't understand when I had to break a date." Their soup arrived, and after tasting a spoonful and declaring it wonderful, she said, "So what made you decide to go into law enforcement, Hollis?"

"I think I just wanted to help people. There are cops who are in it for the power and authority, and some who like the violence and the risk-taking. But most of us can look back on an event that made us want to help people."

"And what was *your* event?"

"I guess when Bobby Greenleaf was kidnapped, back in 1987. You were probably too young to remember it."

Carrie stared at him. "I was only four then, but I know all about it. I've known the Greenleaf family all my life. My father and Richard Greenleaf were business partners before he became the general manager at Rich's. The family moved to Tampa after it happened, but we still see them from time to time. They've never gotten over it."

"It was every parent's worst nightmare," Joplin said. "I was thirteen at the time, but I wasn't allowed to go anywhere alone for months."

"According to my mother, Mrs. Greenleaf still blames herself. It was the only time she ever let Bobby walk to school by himself."

"I remember seeing her on TV. It was heartbreaking, even to a kid like me."

"So you decided to become a police officer after that?"

Joplin hesitated, wondering if he should tell her the rest of it. It was actually Atlanta's obsession with Bobby, a white child from Buckhead, when compared with its reaction to the disappearance of several poor black children eight years earlier, that had inspired him to become a police officer. He remembered all the newspaper articles, with interviews of everyone from the Greenleafs' neighbors, to Bobby's teachers, to various law enforcement officials. He remembered watching the nightly news on TV as the anguished parents pleaded for their eight-year-old son's return and various search parties poked through kudzu and dredged lakes. He remembered how quickly a task force, made up of local police, GBI agents, and Special Agents from the FBI had been formed. They had worked round the clock, to no avail. No ransom note was ever sent; no one ever came forward to say they had seen the little boy after he disappeared. Bobby Greenleaf's body was never found. Yet the media frenzy didn't die down for months.

It was a far cry from the apathy shown by both the media and law enforcement in 1979, when poor black children began disappearing. It would take a dozen such disappearances, over a two-year period, before a task force was formed to investigate those cases. Joplin remembered this time as the beginning of his awareness of racism. As more and more publicity was given to the Greenleaf case, the black community in Atlanta had expressed its outrage over the way the Atlanta Missing and Murdered Children case had been handled. He began to see that great injustice existed in the world, and he agreed wholeheartedly with what black ministers and other community leaders were saying, even as he and the other kids in his Sunday school class at the First Baptist Church in Austell prayed for the Greenleaf boy. They had never prayed for Edward Hope Smith, the first black child who disappeared. It was during one such prayer session that he decided to become a police officer when he grew up, so he could help children like Edward. And, of course, Bobby Greenleaf.

Deciding this wasn't the light repartee he had in mind for their first date, Joplin didn't tell any of this to Carrie Salinger. Instead, he smiled and said, "Pretty much. The whole thing made a big impression on me at the time. Like I said, I thought maybe I could help people."

"And do you think you have?"

"Depends on whom you ask. The people I've arrested didn't think so. Neither did their families. Especially the kids. I used to hate it when we had to take someone into custody in front of their kids," he added. Then he shrugged and said, "But, yeah, I got to save some lives, put away some bad guys who might have killed more people. My first week on the job, I found a baby in a dumpster, and he was still alive. That was a big thrill. So was talking some people out of killing themselves or someone else. But most police work is pretty tedious, especially all the bureaucratic stuff. I get tired of all the people who cover their asses instead of doing their jobs. I'm not a very good bureaucrat."

"So is that what you dislike most about the job?" Carrie asked.

"That and the unavoidable hazard of knowing too much about the terrible things people do to themselves and others. But I'm sure you saw plenty of that when you did an ER tour as an intern."

"Not just in the ER," Carrie said. "I did my internship at Grady, and every tour was a lesson on man's inhumanity to man. And so is this one, at the ME's."

Joplin grinned at her. "If you tell me you're prone to having blue funks, I'll know we're perfect for each other."

"I'm not admitting to that until I know what a blue funk is."

"The official DSM definition is 'deep depression, with bouts of pissy behavior.'"

"I don't think I've ever seen anything like that in the DSM," said Carrie, laughing.

"Trust me. Or if you don't believe me, ask my co-workers. I get them about three times a year, and everyone knows to stay away from me. In fact, I felt one coming on until you said you'd have dinner with me."

"Well, I won't take credit for the cure, but what was the cause?"

Joplin told her about Cecil and Mary Heard. From the comments she made, Carrie seemed to understand why their pitiful, unnoticed deaths bothered him so much. He wasn't used to talking so much about his feelings, however, and was silent as the waiter cleared away their soup plates. She seemed to understand this, too, and began talking about the ME's office, sharing her impressions of various co-workers. She was wickedly funny and managed to turn the mood around with apparently effortless skill. By the time their main course arrived, Joplin felt completely relaxed.

By the time the check arrived, he felt as if he'd always known her.

20

MAGGIE PICKED UP THE MANILA ENVELOPE that Halloran had placed between them on the sofa. Tommy and Megan were finally in bed, and after telling her everything he could remember about his meeting with Anne that morning, as well as what little he knew about Anne's affair, Halloran had decided he couldn't put off showing Maggie the photographs any longer. He understood the shock and repulsion playing across her face as she stared at the first one, and he regretted the pain he was passing on to her.

"I'm not sure this is a very good idea, Maggie."

She shook her head and looked up at him. "No, this is something I can do to help. You can tell a lot about photographs just by looking at composition, the type of photographic paper, the developer—things like that. Ben Mashburn must have learned *something* from them. He didn't get anything on Elliot when Anne hired him last fall. But when she gave these to him, things evidently started happening." She gave a little shrug. "Unless it was just the fact that they existed that made them important."

Halloran frowned, considering what she had said. "But according to Anne, Mashburn told her the photographs weren't evidence of anything unless she could connect them directly to Elliot. It would only be her word against his in a court of law."

"For that matter, what proof is there that these photographs are what Mashburn was investigating in the first place?" Maggie asked. "Anne could just be saying that. Mashburn's certainly not around to refute it—and neither is poor Elliot."

"Yes, but, whether or not she's telling the truth about anything these days is something I can't answer."

"Then why not just turn them over to that investigator, Tom? Maybe he can find out what Anne's up to."

"I can't. Not yet anyway. Mashburn's death is making him look at what happened to Elliot in a different light. If I give him these photographs, he'll just see them as proof that Elliot's death *was* some kind of perverted accident—and maybe even that he killed Mashburn before he strung himself up."

Maggie looked down at the photographs. "I guess you're right." Frowning in concentration, she studied each one carefully in turn, then examined the backsides. She didn't say anything for what seemed like a very long time to Halloran.

"Pretty terrible, aren't they?" he said at last.

She nodded slowly. "In the way you mean, yes. They *are* terrible. Worse than anything I've ever seen in my life. But they weren't taken by an amateur. The interplay of light and shadow shows a level of complexity I hadn't expected."

"What do you mean?"

"The composition of each one draws the eye to whatever body part or expression on a face that the photographer wants the viewer to see. It's what I do myself when I photograph children. But where I try to capture their joy and imagination, the mind that created these images wanted to show the pain and fear and helplessness of children in the grip of an evil they don't understand." Maggie closed her eyes and shuddered. "It's as if he considered himself to be some kind of artist or something."

"But aren't most pornographers professional photographers?

"I guess so. At least the ones who make films or even those quickie videos. But they use professional actors, who are in it for the money." She shrugged helplessly. "I don't know, I just think child pornography would have to be different. The children in these pictures aren't *acting*. The expressions on their faces are all too real, God help them. But the shots look as if they were staged." Maggie shook her head. "I don't know if I'm explaining myself very well."

"No, you're doing fine," Halloran responded. "Go on, if you feel up to it."

"I guess what I'm trying to say is that the photographer was *directing* these shots, not just taking pictures of two adult males having their sick fun with little kids. It's as if he stood behind the camera and said to one of the men, 'Okay, now I want Susie to look absolutely terrified. Go over to her and do such-and such.' He was very detached and objective. We can't see the faces of either of the men in the photos—their backs are always to the camera. But I bet if we could, we'd see that same cold detachment."

Halloran ran a hand through his hair and sighed. "I don't think either of us knows anything about child pornography, Maggie. Maybe this is the way it's done."

"You're right," Maggie said. "I'm totally out of my league. I'll try to stick with what I actually know." She picked up the first picture and stared at it. "The light that's playing across this little boy's face has to be coming from a small arc light that would cast those shadows you see in the background. Which means these photographs were taken in a studio of some kind, or at least a room or an office set up like one." She began flipping through the pictures again. "There's a minimal amount of furniture used—a sofa in three of the photos, an armchair in two others, and a bed in the other three. And as you'd expect, there's nothing personal in any of the shots. No paintings or photographs to connect the place where they were taken to the person who took them."

"Do you see anything else, Maggie?"

"Well, just that these are obviously digital recastings of the original photos."

Halloran's confusion must have shown, because Maggie smiled at him and shook her head. "I'm sorry. I keep forgetting you don't know anything about photography, Tom. First of all, I'm pretty sure these must have been taken over twenty years ago."

"Twenty years ago? You mean because they're in black and white and not color?"

This time she gave him a withering glance. "Oh, come on, Tom! People used color film back then. I'm talking about the eighties, not the forties. I think black and white film was used to help minimize any personal features of the children, like hair or eye color, not because color film wasn't available."

"Oh. Right. I was just trying to figure out how you knew they were taken so long ago. That didn't hit me at all."

"Well, the clothes and hairstyles, for one thing. See the barrettes on this little girl?"

"They're Hello Kitty barrettes, like Megan wears," said Halloran, even more confused.

"Yes, but it's the *way* the little girl is wearing the barrettes. Her hair is totally gathered up by them on the sides of her head. It isn't just a little bit of hair near the middle part that she has, like you'd see today. My sisters wore their hair like that when they were in the fourth and fifth grade, and that was in the late eighties. Also, the type of haircut several of the boys have is very eighties—you know, with the ears covered up, but not very long."

"But how do you know they aren't the originals?"

Maggie turned the photo over. "I can tell from the type of photographic paper used. It's Kodak, but made especially for digital cameras. But since there's no additional logo, like from a Fotomat or a pharmacy, it looks like an laser printer was used."

"Well, that makes sense. A commercial printer would have to notify the police if a customer brought in child pornography."

"Whoever did these must have used a scanner on the originals and then printed them on a private printer." She narrowed her eyes and tilted her head to one side. "Unless…"

"Unless what?" asked Halloran.

"I'm not sure. I'd like to look at them tomorrow with a fresh eye."

"Maggie, are you sure you want to spend any more time on this? I mean, it's got to be upsetting for you to even *look* at those pictures, much less study them."

"It is. But after seeing them, I'm more convinced than ever that they never belonged to Elliot. Never in a million years." Maggie gathered up the photographs and put them back in the manila envelope. "I'll lock them in my desk down in the dark room. Is that okay?"

"I hate having them in the house, but I guess that's as safe a place as any."

"The *safest* place for them would be in the middle of a blazing fire," said Maggie, disgust in her voice. She stood up. "In the meantime, my desk will have to do."

Friday dawned as chilly as the morning Halloran had found Elliot's body. He decided to go for a run, hoping the exercise would clear his mind and prepare him for whatever the day might hold. He had chosen another route, however, wondering if he would ever be able to run in Piedmont Park again. So much had changed in two days.

His present route took him south on Peachtree Street, which at six a.m. was just beginning to show signs of life. He ran past the High Museum, its stark, white walls and curved staircase looking somehow sinister in the weak light. He remembered that an exterior shot of it had been used to represent the mental hospital holding the murderous Dr. Hannibal Lector in the movie, *Silence of the Lambs*. At the time, it had seemed an odd choice, but now he noticed what the filmmakers had seen. He wondered if perhaps the light made it look so different or if all that had happened had somehow given him a new perspective on familiar landmarks.

Halloran tried to shake off the feeling of gloom inspired by the museum as he passed the Alliance Theater and Symphony Hall. It returned full force, however, as he neared Colony Square. On Fourteenth Street, opposite the hotel and office complex, loomed Elliot's apartment building. His eyes traveled up to the seventeenth floor and located what he thought would be Elliot's living room. Breathing hard now, he stopped running, shielding his eyes from the glare of the rising sun on glass. It had occurred to him that there might be more than just evidence of autoerotic asphyxia—planted or not—in the apartment. That was all Joplin had been looking for on Wednesday. But maybe he himself could look for clues as to why the Carters had separated or where Elliot might have been between the time he left Mashburn's office and when he died. He wondered why he hadn't thought of it before and then quickly dismissed it from his mind. It had been less than twenty-four hours since he'd promised Hollis Joplin—twice—that he would stay out of the investigation, and here he was, trying to play amateur detective again. Not to mention that he was already withholding evidence of a kind. Besides, Halloran decided, he had enough on his own plate to deal with. He was meeting Olivia at Patterson's at three o'clock to help her with the funeral arrangements, and he also needed to put in more than an appearance at Healey and Caldwell. Then again, it wouldn't really be interfering with the investigation if he stopped by the ME's office some time that day to see if a ruling had been made on Ben Mashburn's manner of death, but that was as far as he would go.

Lost in these thoughts, Halloran glanced right and left, then began to cross the street to head back home. Nearing the curb, he saw a large, dark car out of the corner of his right eye barreling toward him. To his shock, it sped up as it closed in on him. Halloran froze and watched in horror as everything segued into slow-motion, the car inching closer to him in soundless fury. Every sense save hearing seemed heightened: The sun glinted off the windshield in a golden blaze; he could feel and smell the sweat coming from his pores; and the acrid taste of fear coated his tongue. He remained locked in this silent, rigid state for what seemed an eternity, certain that he was about to die. As the irony of his own death coming so soon after Elliot's hit him, Halloran willed himself into motion, with only seconds to throw himself onto the sidewalk before the huge car raced past. By the time he'd gingerly raised himself to a sitting position, his right forearm badly skinned and sharp pains shooting from his right hip to his knee, it was gone. The sound of his heart pounding away in his chest was the only thing he could hear at first, then he realized someone was standing near him, talking to him.

"Are you all right? Sir, can you answer me? Are you hurt?"

Halloran looked up to see a muscular, very concerned young man in a UPS uniform. He took some deep breaths, trying to slow his out-of-control heart. "I… think so," he said finally. "I don't think anything's… broken. Did you see the car?"

"Just when it flashed by. I was coming back to my truck when I saw you dive for the sidewalk. All I could tell was that it was some kind of dark-colored SUV. Man, the people in this town drive like they're in a stock car race! I'm from New Jersey, and I've never seen anything like it! You're lucky to be alive, mister."

Halloran was thinking the same thing, but he wasn't so sure that reckless driving was at fault. He remembered how the car had seemed to speed up just as it reached him. His heart rate began to accelerate again, and he took more deep breaths, trying to calm down.

"Listen, maybe you need to go to the emergency room," said the UPS man, squatting down by him. "Grady's not far away, and I can take you in my truck."

"No, I'll be okay. If you could just help me get to my feet, I'd really appreciate it."

"Okay, but I'm gonna at least drive you home. You're pretty banged up."

Halloran looked down at his right arm, blood covering an area where his warm-up jacket had been shredded. He groaned as he shifted his weight to his left hip so that he could try to stand up. "That might be a good idea. Thanks."

A few painful minutes later, he was sitting in the UPS truck giving directions to his house. Thanking the delivery man profusely as he got out, he asked for his card so he could call a supervisor to commend him. The man wanted to walk him to the front door, but Halloran declined, not sure he wanted Maggie to know what had happened. He needed to process it himself first and decide what, if anything, he could do. Someone had tried to kill him, and it must have something to do with Elliot's death. But he had no clue as to why, or who it could have been.

Or if it might happen again.

21

HOLLIS JOPLIN SAT AT HIS DESK doing paperwork, trying not to look at his watch. David Markowitz was finally back from court and Carrie was assisting him at an autopsy, so Hollis hadn't been able to talk to her that morning. When the phone rang, he was grateful for the distraction.

"Hollis Joplin."

"I was hopin' you'd be in already," said a familiar voice. "I got a couple things for you, if you're interested."

"I'm always interested in anything you tell me, B. J.," Joplin said to the head of CSU. His full name was Beverly James Reardon, but Hollis was one of only a few people who knew that. "Especially if it's about the Carter or Mashburn cases. I'm desperate."

"Well, you might still be desperate when I'm finished, but here goes: All the legible prints on the porno mags, the shoe box from Carter's closet, and the driver's side door of his car belong to Carter himself. The shoe molds you made did show something interestin', though."

"They didn't match the Nikes found near the tree?" asked Joplin excitedly, hoping they might belong to another pair of shoes entirely. That would help move the investigation over to the Homicide Unit.

"Nothin' that good, Hollis," said Reardon in his slow drawl. "But the Nike prints were made by someone whose right foot pronates a good bit.

It might not have been the deceased, because there's no corresponding worn area on the outer edge of the shoe. Course, they were fairly new, so it's not definitive that someone else was wearing them, but it's possible. Also, one set of prints is a lot deeper than the others, which means—"

"That the person wearing the Nikes could have been lifting Elliot Carson to position him in the ropes," finished Joplin.

"Either that or he gained about 185 pounds in just a few seconds," said Reardon. "Then again, a good defense attorney would ask our print technician if the discrepancy could be explained by the fact that the ground was wetter in some areas than others."

"And he'd have to say yes, I take it," said Joplin disgustedly.

"Only if he wants to keep his job," said Reardon. "Science can never be—"

"The handmaiden of the law," finished Joplin. "You've told me that often enough, B.J." He sighed long and hard. "I bet you're also going to tell me that the paraffin tests on Ben Mashburn show he fired the shot that killed him."

"Not me, Hollis. The test only shows that Mashburn's right hand had gunpowder residue on it that is consistent with his firing a gun. Now, if there'd been *no* residue—"

"I know, I know," said Joplin impatiently. "Why can't you come up with stuff like the people on that TV show, *C.S.I.,* do every week? I bet they could have taken pictures of Carter's or Mashburn's eyes and come up with images of the killer."

"You get me their writers, and I will," Reardon replied. "That show is about as realistic as the one with those so-called Atlanta housewives in it. I'll call you if we find anything else, hear?"

"Thanks, B.J." Joplin hung up, frustration roiling his stomach. The five cups of coffee he'd had since getting up weren't helping either.

"I hear you had a big date last night, Hollis." Chief MacKenzie stood in the doorway of his cubicle, giving his Cheshire cat smile. This morning, it got on Joplin's last nerve.

"Nothing gets past you, does it, sir?" he said, mimicking the smile.

"You'd be surprised, son," said MacKenzie. "She any good in bed? I've heard women doctors are even better in the sack than nurses." He grinned and shook his head. "Never had one myself—a doctor, I mean. Guess I'm just not educated enough. But if they're anything like the nurses I've been with, you musta had yourself a good ole time."

Joplin balled his hands into fists under his desk. "Can't help you, Chief," he said, looking MacKenzie straight in the eye. "I took Dr. Salinger home around nine o'clock and spent the rest of the evening with your ex-wife." Joplin knew he was pushing things, but he didn't care.

The chief investigator's eyes narrowed dangerously, but the smile never disappeared. "You got me there, didn't you, son?" he said, shaking his head. "I'll have to remember that one," he added, his tone making it clear it was something he didn't plan on forgetting. "By the way, you through with the Mashburn report? I want to read it."

"Any special reason?" Joplin asked, surprised. MacKenzie hadn't read anyone's reports in years. "I still have some loose ends to tie up."

"Ben Mashburn used to be on the force. We were partners once. And friends, although I hadn't seen him in a long time."

"I'm sorry. I didn't know that."

MacKenzie shrugged. "It was a long time ago."

"Was he the type to put a bullet in his brain?"

"Who knows? As I said, I hadn't seen him in a long time. He used to have a helluva drinking problem at one time, though."

"So I've heard. I plan to go see his wife sometime this morning."

"Why don't I do that? She might feel better talking to me instead of a stranger."

"Well, sir, I'm kind of involved in this one, and I—"

"Consider it an order, then," said MacKenzie, grinning again. "You just let me handle things from here on out."

"But Dr. Minton told me to focus on the Carter case and the Mashburn case exclusively," protested Joplin.

"Yes, but you don't report to Dr. Minton, do you, Hollis? You report to me. And I've given you a specific order." MacKenzie turned and walked past Joplin to his office.

"Yes, sir!" shouted Joplin, making himself sound like a new recruit at Fort Benning.

"Damn MacKenzie!" said Joplin, bursting into Jack Tyndall's office.

Tyndall looked up from his computer. "And what has the good chief investigator done this time?"

"He took me off the Mashburn case." Joplin slumped onto the battered sofa.

Tyndall's eyebrows arched high at this. "Why would he do that?"

"I have no idea. He asked to see the report when I was through with it, and I—"

"MacKenzie wanted to see a report?" Tyndall shook his head, looking amazed. "The man doesn't give a shit about what happens around here. He's got one more year till he can retire and get his pension. So what happened?"

"I told him I was going to see Mashburn's wife this morning, but he insisted on doing that himself. Told me he and Mashburn used to be partners when Mashburn was on the force, and the wife might be more comfortable talking to him. When I protested, he told me to consider it an order."

"That's the biggest problem with having nothing but former detectives as investigators here," said Tyndall. "Technically, you all work for Lewis Minton, just like me. But you *feel* like you have to answer to MacKenzie because you're all so paramilitary. I told Lewis we should use the civilian model like Fulton County when this office was created, but he wouldn't go for it. He thought that might discourage homicide detectives from applying here."

"Times like this, I agree with you, but it would still be a real conflict for me. I like working with investigators who've been homicide detectives, and I think Lewis was right that a different model might affect applications. It would also be a huge change."

"Sometimes change is good, Hollis. Sometimes it's even necessary."

Something in Jack's voice made Joplin look at him closely. The pathologist looked almost haggard. His stubble was worse, and the bags under his eyes more prominent.

"You've got to quit burning the candle at both ends, Jack. It's killing you."

"My candle's only burning at one end these days. Work is all I have since Janie left."

"Where's the girl you were seeing when Janie found out and left you?"

Tyndall winced and rubbed his face. "She left me, too, when she found out about all my children and alimony payments. Anyway, we were discussing your problems, not mine. Specifically, Chief MacKenzie. Going to see the widow, is he? The randy little bantam rooster! She must be hot stuff."

"I don't mean to poke holes in your theory, Jack, but the lady's in her sixties."

"Yeah, but maybe MacKenzie's had a thing for her all these years."

"Get a life, Jack. Better yet, get another girlfriend. I'm worried about you."

"Then you'll be happy to know that Dr. Salinger is going to lunch with me today."

Joplin wasn't prepared for the way this hit him. Luckily, the phone rang. Tyndall picked it up, and Joplin saw a quizzical expression on his face.

"It's Keisha," Tyndall said, holding his hand over the receiver. "Tom Halloran is in reception asking for either you or me. Shall I have her send him back?"

"Sure, although I have to say I wasn't happy that the senior partner at his law firm dragged Dr. Minton into this. But you should meet him. See what I've been up against."

"I've already talked to him over the phone, I felt like I was on the witness stand. Did I ever tell you I hate lawyers, Hollis?"

"Just about every day, Jack. At least this one won't be trying to get money from you."

Joplin watched Halloran take in Jack's office as he shook hands with both of them and accepted a seat on the sofa. He still looked tall sitting down.

"I'd like to know if you have any preliminary information on Ben Mashburn's death," the attorney said.

"Dr. Minton came in yesterday to do the autopsy himself," Joplin said pointedly. "I'm afraid you'll have to talk to him about that."

"Hollis, I've already let Mr. Halloran know we weren't real pleased about Alston Caldwell contacting Dr. Minton," said Tyndall. "I think you can cut him some slack."

Joplin shrugged. "There really isn't anything to report yet. Dr. Minton's findings were consistent with a suicidal death, but he's waiting on the histology and tox reports."

"Do you have any idea when they'll be completed?" Halloran asked.

"It'll probably be several weeks."

Halloran didn't look happy about this, but he nodded slowly. "Elliot Carter's mother has arranged for Patterson's to pick up his body today. I was surprised it was being released so soon. Does that mean I can get a copy of your autopsy report, Dr. Tyndall?"

"I'm afraid not. I released the body because we've gotten everything we can from it. But I'm also waiting on a toxicological analysis, and I can't give an official ruling as to manner of death until then. And until Hollis is satisfied about the question of foul play."

"But you seemed so sure yesterday that this was an autoerotic death."

"I still am, based upon the autopsy I did. But an official ruling is predicated on several things, not the least of which is circumstantial evidence uncovered by the investigator. Hollis seems to have a gut feeling that Ben Mashburn was murdered. And I trust Hollis's instincts. He thinks that if Mashburn was murdered, then Carter was too."

"But you don't?"

"You just don't understand how difficult it is to fake an autoerotic death. And be able to fool a medical examiner," Tyndall added. "As I've said before, it would have to be done by someone with a very sophisticated knowledge of this type of perversion, as well as the forensics."

"What about a psychiatrist?" Halloran asked. "A psychiatrist would certainly know about autoerotic asphyxia, maybe even have researched it if he had a patient who was into this. And as a medical doctor, he'd also know something about autopsies, right?"

"It's conceivable," said Tyndall. "But highly unlikely."

"It just so happens that Anne Carter's been seeing a psychiatrist for the past six months, and there's a strong possibility that she's romantically involved with him."

"You mean that cold fish who brought her here on Wednesday?" asked Joplin. "His name was Woodley, right?"

"That's the one. Dr. Paul Woodley."

"I knew a Paul Woodley in pre-med at UGA," said Tyndall. "If it's the same guy, he *is* a cold fish. What makes you think he and Mrs. Carter are involved?"

"The proprietary way he acts around her, for one thing," said Halloran.

"I'll admit he seemed pretty protective of her," said Joplin. "But even if they are involved, what would be the motive for him to kill Elliot Carter? The Carters were getting a divorce, and Anne Carter had been cut out of his will."

Halloran shook his head. "I've asked myself the same questions. One thing I keep thinking about, though, is something Alston Caldwell said. That whoever did this did it out of great malice toward Elliot."

"If, in fact, Carter was murdered," said Tyndall. "It's more likely that only Mashburn was murdered—by Elliot Carter. Probably after he'd agreed to destroy his files on Carter in exchange for a considerable amount of money. Maybe Carter didn't want to risk being blackmailed in the future. He might have lured Mashburn to that motel with the promise of money, then gotten him drunk and killed him."

"Jack, as I told Mr. Halloran earlier, I really don't think that anyone in the business as long as Ben Mashburn would actually sell out a client," Joplin said.

Tyndall shrugged. "Well, maybe he contacted Elliot Carter as part of his investigation. He could've *told* him he'd found something, whether it was the truth or not. Maybe in an attempt to help Mrs. Carter get a better settlement. And then Carter decided he'd better get rid of him. So he talked Mashburn into meeting him at that motel to discuss things, then killed him."

"Your logic's a little off, Doctor," Halloran said. "If Ben Mashburn *didn't* sell Anne out, then why did he have so much alcohol in his system? He wouldn't have had any reason to 'celebrate' by getting drunk at his meeting with Elliot."

"Maybe Carter put a gun to his head—literally."

"But how did he even know Mashburn had an alcohol problem in the first place?" asked the attorney.

"I asked *Mrs.* Carter that very question," Joplin said, "when she suggested Mashburn might be out on a 'bender' before his body was found. And she said he told her all about it one night during a phone conversation. Maybe it somehow came up when Elliot Carter came to his office."

"That's a pretty big 'maybe,'" Halloran said sarcastically. "Especially since it's crucial to Dr. Tyndall's murder scenario."

"Look, Mr. Halloran, I admit Jack's theory isn't perfect, but it addresses the two things that have been bothering me about both deaths: I couldn't understand why a man like Elliot Carter would do something so apparently out of character like practicing autoerotic asphyxia in such a public place. I also couldn't believe, as I said a few minutes ago, that Mashburn would sell out his client. But if Carter killed Ben Mashburn—for whatever reason—I can see how the tremendous stress of doing something like that resulted in his needing to find relief in a much more spectacular and riskier way than just on the door of his closet. He decided to go to Piedmont Park."

"Exactly," said Tyndall.

Halloran stood up, scowling angrily. "The two of you are basing this ridiculous theory on what you *think* you know about Elliot Carter. I'm basing my refusal to accept it on what I *do* know about him: that he was an extremely ethical and moral person. He wasn't into autoerotic asphyxia, and he wasn't into—" Halloran's mouth snapped shut.

Joplin cocked his head to one side. "He wasn't into what, Mr. Halloran?"

"Does this mean you're going to close the book on Elliot's death?" the attorney asked Joplin, ignoring his question.

"Not at all," he answered. But the truth of the matter was that Jack's theory made a lot of sense. Joplin's face must have betrayed his feelings, because Halloran's expression tightened even more.

"What if I told you that someone tried to kill *me* this morning?" he asked.

"What do you mean?"

Joplin and Tyndall listened intently as the attorney told them what had occurred on his early morning jog. When he had finished, Joplin looked at Jack, then cleared his throat and thought carefully about what he would say.

"Did you call the police, sir?" he asked finally.

"No. The car was long gone, and besides a scraped arm and a sore hip, I was okay."

"It doesn't sound like the UPS guy actually witnessed what happened. Were you able get the car's license number?"

"No," Halloran shot back. "You don't believe me, do you?"

"I believe what you say happened *did* happen," Joplin replied carefully. "But I don't think it adds up to attempted murder, no."

"Mr. Halloran, we see way too many pedestrian fatalities in this office," Jack Tyndall interjected. "In fact, Atlanta ranks tenth in the nation in that area. I think what Hollis means is that—"

"I know exactly what he means," the attorney said curtly. "Thank you both for your time," he added, then turned and left Tyndall's office.

22

CARRIE WAS JUST PUTTING ON HER LAB COAT in the autopsy room when Hollis Joplin came in. The look on his face was uncharacteristically grave this morning.

"Don't go to lunch with Jack today," he said to her. "He's only after one thing, and I don't want to see you get hurt."

"You mean sex?" she asked, trying not to laugh as she pulled on latex gloves.

"No, I'm talking about your writing skills. I've seen him operate on hundreds of innocent young residents over the years. He'll take you to the Varsity, let you order anything on the menu, and then talk you into collaborating on a forensic article. Except *you'll* do all the work. All you'll get is having your name as first author."

Carrie began taking dissecting tools out of a nearby autoclave and laying them out on a tray. "Actually, I've already agreed to do an article with him. I'm going to start the lit review this afternoon." She glanced sideways at him. "And we're not going to the Varsity, for your information. He's taking me to Magnolia."

"God, it's worse than I thought," said Joplin. "He's not just after your mind."

"What are you talking about?"

"Both his wife and his girlfriend left him recently. It must be troop replacement time."

This time she did laugh. "Don't worry, he's not my type."

"That's what they all say, but, believe me, he's every woman's type when he wants to be. The man has charm. I've seen him in action."

"I assure you, that kind of charm doesn't do a thing for me," Carrie replied. But even to her own ears she sounded unbelievably prim, and the memory of the very real attraction she'd felt to Jack caused the blood to rush to her cheeks. Turning her back to Joplin, she began pulling more tools out of the autoclave.

"Well, that's good news. But let me give you my cell phone number, just in case."

"In case of what?" Carrie asked, pivoting around to him.

He tore off a page of his notebook and handed it to her. "In case you need an antidote to the famous Tyndall charm. We stay open twenty-four hours a day. And there's never a problem with insurance."

"Hollis, I—"

"Don't worry about it," he said, winking at her. "Have a nice lunch—I mean that. Order something expensive." On his way out, he paused at the door, glancing back at her. "Listen, when you're doing the lit review for Jack's article, could you do a search on Paul Woodley and see if he's published anything? He's a psychiatrist who's been spending a lot of time with Elliot Carter's widow."

"You haven't closed that one out yet, have you, Hollis?"

"Not quite. A few things still bother me."

"How does this Dr. Woodley fit in?" asked Carrie.

"Actually, I'm just playing a hunch, and it's not even mine. It was Tom Halloran, Carter's law partner, who suggested Woodley as a suspect. Jack told him it would take someone with expert knowledge of autoerotic asphyxia to fake a death like that, and Mr. Halloran thinks Woodley might fit the bill. So if anything jumps out at you, like something titled, 'Autoerotic Deaths I've Faked,' call me immediately, okay?"

"I'll be sure to do that," said Carrie.

When he was gone, Carrie tried to sort out her feelings. She'd once been told by an ex-boyfriend—a PhD candidate in clinical psych—that she intellectualized everything.

"You just *report* on your feelings, you know, Carrie," he'd said in his most arrogant, supercilious voice. "You never really let yourself feel anything until you've gotten some distance from it. But by then it's too late."

She'd been stung by his words, and angry enough to break up with him, although things hadn't been good between them for some time anyway. She and Stephen had met at a Hillel group when she was a junior at Brown, and the relationship had lasted through her first semester of med school at Emory. But more times than she'd like to admit, Carrie realized that he was right. It *was* easier for her to analyze a situation than to actually experience any feelings that situation evoked. Lately, however, she was making an effort to work on that aspect of herself; she'd been ambushed too often by feelings she didn't even know she had.

Like her attraction to Jack Tyndall.

Carrie quickly switched her thoughts back to Hollis Joplin. She hadn't ever dated anyone like him. It wasn't just that he wasn't Jewish, although that certainly was a factor. She'd never made a conscious decision not to date Gentile men; it had just seemed natural for her to stay within the circle of friends she'd made in Hebrew school and temple. They were the sons of her parents' friends or the brothers of her girlfriends, and they all came from a world where expensive schools and summers in Europe or on kibbutzim in Israel were taken for granted.

She remembered her embarrassment when Hollis asked if she only dated lawyers. She realized now that it had exposed a kind of snobbery she didn't know she had. It was also why she'd agreed to go out with him. And yet, once she'd begun to talk to him, Carrie found herself enjoying the evening immensely. And not just because he could be very funny. What he'd told her about his "blue funks" made him seem pretty vulnerable, despite all his joking. She had asked him later why, given how it affected him, he had sought out this type of work—not just police work, but the aspect of it that dealt exclusively with death and violence.

"There aren't any happy endings at the morgue," she had said over dessert. "No chances to rescue any abandoned babies or to talk anyone out of jumping off a bridge."

"I had my years of that," he'd told her. "But I found myself wanting to focus on the victims, not the killers—and not just the victims of violent crime. A lot of what we do at the ME's office is just fodder for the insurance companies and the lawyers, but it's important to know how and why somebody died, if it's not a clear-cut case of natural causes. I know death is a part of life, but it seems like these days we treat it too lightly. We should be outraged by the number of people who die in car accidents or overdose on drugs or kill themselves because they're old and lonely."

"'Any man's death diminishes me, for I am a friend to mankind,'" Carrie quoted.

"Shakespeare?"

"Actually, it's from an essay by John Donne. While other girls were going nuts over rock groups, I was listening to Bach and reading the metaphysical poets."

"Sounds like you know something about blue funks, too," Hollis had said.

Carrie realized now that in spite of their obvious differences in background and religion, she had felt more at ease with Hollis than most of the men she'd dated. She liked that feeling a lot. Smiling to herself, she finished setting up for the first autopsy of the day. A few minutes later, Jack Tyndall strolled in, unshaven and sleep-deprived. Resisting Dr. Tyndall's famous charm would be easy, she thought.

And then she noticed how blue his eyes were.

By the time he came to get her for lunch, Jack Tyndall had not only showered and shaved, he'd also changed into crisply pressed khaki pants, a blue oxford shirt, and a well-tailored navy blazer. He was wearing cologne, too. Her surprise must have shown.

"You didn't think I'd clean up this well, did you?" he teased.

Carrie started to protest, then gave up. "Actually, I didn't know what to expect."

He sighed. "I've been a real pig, lately. Guess I've been feeling sorry for myself."

"I heard about...your wife."

"Yeah, you probably heard about my girlfriend, too."

"Oh, no, I—"

He waved a hand in the air. "Don't apologize, it's all true. But I'm turning over a new leaf, and you can be a witness to this historic moment." Offering her his arm, Jack led her gallantly out to the staff parking lot.

David Markowitz, who was just coming back from his own lunch break, honked his horn and lowered his window. "Didn't your mother warn you about men like him, Carrie?"

"I assure you my intentions are strictly honorable, Dr. Markowitz," said Jack.

"Honorable, my ass," said David. "Don't say *I* didn't warn you, Carrie."

"I'm a big girl, David," she said, laughing. But as she got into Jack's dilapidated Suburban, Carrie felt about sixteen.

23

ALTHOUGH STILL ANGRY OVER HIS MEETING with Joplin and Dr. Tyndall, Tom Halloran tried to put his near run-in with death and their easy dismissal of it out of his mind. He spent most of Friday morning on work for Healey and Caldwell for a change.

Joan had carefully arranged the piles of letters and files in order of the need for his immediate attention, but he'd been shocked by the sheer volume of it. Aware that the last time he'd billed even any quarter-hours for the firm had been Tuesday, he asked the secretary to screen his calls, giving her a very short list of people to put through. Halloran hoped none of them would call him for at least a few hours. His luck held until around eleven, when Maggie called.

"How are you feeling?" she asked.

"I'm fine. Hip's still a little sore, but you did a great job on my arm."

"Good, but I don't want to have to do any more doctoring in the near future. You need to start triple-tying your Nikes when you jog, Tom."

"I will," promised Halloran, feeling guilty about the story he'd told her. "What's up?"

"I'm actually on my way to a new client's house—can you believe it?"

"Really? That's a better sign that the economy's improving than the jobless rate! We'd better alert the media, don't you think? Better yet, Tim Geithner."

"*Anyway,*" Maggie responded, ignoring his feeble attempt at humor, "I've had a chance to look over those photos again. I can't prove it, but I'm pretty sure they weren't reproduced using a scanner. The clarity's too good. Each time a picture is reproduced without using the negative, like on a scanner, it gets more pixelated."

"Pixelated?"

"The resolution gets poorer," Maggie explained. "There's a graininess that's obvious to professional photographers. I think those photos were made by someone who took pictures of the originals with a digital camera and then printed them on a laser printer."

"But why? I mean, wouldn't it have been easier just to scan them?"

"Of course it would. That's my whole point. There must have been some reason why the person who made these copies couldn't do that."

"Maybe he didn't have a scanner—or access to one," suggested Halloran.

"Possibly, but it still doesn't make much sense to me. By the way, Tom, there was one little boy who looked so familiar to me, but I don't know why. I've tried to think if maybe he just reminded me of one of my brother David's friends, but I don't think so. He had such a sad face and such…dead eyes. I can't seem to get him out of my head."

"I shouldn't have given those pictures to you, Maggie. They're too upsetting."

"But I want to help. I just don't know if anything I've discovered will do that. Listen, I've got to go, but Mother invited the kids to spend the night tonight. Why don't you ask Olivia to come to dinner when you see her today? I haven't been able to get hold of her."

"That's a great idea. She may have other plans though."

"Just let me know," said Maggie.

"I will. Bye, sweetie. Thanks."

Halloran didn't get back to work right away. He wondered about his decision to tell Maggie he'd tripped over a shoelace that morning when he limped into the house. He'd rationalized it by deciding the truth would only upset her, and despite what he told Tyndall and Joplin, he'd begun to have doubts himself about whether the incident had really been an attempt on his life. Still, he was uncomfortable keeping things from her.

Shaking off these debilitating thoughts, Halloran considered Maggie's theory that the photographs were "pictures of pictures" and its

significance, if any. Probably none. But maybe she would know something more by that evening.

Magnolia was in the Hurt Building, an Atlanta landmark in the heart of
downtown. Carrie had never been there, and as they climbed the wide,
curving staircase, she found herself staring up at the chandeliers and
feeling as if she had stepped back in time. The atmosphere was definitely
Old World; she felt as if she were in wartime Germany. Tables were laden
with expensive crystal and silver, and ramrod-straight waiters glided
around and through them with practiced ease. Classical music (she
was sure it was a Wagner piece) played softly in the background. She
almost expected to see a small orchestra tucked away in a corner, gamely
prepared to play through the bombs.

"Nice to see you again, Dr. Tyndall," said the pretty young hostess,
beaming at Jack.

"Nice to see *you* again," said Jack, beaming back. Then he glanced at
Carrie and said, in a brisk, businesslike tone, "I had a reservation for two
at one o'clock."

"Of course," said the hostess. "Your table is ready."

She led them—with a little too much hip action, in Carrie's opinion—
to a table for two near a high Palladian window. Smiling at Carrie, but
with an appraising eye, she handed her an enormous menu. Carrie saw
her wink at Jack when she gave him his menu.

"Enjoy your lunch," she murmured, then turned. More hip action.

"Come here often?" Carrie asked dryly.

"Not really—once or twice," said Jack, studying his menu intently.

"Well, it certainly isn't the Varsity. Although that would have been just
fine."

Jack looked puzzled, then his expression cleared. "Hollis has been
talking to you, right? Telling you how I seduce young residents into
writing forensic articles with me."

"Actually, he said *for* you, not with you, if you really want to know."

Frowning, Jack set his menu on the table. "Listen, I might be butting
in where I shouldn't. I didn't know this when I asked you to lunch, but I
heard today that you and Hollis went out last night."

"And?"

"Hollis is a good friend. I wouldn't want to cut in on him."

Carrie stared at him. "Let me get this straight: I go out to dinner one time with a co-worker, and you think that gives him some kind of 'dibbies' on me. Or you think *he* thinks it does. Then, to add insult to injury, you're so convinced of your own charm, you're afraid that I'll fall madly in love with you over lunch and drop him entirely. Does that about sum it up?"

She was gratified to see Jack Tyndall look embarrassed.

"Sounds pretty damning, putting it like that," he admitted. "I apologize profusely."

"I accept your apology. Is it okay if I order lunch now? I promise to let you know if I feel a swoon coming on."

Jack threw back his head and laughed, sounding genuinely amused. "I think we've established that you've got some kind of innate immunity to my famous charm, Doctor. In my professional opinion, you'll be quite safe right through the cappuccino."

"Great, because I'm starving."

24

JOPLIN KNEW HE WAS TAKING a chance going back to Ace Investigations to ask Janna Helms, Ben Mashburn's secretary, more questions. He had decided not to go to Lewis Minton about MacKenzie's orders to drop the Mashburn case and get him to intervene, so the chief investigator would be pissed if he found out what he was doing. And yet, the likelihood that MacKenzie would interview the secretary himself was pretty small. The man hadn't made chief because of his thoroughness. Or his honesty and integrity, for that matter. Joplin had to admit, however, that his boss had a way of intuiting whatever it was that people were most ashamed of or fearful about and wanted to keep hidden. It was a singular talent—and one based on MacKenzie's own vices and weaknesses—but Joplin had seen it in practice quite often.

"Cherchez la femme, Hollis, ole buddy," MacKenzie might say with a leery wink in the middle of some complex investigation. "Which to us country boys means, 'Look for the pussy.'" And it would turn out that the businessman who'd rammed his Mercedes into a telephone pole at seventy miles an hour had a mistress who was about to end his career and his marriage, or that the priest who overdosed on Ativan and scotch hadn't been as celibate as he should have been.

But the odds that the chief would even think about Mashburn's secretary were pretty low. And so, despite Joplin's belief that Jack's theory about Elliot Carter murdering Mashburn was hard to reject, he had called the secretary and asked to see her sometime that day. She'd told him to come anytime, as she was taking care of the office while Jim Ferguson helped Mrs. Mashburn with funeral plans. He arrived a little after one p.m.

"I'm sorry about your boss," Joplin said to her when he walked into the outer office. "And about having to bother you again."

"There's nothing else I need to be doing that's more important than this," Janna Helms said. She motioned to a chair next to her desk. "What can I tell you?"

"I guess what I really need to know is, do you think Ben Mashburn killed himself?"

Her eyes opened wide, then she smiled and shook her head. "You sure don't waste any time getting to the point, do you?" Her chin came up, and she studied him for a few seconds. "That's okay, neither did Ben. And my answer is no, he didn't kill himself. I've known that man for the past ten years. I was a twenty-nine-year-old mother of three going through a very bad divorce when I met Ben. I came looking for a job and was hired on the spot, because I told him I was desperate." The chin came down, but she leveled her eyes at him. "Ben Mashburn was one of the best people I've ever known, Investigator Joplin. He loved his wife and his daughter and his grandchildren, and he would never have done something like that to them."

Tears began to course down Janna Helms's cheeks, and Joplin said, "I'm sorry."

Janna composed herself, taking a tissue out of a box on her desk and wiping her eyes. "What else do you need to know?"

"Do you happen to know whether he drank Scotch?"

"Yes, he did," she answered slowly. "The subject came up frequently. He'd say things like, 'When I was drinking, I thought my two best friends were a bottle of Scotch and a bottle of Maalox.' Or, 'The only answers I ever found in a bottle of Scotch I forgot by the next day.' That sort of thing."

"I know he fell off the wagon a few years back. What makes you think he didn't do that on Tuesday?"

"Because of what he told me after that happened," Janna said. "His granddaughter almost died in a car accident. He couldn't do anything to help her, and it nearly killed him. He disappeared for three days, and we finally found him holed up in a crummy hotel. Luckily, Jenny was out of danger by then. When Ben could finally talk about it, he said there was nothing that could ever make him drink again. *Nothing.* He said that he'd realized that Jenny might have died while he was off somewhere stinking drunk, making things even harder on his wife and daughter, and that he'd never let them down like that again."

"Drunks make a lot of promises they don't keep."

"I know that," she said a little defiantly. "But I believed him. I still do."

Joplin decided to switch the subject. "Did Mashburn ever discuss his cases with you?"

"Not really. Ben did all his reports to clients on his computer. I knew bits and pieces about his cases, though, because I still typed up any correspondence he needed. I also kept his books, so I knew what types of jobs he was doing for clients. But the general rule was that he didn't tell me much, unless I specifically needed to know."

"But you did know why Anne Carter hired Mashburn last fall?"

"Yes, because I itemized the charges for her bill. It was a typical divorce investigation."

"What about the second time she hired him?"

Janna shook her head. "Ben asked for a retainer when he took a case, but he only sent out bills when it was over. Obviously, he didn't get to finish that one." Her eyes filled with tears again, but she didn't give in to them. "I do know that this time seemed to be…different somehow."

"How so?"

"I'm not sure if I can express it." Her eyes moved left to the wall behind him. "The first time Mrs. Carter came to see Ben, she seemed…desperate. She looked very tense and tired, and she was constantly calling him. But when she came to the office a few weeks ago, it was like she was a different person."

"In what way?"

"Well, she really had it together. She looked great, and she was so… in charge, you know what I mean? It was like, this time she didn't need information, she *had* information. And she couldn't wait to tell it to Ben."

Joplin immediately thought of the things he'd found in Elliot Carter's closet. If his wife had found out about his sexual perversion, she'd have a lot to tell Ben Mashburn. But then he realized that didn't make any sense. If Anne Carter had been the one to discover her husband's autoerotic asphyxia, why did she need Mashburn? Why not just threaten to go to his partners or a judge, if he wouldn't give her the money she wanted? Then again, unless she had actual pictures of Carter dressed in women's underwear, it would be her word against his. And maybe no one would care anyway.

"I know that everything to do with the Carter case was deleted from Mr. Mashburn's computer files and his file cabinet, but was anything else missing?"

She hesitated for just a second. "Not missing."

"Tampered with?"

"I'm really not sure. Ben kept a drawer full of manila folders with clippings from cases he worked on when he was a cop. Not anything official, of course."

"A good cop never gives up on a case," said Joplin reassuringly.

"Exactly," she said, nodding in agreement. "That's exactly what he told me. And he'd talk to me about those cases sometimes."

"War stories," said Joplin, hoping to encourage her. He leaned forward a little and clasped his hands together. "So it looked like someone had gone through that drawer?"

"Yes. It was open just a little, and the files were uneven, as if someone had pulled them up, looking for a particular one. But I didn't say anything to the police because it didn't look like anything had been taken."

"Mind if I take a look?"

Mashburn's office was very plain, with a desk, two chairs directly in front of it, a sofa on the wall to the right, and two file cabinets on the wall to the left. Janna went to the cabinet on the right and stooped down to open the bottom drawer. He stooped down, too, and peered in. The names on the folders before him were like a trip down Memory Lane. A very bad trip. They were all unsolved cases from Atlanta's past: the disappearance of newlywed Mary Little from Lenox Square over thirty years ago; the murder of Judge Albert Singleton in his chambers in 1985; the rape and decapitation of Janice Wainwright at the Ski Lodge Apartments in 1976, to name a few.

"Mind if I take these with me? I'll give you a receipt."

"Sure, why not? Ben was the only one who cared about those clippings." She smiled, but her eyes were bright with tears again.

"I'll take good care of them," said Joplin.

***

Jack Tyndall was in his usual position, hunched over the keyboard of his computer, when Joplin walked into his office around four o'clock that afternoon. The pathologist was decked out in a blue shirt with the sleeves rolled up and a striped tie at half-mast. A navy blazer was draped over the chair in front of his desk. Joplin couldn't remember the last time Jack had worn a jacket and tie outside a courtroom. It meant he had considered his lunch with Carrie to be a real date.

Just as he'd feared, troop replacement had begun.

"You ever take any time between relationships to figure out what went wrong?" Joplin asked, leaning against the door frame in what he hoped was a nonchalant pose.

"I already know what went wrong, Hollis. It was all my fault, as usual. I'm the scum of the earth. But I think I've found the right woman to help me turn my life around."

"That's what you say every time, Jack."

"Yes, but this time is different, Hollis. You have to admit Carrie isn't like anyone else I've been attracted to. I think I'm finally beginning to mature."

"That's what worries me, Jack. Even a little bit of maturity will add a lot to your already considerable charm where women are concerned."

Tyndall's expression turned serious. "Listen, Hollis, I know you told me you were okay about my taking Carrie to lunch, and I almost got my head bitten off by her when I suggested you and she might be an item, but maybe I need to back off anyway."

"What did she say?" Joplin asked quickly. Nonchalance was now out of the question, but he'd settle for not sounding quite as pathetic as he felt.

"Basically, that she's a free agent and that I'm not quite as charming as I think I am. Or even as charming as *you* think I am, for that matter."

Joplin grinned at him. "Well, I guess we've both been put in our places."

"Yeah, it looks like it. Made me want her more than ever."

"Go for it, Jack. I'll enjoy the competition."

For a split second, Tyndall looked surprised, then he frowned again. "Listen, Hollis, I meant what I said about backing off, if you've got a thing for her."

"Like she said, she's a free agent, and there's no reason for either of us to bow out. It's up to her, isn't it?" Wanting to put an end to the subject, he said, "Listen, I just got the LUDS on Carter's and Mashburn's phones, and you'll never guess who Mashburn called this past Monday. I almost fell out of my chair when I recognized the number."

"Okay, I'll bite—who?"

"MacKenzie."

"No shit! *Our* Mackenzie? As in *Chief* MacKenzie?"

"As in," Joplin said, grinning. "It was to his direct line here in the office. The call came in at 10:05 a.m. and lasted fifteen minutes."

"You're kidding. And MacKenzie never told you about it?"

"No. In fact, he told me he hadn't seen Mashburn in a few years. There's another, very brief call logged in at four-thirty Tuesday afternoon, but it's less than ten seconds. I'm figuring MacKenzie had left for the day by then, and Mashburn got his voice mail. Almost immediately after that, he called the front desk, maybe looking for MacKenzie. I checked with Keisha, and she has a vague memory of someone calling that afternoon and asking if MacKenzie was still somewhere in the building, but whoever it was, he didn't identify himself."

"Why would Ben Mashburn be calling MacKenzie? Have you asked him about it?"

"Jack, MacKenzie took me off the Mashburn case, remember? I'll have to get Ike Simmons to follow up on this or my ass is grass."

"Right. Forgot about that. Any calls from MacKenzie's line show up on the LUDS?"

Joplin nodded. "It gets even more interesting on that end. MacKenzie called him from here about eleven a.m. on Tuesday; that one lasted about ten minutes. Then, beginning around seven that night, there are no fewer than three calls from MacKenzie's home phone. None of them lasted longer than a few seconds, so he probably got voice mail each time and hung up. The last one was about eight-thirty."

Jack Tyndall rubbed his face. "Jeez, Hollis, this is the goddamnedest case I think we've ever had. What the hell is going on?"

"Damned if I know. Every time I think I've got it figured out, another piece of the puzzle comes along that changes the whole picture. I went to see Mashburn's secretary today, and she is absolutely convinced that the man wouldn't touch alcohol again or kill himself. Yeah, I know, I know," Joplin added when he saw Jack open his mouth. "We hear stuff like that every day." He sat down on the arm of the couch. "But there are just too many conflicting pieces of evidence in this case." He told Tyndall about his call from B.J. Reardon that morning and the analysis of the footprint molds.

The pathologist sat back in his chair and seemed to be considering everything that Joplin had told him. "Well," he said finally, "I have to agree with B.J. that it wouldn't hold up in court, and it's certainly not enough to tip me toward a homicide ruling. But it *is* suspicious. What about Elliot Carter? Did Mashburn call him?"

"A call to Carter's cell phone was logged in at 3:10 p.m., shortly before Carter showed up at Ace Investigations. Then he made another call to the cell phone at six that evening. By the way," added Joplin, "besides calling Mashburn's office at 4:40 on Tuesday, Anne Carter also placed calls to his office number at around seven that night, and again around eight. The last one was on her cell phone. Neither of them lasted more than ten seconds, so I don't think she got him. It looks like that part of the story she told Tom Halloran is true."

"Yeah, but whatever she told Halloran doesn't make up for the fact that he tipped her off about Elliot Carter being in Mashburn's office the day before his body was discovered." Tyndall shook his head, looking disgusted. "That guy is really getting on my nerves, Hollis. Who the hell does he think he is?"

Joplin shrugged. "My guess is either F. Lee Bailey or Atticus Finch. He certainly has a high opinion of himself."

"Well, in my opinion, the apple didn't fall too far from the tree."

"What do you mean?"

"I Googled Halloran after he stormed out of my office this morning. Did you know his father was Robert J. Halloran, the CEO of Amitron Electronics? He and the CFO looted the employees' pension holdings to pay off some loans, then overstated the value of the company's assets to keep the stock value up. It was like Enron, only worse."

Joplin nodded slowly. "Yeah, sure, I remember that case. And there was a lot about it in the *AJC* when Halloran first started getting press. Didn't Robert J. kill himself before it went to trial?"

"Yeah, although he was in poor health anyway. I think he'd had a heart attack when the shit first hit the fan. But that didn't make him any less a coward. And with a background like that, Tom Halloran shouldn't try to be some kind of avenging hero."

"Maybe not, although he's never been linked to any scandal or corruption of his own. Or do you know something I don't?"

"Naw. I'm just venting, that's all. But I hope you read him the riot act about talking to Mrs. Carter. He could screw this case up if it's ultimately turned over to Homicide."

"I did. And that's exactly what I told him."

Tyndall looked at his watch. "I've got to wrap up this report, Hollis. Why don't we go have a drink in about an hour, and we can discuss this further. Unless you've got a hot date with Carrie."

"No, she's got to start the lit review for your article," Joplin shot back. "But I think I'll invite her to my place for Sunday brunch. I'm a pretty good cook, you know."

"Yeah, you've got me beat to hell there. Who taught you how to cook anyway?"

"My grandmother. She was one of the best country cooks around."

"Mine couldn't cook worth shit. And my mother was just as bad."

"Lisa could cook," said Joplin, referring to Tyndall's first wife.

"Yes, she could, couldn't she?" said the pathologist. "Why did I ever leave her?"

"You found Deidre, who left you over Tammi. And then you married Janie."

"And none of them could cook worth a damn," said Tyndall, slapping the table. He looked up at Hollis. "Can Carrie cook?"

"I don't know, but I hope I find out first," Joplin said.

25

THE MEETING WITH OLIVIA CARTER at Patterson's went as well as could be expected, but Halloran was relieved when it was over. The funeral was to be on the following Wednesday, so that close friends from Charleston could be there. He felt Elliot's loss even more as he tried to guide his friend's mother through writing the obituary, the selection of the coffin, music, pallbearers, and the myriad other details involved. The only instructions Elliot had left stipulated that the service be held at St. Phillip's Cathedral in Buckhead, with interment at Arlington in Sandy Springs. Olivia had also sidestepped Anne's offer to have family and friends to her house afterward by arranging a luncheon in a private banquet room at the Buckhead Ritz-Carlton.

"How are things going with Anne?" Halloran asked her as they walked to his car.

Olivia grimaced behind her sunglasses. "Luckily, I haven't had to spend much time with her. I'm trying to maintain a cordial relationship for Trip's sake, but it's not easy."

"Listen, we want you to come to dinner tonight. Maggie hasn't seen you yet."

"I'd like to, but Trip is coming to me again tonight. I promised him I'd have dinner sent up to my suite. It was the only way I could convince him to leave the house."

"It goes without saying that we'd love to have both of you."

"Can I ask him about it and let you know? I'm really worried about him, Tom."

"Of course you can," said Halloran, immediately concerned. "Is Dr. Woodley any help? Anne seems to rely on him."

"A little too much, if you ask me," Olivia said pointedly. "He seems solicitous enough, and he tries to keep Anne from hovering over the boy, but I don't think Trip feels comfortable with him."

Halloran opened the car door for her. "Do you want me to talk to Anne? Get her to understand that Trip needs a neutral third party right now?"

"You're doing enough already, Tom. And I wouldn't rock the boat just now. From what I've observed, Anne isn't far from the edge herself. I plan to stay in town through next week to keep an eye on Trip, so we'll see how it goes."

On the drive to the Ritz, Halloran decided to bring up the subject of the prenuptial agreement Anne had signed. "Elliot showed me a copy of it last September, but I have a feeling she's going to contest it, as well as the new will. Bart Lawson thinks I should handle both issues now that Elliot's gone. So I need to find out as much as possible about the circumstances surrounding it."

"Let her try," said Olivia. "That agreement was drawn up by one of the best law firms in Charleston."

"That could go against us. She might claim that she was intimidated into signing it by such a high-powered firm. She was only about nineteen at the time, wasn't she?"

"Yes, but even at that age Anne was a pretty determined young woman. And she wanted to be Mrs. Elliot Carter. She could hardly *wait* to sign those papers—and it wasn't just because of her condition."

Halloran took his eyes off the road and glanced at Olivia. "Anne was pregnant?"

Olivia looked confused, as if she hadn't realized what she'd said. "Well, now you know all the family secrets," she said finally. "That sort of slipped out. I promised Anne and Elliot I'd never tell anyone about that, for Trip's sake. I know I can count on you to keep that confidential, Tom."

"Of course you can," Halloran assured her. "But I don't really under-stand why it's such a deep, dark secret. Especially in this day and age."

"It certainly never bothered *me*, except that I wanted to make sure that Elliot didn't feel forced to get married. I mean, he'd just finished his second year of law school. But he adored Anne. She was the most popular girl in her freshman class at UGA and had every boy around after her. He told me the baby just made things more wonderful. It was Anne who was so insistent on keeping it secret. Don't forget, this was almost eighteen years ago, and she was from a small town in South Georgia."

"Is that why the wedding was held in Charleston?" asked Halloran, recalling how Anne had talked about marrying Elliot at his family's house on historic Meeting Street.

"Anne didn't want the locals to start counting backwards after the baby was born. She also didn't want all of our friends and relatives to know she came from McRae, Georgia. She said its only claim to fame was a replica of the Statue of Liberty built by the Lions Club in the town square. She seemed almost ashamed of her background."

"And her parents went along with that?"

"Shoot, Tom, you've met the Landrums!" said Olivia. "Those people would do anything Anne wanted. Ray Landrum was just a salesman for the John Deere Company, but every penny he and Lillian had to spare was spent on that girl—clothes, piano and dance lessons, a car when she turned sixteen. And it paid off. According to Lillian, Anne was homecoming queen and president of her senior class and won a full scholarship to UGA. She was also a very bright girl," she added quickly, as if she hadn't given Anne any credit for her accomplishments.

"And very ambitious, too, it sounds."

"Well, I think Lillian had a lot to do with that," Olivia responded. "I've always had the impression that she thought she'd 'married down' so to speak. And she didn't want Anne to make the same mistake."

"Whose idea was it to do the prenup—yours or Elliot's? I know your husband had passed away by then."

"It was the lawyers' idea, actually. Elliot didn't even want to discuss it with Anne, but the trustee at the bank agreed with the lawyers. Elliot wasn't quite twenty-five then and hadn't received the principal of his trust fund, so the trustee had a lot of power. But Anne made it easy for him. She claimed she wanted it herself—to prove she wasn't marrying Elliot for his money. And I suppose $500,000 looked like a lot at the time. So if she tries to say she was pressured into signing it, don't believe a word of it."

"You'll make an excellent witness in court, Olivia," said Halloran, smiling. "If it should ever come to that."

"Let's just hope it doesn't," said Olivia Carter grimly.

Halloran was still mulling over his conversation with Olivia as he walked into the offices of Healey and Caldwell. But the stack of phone messages Joan handed him and the sight of his still-crowded desk forced him to change gears. He was supposed to be going to trial in a month's time on a case involving the estate of a Coca Cola heir and his very disappointed children, who didn't want the bulk of their father's estate going to Emory University School of Law. He sat down and spent the next half-hour returning calls, then tackled the paperwork.

He managed to work steadily for another hour before Olivia's second bombshell intruded once again into his brain and demanded attention. For one thing, Anne didn't impress him as the kind of woman who would be careless enough to get pregnant. Which meant that the pregnancy might have seemed more like a blessing to her than an accident, or might not have been unplanned at all. But, if so, why had she worried so much about what the people in McRae, Georgia would think?

Halloran suddenly felt ashamed for thinking of Anne in such a callous way. He had no business making assumptions about what a young, unmarried woman who found herself pregnant might feel. And coming from a small town might have been something Anne wanted to put behind her, but it might also have had a big impact on her, too.

It struck him how little he'd really known about Anne Carter before her marriage to Elliot. Or afterward, for that matter. He realized now that even during the years of his and Maggie's close friendship with the Carters he'd thought of her more as an adjunct to Elliot, a "law wife" who had devoted herself to her husband's career, rather than as a person in her own right. He had admired Anne for her elegance and her ability to entertain and the reputation she had among Atlanta's social elite. Now he was being compelled to look at what might have been behind those traits, instead of accepting the illusion Anne Carter had presented.

Forcing himself to go back to work, Halloran decided he had enough time before going home to access Lexis-Nexis and research a controversial new ruling on a particular aspect of the Rule Against Perpetuities.

He had just logged onto the Internet when the phone rang again. It was Olivia.

"I'm sorry, Tom, but Trip just isn't up to going out."

"Don't worry about it. We'll try again next week. By the way, I meant to ask you earlier, but I forgot. Was David Healey one of those boys at UGA chasing after Anne?"

"Actually, he was. I remember Elliot teasing her about that when he decided to accept an offer from Healey and Caldwell. Why do you ask?"

"Just curious. You go take care of Trip."

After telling Olivia he'd see her soon, Halloran hung up. But his mind kept replaying everything she'd told him in the past few days: her fear that taking DES might have harmed Elliot in some way; Anne's inability to get pregnant again and her subsequent affair; and the fact that Anne had been pregnant at the time of her marriage to Elliot. Was it possible that David Healey, not Elliot, was Trip's father? If so, had he known it? And if he had, why hadn't *he* married Anne? Then again, maybe it was *Anne* who hadn't wanted to marry *David*. But if so, why not? The Healeys weren't quite as wealthy as the Carters, but they were close to it. Was that why there had seemed to be a constant, underlying tension between the two men? And yet it seemed impossible that Elliot would choose to become an associate at Healey and Caldwell if he had known that David was the father of his wife's unborn child.

Halloran sighed and clicked out of Lexis-Nexis, too tired to focus on the Rule Against Perpetuities. It had been a long day, beginning with a possible attempt on his life. He wanted to go home, have a big glass of Jack Daniels and then enjoy a quiet dinner with Maggie. He felt a little guilty that he was looking forward to an evening without his children, but the feeling was gone by the time he shut down his computer.

Hollis Joplin's phone rang at 10:02 p.m. Quincy, who was stretched out full-length on his back, his feet in the air, opened one eye and looked at Joplin lying beside him. Joplin set aside the Constitutional law book he was reading and reluctantly picked up the phone. He'd be dammed if he'd pinch-hit for Deke again. He had the day shift on Saturday, and the two drinks he'd had with Jack were excuse enough.

"I'm not here," he said into the receiver.

"Then why did you tell me to call you if I found anything on Dr. Woodley?"

"Carrie!" He sat bolt upright, startling Quincy, who scrambled to his feet and leaped from the bed. "How are you? *Where* are you?"

"I'm at home, at long last. I went to my parents' house for Shabbat dinner, and I'm ready to crash, but I came across something I thought you might want to know right away. I hope it's not too late."

"Are you kidding? I'm happy you called. But first tell me what a Shabbat dinner is."

"Shabbat means 'Sabbath.' The Sabbath begins at sundown on Friday evening, and Jews—well, mostly Conservative and Orthodox Jews—have a special dinner with candles and wine as a sort of preparation for it. I try to go over to my parents' house whenever I have a free Friday. It means a lot to them."

"Sounds like you're a good daughter."

She laughed and said, "If I were truly a good daughter, according to my mother, I'd have married and produced grandchildren for her by now. But let's not go there, okay?"

"Okay," said Joplin. "What did you find at the library?"

"Well, that hunch you had was right. Dr. Paul Woodley wrote an article published in the June, 2006 *Journal of Psychiatry* entitled, 'Autoerotic Asphyxia: A Case Study.'"

"Have you had a chance to read it?"

"I scanned it before I copied it, I was so excited. Then I had to rush to get to my parents' house, so I haven't had a chance to really go over it. But, Hollis, the bibliography alone shows that this guy knows a lot about the subject. To top it off, he actually had a patient who was doing this sort of thing, so he had firsthand knowledge. He's exactly the kind of person who could fake an autoerotic death."

"Carrie, I need to read that article as soon as possible. Can we get together tomorrow sometime?"

"Yes, but I can give you the website for the forensic journal it's in, and you can access it right now."

"That's okay," Joplin said quickly. He hated to give up a chance to see her away from the office. "I don't have a printer for my laptop, and you've already got a hard copy."

"Well, I'm on at Grady at six. I still have to put in time at the path lab no matter what my rotation is, but how about lunch? Say, at noon? Do you like hospital cafeteria food?"

"After Italian, it's my favorite. Listen, Carrie, I really appreciate this."

After he hung up, Joplin stretched out on the bed, hands behind his head, and stared up at the ceiling. He felt happy, a feeling that was so unexpected and overpowering that he just lay there, letting it wash over him. In just a few short days, he'd gone from being on the verge of a blue funk to feeling more alive than he had in a long time.

Quincy's nap had been interrupted when the phone rang. Now the cat padded over to Joplin and climbed up on his chest. He lay down, tucking his paws under him and stared intently at Joplin. Joplin knew the drill and began to stroke the cat softly. The purring was almost deafening. Joplin gazed into the cat's eyes and conjured up a memory of Carrie from the night before. She was sitting across from him at D'Angelo's, her head tilted a little to one side, listening intently to what he was saying. He saw her nod her head, then her mouth curved up into a huge smile, and he remembered how he had wanted to get up from his chair and kiss her right there in the middle of the restaurant. The urge had been so strong that he had reached out and gripped the right leg of the table to keep himself from doing it.

Now Joplin let his imagination do exactly what he had wanted to then. He saw Carrie's look of surprise as he stood up and then bent over her, his mouth coming closer to hers. But instead of saying something or even laughing at him, she turned her face up to his and engaged in what turned out to be a very long and passionate kiss. Her mouth tasted wonderful, in the way that first kisses with people you end up falling in love with always do. He wanted to keep on kissing her forever, but Quincy, evidently sensing that Joplin wasn't really concentrating on him, suddenly leaped up, his claws digging into Joplin's chest before he threw himself onto the floor and ran out of the room.

The image of Carrie faded away like smoke, and Joplin reluctantly turned out the light and tried to fall asleep.

26

THE ELEGANT ART DECO FAÇADE of Grady Memorial Hospital always lifted Hollis Joplin's spirits. As he waited for the light to change at Butler Street, he gazed up at and realized that he had probably developed a love for old buildings because there were so few of them in Atlanta. First and foremost, Atlanta was a city of commerce, and preserving what was historic or beautiful had never been a priority. The old made way for the new whenever–and wherever–money was to be made. Grady had been one of the few exceptions, and for that, Joplin was extremely grateful. Besides the way it looked, he loved the hospital's history of care to the city's poor and disenfranchised. A history that might be coming to an end if Grady didn't survive the financial crisis that had been dogging it for the past seven years and had gone from bad to worse during the recession.

Joplin turned right onto Butler, admiring the Deco diamonds and archways that had been added during its latest renovation several years ago. He circled the building and parked on a side street reserved for law enforcement vehicles and EMS trucks. The cacophony that assaulted his ears as he entered the emergency area was a distinct contrast to the beauty of Grady's outer shell. The renovation had also provided the hospital with seven specialized emergency rooms; each one looked full as he passed by. It was only noon on a Saturday, but life—and death—in The City Too Busy To Hate was in full swing.

Joplin rode an elevator down to the basement, where the cafeteria was located. Carrie was sitting with a tray of food at a table not far from the entrance and motioned him to the service line when she saw him. A few minutes later, Joplin made his way over to her, a plate of meat loaf, mashed potatoes and green beans on his tray.

"I've got to be back in ten minutes," she said. "The path lab is short-handed today."

Joplin put his tray on the table and sat down. Disappointed, but trying not to show it, he said, "No problem. I just appreciate your getting me the article."

Carrie was wearing a pale green blouse under her white medical coat. It did something really nice for her eyes, and he felt another overpowering urge to kiss her in a room full of people, but it was cut short when she pushed a pile of papers toward him.

"Here it is," she said. "I also printed out the titles of other books and articles he's written. Nothing else seemed like a connection, but you might see something I didn't."

"I doubt it, but I'll check it out."

"Hollis, I read the article over more closely, and it puts a human face on a very bizarre subject. I just can't see the doctor who wrote it using his knowledge to kill somebody in such a callous way."

Joplin shrugged. "He probably didn't. It's a long-shot, I agree. But you have to admit it's almost too much of a coincidence."

"That I'll grant you." She looked at her watch. "Sorry, I'm going to have to go."

"How about brunch tomorrow? To thank you for getting all this?" he added quickly. "I have the night shift Sunday, but I'm free all day."

"Wouldn't you rather sleep, if you're going to be up all night?"

"I have tonight and all day Monday to sleep." Joplin was about to ask her to his apartment, when he remembered that it wasn't in such great shape. He hadn't had much time for housekeeping that week. "How about the Horseradish Grill at noon?"

"The restaurant across from Chastain Park?"

"Yes. Shall I pick you up?"

"I'll just meet you there." Carrie stood up, then looked down at his tray. "Oh, dear. You got the meat loaf."

"Really bad, huh?"

"Not till later," she said pointedly, and then she was threading through the knots of people that had gathered, trays in hand, as they scanned the cafeteria for empty tables.

Joplin pushed the plate of meat loaf away and picked up the article. It was entitled "Autoerotic Asphyxia: A Case Study." Woodley began with a brief description of the phenomenon of autoerotic asphyxia and followed with a lit review that detailed most of the known characteristics of the syndrome. Next came a statement that this particular case was significant because of the age of the patient, who had only been thirteen when treatment began. Most practitioners of this type of deviance rarely sought help. Those who did were adults, and most had been engaged in the activity for years. They only got treatment after coming a little too close to dying. In the case study being presented, Woodley had the rare opportunity to treat someone quite young who could provide more immediate information about the onset of this type of deviant sexual behavior.

Woodley then detailed his initial meeting with the parents of his patient. Except for noting their general age range and that they were educated and affluent, he omitted any identifying characteristics. He had been contacted by a local hospital where the boy had been admitted after what his parents believed to be a suicide attempt. An alert paramedic, who'd been called to the scene of an autoerotic fatality a few years before, had described what he'd seen in the boy's bedroom to the attending ER doctor.

The parents were in a state of shock. They painted a picture of a happy home life, a prestigious school in which the boy was a good student, and a circle of friends that made him seem anything but a loner. They could think of nothing that might have driven their son to try to take his own life. They admitted to having a pretty active social life due to the husband's job, but insisted the boy hadn't been neglected. A housekeeper was always in the home, and they would arrange for their son to have a friend over whenever they were out on the weekend. On the night of the "suicide attempt," the chosen friend had gotten sick, and the housekeeper had told them the boy had gone to his room around nine p.m. The parents had returned around ten, and the mother went to say good night to the boy. She had found him hanging from a rope attached to his closet door, naked, except for a T-shirt. A small stepladder was underneath him, on its side, and a bottle of Jergen's lotion was puddling on the floor. The boy's face was completely blue. She had screamed for her husband, who had cut the rope and administered CPR.

The parents had been full of guilt, convinced that their son had tried to kill himself. The guilt turned to shock and disbelief when Woodley told them about autoerotic asphyxia. He'd assured them that although the situation was very serious, because of their son's age, the prognosis was good.

Woodley had then outlined the therapeutic process, which lasted for a year. A minimum of two therapy sessions per week were held with the boy during the first three months. The first few weeks were taken up with administering standard I.Q. and personality tests. Joplin skipped over all the graphs, scores, and scales involving correlations and validity that Woodley had provided and cut to the results, which showed the boy to be exceptionally bright, but with poor impulse control and an extremely high propensity for risk-taking. With regard to sexual identity, he demonstrated more confusion than was normally associated with his age. Woodley noted this issue would be revisited in a discussion on cross-dressing later in the article.

The psychiatrist then elicited a personal history. The boy admitted he and various friends drank alcohol whenever they got the opportunity and had also tried marijuana. He had been masturbating for about a year. When Woodley broached the subject of autoerotic asphyxia, the boy was more than ready to discuss it. He explained that when he was about ten, an older boy at school had told him that one could get "high" by cutting off the circulation to the head. He had demonstrated the technique to the patient, who experienced a very pleasurable, "dreamy" feeling. For several weeks, he and a friend had taken turns doing this to each other. The friend finally tired of it, and the game ended. The boy tried several times to choke himself and get the same results, to no avail.

About three months before he ended up in the hospital, he had seen an episode of *Law & Order* that depicted a young female professional's death from autoerotic asphyxia, and he had been riveted by the subject. It was like a light bulb going on in his brain. He remembered the choking game he'd played and wondered why it had never occurred to him to use a rope in his efforts to achieve the "high" by himself. Before the program was over, he had gone to the basement and found a piece of rope. By the time his parents came home that night from another one of their parties, he had experimented with several ways to use it. The first successful one involved tying one end of the rope around his neck and the other around his closet door knob. He then sat down and scooted along the floor until the rope was taut and masturbated almost to the point of climax before leaning forward to cut off the blood supply to his brain. When he did climax, he said it was like hundreds of orgasms exploding all at once over his entire body.

Joplin continued reading the article, but his concentration was broken. Part of his mind followed Woodley's description of the various therapeutic strategies he had used over the next year, the apparently successful outcome of treatment, and his recommendations to practicing therapists involved in treating this type of deviant sexual behavior. But the other part was distracted by the revelation of how Woodley's patient had learned of autoerotic asphyxia.

Joplin had also seen that particular episode of *Law & Order*, but it hadn't portrayed an autoerotic fatality. The plot involved a murder made to look like an autoerotic fatality.

It was one too many coincidences. He reached in his pocket for his cell phone.

Feeling frustrated, Joplin headed back to the elevator. A woman at Woodley's answering service had assured him that she would contact the doctor right away, but he'd heard that before. Despite it's being his day off, he needed to talk to Woodley as soon as possible, because something else had occurred to him: What if Trip Carter were the boy in Woodley's article? The patient's age, the description of the parents, and the home situation all sounded very similar. If so, that would add two more people close to Elliot Carter who knew all about autoerotic asphyxia—not only Trip Carter, but Anne, too.

Joplin glanced at his watch and saw that it was one-fifteen. He decided to call Tom Halloran once he got to his car. It had been the attorney's idea to check out Dr. Woodley, and Joplin thought he would want to know about the article. Telling him about it might also keep him from complaining to Alston Caldwell that he and Jack had made up their minds about Carter's death. He didn't want Dr. Minton bothered again.

The pendulum seemed to be swinging back to murder.

27

At first, Halloran was elated when Hollis Joplin called him and told him that Dr. Woodley had written an academic article on autoerotic asphyxia. It confirmed his belief that the psychiatrist had the expertise to fake such a death. But the feeling of elation began to wane as Joplin described Woodley's young patient and his family.

"Are you still there?" Joplin asked, and Halloran realized he must not have responded to some question the investigator had asked.

He closed his eyes, trying to get his thoughts together. "I guess I'm just…blown away by this. It's one thing to be suspicious of someone, but to discover that he might actually have been capable of murdering Elliot is a little mind-boggling."

"The fact that Dr. Woodley knows a lot about autoerotic asphyxia doesn't prove anything. But it's a pretty big coincidence, I admit, and I need to talk to him about it. He returned my call a few minutes ago, and I made an appointment to see him at his office in Midtown this afternoon."

"Great," said Halloran absently. "By the way, could I possibly get a copy of the article? I'd like to read it myself."

"I can stop at a FedEx and fax it to you, I guess. Do you have a home fax?"

"I have one in my study," Halloran said, then gave him the number.

***

Only ten minutes had passed since he'd talked Joplin, but if the investigator faxed him the article within the next fifteen minutes, Halloran thought he might have a chance to read it before Maggie returned from picking up the kids at her parents' house. He'd promised to take Tommy and Megan to see *The Pirates! Band of Misfits* at the movies and let Maggie work in her darkroom for a few hours. But the thought of sitting through the movie without being able to check out his hunch was intolerable.

What worried him was that the teenage boy in Woodley's article might possibly be Trip Carter. Joplin hadn't said when the article was written, or how old the boy was at the time. A quick reading might assure him that it wasn't Trip at all. The parents sounded very much like Anne and Elliot, but there were lots of affluent parents in Atlanta who led busy lives and left their kids with housekeepers. Then again, Trip himself had seemed to feel responsible for his parents' separation. What if the Carters had engaged Woodley to treat their son, and Anne had somehow gotten involved with the psychiatrist? What if that were the reason for Elliot's moving out?

It also meant that there was one other person who knew a lot about autoerotic asphyxia. Someone who might even have some of the "accessories" needed to make Elliot's death look like the real thing. Someone who was even supposed to be with Elliot that night and who was also the heir to Elliot's very considerable estate.

Halloran could hardly believe what he was thinking. It was insane to think that a kid like Trip could even conceive of something like that, even if it were true that he was the boy in Woodley's paper. Besides, the two families had been so close over the past eight years—well within the time frame that encompassed Woodley's article—that it would have been natural for the Carters to have turned to them if their child had been hospitalized or undergoing therapy. And even if they hadn't been able to do that, feeling that it was an extremely private matter, wouldn't he and Maggie have noticed that their good friends were going through some kind of terrible family problem?

Unable to wait any longer, Halloran headed down the hall to his study. But as he neared it, he remembered his shock and surprise when Olivia had told him about Anne's affair several years ago. That, too, had happened within the same time frame, and he had never suspected that Elliot was going through such terrible pain in his marriage. Maggie had been thrown for a loop, too, when he'd told her about it last night at dinner. She couldn't believe that Anne, who had leaned heavily on her during all the fertility testing and treatment, had never said a word to her about its aftermath. If the Carters had been capable of concealing a crisis like that, it was entirely possible that they had concealed another one, and that Trip *was* the boy in Woodley's article. And if that were true, then maybe Hollis Joplin had been right from the very beginning: that people do things that the people who know and love them would never imagine. Maybe Elliot *had* collected kiddie porn and practiced autoerotic asphyxia.

And maybe Trip Carter was somehow involved in his father's death.

Disturbed by these thoughts, Halloran opened the door to his study and saw the fax light blinking. He grabbed the pages, sat down at his desk, and began to scan them, looking for dates and ages and a certain time frame first. But nothing leaped out at him that would eliminate Trip as Woodley's patient. A few minutes later, he heard the garage door open; Maggie and the children were home. Hurriedly, Halloran gathered up the pages of Woodley's article and shoved them into the top drawer of the desk. He would read the article again when he had more time and could analyze it more thoroughly.

He only hoped that would destroy the latest suspicion that was beginning to fester in his mind.

Dr. Woodley's office was in the Tower at One Atlantic Center. Because it was Saturday, the parking tower, which was on the other side of West Peachtree, was relatively empty, and Joplin found a space on the third floor. He took the elevator down to ground level, then crossed the street to the side entrance of the Tower. In the lobby, on the far left glass wall, two female security officers sat behind a wide marble desk. The front of the desk listed the Tower's tenants. Joplin already knew that Woodley was in Suite 1538, so he walked across the black and white marble floor to the bank of elevators in the center of the building.

The psychiatrist had told him to go into the office and push the buzzer at the window of the front desk, since there would be no receptionist there. Joplin did this and waited only a few seconds before a door to the right opened and Dr. Woodley appeared.

He was dressed in charcoal slacks and a tweed jacket. Pretty formal for a Saturday afternoon, Joplin thought. "Thanks for seeing me on such short notice, Doctor," he said, offering his hand. Woodley's felt limp as he pumped it.

"I needed to come in to the office today anyway to catch up on dictating this week's session notes. The past few days have been pretty hectic. Come on back."

He led Joplin down the hall to a large office with a mahogany desk near the wall opposite the door and two wing chairs in front of the desk. There was another seating area to the right, comprised of a camel-back leather sofa, two leather chairs on either side, and a coffee table. A box of tissues rested prominently on the coffee table. The third wall, on the left, was one big window, with a stunning view of Midtown and part of the downtown area. He could clearly see Ansley Towers, which was only five blocks away.

Joplin was reminded of something Tom Halloran had told him. The attorney had learned from Carter's secretary that he'd had an appointment with a client at the IBM Tower around one on the last day of his life. The secretary had also said that Carter had called her about one forty-five and canceled the rest of his appointments, saying, "Something has come up." Joplin wondered if it had been the phone call from Ben Mashburn. But had Carter also run into Paul Woodley? Or was Woodley the "client" Carter was meeting? Again, there were just too many coincidences.

"Nice view," he said as he walked into the room.

"Thank you," said Woodley in a self-satisfied manner, as if he had personally arranged the skyline. He motioned Joplin to the wing chair on his left, then sat down in the large swivel chair behind the desk and adjusted his tortoise-shell glasses. "I have to say I'm a bit puzzled as to why you would want to see me. I'm sure you know I can't discuss Anne—Mrs. Carter—with you." He gave a tight, condescending little smile.

Joplin smiled back. "Actually, I wanted to discuss an article you wrote for the *Journal of Psychiatry*, Doctor. The one that detailed your treatment of a young boy who was engaging in autoerotic asphyxia."

The smile momentarily left Woodley's face, then returned, the condescension even more pronounced. "I see," he said, taking off his glasses and carefully cleaning them. "And is this because you think I can assist you in your investigation of Elliot Carter's death or because you think I had something to do with it?"

"A little of both, as a matter of fact," answered Joplin easily. "If the manner of death is determined to be a homicide, we have to conclude that only someone with an expert knowledge of this type of sexual practice could fake a death like this."

"Obviously," said Woodley, still smiling. "Then I take it I'm a suspect? If so, I have to tell you I'm enormously flattered. I lead a very dull life."

"Carter's death hasn't been ruled a homicide. So we're not at the point of having suspects yet."

"But I'd be one of the candidates, right?"

"Among others. And the police would need to know the whereabouts of each suspect on the night that Carter died. Would you mind telling me yours, Doctor?"

"Not at all," Woodley said smugly. "I worked late on Tuesday night—here," he added, his right hand sweeping across his desk, "until about eight. Then I went home, fixed myself dinner, and watched a little television. An episode of *Masterpiece Classic* that I'd taped the Sunday before, to answer what I'm sure is your next question. And, no, I have no way of proving this. I neither made nor received any phone calls during that time, and didn't see a neighbor on my way in."

"I see," said Joplin. "Thank you. But to get back to your article, there's another aspect of it that interests me and suggests the possibility that at least one other person close to Elliot Carter had expert knowledge of autoerotic asphyxia."

Woodley's expression turned to one of surprise this time. "What do you mean?"

"I mean that unless you completely changed the details about your patient and his family, they sound a lot like Trip Carter and his parents."

"That's ridiculous!" said Woodley, putting his glasses back on and glaring at Joplin.

"Is it? I think any intelligent person who read the article and knew the Carter family would see quite a few similarities, Doctor."

"Similarities, perhaps," said Woodley in a calmer manner, "but I can assure you Trip Carter was not the patient I wrote about in that article."

"I hope you understand that under the circumstances, I can't just take your word for it. You're too involved with the family."

"What is that supposed to mean?"

"Just that a few people think that you have more than a doctor-patient relationship with Anne Carter," replied Joplin, deliberately trying to provoke the psychiatrist.

"That's even more ridiculous."

"Well, I don't know too many psychiatrists who would accompany a patient to the morgue to identify her husband's body. Were those billable hours?"

Red blotches began to appear on the psychiatrist's face, but when he spoke, his voice was under control. "Anne Carter and I are old friends, Investigator. We knew each other in college, when I was in pre-med at the University of Georgia. We have also seen each other socially throughout the years at various charity balls. In the past few months, she has come to…depend on me in certain circumstances. If that is what you mean by 'more than a doctor-patient relationship,' then it's an accurate description. But we are not romantically involved. That would be a violation of medical ethics."

"Did you know Elliot Carter at UGA, Doctor?" asked Joplin, trying not to show his surprise at Woodley's revelation. "You must have been there at the same time."

"No, I didn't, as a matter of fact. He was in law school, and I was a lowly undergraduate. We were worlds apart."

"But you must have known him socially, too, since you frequently saw Anne Carter at those charity balls you mentioned."

"I knew him, yes," said Woodley, seeming to measure his words. "But not well. I ran into him at various fundraisers and we occasionally chatted, but never at any length. I saw more of Anne because she was often the chairperson at these events, and she made it a point to circulate. Usually without her husband in tow."

"Well, when the two of you were in college together, she didn't have a husband, and you weren't a psychiatrist yet. Were you and Mrs. Carter romantically involved then?"

Dr. Woodley stood up. "I'm not going to answer that or any other questions. If I do become an official suspect, I'll refer you to my attorney."

Joplin stood up, too. "I can promise you it will be asked again. If you become a suspect, of course. Thank you for your time. I can see myself out."

Woodley, however, followed him out of the office, down the hall, and through the waiting room. Without another word, he held open the door for Joplin, then closed it behind him. Joplin could hear him lock it once he was in the hall.

All in all, it had been a very productive session.

28

JOPLIN'S CELL PHONE STARTED RINGING just as he opened the door to his apartment around five-thirty that afternoon. He was carrying five plastic bags from the nearby Publix; all he really wanted to do was unload them, pop a Coors, and turn on the Braves game. Ignoring Quincy, who had just glided into the room and was looking up at him expectantly, he set the bags down and reluctantly answered his phone.

"Hi, it's Janna Helms. Ben Mashburn's secretary?" she added.

"Hi, how are you?"

"I'm okay. I hope I'm not bothering you, but you said to call if I thought of anything."

"You're not bothering me," Joplin assured her. "What's up?"

"Well, you remember that box of files with clippings in them that I gave you?"

"Of course. I have it here at my apartment. Why?"

"I think a file might be missing from it, but I'm not sure. I looked through everything so quickly. And I was pretty upset when the police were here, you know."

"That's understandable," said Joplin. "Janna, I'm going to go to my bedroom, which is where I put the box. Hang on a minute."

Quincy looked reproachfully at him as he left, but Joplin walked quickly down the hallway to his bedroom door. He scooped up the box from the floor next to his bureau and set it on the bed.

"You still there?" he said into the phone. "I've got it right here."

"Yes," said Janna Helms. "See if there's an envelope labeled, 'Bobby Greenleaf.'"

Joplin didn't move. "Mashburn was on that case?"

"Yes. He told me it was the biggest case in his career as a police officer, and one of the most heartbreaking. He was obsessed with it."

"So was all of Atlanta," said Joplin, somewhat stunned by the fact that he was discussing the decades-old disappearance of a little boy for the second time in two days.

"Did you find the envelope?" asked Janna, breaking his reverie.

"I'm looking now," he answered, flipping through the various folders. "It's not here, Janna," Joplin said finally. "But what could that case have to do with Elliot Carter?"

Janna sighed. "I have no idea. I don't even know why I called you about it, because I sure can't see any connection myself."

"Tell me, had Ben Mashburn brought the case up recently?"

"No. The only time he ever talked about it was when we got some new office equipment a few years ago and did some rearranging. I came across the old case files and asked him what to do with them. That's when he told me about the Greenleaf case."

"Did he tell you any details? Like what the FBI ever found out?"

"Not really. He did say that one of his old buddies had told him about a new lead on the case, but nothing ever came of it. I remember he said something like, 'I hope to God that poor kid is dead, because some things just can't be fixed.'"

"What did he mean by that?" asked Joplin.

"I don't know. I wish now I'd asked, but he looked so sad when he said it that I didn't want to keep him talking about it. I wish I could be more help."

"You are helping. I think the fact that this envelope is missing is important. I just don't know why. Was there anything in it besides news-paper clippings?"

"No. Just the clippings."

"Well, it was a thought anyway," said Joplin, disappointed. "Listen, thanks for calling me about this. If you think of anything else, call me again, okay?"

"I will," said Janna. "Just don't give up on Ben. He didn't kill himself, and the person who did is out there thinking he got away with it. Please find him, okay?"

"I'll do my best," said Joplin.

After he hung up, Joplin sat on the bed, lost in thought. Somehow, despite Chief MacKenzie's order to stay away from Mashburn's widow, he had to figure out a way to see her and ask if Ben had brought up the Greenleaf case recently. It was too late to go out to Lilburn, where Mrs. Mashburn lived, but he could at least try to talk to her on the phone, he decided. He got the number from information, then dialed it. When the voice mail came on, Joplin left a message asking her to call and gave his cell phone number.

Tom and Maggie took the kids to Everybody's Pizza in Virginia-Highlands after the movie. Maggie was somewhat subdued, smiling and nodding as the kids discussed their favorite parts of *The Pirates! Band of Misfits,* but not really giving them her full attention. Halloran raised his eyebrows in a silent "You okay?" manner, but she just shrugged.

Later, however, when Tommy and Megan were finally in bed, Halloran poured himself and Maggie glasses of wine and sat down on the sofa next to her.

"Did everything just finally get to you, Mag?" he asked.

Maggie shook her head. "It's those pictures, Tom. I tried to get some work done on the preliminary photos I took for the new client today, but I couldn't concentrate. My mind kept going back to those horrible photographs. I spent the whole time you and the kids were at the movie going through them again."

Halloran pulled Maggie to him. "I should never have given those pictures to you."

"No, I'm glad you did," Maggie said, her cheek resting on his shoulder. "It made me feel like I was helping in some way. Not just Elliot, although I want to do that. I mean, helping those children somehow. Even though they're not children anymore. They'd all be in their late twenties by now. If they're even alive."

"Please don't look at those photos again, Maggie. It's too upsetting for you. Besides, what you've managed to find out about them is something the police can start with. I intend to call Joplin tomorrow and turn them over to him. He can take it from there."

"But you said that would prejudice the police against Elliot."

"Yes, but I just can't afford to hold onto them any longer. Either I have to destroy them, which I'm not willing to do, or I have to turn them over to the police. Besides, we only have Anne's word that they were Elliot's, and I'm having more and more doubts about everything Anne has told me."

"You still think she's somehow involved in Elliot's death, don't you?"

"Yes. And maybe Ben Mashburn's, too."

"All right, but just promise me you'll back off and let that investigator handle things once you give him the photographs."

Halloran stroked her hair. "I *will* promise you I'll think very carefully before I stick my neck out like this again." He knew that wasn't what Maggie wanted to hear, but at least it was a promise he could keep.

29

HALLORAN OPENED HIS FRONT DOOR at nine a.m. that Sunday and walked down the path to the driveway to get the paper. He'd been up for about thirty minutes and had fixed breakfast for Tommy and Megan, then settled them in front of the TV with a DVD of *Wreck It Ralph*. Now it was time for a second cup of coffee and the Sunday paper. He was trying to let Maggie sleep, even though he'd had a restless night himself. He'd read Woodley's article again after Maggie went to bed, but still failed to find anything that took Trip out of the equation. Somehow, he had to find an opportunity that day to go see Anne and ask her point-blank if he'd been Woodley's patient.

And find out the truth about the photographs she'd given him.

Determined to take a break from the stresses and terrible revelations of the past few days, Halloran picked up the paper and scanned the front page as he walked slowly back to the house. Once inside, he headed for the kitchen and found Maggie sitting at the breakfast table. The manila envelope with the pictures lay on the placemat in front of her. "What are you doing up, sweetie? I was trying to let you sleep."

She turned to look up at him. Her face was haggard, as if she hadn't slept at all. "I had this dream, Tom, and it woke me up. I know who the little boy in the photos is."

"Who is it?" Halloran asked, alarmed by her tone of voice..

"I never knew him personally," she said slowly, "even though his house was about three blocks from our house on Cherokee Drive, where I grew up. But I saw his picture every day for weeks in either the newspaper or on TV. I can't believe it took me this long to realize who it was. It's just been so long since...," she added, her voice trailing off. Maggie closed her eyes, then shook her head as if willing the image away. When she opened them again, she said, "Tom, the little boy in the picture is Bobby Greenleaf."

Halloran sat quietly next to Maggie, holding her hand as she told him the story of Bobby Greenleaf's disappearance and the hopeless search that followed. Although the little boy had been an icon of her youth, Tom had grown up in Chicago and knew very little about him. He was familiar with the name, although mostly in connection with Etan Patz, the boy who had disappeared in Manhattan around the same time. Both had been cited repeatedly in the media frenzy of publicity surrounding missing children. He remembered that soon after, the faces of children had started appearing on milk cartons.

When Maggie finished, he put his arm around her, and they sat silently together on the sofa, absorbed in the sadness of Bobby's story. Then Tommy and Megan burst into the room, pleading to go to IHOP for pancakes after church. Halloran quickly shoved the photographs back into the envelope, while Maggie herded the children upstairs to dress. As soon as they left the kitchen, he picked up the envelope, carried it into his study, and locked it in his briefcase, hoping he would never have to see it again after tomorrow.

Carrie was wearing a light blue plaid sheath with a cream-colored sweater over it; Joplin thought she looked even prettier than when they had gone out on Thursday night. She settled into the back of the booth at Horseradish Grill after they'd both given their orders to the server and now she smiled at him.

"So was the article helpful?" she asked, reaching into a basket of biscuits on the table.

"Very. In fact, it was so intriguing, I arranged a meeting with Dr.

Woodley yesterday. And if it turns out Eliot Carter's death was a homicide, he'll be at the top of my list of suspects. He'd certainly have the expertise to fake an autoerotic death."

"But what will it take to tip the scales in favor of a ruling of homicide as the manner of death? The autopsy itself didn't uncover anything conclusive."

Joplin shrugged. "A break in the case. Maybe something to do with Ben Mashburn's death," he added, but stopped short of telling her about his conversation with Ben's secretary. "Listen, let's not talk shop, okay? I'm sitting in a great restaurant with a beautiful girl on a gorgeous Sunday afternoon, and death is the last thing on my mind right now. Why don't you tell me what 'Carrie' is short for? Caroline? Catherine? Carmen?"

"Actually, it's an Americanized nickname for 'Karolya,'" Carrie told him, slathering both butter and jam on her biscuit. "Judaism doesn't make any promises about the afterlife, so it's customary for children to be named after a dead relative or friend. To make sure they're remembered," she added, "and live on, in a way. I was named for a great-aunt who died in a concentration camp in Poland."

"That's a really nice custom. I guess that *is* a kind of immortality, isn't it?"

Carrie nodded, then began to grin. "But we're back to the subject of death again," she said. "How about this: Have you finished your paper for your Constitutional Law class?"

"All but the polishing, which I can work on later, before I go to work. I have the graveyard shift tonight. No pun intended."

"Then I'll let it pass," said Carrie, smiling again. "So what do you hope to do with this degree, Hollis?"

"Become chief investigator, when MacKenzie retires next year. I don't have as much seniority as some of the other investigators, but the graduate degree will count for a lot. And I think I'd be the best man for the job," he added. "I've got a few ideas that I think would improve the system."

"Such as?"

"Well, for one thing, I'd push for having thirty-day residents like you go out to death scenes, not just the fulltime residents. It might attract more pathologists to forensic medicine. The pay sure doesn't."

"I'd love to go out on a scene," said Carrie.

"Then I'll arrange it. You'd learn a lot more from that than just seeing a body on an autopsy table."

"Sounds wonderful." Carrie raised her wineglass. "Here's to seeing dead bodies out in the field."

Hollis started to raise his own glass, then noticed that the waiter was standing next to them, holding their plates. He mumbled something as he served them, then beat a hasty retreat.

Carrie gave a whoop of laughter. "We're not doing too well at not talking about death, are we?" she asked.

"We're lousy at it, Karolya," said Joplin, clinking his glass to hers.

Returning home from Mass and brunch, Halloran changed clothes and told Maggie he was going to walk off the pancakes. He neglected to add that he was also planning to see Anne and get some answers about the photographs before he turned them over to Joplin. He didn't think that would break his promise to Maggie, but he wasn't sure she'd feel the same way.

It didn't take him long to walk the three blocks to the Carter house. The Sunday paper was still in the driveway, even though it was almost one forty-five by then. He picked it up and walked to the front door, which opened before he had a chance to ring the doorbell. Lillian Landrum, Anne's mother brought her hand to her mouth in surprise when she saw him.

"I didn't mean to startle you," Halloran said apologetically.

"Oh, you didn't, Tom," Mrs. Landrum replied, but she reached up nervously to adjust the pink headband that held back her chin-length blond hair. It matched the pink sheath she was wearing, but both were too girlish for her aging arms and too-tight facelift. "I was just coming out to get the paper because it's Pauletta's day off, and I didn't expect to see anyone. We drove up from McRae this morning. Please come in," she added, taking the paper from him and stepping back into the entry hall.

The last thing Halloran wanted to do was visit with Anne's parents, especially since there would probably be no opportunity to talk to Anne about the pictures. "No, that's all right. I won't stay. I'm sure this isn't a good time. Just tell Anne I stopped by."

"But you're welcome to—"

"That's okay. I'll just see you all at the funeral," Halloran said over his shoulder as he made his escape.

He would have to hang on to the pictures a few more days.

***

"Investigator Joplin, this is Jane Mashburn. I'm sorry I didn't call you back yesterday, but I've been staying at my daughter's house. I just got home and checked my voicemail. It seemed important, so I decided to take a chance that maybe you were on duty. I hope I'm not calling too late."

Joplin glanced at his watch. It was a little after eight p.m.; he'd almost finished polishing his paper for Tuesday's class. "I'm at home, but I appreciate your calling me. And I'm really sorry for your loss."

"Thank you. I've already talked to Billy MacKenzie, you know."

"Yes, ma'am, I know. It's just that I need to follow up on something. I went to see Janna Helms on Friday, and she gave me some files that your husband kept at his office, with clippings from some old cases that he had worked on when he was with the APD."

"Yes, she told me about that. I said it was fine."

"Well, what I wanted to ask you was, did your husband mention anything recently about the Greenleaf case?"

"You mean Bobby Greenleaf? The little boy who disappeared?"

"Yes. Janna said he put off retiring because of that case."

"That's right. He did. That case bothered Ben more than all the others. I think it was one of the things that made him start drinking so much back in the eighties."

"Well, did he talk to you about it recently? Maybe in connection with a case he was working on in the past two weeks?"

"Recently?" she said, sounding surprised. "Lord, no. Ben hadn't brought up that case in quite a while. Not since Billy MacKenzie brought those pictures to him. Those terrible pictures with the children in them. I mean, I never saw them myself, but Ben told me about them. They broke his heart."

"Was Bobby Greenleaf in them?" Joplin asked, trying not to sound too excited.

"Yes, of course. That's why Billy brought them to him. They worked that case together. I guess Billy thought Ben might be able to help."

"Was this when Chief MacKenzie was still with the Homicide Unit? After your husband retired?"

"Oh, no. It was only about four years ago."

"I don't understand. How did Chief MacKenzie get hold of these pictures?"

"I think Ben told me they were found in the home of a dentist—no, it was an orthodontist. Anyway, he died suddenly, and the ME's office wasn't sure what the circumstances were, so Billy was investigating it."

Joplin had never heard anything about kiddie porn involving Bobby Greenleaf being found in connection with a death investigated by the ME's office four years ago. "Did he tell you the name of the dead man?" he asked Mrs. Mashburn.

"If he did, I don't remember it. All I know is that he must have been a pedophile. But I'm sure Billy could tell you. I remember I called him up and gave him hell for bringing those photographs to Ben. He went on a three-day binge after that. One of his worst. He never talked about Bobby Greenleaf again."

Joplin thought of what Janna Helms had told him Mashburn said about Bobby Greenleaf: "I hope to God that kid is dead, because some things just can't be fixed." If he had seen pictures of the child being sexually abused, that would explain his remark. In fact, Joplin agreed with him. Even with psychiatric treatment, kids who had been repeatedly physically and sexually abused were often permanently damaged. Without treatment or, at the very least, someone to intervene and stop the abuse, a small percentage of them grew into monsters themselves—pedophiles or serial rapists or even murderers.

"Are you still there, Investigator?" he heard Mrs. Mashburn saying.

"I'm sorry, ma'am. I was just thinking about what you said."

"Well, now it's your turn to talk. I was a cop's wife for a long time, and I know you wouldn't be asking all these questions about a little boy who disappeared twenty-five years ago unless it had something to do with my husband's death."

"It might or it might not, Mrs. Mashburn. All I can tell you is that everything to do with a case he was working on when he died was erased from his computer files. And the only other thing missing was the private file he kept on Bobby Greenleaf."

"Billy MacKenzie never said anything to me about this when he was here Friday."

"He didn't know about the Greenleaf file. Janna just called me about it yesterday. But I'll definitely talk to him about it when I see him."

"You do that. Besides Ben, there's no one who knew as much about that case as Billy did. If there's a connection to the case that Ben was working on, he might know what it was. Just please don't give up on my husband. He was a cop once, and a good one. And an even better man than he was a cop. He had no reason to kill himself."

"I promise you I'll do everything I can to find out what happened, Mrs. Mashburn."

"Thank you," she said quietly and hung up.

Joplin wondered if she would thank him if she knew what he'd been thinking. If the Greenleaf case had started Ben drinking heavily in the first place, and seeing Bobby Greenleaf in some pornographic pictures had set him off on one of his worst binges, might not some new information on the case have triggered another binge? If so, it had to be something connected to the Carter case. Had Anne Carter hired Mashburn a second time because she had suspected that Elliot Carter was into kiddie porn? Was that what Ben had discovered and what had upset Carter so much when he was at Ace Investigations the previous Tuesday?

Deciding he'd better finish up on his paper so he could grab a few hours of sleep before his shift began at midnight, Joplin pulled his thoughts off the Carter case. Hopefully, he'd have time to mull things over some more later that night.

30

THIRTY MINUTES AFTER HE GOT to his desk at the ME's office, Joplin was summoned to a traffic fatality on Piedmont Road. The dispatcher told him it was near the Disco Kroger, which had gotten its name in the eighties when the Limelight, a notorious nightclub next-door to it which boasted a glass dance floor built over a shark tank, had been *the* place to see and be seen during its three-year reign. After letting Viv Rodriguez, his partner that night, know his destination, he gathered his equipment and headed to the scene. Ninety minutes later, he was back at his desk, but Viv was off at a scene of her own. Joplin only had time to write up half a report before he was called to a fatal shooting in Midtown.

It was shaping up to be a busy night. Especially for a Sunday.

By the end of his shift at eight the next morning, Joplin was still working on his last report. He took his time, hoping to talk to MacKenzie before he went home. But by eight-thirty, the chief still hadn't made it into the office. This wasn't unusual, especially on a Monday, and he and the other investigators had no trouble handling things without any help from their often-absent supervisor. But this time, MacKenzie's lousy work ethic really got on Joplin's last nerve.

He stood up and headed for Jack Tyndall's office, his mind cluttered with all of the contradictory threads of the Carter case, as well as new images planted there by Mrs. Mashburn. The Greenleaf case had haunted him, too, for most of his life. Up until now, he'd always assumed that the little boy was dead, killed by a kidnapper who had probably molested him first. Otherwise, a ransom note would have been sent. But what if he had been sold to some kiddie porn ring or raised by his kidnapper, like Stephen Staynor and, even more recently, Shawn Hornbeck and Jaycee Dugard? All three had been given up for dead, then reappeared years later. Staynor had helped another young boy, kidnapped by the same man who had taken him and raised him, to escape, and then the two boys had gone to a police station. Shawn Hornbeck had been found four years after his own kidnapping, the circumstances almost identical. And Jaycee Dugard had survived even longer, living in the backyard of her kidnapper's house with the two young daughters he'd fathered.

Maybe it would help if he ran it all by Jack. He needed to get a handle on things before he talked to MacKenzie.

The door to Jack's office was closed and Joplin opened it without knocking first, something he immediately regretted. Jack and Carrie Salinger were standing in front of the desk, engaged in what could only be called a passionate kiss. Shocked to his core, he was about to make a fast retreat when Carrie suddenly pulled away from Jack. She turned bright red when she saw Joplin.

"I can't do this," she said, looking at Tyndall and then back at him.

Before Joplin could think of anything to say, Carrie rushed past him and hurried down the hall. He was still staring at her retreating figure when he heard Jack say his name. He turned and looked at the pathologist, who seemed as upset as Carrie had been.

"I guess my timing was perfect, as usual," said Joplin. He felt like someone had thumped him on the chest with a baseball bat.

"You might say that," Tyndall said. He walked around his desk and sat down. "What are you still doing here anyway? I thought you'd be home by now."

"Obviously," said Joplin coldly.

Tyndall ran his fingers through his hair and sat up straighter. "What can I do for you, Hollis?"

Joplin struggled to keep from shouting or even leaping across the desk and smashing Jack in the face. Acting like a jealous lover wouldn't do much for his professional reputation. Or his ego, for that matter. But the shock of seeing Carrie with Jack Tyndall was something he couldn't ignore. Especially after yesterday. After what had seemed like the beginning of a relationship between them.

"Well, you could tell me what that was all about, for starters," he said finally, trying to keep most of the rage out of his voice.

"Just a clumsy pass on my part," said Tyndall.

"It looked pretty reciprocal to me. Young doctors in love and all that."

"Don't be an ass, Hollis. I just caught her off guard, that's all. I'm sure she would have slapped my face if you hadn't come in just then."

"I'm not sure I agree with that, but let's drop it."

"No, let's not," Tyndall said. "I asked you the other day if you wanted me to back off, and you said not to. So I'm going to ask you one last time: Do you want me to give you a clear path with Carrie? I'm willing to do that for the sake of our friendship."

Joplin slouched against the door frame. "No. I mean, don't get me wrong, there's nothing I'd like more than to have you out of the picture. But not that way. What I want is for her not to be attracted to you, but that's wishful thinking. I guess I just thought I had the inside track with her."

Tyndall shrugged. "Maybe you do, Hollis. She didn't kiss me. I kissed her."

"I think the jury is still out on that one, Jack. But I don't intend to give up yet." Joplin moved away from the doorway and put his hands in his pockets. "Listen, I came to see you to tell you about a conversation I had with Mrs. Mashburn last night. I think I might know what all the phone calls between MacKenzie and Ben Mashburn were about." He filled Jack in on his phone call Saturday from Janna and the missing Bobby Greenleaf file, as well as Mrs. Mashburn's revelations about the photographs that MacKenzie had shown Ben.

Tyndall shook his head, looking confused. "So you're saying that maybe Mashburn discovered some kind of connection between Elliot Carter and the Greenleaf case? Because of something Anne Carter told him? And this is what he and MacKenzie were talking about during the phone calls that showed up on the LUDS?"

Hollis Joplin sighed. "Doesn't sound very convincing when you put it like that. I guess I just need to confront MacKenzie and find out what his involvement in all this was. But if what Ben Mashburn called him about last Monday had anything to do with Anne Carter's hiring him again, he should have come forward when Elliot Carter's body was found. And certainly when Mashburn's body was found."

"That's a big 'if,' Hollis," said Tyndall. "MacKenzie can easily say they were just trading phone calls about getting together for lunch or something. You don't have any real evidence that he had special knowledge about the Carter case. You need to be very careful about accusing him of anything. He can cause a lot of trouble for you, especially once he finds out you disobeyed a direct order from him. Which brings us right back to that whole paramilitary thing I was talking about the other day," he added pointedly.

Joplin sighed again. "I guess I'll just let Ike Simmons know about all this for the time being." He started to leave, then turned back and said, "By the way, Halloran's hunch about Dr. Woodley might turn out to be right. He published an article about autoerotic asphyxia a few years ago, so he certainly knew enough about it to fake a death scene."

Jack Tyndall shook his head slowly. "As I said before, this is the Goddamnedest case that I've ever been involved with: an autoerotic death that might turn out to be murder, a dubious suicide, and a twenty-year old kidnapping case."

"Yeah, I can't wait to see how it all shakes out," Joplin said. "All of it," he added pointedly, thinking of Carrie.

"Me, too," said Jack Tyndall, meeting his gaze.

Carrie Salinger sat at a table in the Quizno's on Cheshire Bridge Road and stared at her chicken sub, unable to take a bite of it. She had rushed out of Jack's office and taken refuge in the library, intending to work on the lit review for the article she had agreed to co-author. But her jumbled thoughts made concentration impossible and finally drove her to take an early lunch at eleven. She was also afraid she might run into Hollis. The problem was, she didn't know how to explain the situation to herself, much less to him.

How could she be so attracted to someone like Jack? she wondered, picking up her sub and then putting it down again. He was everything she had always disliked in a man: conceited, glib, manipulative, chauvinistic, *and* a womanizer! But as Carrie thought about Jack's faults, she also remembered how his lips had felt on her mouth, and the almost electric surge that spread through her body. Hollis hadn't even tried to kiss her. Not on the lips anyway.

Carrie felt her face flush again as she thought of Hollis. Sunday had been one of the most enjoyable days she'd had in a long time. After they left Horseradish Grill, they'd strolled around Chastain Park, a sprawling enclave that held a public golf course and swimming pool, tennis courts, stables, and a baseball diamond. It was also a Mecca for joggers and fitness walkers, especially on a beautiful spring day. As people passed by them, she and Hollis told each other more bits and pieces about themselves. Then, not wanting the date to end, they'd returned to the restaurant's terrace bar for another glass of wine around three o'clock.

As they waited for the valet to bring her car, Carrie had been very tempted to invite Hollis back to her condominium. Reluctantly, she decided against it; it was only their second date. She was also cautious by nature, and getting sexually involved with a co-worker was never a good idea. But when Hollis took her hand and gently kissed her on the forehead, she'd almost changed her mind. As she drove off, she'd even entertained the possibility that the relationship might go in that direction once her tour at the ME's office was over.

And then Jack Tyndall had suddenly pulled her to him in his office and kissed her.

Disgusted with herself, Carrie snatched up her sub and took a bite. She chewed and swallowed without tasting anything, then took another angry bite, chewing and swallowing again. The whole thing was ridiculous, she decided. She was twenty-eight years old and a doctor, not some teenager with a crush. Yet that was exactly how Jack made her feel, and it was humiliating. She had no intention of getting involved with a man who had been dumped by his girlfriend while in the process of getting a divorce from his second wife. She'd been furious when he'd kissed her; he'd evidently thought she was as available to him as some woman he might meet in a bar or on the Internet. So why was she even giving him a second thought? Why were her body and her emotions attempting to sabotage what her logical thought processes knew to be correct? Was it possible there were depths to the man that she hadn't consciously acknowledged?

He had certainly surprised her at lunch the previous Friday. Carrie hadn't expected the fresh shave and the navy blazer, much less the self-deprecating humor. And after she made it clear that she didn't consider him to be God's gift to women, Jack had turned off the charm and discussed his ideas for the forensic article about suicide deaths among the elderly. Carrie had been impressed by his knowledge on the subject. When she started researching the issue that night at the library, she'd spent part of the time reading some of his previous articles and had been even more impressed. She had to admit that the man had a first-rate mind.

At least the part of it that wasn't in the gutter, chasing blond bimbos.

Unable to eat any more, Carrie shoved the rest of her food back into its paper bag, grabbed her purse, and stood up. Carrying her tray over to the trash bin, she decided to concentrate on getting through her thirty-day tour at the ME's and forget about everything else. Her schedule left no time for a social life, and she shouldn't even have agreed to go out with Hollis. She also didn't need to spend what little free time she had working on a forensic article. That was not the kind of pathologist she was going to be, so why even go down that particular road? No matter how interesting the subject might be.

Carrie dumped the contents of the tray down the hole in the trash bin and felt much better. As if she had gotten rid of a terrible burden.

The rest of Monday passed in uneventful misery for Joplin. He'd left the ME's office without waiting around to see MacKenzie, deciding to take Jack's advice and avoid confronting the chief until he had more information. He only hoped Mrs. Mashburn wouldn't decide to call "Billy" and ask him about the missing Greenleaf file. But once he'd gotten home and showered, he was too keyed up to attempt sleep. Instead, he spent a few hours doing some much-needed cleaning, hoping to take his mind off what had happened that morning in Jack's office. Despite his best efforts, however, images of Carrie and Jack kissing kept bombarding him as he vacuumed and changed sheets and did laundry.

Joplin treated himself to a Coors at lunch, followed by a nap, finally giving in to layers of fatigue and tension. When his head hit the pillow, he felt as if he were falling down into a deep, dark well that had no bottom. He slept, dreamlessly, until eight that night, but didn't feel rested when he woke up. After feeding Quincy, he cracked open a brand new bottle of Jim Beam and poured himself a sizeable slug over ice. Then he headed for the living room, giving himself permission to drown his sorrows. This week's schedule had him working the four-to-midnight shift on Tuesday and Wednesday, then days on Thursday and Saturday. He only had one class at Georgia State the next day, and he figured he could still get himself together by the time it started at one.

Despite the Jim Beam—or maybe because of it—he was unable to keep himself from floating an image of Carrie in front of his TV set as he lay sprawled on his couch, awash in self-pity. He saw her again as she walked away from him to her car in the parking lot of Horseradish Grill; saw her tip the valet, then turn back to him and wave. She was smiling, and the mid-afternoon sun made her squint a little as she looked at him. Then she got in the car and closed the door and drove slowly out of the lot, away from him.

When the car had disappeared through the hedges that bordered the restaurant's property, Joplin started the whole thing over again in his mind's eye, like an instant replay on his DVR.

He was definitely beginning a full-blown blue funk.

On Tuesday, Joplin nursed his considerable hangover with copious amounts of bottled water and a judicious amount of Tylenol. He managed to get through his Constitutional Law class that afternoon, then stopped at the Varsity for a Glorified and onion rings before heading to his shift at the ME's office. Joplin had always been a big believer in the medicinal powers of grease after a night of heavy drinking, and he badly needed a sizeable dose of it.

Just to be on the safe side, he also ordered French fries.

31

WEDNESDAY, MAY 2ND, WAS RAINY, with an expected high of only fifty-seven degrees. Halloran had grown used to the rapid weather swings so typical of springtime in Atlanta; it was still better than a Chicago spring. But it was a lousy day for a funeral, he thought as he backed his car down the driveway, with Maggie in the passenger seat. Then again, he wondered, what *was* the best kind of day for a funeral?

"I guess if it were a beautiful, warm, sunny day it would be even worse," said Maggie, as if reading his thoughts.

"This is bad enough for me," Halloran said. And it wasn't just the funeral. He'd only had one drink the night before, but a restless night's sleep made him feel like he was recovering from a hangover. He also had disturbing memories of a dream in which he was endlessly jogging toward Elliot's body, never reaching it, as it swung slowly from the tree trunk. He hoped he could get through the day in one piece.

It took about fifteen minutes to get to St. Phillip's. The imposing Romanesque cathedral had been built on one of Atlanta's many hills and loomed over the traffic below like a medieval fortress. Halloran turned off Peachtree and drove up to the parking lot. One umbrella did little to shelter them from the pelting rain as they walked quickly to the door of the church. As they entered the vestibule, Maggie looked searchingly at his face.

"How are you doing?" she whispered.

"Okay, I guess. Just stay close."

The handsome mahogany casket Olivia had chosen was already at the front of the church, surrounded by baskets of flowers; she had not wanted to see it brought in by the pallbearers. Halloran and Maggie sat just be-hind the pews reserved for the family, and he watched as they came down the aisle. It was a painfully small group, without the usual collection of in-laws and nieces and nephews that helped to swell a family procession.

The organist began to play the *Fuga Ricercata* from Bach's *Musical Offering*, one of Elliot's favorite pieces. Trip passed him in the aisle as he escorted Olivia Carter and Pauletta to their seats. Halloran wondered if the housekeeper would have been seated with the family if Anne had been in charge, then immediately felt guilty. He caught Trip's eye as he waited for his grandmother to enter the pew and gave him an encour-aging nod. Anne and her parents followed them. Anne was wearing enormous, Jackie-O sunglasses that looked especially inappropriate in the weak light that struggled through the stained-glass windows. Dr. Woodley was conspicuously absent from the family group, but Halloran fought the urge to look around the church and see if he were sitting elsewhere.

The rest of the service was a blur to him. In keeping with Episcopal tradition, there were no eulogies given, and nothing personal was said about Elliot or his life. Despite this, Halloran found it to be a very mov-ing experience, amazed at how the music wrung emotion from him. At one point, as a lone violinist was playing Barber's *Adaggio for Strings*, Maggie squeezed his hand, and he turned to look at her. She was holding a tissue out to him. He took it and wiped his eyes. Soon after that, the ceremony was over.

Olivia had asked him to be a pallbearer. As the family and friends filed solemnly out of the church, Halloran waited with the others se-lected. Alston Caldwell was the only other person from the firm who'd been chosen; the others were friends from Charleston and one of Elliot's clients. Following instructions, they all lined up behind the casket, three on each side, and grasped the handles.

A few minutes later, even that one, small thing Halloran could do for Elliot Carter had been completed. All that was left was the burial at Arlington in Sandy Springs, a suburb about twenty minutes away. He stood in the archway and watched as the doors of the hearse slammed shut on Elliot's casket, then turned to look for Maggie. He saw her talking to one of their neighbors, both huddled under umbrellas in the still-pouring rain, and motioned toward the parking lot.

They walked to the car in silence. Soon they were a part of the funeral procession, moving slowly up Peachtree as oncoming cars pulled off the road in respect until the last of the cortege had passed them.

During the luncheon at the Buckhead Ritz following the ceremony at Arlington, Halloran spent a dutiful fifteen minutes talking to Anne's parents. He was rewarded for this by learning that they were returning to McRae that afternoon.

"Ray needs to get back for a business meeting tomorrow, and I was going to stay on and spend the rest of the week with Anne and Trip," Lillian said as she carefully realigned the charms on a silver bracelet on her right wrist, "but Anne wouldn't hear of it. She's so strong, you know," she added, looking anything but happy about that.

"Well, they *were* separated for quite a while," Halloran offered cautiously.

"But they were going to get back together," Lillian Landrum insisted. "This has just devastated her!"

"Did Anne tell you that?"

"She didn't have to! I just knew. I mean, she's seemed so much happier these last few months, talking about how everything was all coming together." Lillian turned to her husband and said, "You remember, Ray, she told us that just last week. Remember?"

Ray Landrum looked embarrassed. He was a thin, almost gaunt man with a thatch of gray hair. "Whatever you say, Lil. But she *has* seemed happier lately," he added hastily.

"Maybe Dr. Woodley has had something to do with that," Halloran suggested, nodding toward the psychiatrist, who was sitting next to Anne at a table in the center of the room, deep in conversation with her. He'd never actually seen him at the funeral, but there he was now.

Both Landrums looked at their daughter and Paul Woodley for several seconds, then Lillian said, "Yes, he's helped Anne a lot. Now let me go say hi to that pretty wife of yours, Tom, and then we need to get going. Don't we, Ray?"

At five p.m., when he was fairly sure the Landrums had left for McRae, Halloran told Maggie he needed to walk off the stress of the funeral, again deciding not to tell her he was going to see Anne.

Pauletta answered the doorbell. Smiling, she ushered him in and said, "It was a lovely funeral, Mr. Halloran. Mr. Elliot would've been proud."

"I hope so," said Halloran. He hesitated, wondering how inappropriate it would be if he asked Pauletta whether Trip had ever been hospitalized as a young teenager. If she were the housekeeper mentioned in Woodley's article, she would know all about the hanging incident. Deciding he owed it to Anne to talk to her first, he said, "Is Mrs. Carter home?"

"Yes, I'll get her."

A few minutes later, Anne joined him in the living room. "The service was beautiful, Tom," she said, sitting down on one of the white sofas next to him. "You and Olivia did a great job."

"Thank you. It was an honor. Anne, I need to talk to you about those pictures."

She brought her hands up to her eyes and pressed on them as if they were hurting her. "Can't we do this another time? Elliot's barely in the ground."

"I know. I'm sorry, but this just can't wait."

"I shouldn't have given you those pictures. I know that now. It was a mistake. Please forget about them, Tom. Please."

"I can't do that, Anne. Especially now that I know that one of the children in them was Bobby Greenleaf. Does that name mean anything to you?"

She stared at him. "He was the little boy who was kidnapped walking to school."

"Did you recognize him in the pictures?"

"Recognize him? My God, I barely even looked at those pictures! They made me sick to my stomach! I shoved them right back into that envelope and wished I'd never laid eyes on them. And I wish with all my heart that I hadn't given them to you, Tom. You—you didn't give them to the police, did you?" She clutched his arm in a frantic motion. "Please don't do that. I mean, what if I said those pictures never belonged to Elliot? Couldn't you just burn them?"

"You know I can't do that either," he said, grasping her hand in an attempt to calm her down. "Even if what you say is true. And I certainly hope it is. The police still need to see them, and to find out how you got them."

Her shoulders slumped, and she let go of his arm. "Yes, that's exactly what they'll want to know, isn't it?"

"How did you get them, Anne? What's going on?"

"Whatever it is, it's bigger than me, that's for sure."

"What do you mean?"

"I don't know anymore, Tom," she said tiredly. "And that's the truth."

Halloran tried another tack. "Did you know that Dr. Woodley had written an article a few years ago about autoerotic asphyxia? It was about a former patient, a young boy who had been doing this, and described how the parents had come home and found him almost dead."

"Why are you telling me about this?" said Anne slowly. "Do you think Paul had something to do with Elliot's death?"

"Well, it shows he knew a lot about the subject. But what came to mind when I read the article was the boy he wrote about might have been Trip."

Her face turned ashen. "That's crazy! How can you even think that? Oh, God, I think I'm going to be sick," she cried, clapping a hand over her mouth.

"I'm sorry, Anne. Please believe that I'm not deliberately trying to upset you."

She looked at him, slack-jawed, and Halloran realized too late that he had been ruthless in his attempt to find out the truth. He had come at her like a steamroller. Abruptly, Anne Carter stood up and walked away from him. But before he could call out or go to her, she sank to her knees, then fell over sideways, her head hitting the hardwood floor with a sound he hoped he would never hear again.

It was after eleven p.m., but Halloran was no closer to falling asleep than he had been an hour earlier. He'd returned from seeing Anne almost as upset as when he'd identified Elliot's body. To his relief, Maggie had

handled the situation fairly calmly, but after he told her what had happened, interrupting the story several times to blame himself or say what
he should have done, she'd insisted on calling the Carter house. Voice
mail answered each time, so she'd left messages asking Pauletta to call
back.

It was Pauletta whom Anne had allowed to help her sit up as she
lay sprawled on the living room floor. She wouldn't let Halloran touch
her. When he wanted to take her to the emergency room at Piedmont
Hospital, she had ordered the housekeeper to call Dr. Woodley and then
demanded that Tom leave.

Paul Woodley was the one who'd finally called around seven p.m. to
tersely inform Maggie that Anne was "resting" and didn't want to see or
talk to anyone. Although Halloran had been relieved, he was irritable
and on edge the rest of the evening, especially after remembering that
he had an eight a.m. appointment with Dr. Greer, Elliot's urologist, the
next day. Halloran knew he should just cancel it and turn over the photographs to Hollis Joplin; it was one more violation of his agreement not
to interfere in the investigation. But he decided he'd come this far and
might as well have even more to confess to if the urologist confirmed
what he suspected about Elliot's ability to father a child. He had also
been reluctant to call Greer's dragon of a nurse and cancel a meeting he'd
pressured her into arranging.

Now he lay in bed, his eyes closed, but his mind still racing, wishing
he'd never said anything to Anne about Woodley's article or Trip. He
started to wonder just which topic had caused her to react so violently,
then caught himself. If he kept this up, he would never get to sleep.
Turning over on his right side, Halloran tried to empty his mind, taking
deep breaths to relax.

Anne Carter sat propped up on pillows in bed. It was a little after midnight. The Ativan injection Paul had given her had worn off, and she'd
been awake for the past two hours. She didn't want to take any of the pills
that he'd left for her, though. She had slept enough for a while. Enough
to be able to think clearly for the first time in days and to understand,
finally, how stupid she'd been.

She also realized the harm she'd caused. First to Elliot, who had married her and given her things she'd only dreamed about. He'd been a

kind, loving husband and a wonderful father to Trip. And she'd repaid him by cheating on him. Even worse, she'd tried to blackmail him and had been partly responsible for his death. Ben Mashburn's death, too.

And more people might get hurt unless she could think of something to do.

She could go to the police, of course. But though she'd finally had the courage to face what he had done—what *she* had done, too—she shrank from doing that. Despite everyone's perception of her as confident and determined, she knew that everything she'd done in her life had been done out of fear. Fear of being poor. Fear of being alone. Fear of being abandoned. And now, of course, fear of being found out. She dreaded what everyone would think of her. More than that, she dreaded going to prison.

The reality was that she might be the *only* one to go to prison for what had happened. She had no real evidence to give the police. It would be her word against his, and she knew only too well how good he was with words. He could make her think white was black and black was white, even when she knew better. More than that, his position and authority would protect him. She thought of calling Tom. She had almost told him everything today when he'd come to see her. And then, when he'd asked her if Trip were the patient in Paul's article, she'd totally lost it.

She had to protect her son somehow. Protecting him had led her to the life they'd had with Elliot and even the steps she'd taken to maintain that life, but it had also led to the destruction of her marriage and her involvement in two murders. Yet what could she possibly do?

And then she thought of her Flip. She had bought it to use as a video camera, but it could record sound, too. She sat up and clicked on the bedside lamp, formulating what she would need to say and do to get this monster who had ruined her life to incriminate himself on tape. She could put the Flip on her bedside table, and even if she just got an audio recording it would back up her story. Anne reached for the phone, hopeful for the first time in a week. She would get the evidence she needed and then call Tom. He would make the police understand that she had been manipulated into doing what she had done. She might not even have to go to prison.

Before whatever courage she had failed her, Anne Carter pressed the numbers on the phone and held her breath, waiting for it to ring.

32

HALLORAN AWOKE FEELING punch-drunk. He'd slept very little and when he did sleep, his dreams were filled with images of death and destruction. Groaning, he heaved himself out of bed and headed for the bathroom. When he got out of the shower, Maggie was still asleep. He dressed and left the house before her alarm went off, deciding to go to Starbucks for coffee. He wasn't up to eating breakfast yet.

Dr. Robert Greer's office was in the Piedmont Hospital Professional Building on Peachtree, near the border of Buckhead and Midtown. Halloran, feeling queasy from the effects of two cups of black coffee on an empty stomach, got out of his car at ten minutes to eight and made his way to the fifth floor. He was immediately ushered in to see the doctor by his nurse, a short, iron-haired woman with a starched manner, and warned that Dr. Greer had no more than fifteen minutes to spare him.

Dr. Greer, who had a close-clipped, salt-and pepper beard and piercing eyes that were magnified by wire-rimmed glasses, was sitting behind a cluttered desk. "Mr. Halloran," he said, standing up and offering his hand. He was at least Tom's height.

"Thanks for seeing me this morning," said Halloran, shaking his hand.

"Well, Miss Brambley made the appointment, but I have to admit I got a little excited when I saw your name. I've read about some of your cases in the *AJC,* and I DVR'd the Nesmith case when it was on truTV. That was a doozy. By the way, you look a lot younger in person," he added, smiling now.

"Thanks," Halloran responded. It was something he'd heard before and wasn't sure how he felt about it.

Dr. Greer motioned Halloran to a chair in front of his desk. "I've been out of town, but my nurse told me about Elliot Carter. I was sorry to hear about his death. I understand you're his executor?"

"Yes, I am." Halloran opened his briefcase and pulled out a letter testamentary signed by Judge Wainwright identifying him as such. "I brought this along because I need to get some information from you concerning Elliot's medical condition."

"You mean for insurance purposes?" Greer asked, glancing over the letter.

"Not exactly. The ME's office is leaning toward an official ruling of accidental death, but I think he was murdered." Halloran gave him the details surrounding Elliot's death and watched the doctor's expression change from quizzical to grave. Greer didn't appear to be a man who shocked easily, but what he was hearing was evidently surprising.

"I didn't know Mr. Carter well," he said. "He was a new patient, as a matter of fact. But even so, he impressed me as a very intelligent and well-adjusted person. Certainly not the type to go in for autoerotic asphyxia."

"Do you know much about the subject, Doctor?"

Greer shrugged. "Maybe a little more than the average person, but not much more. I went to a seminar on deviant sexual practices when the AIDS epidemic surfaced, and I've read a few articles, but I've never treated anyone who was into it. At least, not knowingly. But you said you wanted information about Mr. Carter's medical condition."

"Yes," said Halloran. "Elliot's mother mentioned that she'd taken DES—diethyl stilbestrol—during her pregnancy. When he told her he was seeing you, she was concerned, because later research showed a high incidence of testicular cancer among the male children of mothers who'd taken this drug. Was that why he came to see you?"

"No, actually, it was for prostatitis. A little unusual in a man his age, but not unheard of. But when he told me about his mother's taking DES, I ran some other tests, along with the test for his PSA level, just to be on the safe side. He showed no signs of any pathology from the DES."

"Was one of the tests you ran for fertility, Dr. Greer?" Halloran asked.

The eyes behind the glasses became even more piercing. "As a matter of fact, I did, although the incidence of sterility from DES has been found to be far less than originally thought," Greer said. "Unfortunately, Mr. Carter was one of those affected."

"You told him that?" Halloran asked, leaning forward.

"Yes, of course. I gave him all the test results."

"How did he take it?"

"He was extremely upset. He insisted that there must be some kind of mistake, because he had a son who was almost seventeen. When I told him that I'd be happy to run another test, he asked me if it could be a recent condition. I knew what was going through his mind. So I told him it was *possible*. But then he asked me for my professional opinion, and I told him I thought that he'd always been sterile. That it was a congenital condition, due to the DES."

"What was his reaction then?"

Greer shrugged. "About what you'd expect from a man who'd just found out that his son wasn't his biological child. He was pretty shaken up. I suggested that he might want to get some kind of counseling, but he brushed that off. I got the impression he wasn't the kind of person who liked to discuss his problems."

"You were right about that," said Halloran wryly.

"Which is why I'm not real comfortable discussing them with you right now, although I know you have a right to have access to confidential information. Tell me, what does any of this have to do with Mr. Carter's death?"

"I'm not really sure. But the Carters separated soon after Elliot's visit to you, and I think part of the reason was finding out about the sterility. More importantly, I think the impending divorce was at least an indirect reason for his death." Halloran stood up. "Thanks for seeing me. I promised your nurse I wouldn't take too much of your time."

"She scares me to death, too," said Greer, smiling and standing up to shake Halloran's hand again.

All Halloran wanted to do now was to get rid of the terrible photos in his briefcase and end his involvement in the investigation of Elliot Carter's death. Joplin would have to find out from Anne where she'd gotten them.

As soon as he was inside his car, he grabbed his cell phone and pulled up Joplin's number.

"Joplin speaking."

"This is Tom Halloran. I'd like to meet with you as soon as possible. There's something I need to give you. Something I should have given to you last—"

"Sorry to cut you off, Counselor, but I'm at a scene. Anne Carter is dead. Looks like she overdosed on something."

33

HOLLIS JOPLIN HELD OPEN the front door of the Carter house for the two morgue attendants wheeling Anne Carter's body to the transport van. As he started to go back inside, he spotted Tom Halloran making his way up the drive. The attorney, looking very somber, edged past the Crime Scene Unit van and an APD car, but waited until the attendants had loaded the body into the van before walking up to Joplin.

"I can't believe this," he said. "I just saw her yesterday."

"Yeah, I heard about that from the housekeeper. She said Mrs. Carter fainted while you were here, and she had to call her doctor. "

"She called Woodley," Halloran said pointedly.

"I heard about that, too. The housekeeper said he gave Mrs. Carter a sedative by injection and then came back later—around nine-thirty—to check on her. He also left her some Ativan samples."

"Is that what she overdosed on?"

"We won't know that till after the autopsy, but it looks like it. All of the samples—about ten—had been used. The empty packets were on her bedside table."

"Was Woodley alone with her at any time?" Halloran asked.

"Look, I know where you're going with this, Counselor, and I admit Dr. Woodley interests me, but I think you're jumping to a very big conclusion. Yes, he saw her alone when he came back last night. But the housekeeper saw her after that and said she seemed fine. No grogginess or word-slurring. I made it a point to ask."

"Was there a note?"

"There might have been, but if so, we haven't recovered it yet. Suicide notes have a way of disappearing sometimes when there's something embarrassing or damaging in them. I understand Ms. Reed, the housekeeper, had been with the family a long time."

"I can assure you that Pauletta would never hide or destroy anything that important," Halloran responded, scowling.

"Maybe, maybe not. But if Mrs. Carter did write a suicide note, it might have dealt with some of the things the two of you talked about yesterday."

"Such as?"

Joplin felt himself getting pissed. "Don't keep screwing with me, Halloran. You've only been telling me bits and pieces of what you know from the very beginning, and that crap is over with. Three people are dead," he added, raising his voice. "Maybe all three were murdered or maybe they did themselves in. I don't know yet, and that's the God's honest truth. But you're not helping me find out. Now, I don't want to lay a big guilt trip on you, but if Anne Carter *did* kill herself, the odds are that something you said to her yesterday set her off."

Halloran didn't respond right away. Then he took a deep breath, let it out, and said, "Don't think I haven't told myself the same thing in the past thirty minutes. Can we go sit in my car to talk? I have something I want to give you. Something I should have given you days ago. And I promise I'll tell you everything Anne and I talked about yesterday."

"I should have brought these to you last Thursday, when Anne gave them to me," Halloran said as he handed Joplin a manila envelope. "My only excuse is that I was trying to protect Elliot."

Joplin opened the envelope and pulled out a stack of photographs. As he examined them, he felt a number of emotions sweep through him: revulsion, pity, and a terrible anger. And then he realized what he was seeing. "These are the Bobby Greenleaf pictures," he said slowly, trying to make sense of yet another twist in the case.

"Yes, Maggie recognized him, too. Not right away, but Sunday she realized why one of the boys looked so familiar."

Joplin's confusion was replaced by shock. "You showed these to your wife?"

"She's a professional photographer," said Halloran, sounding defensive. "She thought maybe she could help me figure out where they came from; see something I might not see. I was desperate for anything to disprove what Anne told me."

"And what was that?"

"That she found these taped to the bottom of Elliot's bureau drawer at their house up in Highlands a few weeks ago. She said she took them to Ben Mashburn and asked him to help her build a case against Elliot. She left three photos with him."

"That's impossible," said Joplin, shaking his head. "These pictures were found in the home of an orthodontist who died of natural causes about four years ago. Mrs. Mashburn said Chief MacKenzie showed them to her husband."

"Who's Chief MacKenzie?"

"He's my boss. He and Ben Mashburn were partners on the police force back in the Eighties. According to Mrs. Mashburn, they worked the Bobby Greenleaf case. When these pictures were found, Chief MacKenzie took them to Mashburn to see if he had any ideas on them. Mashburn was still obsessed with the case. He even kept a file on it in his office. Along with the Carter file, that's missing, too."

"But what could a twenty-five-year-old kidnapping have to do with Elliot Carter's death?"

"I don't know yet, but I would've at least known what questions to ask, if you hadn't covered all this up and tried to play detective."

"Look, I'm really sorry about that. I was just trying to—"

"Protect Elliot Carter," finished Joplin. "Now you can *show* me how sorry you are by coming clean about everything else. What did you and Anne Carter discuss yesterday?"

Joplin listened intently as Halloran told him about asking Anne if Trip Carter were the patient described in Woodley's article. "And if that played a part in her deciding to commit suicide, I'll have to live with that for the rest of my life," he added, looking remorseful.

Joplin stared out the windshield of Halloran's car for several seconds before responding. "I don't think this *is* a suicide," he said finally. "Somebody had to have given her these pictures—maybe for the purpose of blackmailing her husband." Joplin gazed out the window again, lost in thought. Then he turned back to Halloran and said, "On Wednesday, after I found out Mashburn was missing, I went to see Mrs. Carter to find out why she'd hired him a second time, remember? Like I told you, she blew me off, saying she wasn't going to drag her husband's name through the mud any more than it already had been. The next day, though—Thursday—she apparently changed her mind and decided to give you these photographs. Why was that?"

"I went to see her and told her about Mashburn's death. I told her I was more convinced than ever that Elliot had been murdered, and that Mashburn had been, too."

"What was her reaction?"

"She seemed frightened. Then she left the room and came back with the photos."

"Which sent you off in a totally different direction."

"Yes. I guess it did."

"What I don't understand is," Joplin said, "why *these* pictures? Why use pictures of one of the most famous kidnap victims in this country? If she wanted to try to blackmail her husband, why not use more recent kiddie porn?"

"That's a good question," admitted Halloran. "I should have wondered about that myself. I don't see how she could have been trying to implicate Elliot in the Greenleaf kidnapping—he would have still been in high school then. Maybe she just assumed that he would panic if he thought he could be accused of possessing *any* child pornography."

"Maybe," Joplin responded. "Tell me something. You mentioned that you'd given the photographs to your wife. Other than recognizing Bobby Greenleaf, did she discover anything else?"

"As a matter of fact, she did notice something else, but I don't know if it's important."

"Just tell me."

"Well, she thinks whoever the photographer was, he wasn't some amateur. He had to have been a professional, in her opinion, because of the composition and perspective the photographs showed. She also said that these particular pictures," Halloran added, tapping the stack of photos, "are copies of the originals, printed on an laser printer with Kodak paper."

"That makes sense. It's a lot safer for child pornographers to make copies that way than from the original negatives, even if they had them."

"Yes, but Maggie doesn't think they were scanned. She's convinced that whoever produced them did it by taking pictures of the originals with a digital camera and then printing them out." Halloran shrugged. "I really don't know much about photography. It has something to do with pixels and resolution, but you'd have to talk to her."

"Maybe I will. Listen, when you came here yesterday, did you tell Anne Carter that one of the boys in the photographs was Bobby Greenleaf?"

"Yes. It was my primary reason for seeing her. I knew I had to turn the pictures over to you or the police as soon as possible, but I wanted to confront her about that first."

"Had she known that?" asked Joplin.

"She insisted she hadn't. That she never even looked carefully at the pictures after realizing what they were. Then she asked if I'd given them to the police. When I said I hadn't, but intended to now that I knew they involved the Bobby Greenleaf case, she begged me not to. Then she asked me what I would do if she told me that she'd lied about finding the pictures with Elliot's things. She wanted me to burn them, but I told her I couldn't do that. I said the police would still have to know where she'd gotten them. Then I asked her to tell me what was going on."

"Did she tell you?"

"She said something really curious," said Halloran slowly. "She told me she, herself, didn't even know what was going on, but whatever it was, it was bigger than she was, or words to that effect."

"What do you think she meant?"

Halloran shook his head. "I don't know. I wish now I'd made her tell me."

"Did she tell you if Trip Carter was the patient in Woodley's article?"

"No. That's when she fainted."

Joplin rubbed his face with one hand. "Is there anything else you haven't told me?"

Halloran opened his mouth to reply, then closed it. Looking a little sheepish, he finally said, "Well, I did go to see Elliot's urologist this morning to—"

"You did *what?*"

Halloran held up one hand. "Just let me finish before you get angry again. I needed to follow up on something Olivia Carter—Elliot's mother—told me."

Quickly, Halloran told him about the phone conversation Elliot Carter had had with his mother shortly before he and Anne had separated and how that had led to his visit to Dr. Greer. He explained his suspicions that Carter might not have been able to father a child, now confirmed by Greer, and how this might have led to the Carters' separation.

"I don't know how all of this—the pictures, Woodley's article, Elliot's sterility—fits together, or if any of it is even relevant. But we've got to pursue it. And we can start with Paul Woodley. That's his car, isn't it?" Halloran asked, motioning toward a black Jaguar parked in front of the house next to Joplin's own car.

"Wait a minute," Joplin said, holding up both hands now. "What is all this 'we' crap? You're playing detective again, Mr. Halloran. I realize you're a real hot-shot, and if Anna Nicole Smith were alive and living in Atlanta, she'd be your client, but that doesn't give you the right to keep interfering in this investigation. Back off! I know how to do my job, for Christ's sake."

"Then why did it take you so long to believe that Elliot had been murdered?" Halloran shot back, sounding angry himself. "I know I promised not to involve myself anymore in the investigation, but I felt I had no choice when you totally dismissed the idea that someone had tried to kill *me* last Friday and went back to your original assumption that Elliot's death was accidental."

"Point taken," said Joplin grudgingly. "To answer your question, yes that's Dr. Woodley's car. The housekeeper called him when she found Mrs. Carter. He told her to call 911 and then came here immediately. He's being questioned by Simmons and Knox right now; they're treating this like a homicide for the time being. And I plan on asking him a few questions myself. But you're not going to be anywhere on the premises. Is that clear?"

Halloran gave a reluctant nod. "I think I could help, but I guess I'm not in a position to insist. Can I at least see Trip Carter before I go?"

"He's not here. According to the housekeeper, he's been with Elliot Carter's mother at the Ritz-Carlton since the funeral."

"I'd better get over there then. Will you at least let me know what you find out?"

Joplin gathered up the photographs and put them back in the manila envelope. "I'll think about it," he said as he got out of the car.

34

PAUL WOODLEY WAS LOOKING decidedly uncomfortable. He was sitting in one of the loveseats flanking the fireplace; Simmons and Knox occupied the other one. The psychiatrist's hands were pressed out flat against his thighs; his feet were planted on the floor about ten inches apart. His grim expression was highlighted by beads of sweat on his forehead. As Joplin entered the room, Woodley nervously jabbed his glasses back up on his nose.

"Any further instructions for CSU before they leave?" Joplin asked Simmons. "I just checked on them, and they're ready to wrap things up." The Crime Scene Unit had been called in to gather any forensic evidence, but Joplin had taken photographs of his own and tried to determine time of death before Anne Carter's body was removed.

The heavy-set detective looked up from his notebook, then turned to Knox. "Why don't you go on up and make sure they got everything, Ricky, okay?" When the other detective had left the room, Simmons turned back to Joplin. "Hollis, Dr. Woodley here is saying that Mrs. Carter didn't appear suicidal either time he saw her yesterday."

"I would have hospitalized her immediately if I'd thought that," said Woodley. "She was upset, certainly, but not to the extent that she would take her own life."

"Did she tell you why she was so upset?" asked Joplin.

He shook his head, then pushed his glasses up again. "I tried to get Anne to talk about it, but she told me she needed to think some things through first. I felt she would tell me what was disturbing her when she was ready. And she had also begun to calm down."

"Then, why," Joplin asked pointedly, "did you sedate her?"

"Because she told me she needed to sleep!" Woodley said almost desperately. "I knew she hadn't been sleeping very well since Elliot died, but she'd refused any medication up until then. Then yesterday she asked me to give her something. She said if she could just sleep for a while, she'd be okay."

"So what exactly did you give her?"

Woodley pushed his glasses up again and blinked. "Ten milligrams of Ativan."

"Why not by mouth, instead of intramuscular?"

"She was beginning to calm down, as I said, but she was still agitated, and it was a quicker route," answered Woodley, suddenly wary. "And Pauletta was in the room when I administered it. Listen, you can't possibly think I killed Anne. It's bad enough that I might have missed some sign that she might harm herself, but for you to think that I—"

"We don't think anything at this point, Dr. Woodley," interjected Simmons. "We're just gathering information."

"Not from me. Not anymore." Woodley stood up. "Unless you plan on arresting me, I'm leaving."

"You're free to go, Dr. Woodley, but we might have some more questions for you later," said Simmons.

Woodley glared at Joplin. "My attorney's name is James Chambliss. He's at One Atlantic Center, too," he added, then walked out of the room and into the entry hall. They heard the front door slam.

"Reminds me of when we were partners, Hollis," said Simmons, shaking his head. "Folks were always wantin' to lawyer up after just a few minutes with you. Even the innocent ones. The Bar Association should have given you a plaque when you left Homicide, all the business you sent them."

"That's just because I always had to play bad cop, Simmons. You were so lousy at it."

"We all got our strengths, Hollis. Mine was going to Captain Barrow and savin' your ass at least once a week. And speaking of Barrow, he wants to know when the ME's office can give us something definitive on Carter and Mashburn. And now we have Mrs. Carter to add to the list. You know how he likes everything cut and dried, Hollis."

"Tell him we've asked for a rush on Mashburn's tox report. I think Dr. Minton can be pretty sure about Mashburn, at least, once that's in. And if Ben Mashburn was murdered, that means Carter was, too."

"Unless Mr. Carter killed Mashburn over some information he had, then celebrated by having a hanging party. That was one scenario, remember?"

"Yeah, well, the scenarios are getting more and more complicated, Ike. One in particular I think I need Barrow's help with, because it might involve Chief MacKenzie."

"MacKenzie?" said Simmons, looking puzzled. "How the hell does *he* fit into this?"

Joplin filled the detective in on the missing Bobby Greenleaf file, his conversation the previous day with Mrs. Mashburn, and Tom Halloran's revelations. Then he handed him the manila envelope with the photographs. "I wanted you to see these first and get Barrow involved, but then give them to CSU."

"And I'm sure you want me to check with the Cold Case Unit and Property Control to see if MacKenzie ever turned them in and, if so, are they still there?"

"You read my mind, Simmons. If he didn't, we're about to open up a can of worms that might eat us alive. I plan on talking to him when I get back to the ME's office, but I think I better know about that aspect first."

"For real, Hollis," said Simmons. He gave a low whistle. "I hope the Cold Case officers know all about this, 'cause I sure didn't. And this is the kind of thing that usually gets around, you know? Big, high-profile case like that. Do you think MacKenzie kept these to himself?"

"I don't know," said Joplin. "But he didn't want me to talk to Mrs. Mashburn. I just can't figure out what connection he might have to Anne Carter. They sure didn't travel in the same circles. But if she didn't find those pictures among her husband's belongings, she had to have gotten them from someone."

"From what you've told me," said Simmons, "Dr. Woodley treated a kid who was into autoerotic asphyxia. He also might have treated other kinds of perverts, right? Maybe a pedophile. And maybe that pedophile had a set of pictures like this."

"I sure like that scenario better than one that involves somebody where I work. Of course, Dr. Woodley isn't going to tell us."

"And Mrs. Carter can't," added Simmons.

"Don't be too sure," Joplin replied. "In my opinion, the dead tell us a lot more than the living sometimes. And they don't lie," he added as he headed for the door.

By the time Joplin made it to his office, it was almost eleven o'clock. He went directly to Jack Tyndall's office, hoping he wouldn't run into Carrie—there or anywhere else in the building. Since he'd had the night shift on Tuesday and she had left by the time he got to work on Wednesday afternoon, there'd been no danger of seeing her. But today was a different story, and he was still trying to sort out his feelings.

"I heard about Anne Carter," Jack said, looking up at him.

He and Jack hadn't spoken to each other since Monday either, but Joplin decided his working relationship with the pathologist was more important than his own wounded feelings. Carrie would be leaving in a few weeks, and although part of him still hoped he might have a chance with her, he had no idea how things would turn out.

"Simmons contacted me directly when he got the call about her. He didn't want anyone else examining the body, under the circumstances. Mind if I go over a few things with you?"

"Anytime, Hollis," Jack replied, sounding relieved. "You know that."

Joplin walked over to the desk and sat down in the chair in front of it. "Are you doing the post?"

"Yes." The pathologist looked at his watch. "Right after lunch."

"Good. The circumstances indicate suicide, but I'm not buying it. Two suicides related to what may not be a true autoerotic death are just too many coincidences for me."

"I'd have to agree with you there. What do you have so far?"

Joplin took out his notebook and went over everything he'd learned at the Carter house. He then related what Tom Halloran had told him and saw Jack's eyes widen when he told him about the photographs the attorney had gotten from Anne Carter.

"Do you think they're the same ones Mrs. Mashburn told you about?" Tyndall asked when he was finished.

"I'd be surprised if they're not." Joplin sighed. "Which brings up a brand-new possibility: If Carter's death *was* murder, there's one other person who would have extensive knowledge of autoerotic deaths and be able to fake one."

Jack looked startled. "Who do you mean?"

"MacKenzie."

Tyndall grinned and shook his head. "You've got to be kidding, Hollis."

"No, I'm not, Jack. When he took me off the case, I'm sure it was because he didn't want to take the chance that I might hear about those photographs from Mrs. Mashburn. By the time I did talk to her, though, I knew about the missing file on the Greenleaf case from Mashburn's secretary, Janna Helms. And today, when Halloran gave me the photographs he got from Mrs. Carter, the circle was complete. She must have gotten them from MacKenzie."

"You don't know that, Hollis. They might be a totally different set of pictures. If one pervert had a set of them, you can bet several more existed. That's what child pornography is all about—to sell pictures or videos to a bunch of pedophiles who'll pay big bucks. Hey, I know you and MacKenzie don't get along, but—"

"It isn't that, Jack, and God knows I don't want to think that someone in this office would be involved in a triple murder, but I've got to consider it. I gave the photographs to Simmons, and he's checking out whether MacKenzie alerted the Cold Case Unit when they were found four years ago. I asked him to bring Captain Barrow in on it, too." Joplin cocked his head, a new thought occurring to him. "Listen, I was still with Homicide, but you were here then. Were you in on that case? Did MacKenzie ever show you those pictures?"

"No, and I would remember something like that," said Tyndall, running a hand through his already mussed hair. "Jesus, Hollis, I can't believe this! I mean, what possible connection could MacKenzie have to Anne Carter? From what I've heard of the lady, she doesn't seem to be the type to get involved with someone like MacKenzie. Besides, I thought she and Paul Woodley were an item."

"According to Dr. Woodley, they aren't—for whatever that's worth. And he refused to answer when I asked if they'd been involved in college. He did go to UGA for pre-med, by the way, so he's the same Paul Woodley you knew. Do you know if they were romantically involved then?"

"I wouldn't have ever seen them together," said Tyndall. "We had some classes together since we were both in pre-med, but we didn't travel in the same social circles. The only real contact I had with Paul Woodley was when I bussed his table in the student cafeteria when we were both freshmen. I was on scholarship, but I still had to work to make ends meet. And then he moved into one of the top fraternities by the end of the semester."

"Just thought I'd ask," said Joplin, standing up. "We're not likely to get anything more out of Woodley."

"Keep me posted on anything you do find out. I swear to God, I've never seen anything like this case, Hollis. I'll let you know if I find anything definitive when I do the post on Mrs. Carter."

"I'll be waiting," said Joplin. Whatever it was that Anne Carter's body was going to tell them, they needed to know it as soon as possible.

35

HALLORAN CALLED MAGGIE to tell her what had happened, then hurried to the Ritz, where he helped Olivia give whatever comfort possible to Trip. After sobbing uncontrollably for several minutes as his grandmother held him, the boy retreated into an almost catatonic state. Halloran was ready to call a doctor when Trip roused himself and asked to be taken home.

"Maggie will be here soon, Trip, and besides, we can't go back to your house just yet. The police are treating this as a possible homicide, so the house is a crime scene."

"But I thought you said she overdosed on some drugs or something."

"She did," Halloran said. "But I think someone else administered the drugs. There have been too many suspicious deaths, Trip. First your father and then the detective your mother hired. Now this."

"You're really freaking me out, Mr. Halloran," said Trip, running his hand through his hair, round and round, the way he'd done whenever he was upset, since he'd been little. "Does that mean someone might kill me, too? I'm the only one left."

"No, of course not," Halloran said quickly.

"You're scaring him, Tom," Olivia reproached him. Turning to Trip, she took both of his hands and looked into his eyes. "No one's going to hurt you, Trip. I'll make sure of that."

Maggie arrived at that point. When Halloran opened the door to the suite, she went straight to Trip and sat on the couch. She held him like she would one of her own children, rocking and crooning to him as he began to sob again.

"I could be talked into a very stiff bourbon and water, Tom," Olivia said as the boy's sobs began to subside. "And I think I should call room service and have them send up some sandwiches."

"That's an excellent idea," Halloran replied as he headed for the mini bar. "Maggie, how about you?"

Maggie shook her head. While Olivia called room service, he fixed them each a Jack Daniels and water, using three mini bottles. Trip seemed to have fallen into an exhausted sleep when Halloran returned to the group and handed Olivia her glass. But the knock on the door by room service a little later jolted him awake.

"I really don't feel like eating anything," he said as the waiter wheeled a table into the room. "I'd like to go lie down, if that's okay."

"That's fine," said Olivia. "I'll be in to see you in a little bit." When Trip had left the room, she turned to Tom and said, "I hate to bring this up, but has anyone notified the Landrums?"

"Oh, God," said Halloran. "I haven't even thought about them. I'll call them right now."

"Better eat something first—both of you," advised Olivia. "Bad news can always wait a little longer. In fact," she added sadly, "hearing that your only child is dead is the last thing any parent wants to hear."

"You would know that better than anyone, unfortunately," Halloran said, sitting down in a chair next to the couch. He reached over and took Olivia's hand. "But I think I'd rather get it over with—especially while I have some liquid courage on hand," he said, nodding toward his drink.

For the second time in a week, Tom had to tell a mother the worst news she would ever hear. Lillian let out a shriek, then handed the phone over to her husband. Halloran did his best to give Ray Landrum as many details about what had happened as he seemed capable of absorbing. He didn't raise any suspicions of murder, telling Landrum only that Anne's death appeared to be an accidental overdose. After assuring him that Trip was being cared for, Halloran gave his cell and office numbers and said he would be happy to help in any way.

Olivia made Tom and Maggie eat something, then told them to go on; she would call and let them know how Trip was doing. She also said she intended to arrange for the hotel's security personnel to monitor the suite. Halloran agreed that that was a good idea, if only to reassure Trip. He was sure that Anne's and Elliot's deaths had to do with money, blackmail, and the fear of discovery—motives that weren't likely to extend to Trip. But he felt better that the boy would be guarded for a while.

Once they were out in the hall, Halloran told Maggie about his meeting with Dr. Greer.

"God, this is unbelievable," she said when he was finished. "But if Elliot wasn't Trip's biological father, then who was?"

"Paul Woodley and David Healey are good candidates. And I almost hope it *is* one of them because then at least Trip would have a biological parent still alive."

"Unless one of them is a murderer," said Maggie.

Joplin grabbed a quick lunch at a nearby Arby's, then stopped by the cleaners to rescue two weeks' worth of clothes; he'd run out of Target shirts. He got back to the ME's office a little before one. When he entered the investigators' room, his eyes slid over to MacKenzie's office in the far right corner. The blinds were open, but the room was empty. As he walked over to his cubicle, the phone began ringing.

"Hollis, it's Simmons. We may have a problem here."

Joplin felt his heart beat a little faster. "What's up?"

"Well, the good news is that MacKenzie *did* contact the Cold Case Unit and turned the photos in four years ago, just like he should've."

"Then why didn't you or I hear anything about it at the time? Something as big as that would've gone through the whole department, for God's sake."

"According to Captain Barrow, that's exactly why he told MacKenzie, as well as the CCU, to keep the information on a need-to-know basis. He didn't want word to leak out to the media unless they came up with a new lead. Said it would just make us look bad all over again. So only the Missing Persons and Crimes Against Children units were involved. And the FBI, of course."

Joplin sighed into the phone. "What's the bad news?"

"On Monday, April 23rd at 6:35 p.m., MacKenzie signed the photographs out. Property Control says he hasn't returned them."

"That was two days before Carter was found in Piedmont Park!"

Joplin exclaimed. "That means that MacKenzie could've been the one to give the pictures to Anne Carter."

"But, Hollis, according to Halloran, Mrs. Carter showed them to Ben Mashburn on the *morning* of April 23rd. MacKenzie didn't check them out until that evening."

"She also said she had found them taped to the underside of a bureau drawer and later recanted that statement. Maybe it was also a lie that the photographs were the reason for going to see Mashburn that day."

"Okay, so what's the connection between MacKenzie and Anne Carter?"

"You got me there, partner. Obviously, we're missing some big piece of what has turned out to be a real goat-roping fucker of a puzzle. There's a connection between Dr. Woodley and Mrs. Carter, and he knows all about autoerotic asphyxia, but how would he get hold of the Greenleaf photos? I know Woodley could have had another patient who's a pedophile, but that's another one of those coincidences I don't like. Then there's a connection between MacKenzie and the photographs, and he certainly would know how to fake an autoerotic death even better than Woodley, but what's the connection with Mrs. Carter? Why would he give her the photographs?"

"Goat-roping fucker of a puzzle is right. Has Jack done the post on Anne Carter yet?"

"Should be starting about now, I think."

"You don't want to observe?"

"No, I don't want to miss MacKenzie," said Joplin. The real reason was that the thought of being in the same room with both Carrie and Jack made his palms sweat.

"I bet you haven't even gone to lunch," Simmons chided him. "You don't take care of yourself, Hollis."

"I *did* go to lunch! And I even went to the cleaners while I was out."

"You still buyin' those cheap shirts from Target?" asked Simmons.

"You don't have to make it sound like I pick my nose in public, Ike."

"You need a wife, Hollis. Some pretty little gal who'll cook and clean for you and iron your shirts. No sense messin' with that lady doctor, though. She'd probably be uppity and want to practice medicine. Just get you a country girl, like I did."

"Alfrieda is from New York and is an ADA. How country is that?"

"Yeah, but she's from the suburbs, and my mama taught her how to make biscuits."

"How did you know I went out with Dr. Salinger anyway, Simmons?"

"Cause I'm a detective, Hollis. And we detectives cultivate informants."

"Well, your informant is a little behind the times. I'm not sure I'll be going out with the lady doctor again. I think Jack is more her type."

"Shoot, Hollis!" said Simmons. "I like Jack a lot, but no intelligent, self-respecting woman would get involved with him."

"Times have changed, Ike. I can play bad cop, but I don't do bad boy very well, and bad boys are what the girls go for these days. Even the smart ones."

As Simmons earnestly refuted this, Joplin heard a door slam, then saw lights go on in MacKenzie's office. Deciding there was no time like the present to ask his boss if he were involved in a triple homicide, he cut Ike off. "MacKenzie's back. I gotta go."

"What is it?" yelled MacKenzie, answering his knock. "I'm busy in here."

Joplin opened the door. "Sorry to bother you, Chief. It's just that Property Control wants to know if you're through with the Greenleaf photos. They need them back."

Billy MacKenzie's jaw went slack, and his face lost its natural ruddiness. "Come in," he said, "and close the fucking door."

36

"WHAT'S THIS ALL ABOUT, HOLLIS?" MacKenzie asked, glaring at him.

"Just what it sounds like," said Joplin. He had closed the door and was now standing behind the chair in front of MacKenzie's desk, his hands flat against the top of it, aiming for a relaxed stance. "The Cold Case Unit needs those photos. Seems some new evidence on the Greenleaf case has turned up."

"What new evidence?" MacKenzie spat out. He had recovered a little of his composure, but not his color.

"Another set of pictures, as a matter of fact. Unless, of course, you happened to misplace the ones you checked out, and they happen to be the same ones Mr. Halloran gave me this morning. Mr. Halloran is the man who identified Elliot Carter's body last week."

"I know who Halloran is. He's an egotistical prick who's been feeding you a load of crap from the beginning. How the hell did *he* get them?"

Joplin sat down in the chair without being invited. "Mr. Halloran says he got them from Mrs. Carter, who first claimed that she had found them taped to the underside of one of her estranged husband's bureau drawers. He said she also told him that she had shown the pictures to Ben Mashburn, who kept three of them. But yesterday, Mrs. Carter took it all back and told Halloran she hadn't found them where she said she had. She wouldn't tell him how she got them, though. Do you happen to know anything about that?"

MacKenzie didn't answer. Instead, he picked up a set of keys from his desk, selected one, and used it to open a drawer to his right. He pulled out a manila envelope and pitched it like a boomerang at Joplin. Joplin managed to catch it before it hit him in the chest. He opened it and carefully drew out a set of 8 1/2" by 11" photographs.

"Count 'em. That's every single sick, disgusting picture we found four years ago."

Joplin counted eleven photos. Exactly three more than in the group Halloran had given him. Presumably, the other three had at one time been in Ben Mashburn's possession, if that part of Anne Carter's story was true.

"Now get out of here," MacKenzie bellowed. "I'll call Captain Barrow and tell him you're bringing the pictures back to Property Control. I'll also tell him I intend to file charges of gross insubordination against you for implying that I might have given those photographs to Mrs. Carter. I've been in law enforcement for almost thirty years, goddamn your eyes!"

"All the more reason for you to be charged with dereliction of duty and obstruction, which is what's going to happen when I take these photographs to APD."

"You've lost your mind, Joplin!"

Hollis stood up. "Have I, Chief? Mashburn must have called you right after Anne Carter brought him those photographs. He knew they were the same ones you showed him four years ago. Mrs. Mashburn told me all about it. But instead of getting them from Ben and taking them immediately to the Cold Case Unit so they could pursue the Carter lead, you told him to keep his mouth shut, then hightailed it over to Property Control to see if the photographs were still there."

"No!" said MacKenzie, looking panicked now. "It was Ben who wanted to keep things quiet, not me! He said it would be our chance to finish what we didn't do twenty-five years ago. When I said I wasn't interested, he begged me to give him twenty-four hours to pursue it himself, before he turned in the pictures. He was supposed to come to my house last Tuesday and give them to me if he couldn't find anything on his own. But he never showed up."

"I only have your word for that, Chief. Maybe he showed up as planned. Or maybe he asked you to meet him somewhere. But he was dead by eight o'clock that night."

"Ben Mashburn was my partner! How the hell could you think I would kill my partner? And what possible reason would I have for killing him in the first place?"

"He hadn't been your partner for almost twenty years, and a lot of water has gone under the bridge. But even if you didn't kill him—and I admit I don't know what the motive would be—you didn't do a thing when he didn't show up last Tuesday. And when Elliot Carter was found, you *still* didn't come forward with what you knew. And when Mashburn himself was found dead, you didn't come forward *then*! If that isn't felony obstruction, dereliction of duty and withholding evidence, I'm a fucking monkey's uncle."

"Wait a minute, Hollis!" MacKenzie said, holding up his hands. "Wait! You're right! I should've done something when Ben never showed up, but I thought maybe he was on to something. Then, when I still hadn't heard from him the next day, I thought he'd gone on a bender and was holed up somewhere. I still thought that, even when Carter was found, and I didn't want to get us both in trouble over something that looked like nobody needed to know about. I mean, I thought Carter's death was an accident. You know it would be really hard to fake something like that! And when Ben was found, I felt like shit about it, but I was sure he pulled the trigger himself. He'd talked about doing that before."

"You're so full of crap, MacKenzie," said Joplin, disgusted. "You've been around a long time, and especially with what you knew that we *didn't* know, these two deaths had to look like homicides to you almost from the very beginning."

"But I can help you turn this investigation around, Hollis!" cried MacKenzie, standing up. He looked desperate. "Like you said, I've been around a long time. We'll go talk to Mrs. Carter right now, and I promise you I'll find out where she got those photographs."

"I guess you haven't heard yet, Chief: Anne Carter is dead." Hollis looked at his watch. "She's probably being prepped for autopsy even as we speak. Besides," he added, "I don't really want to be your partner. I don't much like the way you treat them."

***

When Carrie first saw the body of Anne Carter, it was dressed in a white satiny nightgown that looked like a slip. The nails of the hands and feet were carefully lacquered in a pale pink shade, and the blonde hair was splayed against the metal autopsy table like gold on a silver tray. The face, without any make-up apparent, seemed peaceful. As in the proverbial cliché, she looked as if she were merely asleep.

After photographs of the front side of her body were taken, the nightgown was removed, and she and Jack examined every inch of skin on that side. Carrie found an injection site high up on Anne's right thigh, which was probably where Dr. Woodley had administered the Ativan, Jack told her. But after Tim took a picture of it, they continued to look for a second injection site. The initial report Hollis had turned in warned of the possibility that this was a homicide, not a suicide. If the contents of the stomach didn't show undigested pills, the possibility would become a probability, which meant the killing dose had been given to Anne Carter by another route. They made sure to check between fingers and toes, under the arms, in the labia, and on several flat moles that dotted the body. When no other needle marks were found on the ventral side, however, and Jack had noted the absence of any bruises, ligature marks or defensive wounds, they turned the body over.

It was then that any illusion that Anne Carter was sleeping was destroyed. The dark purplish coloring of liver mortis, where her blood had pooled, stained the entire back side of her body. It wasn't going to be easy to spot any needle marks, thought Carrie.

"Hand us some magnifying glasses, Eddie," said Jack, as if he were reading her mind.

Carrie took hers from Eddie and began to examine the back sides of Anne Carter's legs, while Tyndall concentrated on the upper part of the body. She was careful to check the creases between the buttocks and upper thighs. Again, no needle marks. When Tim had taken pictures of that side of the body, they took swab samples of all body cavities. Then Jack directed Eddie to prep the body for internal examination.

"I'm going to go start developing this roll," said Tim. "Call me when Eddie's through, okay?"

"Sure thing," said Jack. He waited until Tim had left the autopsy room, then turned to her. "I'm going to take a break while Eddie's working. Want to join me?"

Carrie shook her head. "I need to get instruments out of the autoclave and set up."

"Look, the instruments can wait a few minutes, Carrie. I think we need to talk."

"I don't," Carrie said firmly. Although she and Jack had continued to work together, she'd successfully avoided being alone with him for the past few days. She wanted to keep it that way. "I have two more weeks left on my rotation, and I don't want any more complications. That's not what I'm here for, Jack. You're very attractive and charming and so is Hollis. But I just don't want to get involved in an office romance. With either one of you," she added pointedly.

"Well, I'm not happy about it, but I understand." He reached over and lightly squeezed her upper arm. "Listen, Carrie, I—"

Whatever else Jack was going to say was interrupted by the loud buzz of a saw. She turned and saw Eddie making the y-shaped incision into Anne Carter's chest. Jack shrugged, let go of her arm, and headed for the door. Despite her earlier resolution, Carrie felt a wave of disappointment go through her.

When they all reassembled fifteen minutes later, Jack gave her a friendly smile, as if anxious to show her that he understood her decision. The internal examination began, with both Jack and Carrie intent on excising organs, noting their condition, and weighing them. From the lack of pulmonary edema in the lungs, which still looked pink and fluffy, it appeared that they had shut down suddenly, consistent with the effect that a powerful drug would have on the central nervous system. When the stomach was lifted from the abdominal cavity, they both focused on it.

"Well, there aren't any undissolved pills here," said Jack finally. "But there isn't anything else either. No undigested food or opaque liquids that might slow absorption."

"You mean if she took about ten Ativan at the same time on an empty stomach, there wouldn't be any still left in her stomach?" asked Carrie.

"Yes, but another possibility is that death would occur before all of the pills could be digested and absorbed. And given all the doubts that suicide might not be the manner of death, I don't particularly like the odds."

"Then what was the cause of death? There were no petechial hemorrhages, so she wasn't asphyxiated."

"A drug overdose, with death resulting from cardiopulmonary collapse."

"But the anal, vaginal and nasal mucosa appeared normal, so apparently no drug was administered by those routes."

Jack frowned, then turned back to the eviscerated body. "I think I have an idea how it was done, but let's see if there's anything in the brain tissues that might surprise us first."

The examination showed no evidence of any kind of seizure, bruising, or cerebral hemorrhage. After the brain had been weighed and samples taken, Jack replaced it, as well as the circular piece of skull Eddie had carved out, then pulled Anne Carter's scalp and face back into position. "Now hand me one of those magnifying glasses," he said.

"But we've already been over every inch of her skin," Carrie protested.

"Ever hear of the old Indian trick of hiding your trail by putting your footprints exactly where someone else has walked? Or in this case, where you yourself walked several hours before."

"I don't get—oh!" said Carrie suddenly. "You think a second, fatal dose of Ativan might have been administered through the same injection site."

"Exactly," said Jack, bending over Anne Carter's upper right thigh. "Only I can't tell with this thing. Hand me a scalpel." When Carrie had given it to him, he quickly excised a half-inch area of skin and muscle tissue at the site, to a depth that would follow the track of a syringe. Placing it carefully on a slide, he carried it over to the microscope. "Bingo," he said as he peered into the scope. "It's pretty hard to see, since twenty-one-gauge needles were used, but I can just make it out. Come here and take a look, Doctor."

When Carrie looked through the scope she saw what her naked eye couldn't, or even when she'd used the magnifying glass: two minutely overlapping hypodermic marks.

'That's amazing. How did you think of that?"

"It's just like with gunshot wounds," said Jack, looking a little smug. "Sometimes your initial examination of an entry wound seems to indicate a single bullet, but then you find two slugs, with slightly varied trajectories. When you look at the site more closely, you can see it. The histologist can lay it out in more detail."

"I'm impressed," said Carrie, hoping she didn't sound as star-struck as she felt. She was determined not to get pulled back into a relationship with Jack Tyndall. "I mean, that never would have occurred to me, frankly."

Jack smiled at her. "Isn't that what you're here for?"

37

"I THINK LEWIS MINTON needs to be informed of the mess MacKenzie's made as soon as possible, Hollis," said Captain Barrow, his hands flat on the top of his desk. Even sitting down, he was still an imposing man, with wide shoulders and the firm-jawed face of an Irish cop out of an old Cagney movie. "Don't you agree, Ike?"

"Most certainly," said Simmons. "I know Hollis doesn't want to bother the man, what with his recent surgery and all, but he has to know about this."

"I agree," said Joplin reluctantly. His cell phone rang just then, and he quickly answered it, hoping there might be some good news to tell Minton, along with the bad.

"Hollis, it's Jack. Thought you might want to hear about this as soon as possible."

Joplin was elated when Jack told him about the second, overlapping hypodermic mark on Anne Carter's body and his official ruling of homicide as the manner of death. It was the break they needed. "I don't care what they say about you, Jack, you're a good man," he said happily. "What was the actual cause of death?"

"Cardiopulmonary collapse due to a drug overdose. Probably Ativan, but we'll have to wait on the tox report."

"That's okay. The homicide ruling is the important thing. Thanks, buddy," he added, remembering the lingering tension between them earlier in the day. When he clicked off, Joplin filled Captain Barrow and Simmons in. Barrow seemed particularly relieved that they could now focus on the psychiatrist as the prime suspect. They all agreed that Simmons would contact the ADA who'd been following the case and see if they had enough on Woodley for an arrest warrant. At the very least, they would try to get a search warrant for his home and office in an effort to locate the syringe used and, possibly, more child pornography.

"I need to get this set of photographs MacKenzie gave me to Camp and Washington over in the Cold Case Unit, sir," said Joplin, looking at his watch.

"You go ahead," Captain Barrow urged him. "I'll call Dr. Minton myself."

Joplin stood up. "Thanks. Tell him I'll call him later." He turned to Simmons and said, "I'll stop by your desk as soon as I'm through. I want to hear what the ADA says."

"Don't hold your breath." Simmons heaved himself out of his chair. "It's Bernstein."

"Shit. She won't go to a judge for a search warrant unless the perp writes down what room in the house he hid the murder weapon."

"Yeah, she's a little cautious. But I think we've got enough on Dr. Woodley."

"Ike, I think you need to get Billy MacKenzie in here," said Barrow. "Get some kind of written statement from him. I don't know what Dr. Minton is going to do to him, but he's still a material witness in this case. In fact, don't let him know that we're focusing on Dr. Woodley. Let him think he's not off the hook yet."

"With pleasure," said Simmons.

Joplin and the detective walked out together, but parted ways at the end of the corridor. The Cold Case Unit was on the opposite side of the building from Homicide.

Damon Washington and Al Camp were both serious, hard-working detectives who were used to setbacks and dried-up leads and just kept doggedly plugging along. Although Simmons had gone over the case with them earlier in the day, Joplin told them the results of Anne Carter's autopsy and the status of their case against Paul Woodley, then related what Chief MacKenzie had admitted to him.

"These have the Property Control Unit stamp on the back," Joplin said, handing the manila envelope to Camp, "so at least we know that part is true."

"We sent the other set of photographs to CSU, Hollis," said Al Camp, a heavy-set man with broad shoulders and a paunch. "Haven't heard anything from them yet."

"Simmons said they were found taped to a bureau drawer belonging to that guy found dead in Piedmont Park," said Damon Washington, a short, slender, dapper-looking black man who always wore a bow tie.

Joplin nodded. "Actually, we're not sure about that. It was his estranged wife who said that, but she later took it back and now that she's dead, too, we can't follow up on it. CSU could check for tape residue, though."

"You think MacKenzie gave her the duplicates?" asked Camp.

"He says no, and for what it's worth, he checked these out after Mrs. Carter took the duplicates to Ben Mashburn."

"Yeah, but maybe MacKenzie checked these out another time, before last Monday," put in Washington. "Has anyone looked into that?"

"Nope, and that's a good idea," agreed Joplin. "Can you run that down?"

"Soon as we're through here," replied Camp.

"Did you guys ever come up with any leads when you got them four years ago?"

"Nothing that cracked the Greenleaf case, if that's what you mean," said Al Camp disgustedly. "We turned that guy's house inside-out—you know, the guy who died, who had the pictures in front of him when he croaked? Couldn't find a thing that connected him to Greenleaf, and his wife was dead, so we couldn't talk to her. The creep was a retired ortho-dontist, so we got head shots of all the kids in the photos and showed them to his former hygienist, but got nothing. And there'd never been any accusations about the guy molesting any of his patients. Then we posted the shots on the Missing Children's Information Center network. Two of the little girls had been kidnapped, also in 1987. The first one in Mobile, Alabama and the other one in Jackson, Mississippi. Neither one was ever found. They were seven and eight."

"About the only thing we were able to do was establish a motive for the Greenleaf kidnapping," said Washington sadly. "A multi-state child pornography ring. Some comfort for the parents, huh?"

"Hey, you did your best," said Joplin. "Maybe something will come out of the case we're working on."

"God, I hope so," said Washington, staring down at one of the pictures that showed Bobby Greenleaf. "That little boy needs to come home, one way or the other."

"Tom Halloran speaking."

"Mr. Halloran, it's Pauletta."

"Oh, God, I'm so glad you called, Pauletta. I called the house after I left the Ritz, but there was no answer, and I didn't know where you might be."

"A police officer took me to my sister's after they got finished there. Said they had to seal up the house while they were doing their investigation."

"Are you okay? They wouldn't let me go into the house, and I know that whole experience must have been terrible for you. I mean, you've been with Anne and Elliot since Trip was born."

"I'm doin' all right," Pauletta said, but her voice sounded husky with tears. "It's Trip I'm worried about. That boy has lost both his parents. How can God *do* this to that child?"

"I wish I had an answer to that. I guess a priest or a minister could come up with a reason, but I can't. And Trip's pretty devastated by this. Maggie and I spent some time with him, and Olivia's taking good care of him, but I just don't know how he's going to get through this."

Halloran heard the housekeeper blow her nose, and then she said, "It was bad enough when Mr. Carter died, because he and Trip were so close. But at least he still had his mama. Miss Anne was a busy, busy person, but she loved Trip. She truly did. And I just can't believe in my heart that she would kill herself and leave him all alone like this."

"I can't either, and I think Dr. Woodley knows a lot more than he's told the police. They were involved with each other, weren't they? He and Mrs. Carter, I mean."

"Him?" said Pauletta dismissively. "He was all the time acting like he owned the house and Miss Anne, too, but I don't think she loved him. Not by a long chalk," she added firmly, using an expression Halloran had heard many southern people use.

"What makes you think that?"

"Cause she just wasn't all that happy when he was here. I mean, she liked the way he took care of things and all, but I don't think he made her heart beat faster. I could be wrong, though, 'cause sometimes she'd be talkin' on the phone to him and her voice would get all dreamy and such. Like she was a young girl."

"Are you sure it was Dr. Woodley she was talking to then?"

There was a pause, and then the housekeeper said, "I don't know, Mr. Halloran, now you ask me that. But who else would it be?"

"It was just a thought," Halloran said. "By the way, did Trip ever see him professionally? I mean, a few years ago?"

"Trip?" Pauletta said, sounding puzzled. "Why would Trip be seein' Dr. Woodley?"

"I just thought maybe that was how he and Mrs. Carter met," Halloran replied, hoping he hadn't been too heavy-handed. "Listen, is there any way you could go see Trip? I know you'd be a great comfort to him."

"My brother-in-law said he'd take me when he got home tonight."

"That's great, Pauletta. And I want you to call me if you need anything."

After giving her his cell number, Halloran hung up, his mind still on their conversation. From the housekeeper's surprise over his question about Trip seeing Woodley professionally, he was now pretty sure Trip wasn't the boy in Woodley's article. He hadn't asked specifically whether Trip had ever been hospitalized, and possibly Pauletta might not have known the name of his therapist, but he doubted it. He was sure Betty, their twice-a-week cleaning lady, knew more about the Halloran family than he'd be comfortable about. Pauletta had also seemed fairly certain that Anne and Woodley weren't romantically involved, which surprised him. Or at least she didn't seem to think that *Anne* felt the same way that Woodley did.

While Halloran was trying to process all this, the phone rang again. It was Hollis Joplin, calling to tell him the results of Anne's autopsy and the decision to try to get search warrants for Woodley's home and office.

"This information is classified, Counselor," Joplin said. "I'm just letting you know because you were the one who put us onto Dr. Woodley in the first place."

"I appreciate it, although I don't have much hope that Woodley would keep any evidence in his home or office that would convict him of a capital crime. But I hope you get the warrants, and I don't intend to say anything about this to anyone. I'm just glad this whole nightmare might be coming to an end. For Trip Carter's sake especially."

"Well, it's not over yet. We still don't have any hard evidence on Woodley."

"Good luck finding it."

"Thanks," Joplin said.

The door to his office opened just as Halloran hung up. He was surprised to see David Healey and wondered how long he'd been standing outside the door. He hoped he hadn't overheard his conversation with Hollis Joplin about the warrants being prepared to search Woodley's home and office.

"Is it true?" Healey asked, standing awkwardly by the door. "About Anne?"

"Yes, David, it's true."

Healey's whole body seemed to sag. "I've been in a deposition all day and just picked up my messages a little while ago."

Halloran had never seen the man like this. His usual smugness was gone, replaced by a bewilderment that seemed sincere. "Why don't you come in and sit down, David?"

Healey nodded absently and walked to the chair in front of the desk. "I heard it was some kind of overdose." He sat down heavily and patted the pockets of his suit jacket as if looking for a cigarette, then gripped the arms of the chair.

"Probably Ativan," said Halloran noncommittally.

"God, I knew she was upset over Elliot's death, but I had no idea she'd do this."

"Had you talked to her lately? I mean, besides at the funeral?"

"Yes, of course! I told you we were friends, Tom. I've talked to her a couple of times since Elliot died. And she was distraught, but I never thought she might kill herself!"

"Neither did I," said Halloran.

"You know, I never believed your theory about Elliot being murdered. I still think the whole thing is preposterous. But I just *can't* believe this about Anne."

"Well, the police are looking into it."

"Good. And I hope they're taking a long look at Paul Woodley."

"Why do you say that, David? I didn't even know you knew him that well. Did you know each other at UGA?"

"I was in my second year of law school at UGA when Paul was a freshman in pre-med there, so we didn't see much of each other, but our families were connected socially."

"And Elliot was also a second-year law student then, right?"

"Yes."

"And you were all dating Anne that year—her freshman year."

Healey suddenly looked wary. "Why are you asking all these questions, Tom?"

Halloran shrugged. "Just trying to get a handle on the way things were then. I thought maybe it might help me understand Anne's relationship with Woodley. I haven't been able to figure out whether it was personal or professional."

"Well, it started out as purely professional, but Paul pushed the envelope, according to Anne. He's had the hots for her ever since college."

"But why would Anne even choose an old boyfriend as a therapist in the first place? And why would Paul Woodley accept her as a patient if he'd had a relationship with her in the past?"

David Healey stared out the window behind Halloran's head. "Anne was…insecure in many ways. I think she wanted a shoulder to cry on more than a therapist. And it stroked her ego at a bad time in her life to have Paul Woodley still interested in her. You'll have to ask him why he didn't think it was unethical for him to treat an old flame."

Halloran knew he was about to fall back down the slippery slope of playing detective, but he couldn't help himself. "Did she cry on his shoulder about seven years ago when she found out she couldn't have any more children, David?" he asked.

Healey's eyes flashed at him. "What the hell do you mean by that?"

"Olivia told me that Anne had an affair after she'd consulted a fertility specialist. It sounds to me like Paul Woodley may have been the man she was involved with."

"Not on your life! She may have let Paul think he had a chance once Elliot left her, but she wouldn't jeopardize her marriage with a cold fish like that."

"Then who, David? Was it you? Was she willing to jeopardize it with you?"

"Why the fuck are you doing this, Halloran?" Healey said, jumping up. "Anne is dead! What good does it do to bring all this up?"

"It's *because* she's dead, that's why. I think Anne *and* Elliot were murdered—and Ben Mashburn, too. And I'm convinced that it had something to do with the affair she had and the reason that Elliot left her. This morning I met with a Dr. Greer, Elliot's urologist. He told me that last summer he gave Elliot a battery of tests, including a fertility test, and that he told Elliot that he'd been sterile all his life. I think that's why he left Anne. He found out he could never have fathered Trip. That she had lied to him to get him to marry her."

"Elliot loved Trip," Healey insisted. "He wouldn't have cared if he weren't his biological son."

"I agree with you. But I don't think that was what finally drove Elliot away. Even the affair she'd had hadn't destroyed the marriage. But when he realized the real reason for the affair—I'm pretty sure now that it was with you, David—when he realized that, he found out he couldn't stay with her, no matter how much he loved Trip."

"And what was the *real reason* for the affair, Tom? Couldn't it have been because she cared about me? I know you don't think I'm a very lovable guy, but maybe Anne did."

"Oh, I'm sure she did, especially when you agreed to help her. She didn't think she was jeopardizing her marriage when she slept with you. She was trying to save it."

Healey barked out a laugh. "That's the craziest theory you've had yet, Tom."

"Is it? What if Anne found out from all the fertility testing she went through that the problem wasn't with her? The next step is to test the husband. And Anne must have heard Olivia talk about taking DES when she was pregnant and realized that it had made Elliot sterile. They'd been trying to have another baby for years. But if Elliot found out he'd always been sterile, he would know she'd lied about Trip being his. So she asked you to do her a little favor. To get her pregnant. And when it hit Elliot after he'd been to see Dr. Greer that she had lied to get him to marry her and then lied again when she told him why she'd had the affair seven years ago, he couldn't handle it."

"She thought that he would forgive her again," said Healey, sounding tired now. He sat back down heavily in his chair. "But he didn't—couldn't, I guess."

"So she hired Ben Mashburn to try to find something that would help her negotiate a settlement. Only he couldn't find anything on Elliot."

"No, and she started to really panic after that. She was sure that even though Bart Lawson was representing Elliot for the divorce, that you'd be calling all the shots. She was terrified of that and thought she'd end up with nothing."

Halloran was stunned. His mind raced to the inevitable conclusion that he, himself, might have been the trigger that set Anne and whoever had conspired with her on a course that led to three murders. And that other person might be looking at him right then.

"Are you Trip's father, David?" he asked.

Healey gave a long sigh. "I honestly don't know. I *think* I am, from some things Anne said to me. But she was involved with a few other guys back then."

"So even Woodley could be his father?"

He shrugged. "It's possible."

"Did she try to get either one of you to marry her?"

"Yes, God help me, she did. But I was already engaged to Eleanor by then, and both our families expected us to marry. I told Anne I'd pay for an abortion, but she didn't want that kind of help. I have no idea if she approached Paul. The semester ended in May, and she married Elliot in June. And although I've carried a little bit of a torch for Anne all these years and even agreed to help her when she wanted to get pregnant again, it never went any further than that. I didn't have anything to do with Elliot's death, Tom."

"So you say, David."

"I've been very honest with you about all of this," said Healey, standing up again. "But you're way out in left field if you think I had anything to do with Elliot's death. Or Anne's, for God's sake. I loved her. Part of me will always love her," he added, then turned and walked out the door.

38

JOPLIN RETURNED TO THE ME'S OFFICE a little before five o'clock. His shift was technically over, but he still had some paperwork to do, and his years as a homicide detective had caused him to see shift times as mere suggestions. When he was finished, however, he intended to go have a drink before going home. Maybe two drinks, he decided; it had been a hell of a day.

Passing through the administrative department, he saw that Jack Tyndall's office door was open. The pathologist was hunched over his computer as usual, but looked up when Joplin entered the room. "Hey, Hollis. Anything new? Dr. Woodley in custody yet?"

"I wish. Janice Bernstein is being her usual tight-assed self. She claims we don't have enough to arrest him yet, and she wants to review everything before she requests a search warrant. Says it has to be very specific or her judge won't even consider it with someone as prominent as Woodley. Listen, you want to go have a drink in about an hour? I think we both deserve one."

Tyndall stretched out his long arms and yawned. "You're right about that, Hollis, but I just can't do it. I need to finish what I can on this Carter report and head home. All I want to do is sleep."

"You're getting old, Jack," said Joplin, shaking his head, but he wondered if Tyndall still felt awkward over the Carrie situation. "You've never turned down a drink before."

"Maybe I'm finally growing up, Hollis. You think that's possible?"

Joplin eyed the pathologist. "You're serious, aren't you, Jack?"

"Yeah, I guess I am. It's about time, wouldn't you say?"

"I have a sneaking suspicion this has more to do with Carrie than anything else."

"Maybe it does. But I'm also going through a second divorce, and I turned forty last year. And if that's not enough, I'm surrounded by constant reminders that life is altogether too short." Tyndall grinned self-consciously, as if embarrassed by his own feelings. "Is that profound enough for you?"

"It's beyond my wildest dreams," Joplin replied, trying to keep his tone light. "In fact, you're scaring me. The next thing I know, you'll be on the Dr. Phil show."

"Don't worry." Tyndall turned back to his computer. "It probably won't last long."

But as he walked to the investigators' office, Joplin did worry. He'd never seen Jack like this before, and he was certain Carrie was the reason. The worst thing was, Jack was his friend, and he really wanted him to find some kind of lasting happiness. He'd been especially worried about him when he'd jumped into the latest affair with Bambi or Candy, or whatever her name was, and screwed up his current marriage. Since then, Jack had become even more of a workaholic, practically living at the ME's office. And he'd begun throwing out comments about Lewis Minton's health and the fact that he should retire, as well as ideas on how the office should be run. As Chief Deputy ME, he was next in line for Minton's job, and his impatience had been showing lately.

Now it looked like Jack had a chance to get his priorities in line. Joplin felt he should be happy for him, but not if it meant he couldn't go on seeing Carrie. In some ways, he was just like Jack, certainly as much of a workaholic. The few times he'd spent with Carrie, however, had expanded the shrunken universe he'd created for himself when his own marriage imploded.

Joplin continued to brood at his desk. He was the only one in the office; both of the evening shift investigators must be out on scenes.

MacKenzie's light was out, too. Joplin hoped Ike Simmons had been able to talk him into going to the station and making a statement. He wondered briefly what had gone on at that meeting, if so, then he was back to his brooding. While he was contemplating whether to call Carrie at home that night, his desk phone rang.

"Don't you ever go home?" asked Simmons, when he answered it.

"Soon, Ike, I promise. And I've decided you're absolutely right: I have no life and I don't take care of myself."

"Well, we can't fix that today, so I'll tell you why I called: First of all, MacKenzie got down off his high horse and had a heart-to-heart with me. Admitted it was pretty much the way you put it to him this afternoon. One thing he remembered is that Mashburn told him that he planned to contact Elliot Carter. MacKenzie said that was a bad idea, but Ben thought he could find out more about the photos, and he didn't seem to think Carter was a threat."

"Well, we know that's true from the phone records. But it doesn't explain how the two of them ended up dead the next morning."

"Maybe Elliot Carter called or went to see Anne, who then contacted Dr. Woodley," suggested Simmons. "Or maybe Mashburn said something to scare her when she called his office at four-forty that day, and that's when she called Woodley. Then he arranged a meeting or separate meetings with Carter and Mashburn and killed them both."

"But why? In the first place, I don't understand why Woodley would be helping Anne Carter to blackmail her husband. He had money of his own, from what I can tell."

"Yeah," said Simmons. "He had some family money and a successful practice, but according to what we've heard, it was his former wife who had the big bucks. She was the daughter of a former CEO of Coca-Cola during the sixties. And the rumor is, Woodley lost a bundle in the stock market when the bottom fell out in '08."

"And Anne Carter wasn't going to get much of a settlement, according to Halloran," finished Joplin. "Okay, so Woodley was helping her blackmail her husband by providing her with the photos. Then, the whole thing starts falling apart once Anne takes the pictures to Ben Mashburn and he recognizes them as the ones MacKenzie showed him four years ago. Question: Why take them to Mashburn in the first place? Why not just show Carter the pictures and threaten to go to the police unless he pays up?"

"We asked MacKenzie the same thing. He said Mashburn thought Mrs. Carter was usin' him. She knew he was a retired cop and thought he could scare Elliot Carter into paying up, but without goin' to the police for real. She wanted a middleman and thought he'd go along with it for enough money. What she didn't know was that he'd been one of the detectives on the Greenleaf case and that he'd seen those pictures before."

"She also didn't know he was an honest man," said Joplin. "Okay, so the blackmail scheme backfires. But why would Woodley step out of the shadows and contact Carter and Mashburn?"

"Maybe they made it clear to Anne Carter that they weren't goin' to let the thing go and pretend it never happened. If it was somehow proven that Woodley had given the photos to her, his goose was cooked without even throwin' in the blackmail scheme."

"Because possession of child pornography is a federal offense, and he's also a mandated reporter if he discovers evidence of child abuse," finished Joplin. "I mean, if he actually did get those photos from one of his patients."

"Exactly. He would have lost his license *and* faced criminal charges."

"Well, I know Anne Carter was a willing participant in the blackmail scheme," Joplin said, "but I just can't see her going along with murder. When I interviewed her after Carter died, I felt she knew more than she was telling me, but I thought she might be protecting someone. And she gave Halloran the impression that the whole thing was like some kind of runaway train that was steamrolling her, too."

"I can't answer that question, Hollis. The fact that she was murdered means she became a danger to Woodley at some point. Maybe he'd been able to convince her for a while that Carter's death was just what it looked like, and that Ben Mashburn fell off the wagon and killed himself. But when Halloran told her that Woodley had written an article about a patient who had practiced autoerotic asphyxia, she totally lost it. I figure she told Woodley that she knew what he had done. So he knocks her out, then goes to her house that night and finishes the job." Simmons paused, then said, "Of course, another scenario is that she was in it up to her neck, the whole time. The way Carter died showed real hatred on the part of someone, and a rejected wife sure fits that bill. Blackmailin' him with child pornography was pretty damned nasty, too."

"You're right about that," said Joplin. "I guess I just still feel like I'm missing some piece of the puzzle, that's all."

"Go home, Hollis. Call that pretty doctor and let her know you're still in the game."

"I think I will, Simmons," said Joplin. "I think that's exactly what I'll do."

Quincy was happily eating some of the fried chicken tenders Joplin had picked up at a Mrs. Winners on the way home, and Joplin was sipping a not-too-strong glass of Jim Beam and water when his cell phone rang. He'd left a message for Carrie before fixing the drink and for a few seconds, he was able to hope that she was returning his call. Then Tom Halloran identified himself.

"What's up, Counselor?"

"I had a conversation with David Healey that I think you should know about."

Joplin listened as Halloran told him about Anne Carter's involvement with Healey in college and her affair with him seven years ago.

"David admitted that Elliot confronted Anne when he found out that he couldn't have been Trip's father, and he accused her of sleeping with David back then just to get pregnant again."

"Was he right?"

"Yes, which is why Elliot ultimately moved out. By the way, David is pretty sure *he's* Trip's father."

"Well, all of that *is* interesting," said Joplin, "and it goes along with what the urologist told you. But I just don't see how Healey could have injected Mrs. Carter with Ativan."

"Before he became our managing partner, David headed up the Medical Malpractice department. He still handles the litigation for our biggest client. He knows a ton of doctors, and I'm sure he'd have access to things like syringes and Ativan."

"Maybe," Joplin admitted. "But my money's still on Woodley. Homicide discovered that his financial situation's pretty rocky. It was his ex-wife who had all the money. From what you've told me about David Healey, his personal fortune is pretty significant. He wouldn't care how much money Anne Carter got in a settlement, but Dr. Woodley definitely would. And I'm convinced that Elliot Carter's murder—and Mashburn's and Anne Carter's, too—was the result of a blackmail scheme that backfired."

"Look, I know I'm the one who's been pushing Woodley from the very beginning, but I'm starting to have some doubts. If Paul Woodley were the type of person who could cold-bloodedly murder three people, why didn't he just kill his wife before she could divorce him? He would have ended up with a lot more money that way."

"True," said Joplin. "But the three murders were committed to keep the murderer from being exposed—out of necessity, in a way. That's a lot different from a premeditated murder for money. But I'll pass everything you've told me on to Detective Simmons. He's in charge of the case now. And I have to admit, you've made a pretty credible case for David Healey as a suspect. I promise I'll talk to Ike about this in the morning."

"I appreciate that. Sorry I bothered you at home."

"No problem," said Joplin. But after he hung up, he wondered if what Halloran had told him could, in fact, become a problem. They didn't really have any hard evidence on Woodley— everything was entirely circumstantial at this point, as Janice Bernstein had made clear. If Ike thought David Healey looked just as good for the murders as Paul Woodley, he would have to share that with Bernstein, who would be even more reluctant to ask her judge for an arrest warrant or even a search warrant for the psychiatrist until they had narrowed their sights and/or had more evidence.

Joplin took another long sip of his drink and decided to call Jack Tyndall. Maybe he could help eliminate Healey in some way. But when he punched in Jack's home number, the voice mail clicked on after three rings. He remembered that Jack was already gone by the time he himself had left the ME's office. The Jim Beam roiled his stomach as he considered the possibility that he and Carrie were together somewhere. His mind searched for more palatable explanations after he once more tapped out Carrie's cell phone number, only to get her voice mail again: Jack had stopped off somewhere to get something to eat. He had gone to see his children. He had been in a car accident on the way home and wasn't dead, but he wouldn't be able to date anyone for a very long time.

"You are one sick bastard, Hollis," he said aloud as he got up and trudged out to the kitchen. He didn't feel like eating anything, much less fried chicken, but it was the only way he could justify having another drink.

And he really needed another drink.

39

CARRIE SALINGER FELT A curious mixture of guilt and anticipation as she sat at the bar of Twist in Phipps Plaza and waited for Jack. The guilt, she knew, was because of her parents and Hollis Joplin. Her parents would never approve of a Gentile who'd been married twice. Not that they'd be any happier with Hollis either. As for Hollis himself—well, she knew what Hollis would think about her meeting Jack. Frankly, she wouldn't blame him. But the anticipation she felt as she kept glancing at the revolving door on the Peachtree entrance was just as powerful as the guilt. Maybe more so.

She knew she was acting like a silly teenage girl, but she couldn't seem to help it. She had never allowed herself to be that way during her adolescence, and that, she knew, was part of the reason she was there. At first she had held firm, telling Jack when he called that she couldn't see him. But he had worn her down, saying, "Just hear me out, Carrie, that's all I ask." She heard the yearning in his voice, and it was matched by a yearning in her own heart and body. Finally, she agreed to meet him at Twist. But later, when the sound of his voice had faded, she began berating herself for being so easily swayed.

Carrie took a cleansing breath of air, followed by a very big swallow of her pinot noir, and forced herself to look around. She had never been in Twist, a fusion tapas restaurant that was wildly popular with young professionals. Carrie liked the energy generated by the long bar, which snaked from one side of the wide room to the other in an undulating curve that incorporated a raw bar and a sushi bar. She had noticed it once during one of her very rare shopping trips to Phipps and thought it looked sophisticated and hip.

The revolving door spun round, and she looked over to see Jack scanning the room. His eyes found her, and his face creased into that smile that made her feel like anything was possible. Carrie began to smile, too, and watched as he crossed the room to her.

The next few hours passed in a blur of talking, drinking and ordering food, but eating very little of it. She finished off the pinot as Jack sat down next to her and thanked her again for meeting him, then said yes to another glass when he gave his drink order to the server. They settled on a few tapas when the server returned, and Carrie willed herself to sip her second wine slowly. But when the food arrived, she barely touched it, only nibbling from time to time on a piece of pita bread without the hummus.

Jack had to lean close to her to be heard above the raucous din of the restaurant. He was wearing the same cologne he'd worn when he'd taken her to lunch, and it suddenly seemed as intoxicating as the wine. He wasn't sporting a navy blazer this time, but he'd rolled down the sleeves of his yellow oxford shirt and combed his hair since Anne Carter's autopsy. What was most in Jack's favor, however, was that he wasn't trying to be witty or charming. Instead, he seemed to be letting his guard down, revealing himself to be far more sensitive—even vulnerable—than she'd ever seen him. Carrie had seen glimpses of this other side of Jack in the past few weeks, but now she felt as if she were getting to know him for the first time.

"I had no right to do that to you this morning," he said slowly, emphasizing each word. "Kiss you like that. Without asking you, or at least waiting until you got to know me better."

Carrie felt the usual hated flush, exacerbated by wine, spread over her face. "Well, maybe I overreacted."

"No, you didn't," he said, looking right into her eyes. "I told you when I took you to lunch that I was going to start changing some things in my life, and even though I made it sound like a big joke, I meant it. And then I screwed up."

Carrie broke eye contact with him and gestured toward the appetizers. "We'd better eat some of this," she said nervously. She smeared a piece of pita with hummus and swallowed it quickly, hoping it would absorb some of the alcohol she'd consumed.

But the rest of the food remained untouched as Jack hesitantly began to peel away some of the layers that had kept her from seeing what might be underneath. Carrie listened as he told her about growing up with an alcoholic mother who'd essentially depended on him for everything whenever her current boyfriend grew tired of her.

"What about your father? Was he around?"

Jack shrugged. "He lived in the same town, but he was married when he got my mother pregnant. He paid child support, but made it clear he didn't want anything to do with me. And the check he sent didn't cover much."

"How did you and your mother live? Did she work?"

His eyes shifted away from her, as if he were looking into the past. "When she could. When she felt up to it. Mostly, she let the men who moved in with us pay for things. But those times didn't last very long." He looked back at her. "So I'd do odd jobs for the neighbors and sometimes—"

"Sometimes...what?" she asked when he didn't finish.

"Look, you don't want to know all this," Jack said, running a hand through his hair.

"Yes, I do," Carrie insisted, although she could tell he was very uncomfortable. "It's helping me understand you a little better. But if you don't want to talk—"

"I used to steal," he blurted out. "From the men who stayed with us. Just a little bit. Not so much that they'd notice it; just enough so that we'd have something when they left. And not from the nice ones," he added quickly, as if she might judge the actions of a desperate child. "Unfortunately, they were the ones who left pretty soon."

"I can't imagine growing up like that," Carrie said, thinking of her own very privileged childhood. "Didn't you have any relatives who could help? Or a teacher you could confide in?"

Jack shrugged again. "Not really. And I knew from some kids in school who were in foster care that that could be even worse than what

I was dealing with, so I just…handled it." He ran his hand through his hair again, then said, "Listen, Carrie, I'm not telling you these things so I can blame my mother for my failed marriages or all the running around I've done. She was sick. I knew that even then. But it did make it hard for me to trust people."

"Women in particular, I guess," said Carrie, looking down at the stem of her empty wine glass as she twirled it absently.

"Yes, women in particular," Jack agreed. "And they didn't deserve the consequences of that lack of trust. I accept full responsibility for that. At least, I'm trying to," he added earnestly. "Because of you. I don't want to screw things up with you any more than I already have."

Carrie looked up at him. "That's a lot to put on me, Jack," she said, disturbed by what he was telling her. "I still barely know you, despite everything you've shared with me tonight. And you barely know me," she added pointedly. "I may not be who or what you think I am—or what you want."

Jack nodded emphatically. "You're absolutely right. But that doesn't mean we can't *get* to know each other, does it? My divorce will be final soon, and your rotation at the ME's office will be over in a few weeks. We can wait until then, if that would make you feel more comfortable. Will you at least think about it?"

Carrie was spared having to give an answer by the arrival of the pretty young server. "Another round?" she asked, smiling brightly.

He walked her to her car, which was parked next to Nordstrom's. Carrie had made herself eat some more, but the closer they got to the lot, she knew it wasn't enough to combat the effects of three glasses of wine in an hour and a half. Jack must have realized this, too, because as she fumbled for her keys, he insisted on driving her home.

"I just live right down Lenox Road," she said, certain that she could at least navigate the half-mile to her condominium. "I'll be fine. Really."

"I'm not so sure of that. And since it's so close, I can just drop you and your car off and walk back here."

Carrie wavered, preferring to go home by herself, but not wanting to run the risk of getting a DUI. Or worse. She'd seen too many drunk drivers—or their victims—at Grady to take that kind of a chance. Why, she wondered, couldn't she have stopped at one glass of wine? Or even two? The stress of the week, plus everything Jack had told her, had certainly gotten to her.

"I guess that might be a good idea," she admitted. "I do feel a little light-headed."

As they drove past Lenox Square, the even larger mall catty-cornered to Phipps Plaza, and then past the Marta station, Carrie was glad she'd accepted Jack's offer. She couldn't remember the last time she'd had too much to drink; it just wasn't something she did. Her internship and residency had been too grueling, without also having to deal with hangovers. And she'd never liked the feeling of being out of control.

"It's just down this hill on the left," she directed Jack. "The Regency," she added, pointing to a gated entrance. She gave him the code, and the gates swung into a small complex of three-story brick townhouses. "Mine's the fourth one on the right. You can just park in the driveway."

"Very nice," said Jack. "And you're only about ten minutes from the ME's office. Sure you won't reconsider applying for a fellowship there?"

"You've given me enough to think about for one night, Dr. Tyndall, don't you think?"

"You're absolutely right," he answered, opening the car door. "And I'd rather you concentrate on that." He came around to her side and took her hand to help her out, then handed her the keys. "I give door-to-door service," he added, then escorted her up the four brick steps.

Carrie managed to open the door without too much fumbling and turned back to thank him. Instead, Jack leaned toward her and gave her what started out to be a sweet, almost chaste kiss, but quickly turned into a replay of the one in his office. Only this time it was Carrie who was more insistent, compelled by needs and feelings she had repressed for far too long. She felt his hand begin to caress her left breast through her silk sweater, then he slipped it under the thin fabric.

They didn't make it to the bedroom. He pulled her carefully down to the floor in front of the fireplace, his face suffused by a tender intensity that she had never seen on him. Lifting up her sweater, he began to kiss her breasts, and Carrie thought she might come right then. She tilted her pelvis upward, and he responded by forcing her narrow skirt up over her thighs until it was bunched around her waist. His mouth found her breast again, then he slid his hand into the leg opening of her bikini panties, massaging her with his thumb in soft, slow strokes. Carrie let go and surrendered herself to the orgasm, feeling liquid spasms gripping her over and over. She came again as soon as he entered her, a shorter but more intense orgasm this time. Carrie rocked with him as his thrusts grew harder and deeper. She came one more time, just before he did, gripping his shoulders and half raising herself up as the knife-like intensity hit her. He crushed her to him, crying out something unintelligible before collapsing on top of her.

40

FORTUNATELY FOR HIS ACHING HEAD and queasy stomach, Joplin was off that Friday. He managed to sleep until a little after eight, when Quincy began his bag-rustling routine. Groaning, he lurched out of bed and into the kitchen as he tried to shush the now meowing cat. The smell of the Whiskas canned chicken and liver really got to him as he dumped it into a clean bowl, and he decided against bending over to put it on the floor. Instead, he set it on the table and made coaxing noises to Quincy until the cat got the point and jumped up beside it.

Joplin sat down heavily in one of the kitchen chairs and massaged his temples, wondering if he should make some coffee or try to settle his stomach with a Coke instead. The Coke won out, but before he could get it, his cell phone rang. He answered it, hoping this time it *wasn't* Carrie returning his call. He hadn't had a chance to use his voice yet.

"Hello," he croaked, glancing at the woefully low level of bourbon in the bottle of Jim Beam on the kitchen counter.

"I sure hope you sound so bad because you were out late with a certain female pathologist last night," said Ike Simmons.

"I wish."

"I just wanted to let you know that Washington talked to someone at Property Control, and MacKenzie did *not* check those photos out before last Monday. So he couldn't have made copies beforehand and given them to Anne Carter. I know he's not your favorite person, Hollis, and he's certainly guilty of dereliction and suppressin' evidence, but I don't see him for these murders. Woodley's our man; even Janice Bernstein believes that. She's just makin' sure we have all our ducks in a row before she takes a warrant to her judge."

Joplin sighed. "Well, we might have one more duck to add to the row," he said and told Simmons about Tom Halloran's conversation with David Healey.

Simmons gave a long, low whistle. "That lady sure did get around, Hollis."

"Tell me about it. And Halloran made a pretty good case for putting Healey on the short list of suspects. Ahead of Woodley, even, so I guess you better fill Bernstein in."

"Yeah, but that means she'll hold off on requestin' the search warrants on Woodley until we rule out Healey. And we can't ask for warrants on both of them; Judge Hoffman will just say we're on a fishin' expedition."

"Story of our lives, Ike."

"I know that's right! I just wish I hadn't called you this morning, is all."

"And I wish I hadn't answered, believe me. Keep me posted, okay?"

"Will do."

Joplin ended the call, then rooted around in the refrigerator for a can of Coke. After he let Quincy out, he shuffled down the hall to his bedroom, hoping a shower would revive him.

Carrie wanted desperately to call in sick that morning, unable to contemplate facing Jack or, God forbid, Hollis Joplin. She was sure that Hollis would be able to take one look at her and know that she'd slept with Jack, and as for Jack—well, she wasn't really sure why she didn't want to see him just yet.

They had showered together last night after making love. Carrie was still feeling the effects of the wine then, but the water had a sobering impact on her, and she quickly threw on her long terry robe after getting out of the shower. Once she'd handed Jack a clean towel, she had scuttled from the bathroom, announcing as she left that she would make them an omelet.

Remorse had begun to set in. Big time.

It must have shown on her face, because when Jack came out to the kitchen a few minutes later, fully clothed, he started apologizing. "I shouldn't have come in with you tonight," he'd said. "You weren't ready for this."

Carrie mustered up a smile. "I'm a big girl, Jack. I told you that before."

"Yes, but even big girls have too much to drink, and I should've—"

"Fought me off? Unfortunately, despite the alcoholic fog, I can remember everything that happened, and I think *I* put the moves on *you*."

Jack had shoved his hands in his pockets and grinned at her, managing to look both boyish and incredibly sexy at the same time. "Well," he said, "since you put it that way, I guess I'm the one who should be forgiving *you* for taking advantage of *me*. You can make it up to me by feeding me. I'm starving."

Carrie began laughing, unable to take herself so seriously after that. So they had eaten the omelet and then somehow ended up in her bed. They had made love again, but slowly this time, with clear heads and maybe even an open heart on Carrie's part. Jack had left at dawn after kissing her and saying he would lock the door on his way out.

But now, with sunlight bulldozing its way into her bedroom, making her want to pull the covers up over her head, Carrie's doubts about getting involved with someone she worked with resurfaced. Someone who wasn't even *divorced* yet, she reminded herself. Without Jack next to her to distract her from all the reasons why last night had been a huge mistake, the remorse she'd been feeling earlier returned. She wasn't a prude and she hadn't been a virgin for a long time, but she still felt a little…cheap. She wasn't in the habit of sleeping with men on the first date—if their meeting at Twist could even be called a date. And just five days ago, she'd been thinking about the possibility of a relationship with Hollis Joplin once she'd finished her rotation at the ME's office! *What had happened to her?* she wondered. What kind of a person was she anyway?

The kind who gets up and goes to work even when she feels like hell, Carrie thought resignedly as she headed off to the bathroom for yet another shower.

Ike Simmons called Joplin around one that afternoon to let him know that Janice Bernstein was, indeed, going to hold off on submitting their requests for search warrants for Woodley's home and office until they had more evidence—on either Woodley or David Healey.

"Goddamn Halloran!" Joplin said heatedly. "If he hadn't poked his ugly legal nose into this investigation, we'd have those warrants by now."

"Yeah, I hate it when we get too much information on suspects," Ike replied dryly. "Civilians just keep helpin' us out too much lately. Makes us look bad."

"You know damn well what I mean, Ike. This whole line on Healey will turn out to be a dead end, and in the meantime, Woodley is probably destroying evidence as we speak."

Simmons sighed heavily. "Yeah, I know. Think Jack could come up with something more to link Woodley to Anne Carter's murder? Or maybe even the other two, now that we're sure they were homicides?"

"It's worth a shot," Joplin said, remembering that he'd tried to call Jack the night before to see if he could do just that. And then he'd become convinced that Jack and Carrie were together somewhere, and he'd gotten drunk. "I'll call him right now," he added, vowing that he wouldn't let his nonexistent love life interfere with his job from now on.

But when Joplin got Jack on the phone and identified himself, there was a long pause, and all of his fears that Jack and Carrie had been together the night before came flooding back. "You there, Jack?" he asked finally.

"Yeah, Hollis, I'm here," Jack said, sounding very guilty to Joplin's ears. "What's up? I thought you were off today."

"I am, but I just got a call from Simmons."

Joplin pushed aside all thoughts of Carrie and Jack together—at least for the moment—and filled the pathologist in on the latest obstacle with the search warrants.

"Anne Carter was involved with David Healey, too?" Jack said when he'd finished. "My God, that lady makes me look like a choir boy! I really wish I'd had a chance to meet her. Alive, I mean," he added.

"Yeah, I know what you mean, Jack." Joplin said, suddenly wishing he'd introduced Elliot Carter's beautiful widow to Jack the day she'd come to identify her husband. Maybe his friend would have set his sights on her instead of Carrie Salinger. And maybe she'd still be alive, he thought, although that didn't seem likely. "Do you think you could go through the Carters' autopsy reports and see if anything hits you? Anything that might point to Woodley as the prime suspect? I'll go through Dr.

Minton's report on Mashburn tomorrow when I get into the office. I know you're probably up to your ears today, but maybe sometime this weekend? You got anything important going on this weekend?"

There was another long pause, and Joplin closed his eyes, certain now that Jack would be spending time with Carrie on the weekend. And certain that Jack knew that he knew.

"I think I can find some time, Hollis. I'll call you if anything turns up."

"You're the best, Jack," Joplin said and hung up.

There was no phone call from Jack on Friday night. Joplin thought about calling him around ten and even picked up the phone, but decided against it. And since Carrie hadn't bothered to respond to his message from Thursday, he knew better than to call her. Making a superhuman effort to get some control over his life, he managed to make it through the evening with only two drinks, albeit strong ones. He got through his shift the next day by concentrating on work, going out on a homicide scene in Alpharetta, then a traffic fatality in Midtown. After writing up his reports, he spent some time poring over Ben Mashburn's autopsy report, with disappointing results. Nothing at either the scene or during the autopsy tied Woodley directly to the murder.

When his shift finally ended at four, he stopped at the Publix near Lenox Square on his way home and stocked up on things he'd been out of for days. He also bought some bagged salad greens, a sweet potato, and a rib eye steak; he'd been eating too much fast food lately. Once back at his apartment, however, Joplin put away the groceries, fed Quincy, and sat down in front of the TV with a bag of Nacho Doritos and a drink. He didn't want to jump into healthy eating too quickly; he needed to ease into it, maybe after another drink, he decided. The six o'clock news, with its coverage of more deaths in Afghanistan, more ups and downs in the stock market, another local bank going under, and rising gas prices for the coming summer months, depressed him even further. He got up and slumped off to the kitchen to make another drink, wondering where the hell Jack and Carrie were.

And, most especially, what the hell they were doing.

***

Carrie was making dinner for Jack that night. Something Italian, she decided as she walked into the Fresh Market on Roswell Road. Pasta? she wondered. Maybe rack of lamb slathered in garlic and rosemary? She wandered down the produce aisle, picking up raspberries to top chocolate gelato, a small container of peeled garlic cloves, and arugula and pears for a salad. Those items she knew she would need; she'd come back for anything else once she decided on the main course. And once she got to the fish counter and saw the large, pink shrimp and the glistening sea scallops, she knew she wanted to make Jack the seafood stew in a cookbook by Giada De Laurentiis that she'd made a few times before. Carrie added two pounds of mussels to her order and moved on to the bread department, plucking a round rosemary loaf from a table and breathing in its rustic perfume before putting it in her cart. She zipped back to the produce section to get some fresh basil, then found a nice block of parmigiano reggiano in the cheese area. After gathering a can of San Marzanno tomatoes, some Pellegrino water, the gelato, and a few bottles of Prosecco, she had everything.

Everything but flowers, she realized, and hurried back to get them. She found a nice mixed bouquet and then got in line to check out. She had about an hour before Jack would get to her condominium, and she could cook once he arrived, but she wanted to shower and change clothes before that. Her body was still humming from the sex they'd had Friday night and again this morning, but she was already anticipating being with him that night. The thought of being wrapped in his arms when she opened the door and then kissing him hello made her smile. The cashier smiled back at her and motioned her forward, and she realized that the people in front of her had already checked out while she'd been daydreaming.

She was going to hell in a wheelbarrow, that was for sure.

And she didn't care.

By Sunday afternoon, Joplin's blue funk was more pronounced than ever. He was hung over and tired after another night of drinking and not sleeping well; he was also still waiting on a phone call from Jack. Although he'd admitted to himself that Jack had simply been unable to find anything in either of the Carters' autopsy reports to nail Dr.

Woodley, he didn't believe it. He was sure the pathologist was just way too busy with Carrie Salinger to give catching a murderer any thought.

Determined not to call Jack, Joplin started happy hour early instead. He knew he was getting into a very bad rut, but he couldn't seem to care very much. Why, he wondered, did the whole Jack-Carrie thing bother him so much? He had fallen pretty hard for Carrie, but he'd really only known her about three weeks. Then a blindingly vivid memory of her across the table from him at D'Angelo's the week before made him pause as he lifted the glass of Jim Beam to his lips. She was smiling at him as she stood up to go to the ladies' room, and as she walked away, her cute little behind swaying ever so slightly, he remembered feeling that he had always known her. That he had dreamed about her before he even met her. That he had been waiting for her even when he'd been married to Beth Ann. That everything he had seen and done and thought about was only a prelude to the day that he had walked into the conference room at the ME's office and met her for the first time.

The image of Carrie walking away from him seemed to go on forever. When it faded, he realized that, however long he had known her, keeping her in his life had somehow become more important to him than anything else.

And so far, he had failed miserably.

41

JACK WAS ACTUALLY WAITING for him in the investigators' room when Joplin got to work Monday morning. He couldn't help but notice that the pathologist looked happier and more rested than he'd seen him in a long time. He also couldn't help attributing Jack's improved appearance to a weekend spent with Carrie Salinger. Fighting the urge to knock the stupid, shit-eating grin off his friend's face, Joplin strolled over to his desk and sat down.

"I think I've got something Ike can take to Janice Bernstein," Jack said excitedly.

"Great," said Joplin, trying to muster up some enthusiasm.

Tyndall eased his lanky frame into the chair next to Joplin's desk. "I read through both of the Carters' autopsy reports, but nothing jumped out at me. Then I started thinking about what led to the homicide ruling in Anne Carter's death—"

"You mean the two separate needle marks at the same site?"

"Exactly."

"Are you saying that only a doctor could have thought of something like that?" Joplin asked. "That that would give us probable cause for a warrant to search Woodley's house and office?"

Jack grinned and shook his head. "It's more than that, Hollis. I'm saying that the evidence will show that only the doctor who administered the first injection could have administered the second one. I came in early this morning and went through the photographs the histologist took of the slide I prepared at autopsy showing the two distinct punctures in Anne Carter's thigh. And it's amazing that I was even able to distinguish them in the first place, because the trajectories are almost identical."

"You're losing me, Jack. Hypodermic needles aren't bullets. How can they have trajectories?"

"Same principle. A needle, before it enters a body, is held in a human hand just like a gun and 'fired' if you will via the action of the person's thumb depressing the plunger of the syringe. Just like a gun, a syringe is held at a certain height and angle in relation to the body and the needle leaves a 'pathway' from the epidermis through the muscle—the trajectory."

"But wouldn't the height and angle of a syringe be pretty standard for an intramuscular injection? I mean, to make sure the needle doesn't go into a vein or artery? Don't doctors and nurses and techs have to practice on oranges or something like that to learn how to do it safely?"

Tyndall nodded. "Yes, but 'standard' doesn't mean 'fixed' or 'exact' in this case. Muscular tissue is just under the layers of fat and dermis and presents a fairly large target for a needle. And there are always little differences in the way medical personnel hold syringes and give injections. So the odds that a second person administering an injection into Anne Carter at the exact site of the original one and leaving the same trajectory are extremely low. And although that wouldn't be enough to convict Woodley, I think it *is* enough to give the police probable cause for the warrants."

Now Joplin began to get excited. "It's good enough for me," he said. "I just hope Janice Bernstein and Judge Moreland will think so. Would you be willing to take the slide photos to the judge in person and make the case if they don't?"

"You bet. I want to catch this guy *almost* as much as you do, Hollis. Just give me a call if you need me." Tyndall stood up and looked at his watch. "People are still dying to see me, buddy. I need to get going."

"Thanks, Jack," said Joplin. "I really appreciate this," he added, squelching a burning desire to ask the pathologist how his weekend was. "I'll keep you posted."

Joplin lost no time in contacting Simmons to let him know the new information Jack had given him. Ike, too, thought it would be compelling enough for Bernstein to take to her judge and promised to get on it right away.

"Tell her to call Jack if she needs further convincing," Joplin said.

"Will do."

Joplin's elation over what might be a break in the case came to an abrupt halt when he rounded the corner into the conference room on his way to get coffee and came face-to-face with Carrie Salinger. He stood there just staring at her, and she in turn took a step back. It was one of the most awkward moments he'd ever experienced. Again, he wondered just what it was that made him feel so connected to Carrie; why it was that he was so devastated at the thought of never seeing her again. Or worse, seeing her become a part of Jack Tyndall's life.

"Hollis," she said, finally breaking the silence between them.

There was emotion in her voice. What it was he wasn't sure, but it gave him a little hope that she had felt the connection, too. A hope that was dashed by the realization that she seemed to have undergone some material change. At least, if brighter eyes and creamier skin and glossier hair were any indication, he told himself.

Sex was a very powerful cosmetic.

"Did Jack tell you that he came up with a great piece of evidence to help Simmons get the search warrants on Paul Woodley?" he asked, plastering a smile on his face.

"No. I…I haven't seen Jack yet this morning."

"Well, get him to tell you all about it. When you *do* see him," Joplin added as he moved past her toward the coffee machine.

"Hollis!"

The combination of anguish and frustration in Carrie's voice stopped him dead in his tracks. He turned to look at her and saw the same combination of emotions on her face.

"Please talk to me for a minute. Please."

"Sure. What's up?" he responded, still hoping to bluff his way through the awkwardness.

"I want you to know that I feel really bad about…all of this," she said. "About you and Jack and me. There's no use pretending that something hasn't happened between us. Jack and me, I mean. But it wasn't what I *wanted* to happen, Hollis. It's just that—"

"You don't need to explain anything to me, Carrie," he said quickly. "And quit beating yourself up over this. We only went out twice, and I knew Jack was interested in you, too. Who wouldn't be?" he added, smiling at her. "You're a terrific person, which is why you should be happy. And if being with Jack can make you happy, then I'm all for it. Really."

She seemed to search his face, as if trying to determine whether he was telling the truth. Then she said, "Thank you," and turned and walked out of the room.

There was still no word from Janice Bernstein about the search warrants by the time Joplin's shift ended at four that day. Simmons had called him around two to say that Bernstein's judge was presiding that week and they had a very heavy plea calendar Monday and Tuesday, but she had promised to get him to look at the warrant requests before he left for the day. Whether he would sign them was another question. In fact, she had advised Ike to have Jack Tyndall ready to meet with the judge sometime the next morning. Ike had already contacted Jack.

Not wanting to jeopardize what he had come to think of as a stunning Humphrey Bogart/*Casablanca* gesture with Carrie that morning, Joplin had decided not to go discuss the warrant situation with Jack. He wasn't sure he had any more valor or self-sacrifice left in him. At five, he said good night to Glenn Martin and Viv Rodriguez, who had the evening shift that night, and headed to Tacqueria del Sol, a Tex-Mex restaurant down the street. He would have one drink and order something to go, he decided. Then he would go to bed early and be bright-eyed and bushy-tailed for his classes the next day. His work on the Carter/Carter/Mashburn cases was essentially over; so was his non-relationship with Carrie Salinger. It was time to move on to new bodies and new crime scenes and new romantic possibilities.

He just hoped Jack wouldn't ask him to be best man at his next wedding.

Joplin's cell phone rang as he was taking his first sip of Jim Beam. Caller ID flashed Tom Halloran's name on the screen, and he was tempted to ignore it. There was no reason for him to have any further involvement with the man now that the death investigations were over. And although he'd come to respect Halloran's dogged determination to find out what happened to his friend, enough was enough. He started to reject the call, then changed his mind. Maybe he could at least impress upon the attorney that their unofficial collaboration was over.

"What's up, Counselor?"

"Well, I haven't heard from you since I passed on that information about David Healey, and I was just wondering if Detective Simmons had followed up on it. Or if the judge signed those search warrants on Dr. Woodley."

"I can't really tell you anything about that, Mr. Halloran."

There was silence for a few seconds, and then Halloran said, "Okay. But can you tell me anything about the photographs I turned over to you on Thursday? I mean, where they came from? Obviously, Anne wasn't telling the truth about how she got them."

The bartender came over with the fish tacos that Joplin had ordered to go, and he handed him his Visa. "Mr. Halloran, I'm out of this now that cause and manner of death have been established in all three cases. But you can contact Detective Simmons if you want to." Joplin paused; Halloran's query about the photographs had reminded him that there was still one very big loose end in the case. "By the way, what was it your wife said about those pictures? That someone had taken *pictures* of the originals and then printed them out, not downloading them or scanning the originals?"

"Yes, she thought that maybe he—or she—couldn't physically take the original photographs to a printer that had a scanner for some reason. But that still posits access to an original set and doesn't explain how Anne could have gotten them. Or from whom."

"You're right about that," Joplin said slowly, an idea beginning to form in his mind. One that might explain how MacKenzie had obtained *two* sets of pictures. He still had no idea why his boss would have had any involvement with Anne Carter, but it might be important to find out if he could have been the one to give her the set she had shown Ben Mashburn. "Listen, if I hear anything that I think I can pass on to you, I'll give you a call, okay?"

"Sure," Halloran responded, sounding a little surprised. "I'd appreciate that."

Joplin hung up, then got out his notebook and looked up the number for the Property and Evidence Control Unit at APD. He was happy when

Frank Donnelly, an evidence tech that he'd known since his days as a rookie, answered the phone.

"It's Hollis Joplin, Frank. Can you check the log for a name for me?"

"I already told Damon Washington that MacKenzie only checked the Greenleaf photos out that one time, Hollis," Donnelly said, sounding irritated.

"I know, Frank, but I need you to look at the other log, the one that everyone signs just to go back in the stacks."

"Can't do it. At least not for a while. I'm having to turn the place upside down trying to locate some evidence they need over in Judge Hyatt's court for a murder trial. He said he'd hold me in contempt if I can't find it. And he will, Hollis."

Joplin looked at his watch. It was a little after six, and he didn't really feel like going home yet anyway. "Why don't I just come by and look through the log book myself, Frank?"

"You don't mind, Hollis? You know I'd help you out if I could, but—"

"I don't mind, Frank. I'll be there in twenty minutes."

42

"HEY, HOLLIS," SAID FRANK DONNELLY, a short, compact man with reddish blond hair and freckles. "Told you I had a lot going on tonight," he added, gesturing toward several boxes on the counter in front of him. "I got the sign-in log for you, though."

"I appreciate it, Frank. I'll just stand here at the counter and flip through it, okay?"

"Sure thing, Hollis. You take your time."

The APD used a computerized records management system to oversee the handling of confiscated property and evidence. This had significantly tightened security and made mandatory audits a lot easier in the past few years. Authorized visitors still had to sign in and out, however, and when they were allowed to take evidence with them, they had to sign yet another log to ensure chain of custody. Information from both books was then inputted into the computer, but that sometimes took a back seat to more pressing duties. Joplin knew he'd get more current info from the actual log. He opened it and began paging back until he had reached a date about a month before Elliot Carter had been killed, then started scanning the pages. Ever since Halloran had given him the photographs of Bobby Greenleaf, part of his mind had been working on the mystery of how Anne Carter had gotten hold of them. And while he'd been talking to the attorney a little while ago, a possibility had oc-curred to him: What if MacKenzie had brought a digital camera with him several weeks ago and taken pictures of the originals to give to Anne Carter?

It took Joplin about twenty minutes to determine that MacKenzie's name wasn't there. He was about to close the book, when he realized that he had seen a name in passing that hadn't registered until just then. He hadn't been looking for it, so he'd just glossed over it. It wasn't that un-usual anyway. Besides police officers and investigators, there were several categories of people—prosecutors, MEs, ADAs, and private attorneys for both civil and criminal cases, for example—who had access to evidence in the stacks. The protocol, especially for defense attorneys, required that a technician or supervisor accompany them to the evidence stacks. But budget cuts had reduced manpower across the board, and that wasn't always feasible. Nor was it always considered necessary, if the authorized visitor was a familiar face. Joplin skipped back to where he thought he'd seen the name, and there it was, about midway down on the April 12th page. There was a case number next to the name, something that would have to be given even if the evidence weren't going to be taken from the unit. With a growing sense of shock, he realized that it was the same number that he'd seen on the back of the photos MacKenzie had given him.

Joplin left without waiting to see Frank Donnelly and walked slowly back to his car. It was now dark outside, but the bright lights of the parking lot made him feel as if he were enclosed in a bubble, their glow making the sky a milky haze. He opened the car door and eased into the driver's seat. Tom Halloran had been right: Dr. Woodley might not be the prime suspect after all.

What had been an especially long and stressful day was now shap-ing up to be an even longer and more stressful night. He found his cell phone and dialed Jack's number again, fervently hoping the pathologist would now be at home. He needed to discuss this with him as soon as possible. Time after time, Jack had helped him think things through or come up with a different spin on a set of facts. He'd be able to come up with an explanation for this, too.

Jack's voice mail came on after several rings, and Joplin left a message for him to call back. He reached for the plastic bag that held the food from the Tacqueria del Sol and opened it. After unwrapping the tacos, he made himself take a few bites. He needed to slow the processing of the alcohol in his system, to make sure he'd be able to think things through clearly. All the while, his mind went over the whole case, everything that had happened since he'd been called to Piedmont Park to investigate Elliot Carter's death.

This time he didn't see the memories holographically; they came at him too quickly. Instead, images clicked through his brain, as if he were looking through the View Master he'd had as a child: Tom Halloran telling him about Elliot Carter's will in the park the morning that the body had been found; the apprehensive, almost fearful expression on Anne Carter's face as she viewed her estranged husband's body at the ME's office; Ben Mashburn's body slumped over the passenger seat of his car; Jack telling him that the odds of successfully faking an autoerotic death were a million to one; Paul Woodley's flushed face as he insisted he and Anne Carter were not sexually involved; opening the manila envelope that Halloran had handed him and seeing Bobby Greenleaf's face in that first, hellish photograph; Chief MacKenzie angrily pulling an almost identical manila envelope from his desk drawer and tossing it at him; and the bottle of Jim Beam on his own kitchen table as he listened to Halloran tell him that David Healey thought he was Trip Carter's father.

He knew what had happened. And why.

Joplin shoved the fish taco back in the bag, then started the car. He pulled out of the APD parking lot and headed back to the ME's office. So far, all he had was a theory and a very strong gut feeling, but a few phone calls might find support for both.

Viv Rodriguez was in her cubicle in the investigator's office when Joplin passed through. "What are you doing back here, Hollis?"

"I left my cell phone on my desk," Joplin lied, "and since I was just down the street grabbing dinner, I decided to come back for it. Might try to get a little more work done while I'm here. Glenn out on a scene?"

"I guess so. He was gone when I got back from one of my own." Viv made a face. "A decomposed found in an abandoned house on Hilliard. Looks like one of those prostitute murders," she added, referring to a series of murders that the Homicide Unit had begun to attribute to a serial killer. "I'm typing it up now."

Joplin chuckled. "Glad it was you and not me," he said. "Your perfume smells familiar."

"I can't wait to get into a hot shower," she said. "And burn these clothes."

"Been there," he said, heading for his own cubicle. He sat down and pulled out his notebook, then found the number for the security desk at Ansley Towers.

"Brent Daniels speaking."

"Brent, this is Hollis Joplin, with the ME's office. You working nights this week?"

"Just until eight. I had to fill in for someone."

"Well, that's my good luck. I have a few more questions, if you've got a minute."

"Sure. How can I help you?"

"You told me that the usual procedure when a visitor comes to the building is to first look to see if the owner notified you that that person was to be admitted or, in the event no advance notification was given, to call the owner. Is that about right?"

"Yes, sir."

"But then, that's the extent of your involvement, isn't it?" inquired Joplin. "You don't monitor how long that visitor stays or when he or she leaves, do you?"

"No, sir," answered Daniels, sounding puzzled.

"So you wouldn't know if that person decided to go to another apartment in the building, after leaving the apartment of the owner whom you'd called earlier?"

"Sir, we'd have no control over something like that," said Daniels, sounding alarmed now. "Once a guest has been admitted, it's up to the owner as to how long he stays."

"No need to explain," said Joplin quickly. "I'm just checking on something. Listen, I really appreciate your help here. Thanks, okay?"

"Sure thing." Brent Daniels sounded relieved now.

Viv came out of her cubicle and waved to him. "Got another call to a vehicular death on Peachtree Dunwoody," she said. "Go home, Hollis. *I* sure would, if I could."

"Five more minutes, Viv." Joplin waited until she was gone, then found Tom Halloran's cell phone number. The attorney answered on the second ring.

"Sorry to bother you," Joplin said after identifying himself.

"That's okay. I'm on my way home, but I can talk. Is this about the warrants? Did the judge sign them?"

"No, there's nothing new on that front, but I do have a few questions. About Elliot Carter's will."

There was a long pause, and then Halloran said, "I'll be happy to answer any questions you have, but I'm a little confused. I thought you said that you're off the case."

"I am, but I've been thinking about some of the things you've told me, and I'm beginning to have my own doubts about Dr. Woodley."

"I'm glad to hear that. What do you need to know about Elliot's will?"

"Could Anne Carter have contested it? And would she have had much of a chance if she had?"

"Yes, to both questions, although I wouldn't have made it easy for her."

"You also said that when someone dies intestate, everything goes to the next of kin."

"Right, but that didn't happen in this case."

"I'm not talking about Elliot Carter. What if, say, David Healey really *is* Trip Carter's biological father, and Trip dies without a will? Could Healey legally claim the estate?"

There was an even longer silence on the line this time, and Joplin knew he had thrown the attorney a real curve ball.

"I take it this means you're now seriously considering David Healey as a suspect?" Halloran said finally.

"Maybe," said Joplin. "But I can't tell you any more than that."

"But you *can* tell me if you think Trip is in any danger," Halloran shot back at him. "Please don't play games. Olivia Carter has hired some security through the hotel, but they'll need to know if he's in danger from a specific person. *I* need to know. You're scaring the hell out of me."

"I understand that, Mr. Halloran. But *I* won't really know until you answer my question."

He heard Halloran sigh, and then the attorney said, "The short answer is 'yes.' If David is Trip's father, he would have a legal claim on the estate. But all sorts of obstacles would have to be gotten out of the way first. He'd have to *prove* paternity, for one thing. Then he'd have to fight a claim from the Landrums or even Olivia Carter. But frankly, I can't see his doing any of that. The media would turn it into a circus, and David Healey isn't the kind of man to want his dirty linen aired in public."

"But he *would* have a legal claim to the estate. That's what you said."

"Yes, he would. Now it's your turn. I'm asking you again: Is Trip Carter in danger?"

"Not at this point." Joplin wondered if he should tell Tom Halloran any more. A plan had been forming in the back of his mind since he left APD, but if it went wrong and something happened to him, Trip Carter might need protection after all. "Look, I think I know what happened and why, but I can't prove it. If things work out tonight, maybe that'll change, but if not, you need to make sure the boy is taken care of. Maybe get him out of Atlanta altogether."

"Investigator Joplin, you need to tell me what's going on."

"Why don't you call me Hollis, Counselor? I think we've gotten to know each other well enough to drop the formalities, don't you?"

Halloran gave a short laugh. "Okay, Hollis, but only if you call me Tom. And only if you tell me what's going on."

"I can't, Tom. I just don't have any proof yet."

"Then let me help you. Whatever it is you're going to do, let me go along."

"Thanks, but I don't think that would be a good idea. I'll keep you posted, though." Joplin hung up before Halloran could say anything else. He looked at his watch; it was ten minutes after nine. He picked up a legal pad and began writing out a brief narrative of how he thought the murders had gone down. The phone on his desk rang several times, as did his cell phone a few minutes later, but he ignored them, certain the calls were from Tom Halloran. Finished, he ripped the sheet of paper from the pad, folded it, and stuck it in an envelope, which he stamped and addressed to Halloran. Then he thrust it into his inside jacket pocket and hurried out the door.

Hopefully, he would find a post office box on the way.

43

IMMEDIATELY AFTER HANGING UP, Halloran retrieved the number of the phone Hollis Joplin had used to call him. He dialed it, but got no answer. A call to 411 produced the address for that number, which he knew belonged to the ME's office. After trying Joplin's cell phone, he made a sharp right off Peachtree onto North Avenue and headed for Piedmont, deciding that would be the fastest route to the morgue. He was convinced that the investigator might be putting himself in danger in an effort to trap the killer. With any luck, he might get there before Joplin left.

Impatiently, Halloran waited for the light to change at the intersection of Tenth and Piedmont. Checking his watch, he saw that ten minutes had already passed since Joplin had called him, and the medical examiner's office was at least fifteen minutes away. He tried the investigator's cell phone again and left a message on his voice mail this time, pleading with him to call back. If he didn't, however, and if Joplin had already left on his mission to try to smoke out the murderer, Halloran knew he had very little chance of finding him.

Joplin didn't park in the tiered parking lot across from One Atlantic Center this time. Instead, he left his car on a side street off West Peachtree and walked the three blocks back to the Tower. Looking up at the tall, imposing building that dwarfed its surroundings, he was struck more than ever by some ancient quality that it seemed to possess. It loomed in front of him like a Medieval fortress, illuminated both at its base as well as at its turret. Thick clouds, which had been gathering since late afternoon, were reflected in the light and surrounded the Tower, making it appear almost menacing. He felt suddenly chilly in the night air and stepped up his pace.

Ahead were Fourteenth Street and the Tower entrance. Surprisingly, there were several people milling around the lobby. He remembered that the law firms of Holland and Knight, as well as Alston and Bird, leased several floors; there were also some stock brokerage companies in the building. Going home at six was a luxury a lot of people didn't have these days.

There were no young women in maroon blazers behind the marble desk this time. Instead, a security guard sat at a desk in the elevator area, behind a sign that said, "Visitors Must Sign In." Hollis smiled at him.

"Evening, sir," said the guard, a young, ramrod-straight black man with a "jarhead" haircut that Joplin knew was favored by Marines.

He was careful not to use his own name when he signed in, and in the space for the tenant he was going to see, he gave the name of a lawyer with Holland and Knight that he'd once met on a case. "Gotta give a deposition, can you believe that? Hope it doesn't take all night."

"I hear that," said the guard, nodding his head in empathy. "Good luck."

I'll sure need it, thought Joplin as he entered the elevator.

The front door of the ME's office was locked. Halloran went around to the back and found the morgue entrance. Inside, the attendant told him that Joplin had been there, but had left fifteen minutes earlier.

Walking back to his car, he replayed the conversation he'd had with the investigator, trying to decipher what he might have in mind. It seemed obvious that he had switched from thinking of Woodley as the prime suspect to thinking it was David Healey. But why? What had happened since his earlier conversation with Joplin to change the man's mind? And why wouldn't he come right out and say what he was thinking?

What bothered Halloran the most was that the investigator had implied that Trip might be the next victim. He also seemed to think that the killer would be Trip's biological father. But even David hadn't seemed entirely sure he was the boy's father—or so he'd said. He'd also said that Anne had been involved with "a few other guys" back then.

Halloran forced himself to focus again on how the investigator might be trying to get evidence for his suspicions. Whatever Joplin was doing, he seemed to think it needed to be done that very night. But what could that be? What was going to happen in the immediate future that would explain why he was willing to risk his own safety?

"The search warrants," Halloran said out loud.

Joplin must believe that the murderer would try to plant evidence at Woodley's house or office, just as he'd planted the autoerotic paraphernalia at Elliot's apartment, Halloran decided. And he'd be waiting to catch him in the act. But how would the murderer know about the search warrants? Yet even as the question formed in his mind, he thought he knew the answer, and it sent a chill through his body. He had been afraid that David Healey might have been listening outside his office door while he was talking with Joplin about the warrants. It looked as if he'd been right to be afraid.

Halloran didn't know offhand where Woodley lived, but he remembered Anne saying that his office was at One Atlantic Center. He'd start there, and if he couldn't find Joplin, he'd track down Dr. Woodley's home address. Excited now, the adrenaline pumping through his veins, he switched on the ignition and pulled out onto Cheshire Bridge. Lit up against the night's murky background, he could already see the imposing tower of One Atlantic Center.

He only hoped he could get there in time.

Carrie and Jack had dinner together at Houston's, a popular casual restaurant across from Lenox Square mall. She had told him she needed to make it an early night after spending almost every minute of the last four days together, and he admitted he was a little tired himself. But a good kind of tired, he'd said, smiling at her. She smiled back, happy to be with him, but also looking forward to a good night's sleep. Ever since Thursday night, she'd been on a roller coaster of emotions. Most of them had been part of a long, steep climb that reached a level of happiness and exhilaration she hadn't felt in a long time. Maybe never, actually.

But there'd been a few dips along the way, too: her remorse over having sex with Jack before he was even divorced and her agitation when she'd run into Hollis Joplin that morning. The agitation had dissipated once he'd told her to quit beating herself up over the situation and that she deserved to be happy. That he wanted that for her even if it meant her being with Jack.

That had been a really nice thing to say, Carrie thought now. She remembered feeling a sense of regret, almost verging on loss, as she walked away from him. It was odd how she still felt a pull toward Hollis even as she reveled in her new relationship with Jack. She needed to think about that. But then she heard Jack ask her something, and she made herself focus on him.

"Don't you think that would be a good idea, Carrie?"

"I'm sorry, Jack," she said quickly. "I must be more tired than I thought. What were you saying?"

"I was just wondering if you might want to meet my kids. Not right away, but maybe in a few weeks? I'd really like that."

"Oh…Jack, I don't know about that," she answered, feeling a little panicky. Over the past four days, she had willed herself to forget the fact that he had children. Four children, as a matter of fact. And soon, two ex-wives. How could she possibly deal with all of that? And why was she even considering it? They had really only known each other three weeks. She took a deep breath and said, "I think that's something that should wait until after your divorce, don't you? I mean, for their sakes."

He smiled again, sheepishly this time. "Yeah, I guess you're right. I wasn't thinking. Besides, it's getting late, and I promised you'd get home early."

He walked her out to where the valet attendant stood, then put his arm around her as they waited for her car. Turning to look at her, he said, "Try to overlook what an idiot I can be sometimes. I meant it when I said I was out of my league here."

Carrie felt her panic melt away. Jack seemed to know exactly what she was thinking and had said just what she needed him to say at that moment. She turned her face up to his and kissed him with all the passion and intensity that she'd been feeling since last Thursday.

It would all work out. Somehow.

***

Joplin pushed the elevator button for the nineteenth floor of One Atlantic Center, where Holland and Knight had offices, just in case the security guard was watching. Once there, he quickly headed back down to the fifteenth floor and located Paul Woodley's office. He knocked loudly, then called out the psychiatrist's name. There was no response, so he repeated his actions, waited, then did the same thing a third time. Convinced that Woodley wasn't inside, he moved on to the second part of his plan and began looking for a nearby supply closet. He needed a place to hide with a clear view of anyone entering the psychiatrist's office. With this in mind, Joplin had brought along some lock-picking tools to get into the closet. If the person he was expecting did show up and broke into the office, he could then claim he saw a felony in progress and follow him inside. The rest would be easy. Either he'd be able to observe the suspect in the act of planting evidence, or, once he arrested him, he could search him and find the evidence that was going to be planted. It was a fairly fool-proof plan.

Unless, of course, things got out of hand.

Unfortunately, the only supply closet for that floor was around the corner, on the west side of the tower, which wasn't suitable at all. Joplin walked slowly back to Woodley's office, trying to decide how to proceed. If he let himself in with his tools and got what he needed, he doubted that Paul Woodley would press charges, under the circumstances. But any defense attorney would challenge the admission of evidence obtained that way, even though only Woodley's right to privacy had been breached.

The other option was simply to leave. Tomorrow, he could discuss the whole thing with Tom Halloran. He'd already mailed him a letter laying out his suspicions anyway and, frankly, the attorney had done more to get the investigation on the right track than anyone else involved. Then there was Simmons. Maybe he and Ike could come up with a way to get the son-of-a-bitch in a legal and proper way. And he could also go over everything with Jack and see what he said, just as he'd planned earlier. There were a lot of excellent reasons on the side of being cautious.

The fuck with that, thought Joplin as he got out his lock-picking tools.

Waiting held too much of a risk. If evidence *was* planted tonight, and a search warrant produced it, Captain Barrow might insist on arresting Paul Woodley anyway. But even if he could prevent that, coming up with good, solid evidence would take a while, and in the meantime, someone else—like Woodley or even Trip Carter—might be killed.

It took only seconds to open the outer office door. Within minutes, he was in Paul Woodley's private office. Joplin remembered the layout from his previous visit and decided that the only place to hide was in the bathroom. He would also have a perfect view of the psychiatrist's desk and computer. Moving quickly, he went into the bathroom, leaving the door slightly ajar. He then lowered the toilet lid, pulled his Glock from its holster, and sat down.

He didn't have long to wait. About fifteen minutes later, Joplin thought he heard the outer door being opened, then closed. Quietly, he stood up and moved past the inside of the bathroom door, flattening himself against the wall. He saw a sliver of light suddenly appear at the bottom of the inside office door.

Joplin soon heard the familiar sound of lock-picking tools being used. Then he heard the door swing open and out of the corner of his right eye saw the light come on. Bracing himself for the possibility that the intruder would next check out the bathroom, he held his breath. After several seconds, he heard a rustling of papers and then the sound of the computer being rebooted. Joplin carefully let out the breath he'd been holding. Soon he heard tapping at the key board and knew he was safe—for a little while at least. Slowly, he raised his left arm and looked at the illuminated dial on his watch. It was seven minutes after eight. He would wait exactly two minutes and then leave the bathroom. He didn't want to give the intruder enough time to dispose of everything he might have brought with him to help establish Woodley's guilt; just catching the suspect with them in his possession would give Joplin an edge.

It was the longest two minutes of his life. When the dial finally read 8:10, Hollis walked slowly and quietly out of the bathroom, his weapon raised. It took a few seconds for the man sitting at the desk to register that someone was in the room. When he did, the expression on his face was one of shock.

"Hello, Jack," said Joplin calmly. "Working late again?"

44

THE SHOCKED LOOK ON Jack Tyndall's face slowly disappeared. "I could say the same thing about you, Hollis," he said, smiling now. "I thought you went home hours ago."

Joplin smiled, too. "I never quite made it there, as you can see."

"I did, but just for a little while. Then I met our girlfriend for dinner. Well, actually, I'm sorry to have to tell you this, but she's just my girlfriend now."

"She won't be for long," said Joplin, refusing to rise to the bait. "Not when she finds out you've killed three people."

"Who's going to tell her, Hollis? You? I don't think she'll believe you. I don't think anyone will believe you."

"I think the fact that I caught you planting evidence will convince Carrie. And anyone else, for that matter. You're under arrest for the murders of Elliot Carter, Ben Mashburn, and Anne Carter. You have the right to remain silent. If you choose to talk, anything you say can be used against you. You have the right—"

Tyndall waved a latex-gloved hand at him. "I know my rights, Hollis. I also know that unless you have something else, you don't have shit, because my attorney will make sure you can't use anything you saw or might find here tonight. I seriously doubt that you have Dr. Paul's permission to be here—or a warrant in hand."

"I'll just explain that I became suspicious of you and followed you here. When I saw you break into Dr. Woodley's office, I went in and found you planting evidence."

Tyndall smiled again. "Good plan. But I'm sure you'll be asked what made you suspicious of me in the first place. What was it?"

"I went and looked at the Evidence sign-in sheet to see if MacKenzie's name was there before he checked those photographs out on the twenty-first," said Joplin. "It occurred to me that he could've taken pictures of them with a digital camera and then printed them later," he added, careful to keep Maggie Halloran out of it. "His name wasn't there, but yours was."

"But, Hollis, as Chief Deputy ME, I have every right to review evidence whenever I want. Besides, I might have gone there to see something else."

"Yeah, but you have to list what evidence you're going to review when you sign in, and that particular piece of evidence was pretty damning. So was the timing. That's when I started putting the whole thing together."

"And what do you think that is?" asked Tyndall.

Joplin knew Jack was just pumping him, trying to find out what he knew, as well as to buy time and maybe think of a way out. But he wanted the pathologist to know just how much he had figured out, hoping he might confess.

"That you knew Anne Carter when you were both at UGA; in fact, you'd slept with her. I think she went to you when she was pregnant, but you wouldn't marry her; she got Elliot Carter to marry her instead. After she and Carter were separated, you ran into each other again. By that time, you were going through your second divorce and had enough money going out in alimony and child support payments to rival the national debt."

"Well, that part is certainly true, anyway."

"So's the rest of it," said Joplin. "Anne Carter wasn't the same young girl you knew in college, was she? Now she had money and social position. Just what you needed these days, Jack. But there was one problem: Her husband was refusing to give her what she—and you—thought was a decent settlement. And you weren't going to saddle yourself with a third wife unless you could get your hands on a lot of money. So you got her to agree to blackmail Elliot Carter with those photographs. You thought an attorney would be scared shitless at the thought of his wife claiming he was into kiddie porn. Then, just to scare him a little more, you and Anne tried to use Ben Mashburn. You knew he was a retired cop, and you thought you could pay him to threaten Carter that he would turn the pictures over to the police. But you didn't know that he'd been Billy MacKenzie's partner and had worked the Bobby Greenleaf case. Or that MacKenzie had shown him the original photographs four years ago. Ben recognized them as soon as he saw them, and he knew something was up."

"Yeah, the pictures were a big mistake. Mashburn remembered that I had performed the autopsy on that pervert orthodontist who had the pictures in his possession when he died. So he called me when he couldn't get MacKenzie that Tuesday, just trying to get a lead on the pictures. Something I said tipped him off; I could tell. But I didn't let him know that and said I'd drop by his office later and talk some more. I knew I'd have to take care of Mashburn, so I brought along a gun. When he saw it, he thought he could protect himself by telling me Elliot Carter knew about the pictures. So I went to Plan B and told him to get Elliot Carter there, too, or I'd kill him on the spot."

"And then you killed both of them," Joplin said.

"What else *could* I do? I certainly wasn't going to go to prison for extortion and possession of child pornography! And the whole thing could've ended right there if that stupid bitch hadn't given those photos to Tom Halloran."

"She was afraid," said Joplin, trying not to betray his elation over Tyndall's admission. "When Halloran told her that Mashburn was dead, it was pretty hard for Anne Carter to believe that *he* had killed himself, too. You'd evidently been able to get her to believe that Elliot really *was* the victim of autoerotic asphyxia. That that type of death couldn't be faked. But when Mashburn died, it was too much for her to believe. She needed to talk to you, have you convince her that you weren't involved. But first she had to throw Halloran offtrack."

"Instead, those pictures led you right to my name on the Evidence sign-in sheet."

"Which wouldn't have happened if you'd succeeded in killing Tom Halloran last Friday," said Joplin, realizing now that the attorney had been right about the attempt on his life.

Tyndall smiled. "Busted again, Hollis. I parked near his house before dawn that morning, hoping he might go jogging again. He told you that he ran every morning, remember? And sure enough, he came out in jogging clothes around six-thirty. Once I realized where he was heading, I doubled around and came at him going north on Peachtree. Unfortunately, he was a little too quick for me."

"But even if you'd killed him, the pictures would have turned up sooner or later," Joplin said. Maggie Halloran had seen them and knew where they came from, although Jack wouldn't have known that.

"Maybe. But what proof would there be to connect them to Anne? If I could have undone the damage she did, we would have been okay." Tyndall shook his head, a disgusted look on his face. "Anne could be so clueless sometimes. Like when we were at UGA. She went after all the spoiled rich guys, thinking she could have anyone she wanted, just because of her looks. I was the only one who really turned her on, though. We were two of a kind."

"Then why didn't you marry her?"

"Because I had just been accepted to medical school," Tyndall said, looking at Joplin as if he were a moron. "I didn't have some rich daddy paying my way like Paul Woodley and David Healey and Elliot Carter did. I couldn't have supported a wife and child, for Christ's sake! I told her to get an abortion."

"But she didn't."

"No, and I'll never understand that. Instead, she told Elliot Carter, who'd been chasing after her since she showed up on campus, that the baby was his."

"Maybe it was."

Tyndall grinned slyly. "Nice try. I know all about Carter's fertility problem, Hollis. And besides, Anne didn't sleep with anyone else after she met me, and she didn't start up again with Carter and David Healey until I turned her down. But Elliot bought her story hook, line and sinker, the poor schmuck. The next thing I knew, she was on her way to Charleston to get married."

"Leaving you all alone in Athens."

"Believe me, I didn't lose any sleep over it. I've never had any trouble getting women, Hollis. Ask Carrie Salinger."

Joplin felt the blood rush to his head, but he fought for control. "How did you and Anne get involved again?"

"I ran into her at the courthouse last December. I had just testified at a murder trial, and she had just lost some motion against Elliot Carter. We spent the night together."

"And picked up where you left off eighteen years ago. Didn't it bother you that she was also involved with Paul Woodley again?"

Tyndall's face twisted into a sneer. "Are you kidding? She was just stringing him along, like she did in college. Besides, we had to keep things under wraps for a while, while she worked on Carter to give her more money. Paul was a good cover."

"Did you ever meet Trip Carter?"

"No. But I saw him once with Anne at a restaurant in Midtown. He seems like a great kid. I wish I'd been around while he was growing up."

"But you weren't, Jack," said Joplin, hoping to goad him into talking about Carter's death. "Elliot Carter was. And Trip Carter worshipped his father."

"Elliot Carter wasn't his father!" Tyndall shouted. "I am! He got to raise my son because he was filthy rich. He had everything given to him on a silver platter, the son of a bitch. Everything. Even my son!"

"But you took it all away, didn't you? Trip, his life, his good name. And his dignity. Especially his dignity. The way you murdered him was guaranteed to destroy everything that was important to him."

The pathologist took a deep breath and closed his eyes. When he opened them, the anger that had distorted his face was gone, and he looked at Joplin almost calmly. "I thought making it look like an autoerotic fatality was a stroke of genius, myself. I had to bite my tongue sometimes to keep from telling you, Hollis. I even gave you hints, telling you over and over how only someone with expert knowledge could fake it. Like me."

Joplin felt sick to his stomach. He knew he was seeing the real Jack Tyndall, not the one he had thought of as his friend and colleague. He had always prided himself on being able to read people. To watch their facial expressions and body language, and to know if they were lying. But he had known Jack for years, long before he'd joined the ME's office, and had never suspected that he was dealing with a monstrous sociopath.

"How, Jack? How could you do it? How could you kill two innocent people like Elliot Carter and Ben Mashburn because they got in your way? How could you murder the mother of your child and then calmly carve her up the next day on an autopsy table?"

"That bitch tried to get me to say incriminating things while she taped me! She called me Wednesday night after Paul Woodley left the second time and told me what had happened. She insisted I come over, and she let me into the house after Pauletta had gone to bed."

"Is that how you two usually managed to get together?"

"That was the first time I'd ever been in her house, Hollis. We always met at my place. Janie and I were separated by then."

"But this time she wanted you to come to her."

"She said she couldn't make it one more day without seeing me, the phony bitch. But when we got up to her bedroom, she started acting strangely, going over everything that we'd done and trying to get me to talk about it. Said Tom Halloran was hounding her, and she was afraid he'd go to the police. It didn't take me long to figure out what was going on, especially after I saw her Flip on the bedside table. She was recording me! She was going to turn me in, for Christ's sake! I *had* to do something to stop her."

"You'd made up your mind to kill her before you went to see her that night," said Joplin. "Or do you always carry around a syringe filled with Ativan, Jack? She must have told you Woodley gave her a shot of Ativan, and you had it all planned."

Tyndall gave a nonchalant shrug. "It was getting harder and harder to keep her in line. I knew she was going to crack soon. Anne could act like an ice queen, and I grant you she was pretty ruthless at times—like getting Elliot to marry her and talking David Healey into helping her get pregnant again. She even went along with my little extortion plan to get back at Elliot for changing his will and refusing to give her more money in a settlement. But she didn't have the guts to kill. Or even admit to herself that taking care of Elliot and Mashburn was the only thing to do. I had to do *everything*. Even kill *her* when that became necessary," he added, his voice sounding as normal as if he were talking about fixing a flat tire.

"How'd you get her to lie still so you could inject her in exactly the same site as Woodley had?"

"It was easy," Tyndall said, almost smirking. "She had no idea I was on to her. I went over to her and held her and started kissing her, telling her the police had evidence that Paul Woodley had killed Elliot and were closing in on him. That everything would be fine soon. It wasn't long before we were in the old missionary position, and that's when I put my hand over her mouth and compressed her carotid. When she lost consciousness, I found the injection site and gave her enough Ativan to kill her. Then I flushed all of Woodley's pills down the toilet to make it look like she overdosed. But when I saw that you and Simmons weren't buying that, I decided to 'discover' the overlapping injection during autopsy. I figured it would clinch the case against Paul. And when you wanted me to find something that would tie him directly to her death, I made up all that stuff about needle trajectories. It would have worked, too, if you hadn't checked out that Evidence sign-in sheet, Hollis. As I said, using those photographs was a big mistake."

"Why those particular photographs, Jack?" asked Joplin, suddenly sensing that he was getting closer to one of the mysteries in the case. "You took a real gamble making copies of them and then getting Anne Carter to take them to Mashburn. You didn't know MacKenzie had shown them to him four years ago, but he was bound to recognize Bobby Greenleaf."

Jack glared at him. "I *said* it was a big mistake, Hollis. You don't need to beat it to death. As for why I used them, that's my business. I've spilled my guts enough for one night, and this discussion is beginning to bore me. Let's just get the cuffs on and get this over with, okay?"

Joplin was only momentarily taken aback by this. He hadn't expected Tyndall to concede things quite so easily, but after everything he'd admitted, the man didn't really have a choice. "Okay, but, first kick that duffel bag you brought over to me, Jack."

"You got it, Hollis," said Tyndall, punting the bag toward Joplin's feet.

Joplin carefully held the gun on Jack as he zipped open the bag. Taking his eyes off the pathologist only momentarily, he glanced in it and saw what looked like the manila folders missing from Mashburn's office.

"Just a few things to plant here to make Dr. Paul look even guiltier," said Tyndall.

"Just like the things you planted in Carter's apartment," Joplin said. "Nice touch. Tell me something: Am I right in thinking that once you had Elliot Carter's keys, you were able to get past security at Ansley Towers by going to see someone else you knew there first, Jack?"

"Mimi Caldwell," said Tyndall with a wide grin. "I dated her in between marriages. I left a gym bag with stuff to plant in Carter's apartment out in the hall while I was visiting her on the twelfth floor, then took it on up to the seventeenth floor when I left her."

"Was this before or after you killed Carter and Mashburn?"

Tyndall cocked his head. "Let's see. It was after I got rid of Mashburn, but before I got around to old Elliot. I kept him in the trunk of his car until I had taken care of everything else."

"You mean while you killed Ben Mashburn," said Joplin. "How'd you get him to go to that motel?"

"At the end of a gun. Just like I said last week when Halloran came to my office. We took his car and stopped by a liquor store with a drive-thru window. I knew about his drinking history from Anne. Then we drove to the Urbana. I figured it was the perfect place for an old drunk to die, considering how many autopsies I've done over the years of people who killed themselves there. Got him to keep drinking while we sat in the car, then shot him with his own gun."

"Then you killed Elliot Carter."

"Well, first I walked back to Mashburn's office and got my car; it was only about six blocks away from the motel. Then I bought everything I needed for my little set-piece in Piedmont Park, went back to Mashburn's office parking deck and got Elliot out of the trunk of his car."

"How did you get him to put on the women's underwear and wig?"

"Same as Mashburn: at gunpoint. I also told him I'd kill Trip if he didn't cooperate. So he cooperated. Got himself all trussed up like a lamb to slaughter. It was touching."

Joplin took a deep breath. "I'm sure it was," he said. "Were you planning on killing Trip anyway, once you killed Anne? He's inherited a lot of money now."

Jack glared at him. "Do you really think I would kill my own son, Hollis?"

"I guess not. If you did and then managed to prove paternity, it might make the Homicide Unit take another look at all these murders. Even with Woodley dead and looking guilty as hell." Joplin moved in closer, keeping the Glock pointed at Tyndall. With his left hand, he reached inside his jacket and pulled out a set of handcuffs. "Okay, now stand up and turn and face the wall, please."

Jack Tyndall stood up, but as he began to turn around, his right arm swung out in a wide arc that reached Joplin's midsection in less than a second. Reflexively, Joplin sucked in his stomach and bent slightly at the waist, but it afforded little protection. He felt a tugging sensation that went from the left side of his abdomen to the right, then heard something clatter to the floor and saw that it was a bloody letter opener. Blood was now pouring from the slash Tyndall had inflicted on him. He backed toward one of the two chairs in front of Woodley's desk, clutching at the wound with his left hand, but keeping the Glock on Tyndall. Landing heavily on the chair, a large spurt of blood gushed out, and he used both hands to try to hold himself together. Overwhelming pain suddenly jolted him. He lost his grip on the gun, and it fell to the floor.

Tyndall walked over to him and kicked the gun toward the door. "Guess I'm not the only one to spill his guts tonight, huh, Hollis?"

45

HALLORAN LOCATED PAUL WOODLEY'S suite number in the lobby of One Atlantic Center, then walked over to the bank of elevators.

"Good evening, sir," the security guard greeted him. "If you'll just sign in, please."

As Halloran did, giving the name of an attorney he knew with Alston and Bird as the person he was visiting, he scanned the sign-in sheet for Joplin's name. It wasn't there, but he headed for the elevator anyway, hoping the investigator had used another name. If not, he was wasting valuable time. When the doors opened on the fifteenth floor, he turned to the left and then right again down the hall in the direction of Suite 1538. He listened at the door and thought he could hear someone talking, although the sound was very faint. Twisting the door knob, he was surprised to find that it wasn't locked. Cautiously, he moved into what was an outer office. The voice he'd heard seemed to be coming from behind a door to his right, and Halloran headed toward it.

He put his ear against the door and held his breath, trying to make out what the person was saying. To his surprise, he recognized Dr. Tyndall's voice, and what the pathologist was saying chilled him to the bone.

***

"You didn't really think I would tell you all that and then let you arrest me, did you, Hollis?" asked Jack Tyndall.

Joplin watched through half-closed eyes as Tyndall picked up the duffel bag and put it on Woodley's desk. He wanted the pathologist to think he was going into shock, but he was sure the incision wasn't as deep as he'd thought at first. The slight distance he'd put between himself and the letter opener had probably saved him. It had sliced through skin and fat, but not, he hoped, the layer of muscle that covered his intestines. Still, he wasn't sure he could get to the small, second gun he always kept in an ankle holster on his right leg, an old habit since his days as a rookie. He would wait for an opportune moment and in the meantime, hope that Jack kept talking.

"Sorry I had to do that, Hollis, but this will put the final nail in Dr. Paul's coffin. The police will find you dead and then discover the souvenirs I'm planting, but they won't find Dr. Paul. I'll make sure of that. They will, however, find your gun in his house."

Joplin saw him open the duffel bag and pull out the stack of manila folders. He watched as the pathologist opened various desk drawers before carefully placing files folders in one of them. This done, he peered into the duffel bag.

"Almost forgot these," Tyndall said, lifting out a small manila envelope. "These are the three photographs that Anne let Ben Mashburn keep. I ought to burn them, they've messed things up so badly, but I guess I'm just sentimental." He stood up and walked around the desk, then sat on the edge of it in front of Joplin. He opened the envelope, then held up the pictures so that Joplin could see them. "You wanted to know why I used these, and now that you're going to die anyway, I'll tell you. These are birthday pictures, Hollis. *My* birthday pictures!"

Joplin stared at the photograph, trying to focus on the faces of the children. What Jack had said made no sense to him. He was too old to be one of the children who, along with Bobby Greenleaf, all seemed to be under ten years old.

"No, not them," said Tyndall. He pointed to one of the adults in the right-hand corner. "Here. That's me! I know it's hard for you to tell, because Harry always had us keep our backs to the camera, but that's me, all right. It was my sixteenth birthday. And, boy, what a birthday! It truly was the first day of the rest of my life, as they say."

Joplin raised his eyes to Tyndall's face and saw madness there. The mask he had worn so well had disappeared, leaving the disturbed remnants of a human face.

"I was nine when my mother gave me to Harry and Dan. Harry was a school photographer, but he had a little sideline selling drugs. He was also a pedophile. Then he got into kiddie porn and made even more money. Anyway, my mom was a crack addict and used me to pay off her drug debt."

"I'm sorry about that, Jack," said Joplin, meaning it.

"Yeah, well, life's a bitch, isn't it? I found out real fast that most kids didn't last very long with Harry and Dan, so I did everything I could to stay alive. I knew how to cook and clean and steal things, because of the way my mother was. But the best idea I had was to help them get more kids when they needed them. See, children are warned not to talk to strangers, but they're not afraid of another kid. Bobby Greenleaf wasn't, even though I was a teenager by then. We spotted him that morning and Harry had me get out of our car about half a block behind him. I caught up and started talking to him, and then Harry pulled up and I hustled him into the car with me."

"Is he...alive?" asked Joplin, trying to sound weaker than he felt.

"Bobby?" Tyndall shook his head. "None of the kids in these pictures is alive. And they were killed not too long after this particular photo session." Jack lowered the photos to his lap and scooted back a little on the desk. "See, I told you, it was my birthday that day. So Harry gave me some beer. I fell asleep watching some videos in my room down in the basement, and when I woke up, it was real quiet. I mean, *real* quiet. Nobody was in the house. I kind of had an idea what was happening—I mean, I'd been with Harry and Dan for almost six years and they didn't keep the kids they abducted for more than a few weeks. So I went and found Dan's rifle and crept out into the backyard. See, they had this house in a little town called Borden in South Carolina. It was a vacation house, so they never had to get to know the neighbors. Anyway, it had a lot of woods around it, and sure enough, I found them out there, burying all the kids. I knew it was just a matter of time before I was next, because I was getting too old to be much use to them. So I waited till they were done, and then I came out from behind a tree." Tyndall smiled widely, as if remembering. "I'll never forget the looks on their faces! I made them dig two more holes, and then I shot them both."

Tyndall got up and walked back around to the other side of the desk, then shoved the photos back into the envelope. "I need to wrap this up, Hollis, but I know you want to hear the rest of the story, so I'll keep talking." He pulled out a drawer on the left side of the desk and placed the envelope with the photographs in it, then began going around the room, checking for any evidence that shouldn't be left behind. He also picked up Joplin's Glock from the floor. "After I buried those two perverts, I went back in the house and gathered up anything that could lead to me, then found where they kept their money. There was only about $10,000 in the house, but I didn't want to risk getting more out of the bank, and it was enough to get me started on my new life."

Tyndall put the Glock and the computer disc he'd brought in the duffel bag and zipped it. "It wasn't hard at all to create a whole new identity," he continued. "I looked a lot older than I was, so people didn't question my being on my own. I'd seen a movie about how this prison escapee got the birth certificate of someone who had died and used that and the person's Social Security number to get a driver's license. It worked like a charm. Then I started reading every book I could get my hands on, and I got a better education than a lot of kids at those elite private schools. I got a GED and then I took the SAT exam. My score was good enough to get me a scholarship at UGA."

Joplin closed his eyes completely now, feigning unconsciousness. He heard Tyndall walk toward him and could sense that he was leaning over him.

Tom Halloran stood outside Woodley's office door, frozen by doubt over what he should do. If he burst through the door, Dr. Tyndall might shoot him; if he did nothing, the pathologist would surely kill Hollis Joplin. If he weren't already dead or dying. The few times Halloran had heard him speak, Joplin's voice had sounded very weak. Deciding he had to do something, he backed slowly away from the door. When he was on the other side of the room, he pulled out his cell phone and punched in 911. He could at least alert the police and get them on the way. But as soon as the emergency dispatcher answered, she put him on hold. As the seconds ticked away, Halloran remembered the stories in the *AJC* that had reported serious problems with Atlanta's 911 service. Some had revealed the incompetence of employees; others had warned the public of the "lag time" police stations were forced to use because there weren't enough officers to send to scenes. Even if the dispatcher came back on the line in the next few minutes, there was no guarantee that help would arrive in time to save Hollis Joplin.

"I know you can hear me, Hollis," said Tyndall. "Hearing is the last sense to go. Don't you want to know why I became a doctor?"

Joplin could feel Tyndall's hands on his chin and the top of his head and then the sensation of his head being moved up and down in a nodding motion.

"I thought so. Well, here's the answer: to help people, of course! Even though I was just the kid-wrangler in the pictures we made—I want you to know I never diddled them myself, Hollis—I decided I could make up for all the years I was forced to work with Harry and Dan by going into one of the 'helping professions.' So I declared a pre-med major and found I had a real knack for taking out all the cat hearts and frog brains in biology labs. Then, when I was doing my internship, I discovered forensic pathology. It occurred to me that I could be a doctor *and* catch criminals like Harry and Dan. I'm pretty big in the field now, what with all those forensic articles I've published. When Lewis kicks off, I'll be even bigger. The only problem is that it doesn't pay as well as other fields. But that's where Carrie and her rich family will come in handy. Especially after her parents pass away. I want you to know that I had to really work hard to land Carrie, Hollis. She's head and shoulders above my usual type. Remember that bet we had about whether she can cook? Well, she can. She can also fuck like a bunny."

Unable to stop himself, Joplin opened his eyes and tried to heave himself out of the chair, then fell back heavily. Tyndall grinned and said, "Not quite as near death as you look, are you, Hollis? Sorry, but I can't take a chance that you might survive." He went over to where the letter opener lay on the floor and picked it up. Then, still smiling, he turned back to Joplin.

Hollis had waited until Tyndall's back was to him, then tightened his hold on his abdomen and bent down to retrieve his ankle gun. Excruciating pain hit him as he sat back up, but he had the gun hidden under his right thigh when Tyndall headed back over to him. Allowing himself the luxury of a groan, he waited for Jack, who was holding both the gun and the letter opener now, to make his move.

"I really hate doing this, Hollis, believe me," he said.

The door burst open at that moment, and Joplin couldn't believe his eyes as Tom Halloran came charging in. Tyndall must have been just as shocked because he didn't react for several seconds.

"The police are on their way, Dr. Tyndall," Halloran said, sounding almost calm. "I told Detective Simmons you were holding Joplin hostage, so I wouldn't do anything stupid if I were you."

Jack's expression morphed back into a smile. "You've already beat me to it, Mr. Halloran, by barging in here. As you can see, I've got *two* weapons to your...none. So if you don't want me to shoot Hollis, you'll go stand behind him. *Now!*"

As the attorney began to move slowly toward him, Joplin inched his gun out and began to raise it. Tyndall caught sight of it and instantly lunged toward Halloran, grabbing him by his suit jacket and maneuvering him into place as a human shield.

"I know you don't like lawyers any more than I do, Hollis," he said, jabbing the gun into Halloran's rib cage, "but you're too much of a boy scout to get a civilian killed. I'm going to back toward the door, and I suggest you let us get out of here." He moved Halloran and himself to the door, then said, "Tell the police I'll kill him and as many people as I can if they get in my way."

"Jack, don't do this," Joplin said, still pointing his gun at the pathologist. He saw Tyndall take aim and ducked as a bullet whizzed past him.

Then the door slammed shut.

46

JOPLIN HEARD SIRENS IN THE DISTANCE as he stumbled into the bathroom. He was now in considerable pain and grateful that Halloran was apparently telling the truth about the police being on the way. Moving carefully, he grabbed a large handful of paper towels from the dispenser next to the sink. After setting the gun down on the ledge, Joplin undid his belt and trousers. He took a deep breath and stuffed the paper towels down the front of his briefs, then cinched his belt as tightly as he could. Next, he found his cell phone and called Ike, relating as quickly as he could what was happening.

"I'm only a few blocks away, Hollis, and the paramedics are on their way. Just lie low till they can get to you, okay?"

Instead of answering, Joplin switched off his phone.

The hall outside Woodley's private office and the reception area were dark. Cautiously, he made his way to the outer door and opened it. Then, holding his gun in both hands, he stepped into the hall. No one was there, so he moved over to the opposite wall and advanced toward the bank of elevators, every nerve in his body on alert. Joplin listened intently for any sounds before turning the corner into the elevator area; there was no sign of Halloran and Tyndall there either. After debating whether to take the stairs, he punched the down elevator button. When the doors of the car on the left opened, Joplin slowly entered it, the pain becoming stronger. He thought he could hear the faint sound of more sirens as he descended to the lobby.

Joplin kept his gun down near his right thigh as he left the elevator. There was no one in the immediate area, not even the security guard, and it was eerily silent. He saw three men going out the front doors and thought he'd just missed Tyndall, when a door to his left, beyond the elevators, opened. Two thoughts hit him simultaneously: that Tyndall had stopped on the first floor and walked down to the lobby, and that Tyndall would shoot him as soon as he saw him. He dropped to the floor just as a shot rang out, mind-numbing pain gripping him as he did, then heard shouts of "Police!" and "Drop your weapon!" Since his own gun had skittered away from him as he hit the floor, he figured they were yelling at Tyndall, and looked up. Four uniformed police officers, who must have been waiting out of sight, stood at the edge of the elevator bank with their guns drawn. Standing next to them was Ike Simmons, also with his gun drawn.

"I'll kill Mr. Halloran if you get any closer, Simmons," said Jack Tyndall.

"Yeah, but then we'd have to shoot *you*, Jack," said the detective.

"This is just déjà vu all over again, isn't it, Hollis?" Tyndall said.

Joplin turned his head so that he could see Tyndall and Halloran. His vision was blurring a little, but he could tell that Jack had the Glock in his hand. "You're never going to make it out of here alive, Jack," he told him, breathing hard now. "I know you're smart enough to know that."

"Why don't we work out something where *nobody* gets shot, okay?" asked Simmons.

"Fine with me, but only if it involves my getting away, free and clear."

"That's cool. Just let the man go."

"No way, Ike. He'll have to stay with me until there's no chance you'll shoot me."

"Why don't you take me instead, Jack?" suggested Joplin. "As you said before, Mr. Halloran is just a civilian, but I know where all the bodies are buried. I know all those things about you that you told me when you thought I was dying. Things you'd rather not have people know," he added, hoping he would hit a nerve.

Tyndall stared at him, apparently considering the proposal. "You've got a point there, Hollis. Let me think a minute."

"You mind if I sit up while you do? I'm not feeling too good on my stomach, and my gun's way over there," Joplin added, jerking his head in the direction of the second gun.

"You can get to your knees," said Tyndall. "Facing me." He waited until Joplin had done this, then said, "I've decided to accept your offer, Hollis, but Halloran's going with us. I need all the protection I can get, and it'll keep you from trying anything funny."

"I don't think this is a real good idea, Hollis," said Ike Simmons.

"And *I* don't think anyone asked for your opinion, Ike," Tyndall spat out. "Now, Hollis, I want you to listen to me very carefully. When I give the word, I want you to stand up, walk over here and get behind me. I'll have this gun pointed at Mr. Halloran's back the whole time. Then I want you to reach around me and grab hold of his arms. We're going to make a human sandwich, with me as the filling. Try anything funny and I'll shoot Halloran. I don't have anything to lose now, and I'm not going to jail. You understand?"

"I understand," said Joplin, although he'd had a little trouble focusing on what Jack was saying. His voice had seemed far away.

"How about you, Simmons? Are you real clear on this?"

"I'm clear. Just don't hurt anybody else, Jack."

"All I want to do is get away. Okay, Hollis, walk on over here and do what I just told you to do."

Joplin stood up slowly, wincing at the pain. Blood had soaked through the paper towels and was smeared on the marble floor. He could also feel it running down his legs.

"You okay, Hollis?" Simmons called out.

"Yeah," said Joplin, but his voice sounded funny, even to him. He'd lost a lot of blood and was going into shock. Walking unsteadily to where Tyndall and Tom Halloran stood, he turned and stood directly behind Jack. Then he grasped the attorney's arms.

"That's just fine," said Tyndall, nodding. "Now we're going to take the elevator down and go to the parking garage. Is your car there, Halloran?"

"Yes."

"Good. Don't try to follow us, Simmons. I want safe passage out of the parking deck. When I'm away from here, I'll let these two go, but not before."

No matter what Jack said, Joplin knew he wouldn't let them go. He was resolved to try to free himself and Halloran at the first opportunity.

If not, he would at least keep Tyndall from getting away, no matter what it took. He just hoped he didn't pass out first. His vision was even more blurred now, and he had begun to hear a roaring sound.

Slowly and awkwardly, they made their way to the elevators. About five feet away, the doors to the one on their right suddenly opened. Tyndall jerked his head toward it, and in that instant, Joplin pulled Tom Halloran's arms downward, using every last bit of strength he had left to bring him to the floor as he himself dropped to his knees. Only the pathologist was left standing. A shot rang out, and he felt something warm splatter on his head and face, then Tyndall toppled over. The last thing he saw before he lost consciousness was Tyndall lying on the floor, the back of his head missing and blood everywhere.

Some of the blood, he knew, was his.

47

HOLLIS JOPLIN WOULD LATER LEARN that he almost died twice—once in the EMS truck and the second time on the operating table—and that he was in a coma for ten days. He'd lost a lot of blood tracking Tyndall, and, despite what he'd thought, part of his abdominal wall had been cut and an intestine had been nicked. It was the peritonitis that almost did him in. Joplin never saw Jesus or any of his dead relatives, or even the tunnel and bright light that most people who had near-death experiences remembered. He did, however, recall looking down at himself as a group of medical personnel in scrubs and masks worked frantically to get his heart started again.

Time and space lost all meaning for him. He felt as if he were submerged in a vast ocean, sometimes being scraped along the rocky floor by strong currents, at other times floating serenely through a vivid blueness. If he drifted close to the surface, he could hear voices, but at first they were just murmurs, blown across the sea from some faraway island. Then they began to call him by name, and despite how tired he was, he would try to reach them, pulling his weightless body toward the sounds. Soon, he was able to recognize the voices. He heard Ike Simmons cuss him out for being so stupid, then the sound of sobbing, harsh and rasping over the waves. He heard Tom Halloran thank him for saving his life. He heard Lewis Minton tell him to fight.

Once, Joplin bobbed to the surface and managed to get his eyes halfway open. He thought he saw Carrie sitting in a chair next to his bed, but the brief consciousness proved so exhausting that he sank back down into the water. Sometime later, he surfaced again and opened his eyes all the way. Alone in the room this time, he noticed a number of machines and various blinking lights. Terrible, corrosive pain surged through his body, and he felt himself going under again. The next time he woke up, a nurse was in the room. She smiled and told him he was in the ICU at Grady Hospital with a serious abdominal wound. He flashed back to Jack Tyndall's face and the feel of the blade slicing into him, then, mercifully, he sank back into darkness.

The next time Joplin opened his eyes, a voice was calling him insistently. A man in a white coat said he was Dr. Chatham and repeated what the nurse had told him before. The doctor also said he was going to be just fine.

Joplin didn't feel fine. The pain, which he had felt off and on while he was unconscious, was now unrelenting. It never fully left, even after the nurses had given him morphine. Although he had finally come out of his coma, he spent a lot of time sleeping. Yet even in this state, the pain would find him. He would awaken with tears leaking from his eyes, praying that a nurse would be nearby and he could ask for more morphine. It hurt too much to grasp the buzzer next to him and summon help.

On one of the times he awoke like this, Simmons was sitting by his bed. He took one look at Joplin and said, "I'll go get someone," then hurried from the room. He returned with a nurse, who injected morphine into his IV tube. Soon the pain released some of its grip on him, and he took a deep breath. This was a mistake, because the movement of his diaphragm jarred his abdomen, causing the muscles around his incision to spasm.

"God...dammit," he said, through clenched teeth.

"I should have known your first words to me would involve takin' the Lord's name in vain, Hollis," said Simmons. He was smiling, but Joplin saw that he had tears in his eyes.

"Screw...you...Ike," said Joplin, trying to smile, but not sure he'd succeeded.

"You cuss all you want, Hollis. I know you hurt bad. Besides, I've spent a lot of time cussin' *you* out for bein' so stupid, goin' after Tyndall alone, like some rookie hot dog."

"I… heard you."

"You did?" said Simmons, sounding surprised. "The doctors told us that people in comas can still hear things, but I wasn't sure. You remember me talkin' to you?"

"Yes. You also told me you went… and got Quincy. Thanks."

"You're welcome, but you owe me big time. That cat's a mess! Did you know he likes fried chicken? I have to get him his own snack pack when I go to KFC."

Joplin smiled at this. Then he remembered something else. Something he needed to tell Ike right away. He closed his eyes, then opened them and said, "Bobby Greenleaf."

Ike stared at him. "What?" he said sharply. "What about Bobby Greenleaf?"

Haltingly, Joplin told him everything that he could remember about the house in Borden, South Carolina, and what might be buried in the backyard. He forced himself to recall the names of the kidnappers and any details about Bobby Greenleaf and the other children that Jack Tyndall had told him. Then Ike took over, asking him questions that pulled any remaining shreds of information right out of his brain. Finally, Joplin closed his eyes, completely exhausted, and gave himself up to the morphine.

When he awoke, it was morning. He was in pain again, but Lewis Minton was now sitting in the chair next to his bed.

The pathologist's face broke into a big smile. "Well, hello, there. How are you feeling?"

"Okay," Joplin answered, but he must not have been very convincing, because Minton reached for the buzzer to call the nurse.

"I think you could do with some meds," he said.

A middle-aged black nurse whose name he couldn't remember, but who had been especially kind, came in to give him morphine. Cheerfully, she told him it wouldn't be as much as the last dose, because the doctor was going to begin weaning him off the drug, but they would try to keep him "comfortable."

"I'd settle for 'excruciating' right about now," he told her.

She looked at him searchingly. "You let me know if it gets too bad, and I'll talk to Dr. Chatham. You've had a good bit of your intestines removed, Mr. Joplin."

"I'll be okay," said Joplin. When the nurse had left, he closed his eyes, waiting for the morphine to work. He also had no idea what to say to his boss.

"I better go and let you get some rest, Hollis."

"I think that's all I've done for the last ten days," he said weakly.

"The more you rest, the sooner you can get out of here and start recovering. And then you can get back to work."

"Yeah. Maybe." Joplin was sure Lewis Minton was just saying that because he was in a hospital bed.

"Hollis, I promise you, it'll take a while, but you're going to be fine. You're not going to have that colostomy bag forever, you know. It's temporary."

"I know," he said, sighing. "But even if I can work again, you know you won't be able to take me back, Doc."

"And what makes you think that?"

"It's not just because of any disability, but because of some things I've done. You know that. I broke into Woodley's office and went after Jack on my own, without following proper procedure. You're a great guy, Doc, and I appreciate what you're saying, but even if you wanted me to stay at the ME's, the higher-ups will have the last say. It's my guess I'll be asked to resign—if they don't fire me first."

Instead of answering, Lewis Minton bent over and pulled an armful of newspapers out of a briefcase on the floor next to him. "I've saved these for you. Maybe now's a good time for you to see them. Don't worry—I'll read them to you."

The first article he read was on the front page. It recounted the three murders, as well as all the twists and turns in the investigation. Halloran's efforts to vindicate Elliot Carter were detailed, but it also focused on "Investigator Joplin's dogged determination to uncover the truth" and his dedication to his job. The article ended by stating that he might even lose his life because of that dedication.

Two subsequent articles stayed on the front page; the rest appeared in the Metro section. They were studded with excerpts from interviews with law enforcement and judicial officials around the state, detailing the efforts made to ensure that Jack Tyndall's work for Milton County would be thoroughly investigated. The governor declared that he had created a special task force for that purpose, assisted by the GBI. He had also been quoted as saying that, "The terrible discovery of Dr. Tyndall's heinous crimes is mitigated only by the bravery and devotion to public service shown by Investigator Joplin, who also works at the Milton County Medical Examiner's Office." He then urged the public to keep in mind the dedicated service that forensic pathologists throughout the nation had given through the decades. As he read this, Minton winked at Hollis.

In all the articles, Joplin's status and progress were updated. Dr. Chatham declared that Joplin "…has a long and difficult recovery ahead of him, but he's a fighter, I can tell you that." Members of the Carter and Mashburn families publicly thanked him, as well as Tom Halloran, for their efforts to solve their loved ones' murders. Minton then read what he himself had said in answer to a reporter's question: "'Investigator Joplin's job will be waiting for him whenever he recovers. I don't think I need to tell you that he's an asset to the ME's Office. Chief William MacKenzie, however, has been fired and charged with obstruction and dereliction of duty.'"

Lewis Minton folded the last newspaper and stood up. He was smiling, but his eyes looked a little moist. "I hope that takes away any worries about your job, Hollis. That said, I have to ask you: What the hell were you thinking, son? You almost got yourself killed and caused everybody a lot of grief! That letter you sent to Tom Halloran was a good idea, but it would have been cold comfort if Jack had succeeded in killing you."

"You're right, sir. I did a lot of stupid things."

"Well, as long as you realize that, I won't say any more." The pathologist reached out and patted Joplin's hand. "Just don't do anything like that ever again."

Joplin smiled for the first time in days. "I promise, Doc," he said, then closed his eyes. It was suddenly a huge effort even to talk. The morphine had kicked in big time.

"Get some sleep now, son."

Joplin was too exhausted to answer him.

48

Tom Halloran rode the elevator up to the surgical floor of Grady Hospital, something he'd done several times in the past twelve days. This time, however, Maggie was with him, and they were hoping to be able to talk to Hollis Joplin. The door to Room 982 was open, and Joplin was sitting up in bed, his now clean-shaven face doing wonders for his appearance. He was still gaunt-looking, and Halloran could see the effects of drugs and pain in his eyes, but at least they were open now.

"Hello, Counselor," he said. "Is that Mrs. Counselor with you?"

"I'm Maggie, Hollis," she said, taking Joplin's hand and holding on to it. "Thank you for saving my husband's life."

"Well, he pretty much saved mine, too, ma'am."

"But I made things a lot more difficult for you, didn't I?" said Halloran. "Being taken hostage, I mean."

Joplin turned to look at him. "Yeah, but you were trying to help me, and that took a lot of courage. So did keeping your cool with a gun in your back. Besides, if you hadn't burst into Woodley's office when you did, I might not be here. I'd gotten hold of my other gun, but I was moving kind of slowly that night."

Halloran shook his head, remembering. "I don't know how you did it. I could tell you'd been injured when I first saw you. I just didn't know how badly."

Joplin grinned. "Neither did I, thank God. Now let's cut all this back-slapping and move on, okay? Do you know yet what's going on in Borden, South Carolina? I asked Ike Simmons to fill you in. Both of you," he added, looking at Maggie, "since you'd already seen all the photographs. I wanted you to know that we found those children."

"He did," Halloran responded. "He also said the FBI is planning to release the information at a press conference next week."

"They want to make sure they've discovered and identified all the bodies and notified the parents first," said Joplin. "Richard and Susan Greenleaf were told yesterday." He shifted his position, wincing as he did. "About the only good thing to come out of all this is that there'll finally be some closure for all those families."

"Not the only good thing," Maggie insisted. "The families of Ben Mashburn and Anne Carter know now that they didn't kill themselves, thanks to you."

"And you gave Elliot back his dignity and good name," said Halloran. "I can't tell you how much that means to Trip," he added, remembering what he'd gone through when his own father had killed himself. He thanked God that Trip wouldn't have to deal with that kind of legacy.

"Does he know about…Jack? That Jack—"

"Was his father?" Halloran shook his head. "Olivia and I decided he doesn't need to know that right now. Luckily, the media weren't given that piece of information."

"I guess it was bad enough finding out that his mother had blackmailed the man he thinks was his father."

"Exactly," agreed Halloran. "But at least I was able to tell him that she hadn't taken part in Elliot's murder. She made some terrible mistakes, but she wasn't a murderer, and when she realized what Tyndall had done, she tried to stop him. I think she was terrified that he might try to harm Trip, too, so she put her own life in danger to protect him."

"Well, that still doesn't make her Mother of the Year, in my book," said Joplin.

Halloran sighed. "I'd have to agree with you on that. Anne was a very flawed and surprisingly insecure person, who did some terrible things. But at least she wasn't a monster like Tyndall." Switching the subject, he said, "Speaking of 'Mothers of the Year,' has the FBI been able to find out if what Tyndall said is true? That his mother gave him to those pedophiles to pay off a drug debt?"

"Not so far. His fingerprints aren't on record anywhere, so there's no way to trace his real identity. And nothing was found among his personal effects. The only thing they've been able to establish is that he *wasn't* the Jack Tyndall born in April of 1971 in Montgomery, Alabama, as he claimed. That person died in a car accident in 1979. But they're hoping to find out more by tracking the activities of Harry Stringer and Dan Garvey—the kidnappers' full names—during the time Jack claimed he was given to them. They've each got long records for drug use and sales, and Harry had a conviction for taking indecent liberties with a child in Mississippi. From what the Feds can tell, they operated mainly in that state, as well as Alabama and Tennessee, and most of the kids buried in South Carolina had gone to schools where Harry took pictures each year."

Maggie shook her head in disgust. "I guess they didn't do many background checks on people who worked with children back in those days."

"I don't even know if they check out school photographers *today*, Maggie. Do you, Tom?"

"Actually, I don't," said Halloran, making a mental note to find out. "And there seem to be all sorts of cracks that pedophiles can fall through to gain access to children. But what strikes me here is that so far, everything Tyndall told you that night has proven true: the house and the bodies in South Carolina; two men named Harry and Dan whom he said were the kidnappers; and the fact that Harry was a school photographer. So it's entirely possible that what he told you about his mother was true, too."

Joplin closed his eyes for a few seconds. "In a way, I hope it *is* true. It would help explain how Jack became what he was. Don't get me wrong, I think he was a monster, too. But when you think of what he went through as a child..." He shook his head. "He didn't tell me this, but I think that's why he arranged for Elliot Carter to die in the Playscapes at Piedmont Park."

"You mean because it might have represented the childhood he never had?" asked Maggie.

"Yes," said Joplin. "Jack never had any kind of help, either. I think he was eaten up all those years by guilt and shame and anger over what had happened to him, and the fact that he helped those perverts kidnap the other kids. I think that's why he told me everything he did that night. He wanted someone else in the world to know what he'd been through."

"He also thought he had mortally wounded you, Hollis!" Maggie said. "Have you forgotten that?"

"No, of course not," said Joplin, sounding very tired. "But I have to accept part of the blame for everything that happened."

"Why in the world are you blaming yourself?" Halloran asked.

Joplin looked out the window for several seconds, then said, "The very first time I met you—that morning in the park—I remember telling you so smugly how none of us really knows everything about another person. Especially the shameful things they try to keep secret. Even the people we care about the most."

"And you were right," said Halloran.

Joplin waved his hand dismissively. "I was trying to convince you that your best friend had killed himself while practicing kinky sex, Counselor. But I was wrong. And if you hadn't kept after me, this whole thing might have been a lot more tragic."

"But I understand that. All your experience in law enforcement had—"

"Screw my experience! Excuse my language, Maggie," he added quickly, "but that's how I feel. My 'experience' sure didn't help me see that *my* best friend was a murdering sociopath, did it? Or even pick up on all the clues he kept giving me."

"What are you talking about? What clues did he give you?"

"That he'd been at UGA the same time as Anne Carter. That he knew Woodley. He even kept telling me that only someone with a lot of expertise in forensics could have carried out a murder made to look like an autoerotic death. And I didn't get it! I didn't get it until it was almost too late. *Was* too late for Anne Carter," Joplin added bitterly.

"Hollis, listen to me," said Halloran, trying to come up with the right words. "You didn't see what Tyndall was because you trusted him. He wasn't a suspect; he was a co-worker and a friend. We all have to trust people, especially the ones we're closest to. I wish...I wish Elliot could have confided in *me*. If he had told me what he'd found out that day in the urologist's office instead of keeping it all inside, maybe none of this would have happened. The fact that you were wrong about Tyndall shouldn't keep you from trusting everyone else. And you also have to keep on trusting yourself, Hollis—your instincts *and* your experience. Because those two things ultimately made you realize that Jack Tyndall was a murderer."

Joplin laughed weakly and shook his head. "I appreciate the kind words, Tom. Really. In spite of the fact that you're a lawyer—and a Republican, too, for all I know—I'm starting to like you. But what actually put me on to Jack was what your wife, here, said about those photographs—that they were 'pictures of pictures,' not scanned. That's why I decided to go look at the sign-in sheet at Property Control to see if Chief MacKenzie's name showed up before he checked the photos out on April 21st. Only I found Jack's name instead, and he had claimed he never knew about them. So you're the one who deserves all the credit," he added, turning to Maggie.

"Wow," she said, clearly thrilled by this. "Thanks for saying that, but it was just one little piece of the puzzle."

"Yeah, but it was a really important piece. I had turned everything over to Detective Simmons by then and thought the case against Dr. Woodley was pretty damning."

"I had no idea you suspected Tyndall before you went to Woodley's office," Halloran said. "I thought you were just hoping to catch the killer—whoever it was—planting evidence."

"Nope, it was your lovely wife, here," said Joplin, grinning. But the grin turned into a yawn, which he was unable to get under control.

"We'd better go," Maggie said, patting his hand. "You look like you need to rest."

"Yeah, they switched me over to Vicodin," Joplin held up the button that allowed him to self-administer the drug. "I just gave myself a big squirt of it, so I'm feeling a little sleepy. By the way, thanks for the flowers." Joplin nodded toward a huge bouquet on his nightstand.

"Our pleasure," said Halloran. "I'll come by to see you again in a day or so, if that's all right."

"I'd like that a lot. But, Tom? Can I ask a favor?"

"Anything."

"Don't play detective anymore, okay?"

"I think he's learned his lesson," said Maggie. "He'd better have, anyway."

Halloran smiled down at him. "I give you my word on that. No more playing detective."

"I trust you," said Joplin, closing his eyes.

***

In what seemed like only a few seconds later, Joplin heard a gentle knock at the door.

He opened his eyes, wondering if the Hallorans had forgotten something, then opened them even wider when he saw who it was.

"Hello, Hollis," said Carrie Salinger. "May I come in?"

Author's Note

There is currently no Milton County in Georgia. Up until 1932, however, Milton County did exist, having been created in 1857 from bits and pieces of Cobb, Cherokee, and Forsyth counties. It was then merged with Fulton County to save it from bankruptcy during the Depression. Recently, there has been a strong movement to recreate Milton County, which has so far been unsuccessful. But its supporters vow to continue and have recently managed to make the changes in the Fulton County Board of Commissioners described on page ten of this book. They are also working to get the necessary votes to change Georgia's constitution, which prohibits the existence of more than 159 counties. My Milton County extends much further south than the original, but, in my opinion, reflects the racial, political, and financial concerns of many of those who wish to bring it back to life. My main intention, however, was to have more creative control over the medical examiner's office where Joplin, Tyndall, and Carrie Salinger work and be able to differentiate it from the ME offices in both Fulton and Dekalb Counties.

ABOUT THE AUTHOR

While completing a Master of Science degree in Criminal Justice at Georgia State University in 1987, P. L. Doss served a graduate internship at the Fulton County Medical Examiner's Office. Assigned to the investigative division, she discovered how important the duties of the investigators were in helping the forensic pathologists determine the cause and manner of death. She was also able to observe many autopsies—an experience that proved to be invaluable in toughening her up for her career in law enforcement, first as a volunteer analyst in the Missing Children's Information Center at the Georgia Bureau of Investigation, and then as a probation officer and supervisor of officers at the Georgia Department of Corrections. She currently lives in Atlanta with her cat, Teddy, and is hard at work on her second Joplin/Halloran mystery.